DESIRE'S KISS

"In time, you'll learn our ways. You'll know when to speak, and when to remain silent."

A shiver ran through Kristy at Jared's words, and at his nearness. "You speak as if you don't believe there's a way for me to return to my own time—as if you think I'll be here for the rest of my life."

"Forgive me." She warmed to his comforting tone. "It's only natural you'll be wanting to get back to your family." He paused, then added, "Your husband, your children, perhaps."

"I'm not married."

"But you're of marriageable age—"

"I'm only twenty-five."

"And still unwed? Surely, with your fair face and your other charms, you must have been sought after by more than one man." He leaned closer as he spoke, and she found herself aching for his touch.

"There was a man who wanted to marry me. I couldn't go through with it."

"Your parents allowed you to break off your betrothal?"

"I have no parents." He was ever so close now.

His mouth brushed hers. He parted her lips and his tongue slid inside, touching, teasing, savoring.

A Love Beyond Forever

Diana Haviland

LOVE SPELL BOOKS NEW YORK CITY

To my husband.

LOVE SPELL®

January 1999

Published by

Dorchester Publishing Co., Inc.
276 Fifth Avenue
New York, NY 10001

ISBN 0-505-52293-4

A Love Beyond Forever

Prologue

The flat stone slab felt rough and damp under Kristy's out-stretched body, and her thin shift could not shield her from the penetrating cold. An icy, salt-scented wind lashed her hair across her face. She tried to push the tawny strands aside, but she couldn't reach them. What was it that gripped her wrist, restraining the movement of her arm?

She drew in her breath sharply, and felt the first stirring of uneasiness. She tried to move her arm once more, and heard the harsh clank of metal.

Turning her head, she caught sight of the iron band encircling her wrist, and the heavy chain to which the band was fastened. Her heartbeat quickened, and she tried to cry out. But she could make no sound.

Move the other hand, then. But it was futile. She tried to move her legs, only to wince as the iron bonds scraped against her bare ankles. Raising her head as far as she could, she saw she was chained to the rock slab. A chill gust of wind explored her thighs, her taut belly, the curves of her breasts. A shiver ran down the length of her body. She drew on all her strength, and cried out, "Help me—somebody, help me!"

Her cry was answered only by the sound of laughter, harsh and pitiless. She twisted her head and saw the red glow from a circle of flaming torches. A crowd milled around the rock on which she lay. Who were these figures in their wind-tossed garments? Their faces were concealed by animal masks: horned goats, sharp-fanged wolves, hook-beaked birds.

She struggled against the tide of terror that threatened to engulf her. How had she come to find herself a prisoner, bound hand and foot, under the night sky? She tried to cry out again, but the acrid smoke from the torches turned her plea for help into a wordless, strangled sound. Again, the only answer was an outburst of unholy laughter.

But now she saw another face, a man's face, close to her own. Although he wore no mask, his feral green eyes were like those of a forest beast, a lynx or a panther. She stared up at the angular planes of his face, his square chin, the hard slash of his thin-lipped mouth. Her gaze locked with his, and she could not look away.

He was not laughing like the others, and instinct told her that he was not one of them. His eyes deepened into a darker green, the fathomless color of the sea. Although he did not touch her, she felt a warm, liquid sensation stir, deep in her loins. An unfamiliar heat flowed through her. It was as if, just by looking at her, he penetrated the hidden depths of her being. Her nipples peaked against her shift. Fear gave way to another, equally primitive emotion. A fierce, overpowering need.

"Touch me." Her lips shaped the words. "Hold me." Her body arched upward and now he was reaching out for her. Friend or foe? Destroyer or deliverer? At that moment, she did not know, she did not care.

Even as his hands cupped her breasts, the masked figures moved in closer, torches blazing. The green-eyed man turned on the crowd and fought them off, but there were too many of them. They were dragging him away into the darkness. She could no longer see him. . . .

She tugged at her bonds with a strength born of desperation, felt the iron cutting into her wrists, her ankles. The metallic clang of her chains grew louder. She screamed. . . .

And sat up in bed, the sheet tangled around her body. She pushed it away, her hands shaking. Her silk nightgown, damp with perspiration, clung to her body. Once again, the dream had taken possession of her being. But it had never been so vivid, so real before.

She reached out and switched on the bedside lamp, then glanced at the clock. It was only four-thirty; she wouldn't have to leave for Kennedy Airport for another two hours.

Turn over and go back to sleep, she told herself. Her lips curved in a derisive smile. As if she could fall asleep and risk entering into the alien world of that now-familiar dream.

Even fully awake, she could remember every detail. The menacing crowd, their torches flaring; the animal masks that covered their features. The sound of their laughter, filling the night, taunting her, mocking her cries for help.

And always, the face of the green-eyed stranger, close to hers. The response of her body to his nearness. Never in her waking hours had she responded to any man with all her being.

Stop it! Think about something else. Go over the preparations for the flight.

Her luggage was already packed, the large suitcase labeled with her name and address. Ms. Kristy Sinclair, West 75th Street, NYC. The Donna Karan beige pantsuit she'd chosen to wear on the flight hung on the wooden rack opposite the bed, along with the honey-colored silk blouse. Her dark brown Mark Cross handbag lay on top of her dresser. She tried to draw reassurance from these practical details. Gradually the memory of the dream was receding. Reality was taking over.

As soon as she landed in England, there would be plenty to keep her occupied. Once she immersed herself in her demanding new assignment, she would be far too busy to brood over the dream. She would be a competent, well-organized junior executive respected by her coworkers at Marisol. Reliable, efficient Kristy Sinclair.

She would forget all about those bizarre dreams that had troubled her since her breakup with Brian. She'd been right to put an end to their relationship; she was sure of it. Although she'd been closer to him than to any man she'd known since arriving in New York, his proposal of marriage had forced her to realize that she did not love him. That she certainly was not prepared to be the kind of wife he deserved. Still, perhaps their parting had shaken her more than she wanted to admit.

A sudden thud at the foot of her bed caused her to start and catch her breath. A pair of luminous green eyes were fixed on her face. She blinked and then gave a shaky laugh as she reached down and felt Macavity's thick, soft fur beneath her hand. She rubbed his jowls and heard his loud, appreciative purr.

"Will you miss me while I'm away?"

He leaped down to the floor, and stared fixedly in the direction of the kitchen. All right, she might as well get up and feed him. She opened a can of 9-Lives Ocean Whitefish, his favorite. No need to worry about the cat pining for her; so long as Liz came in each day to fill his food and water dishes and change his litter, he'd be fine for the next two weeks.

She swung her long legs over the side of the bed and slid her feet into her slippers. For a moment, she felt a pang of uneasiness; her body was still a little damp with perspiration, a reminder of the dream.

She'd told no one about the recurrent dream, not even Liz, her only close friend. If she had, Liz would probably have recommended that she see a therapist. Someone who'd go digging into her past, her early childhood. She flinched at the prospect, for she could just imagine what a therapist would make of the fact that she had no memories of the years before she was six.

Forget the dream, she told herself briskly. Feed Macavity and take a long, hot shower. Finish packing the carry-on bag with a few last-minute items.

Think about the assignment, the hefty raise that went with it. Think about doing over this whole apartment. Or maybe she should move to a new one. If she was really lucky, she might even find one with a working fireplace and a view of the river.

It was nearly five o'clock when she stepped out of the shower and dried herself with a thick, soft towel. The full-length mirror, although hazy with steam, reflected her high, firm breasts, her narrow waist and gently curving hips. Regular sessions of aerobics three days a week at her health club helped to keep her in shape.

Her gaze lingered on her steam-clouded mirror image: shoulder-length tawny-blond hair, amber eyes. Had she inherited her coloring from her mother or her father? She would never know.

She didn't have the slightest memory of either of them. They belonged to those first and completely forgotten years. The lost years, before that night the state troopers had discovered her alone, standing on the road outside her aunt's house, dazed and silent.

She returned to the bedroom, got into her clothes, then checked the contents of her carry-on bag. Her Toshiba laptop was already inside, packed in its own case along with extra backup disks and batteries.

She went on checking the items in the bag. Here was the small, high-intensity flashlight she'd picked up at Sharper Image. Packets of instant tea and coffee bags. Immersion heater and cup. Her cosmetic case, with all the basics, plus three shades of lipstick, to go with whatever outfit she might choose to wear. Ms. Efficiency—that's what Liz called her.

Perhaps she should pack an extra nightgown, the pale blue nylon one. Another pair of panty hose. Should she also tuck in an extra bra?

Although she'd often traveled on company business, the airlines had never lost her luggage; still, there was always a first time. When she walked into the office of the newly established Manchester branch of Marisol, she had to look and feel absolutely self-confident. She had been entrusted with the responsibility for checking out the management of the shop, the efficiency of its sales staff and office personnel. Only twenty-five—and she was climbing the executive ladder fast.

Carry off this assignment, and you're definitely on your way to the top, she told herself.

Her hand brushed against something soft. She drew back her fingers. Even before she looked into the drawer, she knew what she'd touched. The black velvet bag. She felt a shudder of revulsion.

Leave it alone, Kristy. Forget it. But she couldn't.

Driven by a force she didn't understand, she was taking it out, putting it on top of the dresser. *All right, then—throw it away. Do it right now. Go out to the back hall and toss it in the trash can.* But it was no use. As if controlled by some alien force, she already was opening the drawstrings, and taking out the mirror. The "scrying mirror."

Why had she bought it? Why had she allowed Liz to drag her into The Magick Caldron that snowy afternoon three months ago? She probably wouldn't even have noticed the shop if she'd been alone. It had been inconspicuous, sandwiched in between a secondhand bookstore and a copy center, on a side street off of Broadway. The self-consciously quaint spelling of the name on the window had irritated her.

"My aunt's into this New Age stuff," Liz had explained. "Crystals, autohypnosis tapes, aromatherapy. Maybe I can find her a Christmas present here."

While Liz had hunted for a gift, Kristy had passed the time scanning the hodgepodge of stone gargoyles; tarot cards; and books about reflexology, channeling, love potions, and witch-craft.

Then she'd stopped short, her gaze caught and held by a black velvet drawstring bag on the counter in front of her. The velvet looked dusty and slightly frayed, but she picked it up, moved by an impulse she couldn't explain.

She undid the strings, reached inside, and drew out an ebony frame with a handle. Was it a mirror? But this was like no mirror she had ever seen. In the oval where her face should have been reflected, she saw only an opaque, dark surface.

She wanted to put the mirror back in its bag, but her fingers remained wrapped around the curved ebony handle. It took all her willpower to push it back inside the velvet bag, to lay the bag on the counter.

A stout woman, her arms already laden with packages, reached for it, but the saleswoman had quickly intervened. "I'm sorry, ma'am. The scrying mirror is for the young lady. It would be of no use to you. It is for her, only." She pointed at Kristy.

Scrying mirror? What was a scrying mirror? Kristy had protested that she didn't want it. The saleswoman ignored her words, and kept insisting that the mirror was meant for her. "You may have it at whatever price you wish to pay," she said.

"How about a dollar?" Surely, that would put a stop to the saleswoman's pitch. To Kristy's surprise, the woman had already started to wrap the piece. "It's yours for a dollar, miss."

"You can't refuse—not at that price," Liz urged.

As they left the shop, Kristy had tried to convince herself that Liz, the dedicated bargain hunter, had been responsible for getting her to buy the mirror. But she knew perfectly well that no amount of persuasion from her friend or the saleswoman could have forced her to make such a purchase against her will. Was there some hidden force in the mirror itself that had made her unable to leave it behind?

Ridiculous! Kristy wouldn't let her thoughts wander into such fantastic bypaths. She'd wanted to get out of that weird shop and away from the saleswoman, who had stared at her as if expecting her to perform some feat of magic on the spot.

Then why hadn't she just walked out? Why had she felt the need to buy the mirror? All right, so she'd given in to a foolish impulse. So what? Forget it.

But even after she and Liz were seated in a booth at the coffee shop next door, her friend had gone on talking about the mirror. "Only a dollar! And who knows, maybe it really is an antique like the woman said."

"Maybe it is. Why don't you take it, and give it to your aunt for Christmas." She had forced an unconvincing laugh.

Liz had shaken her head. "The mirror's only for you, remember?"

Chapter One

Kristy drove the rented Toyota along the narrow road through the Yorkshire moorlands. For the first time in months, she relaxed, completely at ease. After arriving in England, she'd immersed herself in her work, and, as she'd hoped, she had slept soundly each night, untroubled by those bizarre dreams that had tormented her back in New York. She'd needed a change of scene, that was all.

She certainly would have made better time had she chosen the main highway, but she preferred this side road, where she could take in the austere beauty of the countryside. On this March afternoon, the broad sweep of the moors showed a subtle blending of brown and grey, dotted here and there with fronds of bracken; leafless, gnarled oak trees; and grotesque outcroppings of rocks, shaped by the centuries of wind and rain. From time to time, she caught sight of a herd of black-faced sheep, or a small, thatch-roofed farmhouse.

The moors offered a welcome change from the jostling crowds and the heavy traffic she'd left behind in Manchester.

She'd carried out her assignment with her usual efficiency; she'd checked the new branch of Marisol; then she'd faxed a brief letter to the home office in New York.

Tonight, after she checked into the hotel in Scarborough, she would make out a more detailed report. She'd have dinner in her room and go to bed early, so as to be ready to get on with the rest of the job: to scout for possible locations for new Marisol shops.

But for now, this quiet interlude belonged to her and she would make the most of it. She savored the brisk, refreshing breeze; it blew in through the half-open window and set a few white clouds drifting across the deep blue sky overhead.

With a sigh of pure pleasure, she reached out to put her Andrew Lloyd Webber CD into the slot. She drew back her hand as she caught sight of a sharp turn up ahead. A steep wall of jagged rocks rose on either side of the narrow road.

She rounded the turn, then caught her breath as she saw she was heading straight into a heavy fog. She blinked, then glanced upward. The sky overhead was the same deep, sunlit blue as before, the breeze still fresh and brisk. But the fog surrounded the car, blotting out her view, forcing her to slow down. Although she'd seen little traffic, she didn't want to run into a stray sheep, or a pheasant leading its brood across the road.

The fog was heavier now; she shifted uneasily, her hands tightening on the wheel. Maybe the weather changed quickly here on the moors, but this fog had appeared from nowhere; it enveloped her car like a thick, clinging shroud, so that she could scarcely see a foot ahead.

She drew a deep, steadying breath. All right, so she'd run into some unusual weather. She'd soon drive through these veils of billowing grey—Grey? Her muscles tensed. The fog now burned with a reddish glow, as if shot through with tiny, glittering sparks. She closed her eyes, opened them again. The fog was heavier and the sparks whirled upward in an eerie dance.

She gave a small, wordless cry as she caught sight of a dark shape looming up in the road ahead. A man or a woman? She wasn't sure. Certainly no shepherd, no farmer's wife, would go wandering around the moors in a long, hooded cloak.

She pressed down on the horn. The figure turned, raised a slender white hand, and pushed back the hood.

The woman made no move to get out of the path of the car. She nodded, and her lips curved in a mocking smile. It was as if she'd been waiting for Kristy here on this deserted road.

Kristy pressed the horn again. Still the woman didn't move. Kristy turned the steering wheel left, heading straight into the fog. She heard the sound of the woman's laughter.

She hit the brake. Too late. The car was veering out of control. As it swerved past the woman, Kristy had a moment's glimpse of dark hair, red lips, and silvery-grey eyes. Then, metal hit solid rock and she cried out. The seat belt pressed hard against her chest. She fought for breath. The air bag opened like a great white blossom and the inside of the car was filled with a powdery dust.

She was dizzy and trembling, her heart jerking unevenly. Her hands shook as she unfastened the seat belt. The door beside her was hopelessly jammed, but she managed to get out through the passenger's side. She fought off a wave of vertigo, and filled her lungs with the clean, cold air.

Where was the fog that had hidden the road only moments before? It had disappeared as quickly as it had come on. And the dark-haired woman—she, too, was gone.

Kristy shaded her eyes against the brilliant sunlight and stared out over the moors. Although she looked in all directions, her gaze moving over the gently rolling stretches of grey and brown, the woman was nowhere in sight. It was as if the silver-eyed stranger had conjured up the fog, then disappeared along with it.

This was no time to let her imagination run away with her.

Later, she'd find a logical explanation for all that had happened. Right now, she had more immediate problems.

She looked over the car, taking stock of the damage. It hadn't been totaled, but she certainly wouldn't be able to finish her drive to Scarborough. The impact had left the hood bent upward at a grotesque angle; the driver's-side door was jammed.

Cautiously, she rotated her head, flexed her knees and her elbows. No broken bones, not even a sprain or bruise. The car needed repairs, but she was all right. She breathed a silent prayer of thanks, then began to make plans.

She'd have to walk to the nearest town and send a tow truck back for the car. She glanced down at her mid-heel pumps. Not exactly what she'd have chosen for a hike across the moors, but she'd manage.

She retrieved her road map from the glove compartment, studied it carefully, and located the most likely destination. Her lips shaped the name: Glenrowan.

"I'll help you unpack, miss," said the flaxen-haired girl. "Just sit yourself down and rest. You must be worn out, what with the accident and all."

After Kristy had arrived at Glenrowan a few hours ago, she'd been lucky enough to find the Rowan Tree, a small, well-kept inn at the far end of High Street. Mrs. Ainsworth, the landlady, had greeted her with a warm smile. "You can have your choice of rooms, Miss Sinclair. We've no other overnight guests right now. Morag will help you get settled in."

The landlady had gone downstairs to phone the local garage for a tow truck, and now her daughter, who looked about sixteen, was chattering away as she helped Kristy unpack. "We don't get hardly any visitors in March or April. But in summer we get the hikers—American college students, some of them."

Morag stared with wide-eyed admiration at Kristy's burgundy pantsuit and ivory silk blouse. "The hikers don't dress up like you, though. Jeans, t-shirts, boots. That's what they wear."

The young man who ran the local garage had gone out with a tow truck, retrieved the car, and dropped off Kristy's luggage here at the inn.

Now the girl reached for Kristy's suitcase. "Shall I unpack this?"

Kristy shook her head. "I'm only staying overnight."

"How did the accident happen, miss?"

"The fog. It was so heavy, and it came on suddenly."

"But we haven't had any fog hereabout—not for weeks."

Kristy was gripped by a sudden uneasiness. "I saw it, Morag."

"Likely you dozed off for a minute. That happens sometimes, even to folks who're used to driving on these moors."

But she hadn't dozed off. She had seen the billowing, red-tinged fog shot through with those whirling sparks. She'd seen the cloaked woman in the road, too, her black hair tossed back from her face. Even now, she remembered the sound of the woman's mocking laughter.

A swift flash of instinct warned her not to say any more about the red-tinged fog that had appeared out of nowhere in the middle of a sunny afternoon, or the woman who'd stood unmoving in the car's path.

"I guess you're right." Kristy forced a smile. "I must have dozed off."

Morag nodded, only half-listening, for she had already unzipped the carry-on. She was examining its contents, her blue eyes round with wonder.

Kristy understood. Morag wore a serviceable brown wool skirt, starched white blouse, knee socks and sturdy laced oxfords. A plastic barrette held her straight hair back from her face. No makeup, not even lipstick.

Of course the girl was fascinated by Kristy's lacy bras, designer panty hose, and sheer blue nylon nightgown. She was probably a little envious, too. And who could blame her?

Kristy remembered herself, at Morag's age. How she'd longed for the small luxuries her aunt called "a waste of good money." Aunt Vera had never missed a chance to tell her how lucky she was, just to have a roof over her head and three meals a day.

Kristy caught her breath, all thoughts of her aunt swept aside. Now her eyes were fixed on Morag, who'd just picked up the velvet bag holding the scrying mirror. Although Kristy was sure she'd fastened the drawstrings securely, the bag opened. The mirror dropped out onto the bed.

"It's not broken, miss," Morag assured her quickly. She picked up the mirror and stared into the dark oval surface. "Oh, miss! It's a scrying mirror." Swiftly she put it down and took a step back, her light blue eyes fixed on Kristy. "I've never seen one before, but my granny told me about them. She said there were those who could use them to look into the future." She reached out cautiously, then touched the ebony handle with her fingertips.

What a perfect opportunity to get rid of the unwanted mirror. "You may have it if you want it, Morag."

"Oh, no, miss!"

"But you can use it to tell fortunes, take it to a slumber party, maybe." Did they have slumber parties in this remote town? If not, Morag could create a new sensation.

But the girl shook her head. "It's of no use to me," she said earnestly. "It's yours and no other's."

A shudder ran through Kristy's body. The saleswoman at The Magick Caldron had used those same words.

"You all right, miss? Maybe you got a chill, walking across the moors. I'll fetch you a pot of good, strong tea."

She started for the door, then paused. "Please, miss, do you think you could—" Her round cheeks flushed, and her eyes avoided Kristy's.

"What is it, Morag?"

"There'll be a full moon tonight. If you let me leave the

mirror outside in the moonlight, it will draw down the Wiccan power. The power of the goddess, Aradia.''

Wiccan power? Aradia? What was the girl talking about?

"Then we'll draw the curtains and light the candles and you can read my future. Would you do it, miss? Please?''

Before Kristy could assure the girl that she had no such supernatural powers, Morag went on, the words tumbling out. "It's because of Tilda. She used to be my best friend—my only friend, really. But now she's going around with Jimmy— the lad who works at the garage—and she has no time for me. Treats me like I was a child, she does.''

"But even if I could read your fortune, how would that help?'' Kristy asked.

"You could tell me when I'm going to meet a young man of my own. And will he be from hereabouts? Or maybe from far off? And will he be handsome?''

Kristy was touched by the girl's eagerness, able to empathize with her. She remembered herself at sixteen: lonely, friendless, starved for affection. Aunt Vera, her mother's sister, had given her a home, had provided her with the necessities; but deep inside, Kristy had felt an aching void. She was different from the other girls in town, and she had always known it. She'd been an outsider, who couldn't remember the first six years of her life, the faces of her parents. She'd never even seen a single photograph of her mother in Aunt Vera's house.

Kristy had been shunned by the other children in town during her adolescence. *I can't have you at my party. Mama won't let me.* But why?

Morag's voice brought her back to the present. "Will you do it, Miss Sinclair? Will you read my fortune?''

"All right, then,'' Kristy heard herself saying. She'd look into the dark mirror and tell Morag she'd soon have a young man of her own. She slid the mirror back into the velvet bag and handed it to the eager girl.

"I'll put it out in the garden at moonrise,'' Morag said, her eyes glowing with anticipation. She hurried out, clutching the velvet bag.

The curtains were drawn. Two candles in brass holders flickered on a small table beside the window. Kristy and Morag sat opposite one another, the mirror between them. As the candlelight played across the dark, polished surface, Kristy felt a growing uneasiness. Think of it as a game, she told herself. Give Morag the future she longed for.

"How soon will I have a young man of my own?" Morag asked. "Will he be tall and handsome? Will he come from far off—Manchester—or maybe London?"

Kristy kept her eyes fixed on the mirror. Its surface remained dark, empty. What else had she expected? Somehow, she'd have to go through with the charade. She moved the mirror closer to the candles.

Her breath caught in her throat, for now the dark surface was in motion. Only a trick of the candlelight.

From the depths of the mirror, a face appeared for a moment, then vanished. Her fingers began to tremble and she tightened her grip on the ebony handle. The surface of the dark oval was stirring now, rippling like the waves of a midnight sea. Again, the face began to take shape.

"What is it? What do you see?" Morag's voice seemed to come from far off.

Kristy stared at the face in the mirror, a man's face, but his features were not yet distinct. Was it really possible that she had the power to catch a glimpse of Morag's future?

"You see him! I know you do! Tell me, miss—what's he like?"

Kristy bent closer to the mirror and her whole body went rigid. This wasn't the face of a stranger. She'd seen him before: the hard slash of his mouth, the angular planes beneath his tanned skin. Thick black hair, moving as if tossed by the wind. Feral green eyes seeking hers, drawing her into their fathomless depths.

She felt a damp, cold wind, sharp with the salty tang of the sea. It whipped her hair across her face. And the shrill, pitiless laughter—she'd heard it before.

Her dream. It had returned, it was taking possession of her, drawing her to a place far from the haven of this candlelit room. An unholy place, beneath a wide, alien sky.

The mirror slid from her hand and fell to the floor. The candle flames flickered, and were gone. She stood up, clutching at the table. But the floor was shifting under her feet. She was falling through a red-tinged fog. Down, down into infinite darkness . . .

She was lying on the floor. "Morag! Turn on the lights!"

The wind had blown out the candles, but the room wasn't in total darkness. Morag must have pushed aside the window curtains, for the rays of the full moon slanted in. She turned her head; at the far end of the room, a pile of embers glowed in the fireplace. But there had been no fire there before she'd lost consciousness.

Something hard and bulky lay beneath her outflung arm. Her carry-on. She pushed it aside, then got to her feet. "Morag! Where are you?"

Still no answer. Surely Morag hadn't left her here, alone and unconscious. Or had the girl also seen the face in the mirror, felt the icy wind, heard the unearthly laughter? Had fear sent her running from the room?

But Morag couldn't have seen the man's face; he was a part of Kristy's dream. The masked figures with their flaring torches, the laughter, the fierce sea wind . . . all existed only in the dream that had tormented *her* night after night.

Kristy swayed, her legs unsteady. She reached out to grip the edge of the table. Her fingers closed on empty space.

The table wasn't there.

But that was impossible. Only a few moments ago, she'd been sitting at the table with candlelight shining down on the

23

mirror. Yet now the table, the candles, the mirror all had disappeared.

She moved shakily across the room to the fireplace. The light switch was close beside it, that much she remembered. Right now, she needed the bright glow of the ceiling fixture to banish the shadows, to bring her back to realty.

She slid her fingers along the wall. Where was the switch plate? She took a few steps sideways, and stumbled against an iron stand that held a shovel and poker; a coal bucket stood beside it.

She seized the poker and stirred the embers. The fire flared up, and its light flickered over the wall.

She cried out in shocked disbelief. The wall was paneled in dark oak. What had become of the wallpaper with its pattern of cornflowers and ivy? She remembered the cheerful, welcoming air it had lent the room. She tilted back her head and stared at the ceiling; it should have been the same soft cream color as before; but it, too, had changed. She stared at the heavy oak beams. No overhead light fixture.

Fear welled up inside her as she searched the wall again. The switch plate, too, had disappeared. Well, of course, she told herself. It all made perfect sense. No light fixture, no switch plate.

She forced herself to look toward the other end of the room. The bed was higher, wider than it had been before; carved posts supported the canopy; heavy curtains hung down on both sides.

Her hands clenched into fists as she fought back the rising tide of panic. She had to keep herself under control.

Concentrate on the facts, Kristy. On your visit to Manchester, the meeting with the Marisol staff, the report you faxed to the New York office. Think about New York. About Liz. They'd have lunch together when she got home. Wait until she told Liz about this. No, better not. Liz might try to send her off to the nearest shrink.

Tell Brian, then. He's understanding, considerate. She

shook her head. Not Brian, either. She hadn't seen him since their breakup last autumn.

She shut her eyes, squeezing the lids together hard, then opened them again. The oak-paneled walls, the beamed ceiling, the canopied bed, were still there. But there was no round table nearby, nor the two chairs, nor the candles in their brass holders.

There's a perfectly sensible explanation, she told herself. There's got to be. A room changes in a few minutes; solid objects vanish; others take their places. Oh, sure. Happens all the time. She laughed, then stopped herself when she caught the sound. It held the beginnings of hysteria.

You have good sense, Kristy. Use it. Figure out the reason for what's been happening here.

The accident, that was it. She'd been in a car crash only this afternoon, and she still hadn't recovered. A concussion might be causing these weird delusions.

But a concussion came from a blow on the head, didn't it? She hadn't hit her head. The air bag had protected her. Okay, maybe this was the aftermath of some other kind of shock to the nervous system. A delayed reaction.

That would explain the man's face in the scrying mirror the familiarity of his deep green eyes and dark hair. The mocking laughter of the crowd. The salt-scented wind that had chilled her body and lashed her hair against her cheek.

Unreal, all of it. . . .

She forced herself to go over the details of the accident. The curve in the road, the fog. The cloaked woman.

Her heart sank. The fog, the woman in the car's path—all that had come before the accident. Or had she mixed up the sequence of events? Maybe the accident had happened first; maybe the fog, and the woman, were part of the delusions.

She should have brought along a bottle of tranquilizers. Liz swore by Valium for emergencies, but Kristy had prided herself on never needing pills to calm her nerves.

Now she remembered Aunt Vera's old-fashioned remedy:

25

ice-cold water, splashed on the face and wrists. It was worth a try. She headed for the bathroom. Then she stopped short.

From the courtyard below the window came the creaking of wagon wheels, the crack of a whip, the clatter of hooves. Okay, so maybe in this isolated corner of Yorkshire they still delivered produce in wagons. But, after midnight?

She hurried to the window. It was a casement window now, made of leaded, diamond-shaped pieces of glass. It was wide open, and she leaned out on the sill. In the light of the full moon she caught sight of a tall, broad-shouldered man in a heavy cape, who was dismounting from his horse. The wide brim of his plumed hat shadowed his face, concealing his features.

She could make out other dark shapes, too. A line of heavily laden wagons. Horses stamping on the cobblestones of the courtyard. The drivers were climbing down, talking among themselves.

The tall caped man pounded on the inn door. "Open up, Master Prescott! Be quick about it!" His voice was deep and resonant.

Who was Master Prescott? A servant here at the Rowan Tree? Maybe so, but did they still use such an archaic title, even in this remote corner of the moors?

What kind of place was Glenrowan? Both High Street and the inn had seemed a little quaint when she'd first seen them that afternoon, but no more so than a lot of towns in Vermont or Ohio. And as for Mrs. Ainsworth, there'd been nothing unusual about her.

Who were these late-night visitors, dressed in the clothes of a past century? Were the wagons, the drivers, the man in the cape and plumed hat also a part of the delusions caused by her accident? Although she tried to cling to that explanation, it was becoming harder by the minute to do so.

Heavy, lumbering footsteps moved along the hall, past her room. She hesitated, then opened the door a crack and saw a stout man going down the stairs. She slipped out into the hallway, which was lit only by a lantern set in the wall. By its flickering light, she made her way to the head of the stairs, then stopped beside the newel post. Down below, another lantern glowed faintly.

Not only her room, but the whole inn, had changed.

The stout man opened the front door to his visitor, then stepped aside. "I been expectin' ye since last night, sir. Morag had a fine joint of mutton roasted to a turn. Beef pasties, too."

"We were delayed," the caped man interrupted.

"By the Lord Protector's men?" Kristy heard the fear in Prescott's voice.

"A troop of them were lying in wait for us."

"But ye shook them off yer trail, like always."

The caped man gave a brief, hard laugh. "We lost them on the cliffs near Egton."

"Yer sure? If they was to follow ye here, it'd mean a noose around my neck."

"You're safe enough, this time. And you'll be well paid for your risk, as always."

"Ye got a good haul, then, yer lordship?"

"I'm Master Jared Ramsey for now. Don't make it necessary for me to remind you again." The tall man brushed past Prescott and started for the stairs. "Get a couple of hostlers to stable the horses, and change them for fresh ones."

"Right away, sir. Morag'll bring ye hot water, and get yer meal ready. An' if yer wantin' a wench to share yer bed, Della will give ye a warm welcome."

"I'll not be wanting her tonight."

Jared Ramsey had already started up the stairs. Kristy turned and hurried down the hall, back to her room. She shut the door behind her and made her way to the bed. The embers burned low again, and with only the moonlight to guide her, it was slow going.

She could make out the shape of her carry-on, on the floor nearby. Thank goodness she'd packed her high-powered flashlight. She crouched down to unzip the bag, then felt around inside.

She froze as the door creaked open. Looking over her shoulder, she caught sight of Jared Ramsey's tall, caped figure in the doorway. He came striding in, then stopped before the hearth.

He tossed his plumed hat aside, unfastened his cape and dropped it over a nearby chair. She watched as he shoveled more coal into the fire, then thrust at the embers with the poker, stirring up a leaping, red-gold blaze. He turned back to the room.

For the first time since he'd arrived at the inn, she saw his face. She could not hold back her cry of recognition.

His gaze swept the room and came to rest on her, still crouching beside her bag. She stared at him, unable to look away. His eyes were dark green under straight black brows. She was mesmerized by his face, touched as it was by the red glow of the firelight; by that wide slash of a mouth; by those high, angular cheekbones.

Jared Ramsey was the stranger who'd appeared to her in her dreams, who'd looked up at her out of the depths of the scrying mirror tonight. He was no illusion, conjured up out of her fantasies.

He came striding toward her, and now, as he stood over her, his booted feet set apart, she caught the smell of horses, of leather, and of his masculine scent. Jared Ramsey was a man of flesh and blood, and he was here in this room with her tonight.

Chapter Two

Jared stared down at the girl who was crouching near the big bed. Why the devil had Prescott sent Della up here to his bedchamber after he had already declined the offer? Had the greedy landlord brought the wench here to offer her as a distraction, while he and his hostlers diverted part of the valuable cargo for his own profit? Not likely. Prescott was dishonest, but he was also a coward. He wouldn't dare to try such trickery on Jared and his men—not if he valued his skin.

Jared wasn't about to lose even a portion of his freight to a thieving landlord, not after the risks he'd run, smuggling it into England. He had sailed a schooner across the turbulent waters of the North Sea in the teeth of a gale; he'd ridden a stallion along the steep, rocky cliffs above Scarborough and Whitby, then on across the windswept moors, where he'd been confronted by Cromwell's troopers. Only his familiarity with Yorkshire had helped him to make the narrow escape from the Lord Protector's forces, and other dangers still lay ahead.

As soon as he'd eaten a hasty meal, he would have to oversee the inventory and division of his illicit cargo. Before the sun rose over the moors, he and his followers would be on their way again, bound for their various, far-flung destinations. Even now, Prescott's hostlers were rubbing down the exhausted horses and settling on fresh teams for the wagons.

He had no time for Della, not tonight. But she was a warm-hearted girl, generous with her favors, and he had no wish to wound her feelings. A length of Brabant lace and a parcel of embroidered taffeta ribbons would soothe her injured pride.

"Sorry, lass," he began, as he strode past her to the rough-hewn washing stand beside the bed. "I've no time for pleasure, not tonight."

He took flint and tinder from the drawer, then lit the lantern that hung from a hook on the wall. She did not move or speak. "No need to sulk," he told her. "Wait until you see the finery I've brought for you." Still she didn't say a word. "You'll be the envy of every wench in Glenrowan—"

He broke off, then peered at her more closely in the lantern light. He tensed.

She wasn't Della.

If it were not for the long, shimmering waves of her tawny hair, the fine-boned oval of her face and her delicately molded lips, he wouldn't have been certain, at first glance, that she was a female. Even the most shameless trollop would not have come to a man's bedchamber in such blatantly masculine attire. He had to admit to himself that her perfectly-fitted breeches set off her trim waist, the sensuous curve of her hips and the length of her shapely legs in a most enticing manner; her jacket swung open, and her ivory silk blouse clung to her high, rounded breasts. But no female he knew, whether lady or whore, would wear a man's garments.

She stayed motionless a moment longer, still kneeling beside an open canvas trunk. Then, with one fluid movement, she rose to her feet. Although she lifted her chin, and her gaze did not waver, he caught the flicker of fear in her eyes:

amber eyes framed by thick, dark lashes with brows that slanted upward.

Once before, he'd known a woman with such eyes: Liane, who had pledged her eternal love to him. Liane, now lost to him forever. In the deepest recesses of his mind, the long-repressed memories began to stir, but he forced them away.

"Who the devil might you be?" he demanded. "What are you doing in my bedchamber?"

"Kristy Sinclair's my name." Those amber eyes burned like twin flames as fear gave way to anger. "And this is my room!"

Her breasts rose and fell with her quick, uneven breathing. "At least, it was my room—but now it's all been changed." As she went on speaking, her voice began to tremble slightly. "Nothing's where it was before. The table's gone. The bed's all wrong—and so is that window."

Her words made no sense, and it wasn't easy for him to understand her peculiar accent. In pursuing his trade, he'd traveled from one end of England to the other, and across the sea to Holland and France; but he could have sworn he'd never heard anyone speak like that. He was rapidly losing patience.

He glanced around the chamber, with its familiar beamed ceiling and oak-paneled walls. The hearth still stood at the far end of the room. The lantern hung from its iron hook beside the wide canopied bed.

"I see no changes since the last time I stopped here." He advanced on her, trying to restrain his rising anger; the girl stood her ground.

"Oh, but you're wrong. You must be wrong. Because otherwise . . ." A visible shiver ran down the length of her slender body; he saw that she was fighting hard not to lose control.

She spoke more quickly now, her voice tight with mounting fear. "I heard that man—Master Prescott—mention Morag by name."

"So you were eavesdropping, were you?"

She ignored his interruption. "You've got to send for her right now. She knows the Rowan Tree's changed. Maybe she'll be able to explain what happened here, before you came. Surely, she'll tell you—"

"Tell me what?" he demanded. Somehow, he controlled the urge to shake the truth out of her.

"She asked me to read her future. I wanted to tell her I can't read fortunes. But she seemed so eager, and I thought it would do no harm to pretend. To tell her what she wished to hear."

His lips clamped together as he fought down his rising anger. She was making no sense. Was she was deliberately talking in riddles to distract him? Had she been sent to help set a trap for him and his men?

She locked her glance on his, as if she were willing him to listen and believe her. "Later, after midnight, when Morag brought back the mirror, she turned out the lights and lit the candles on the table by the window. She wanted me to tell her when she'd find a young man of her own, what he'd look like."

"And did you?"

She shook her head, her amber eyes haunted. "It was your face I saw. I heard weird laughter, and felt a cold wind sweep through the room. The candles went out and then—"

"That's enough!" He grasped her shoulders. "Who sent you? I want straight answers, now!"

"Take your hands off me!" Her eyes burned with golden fire. As Liane's eyes had burned, when she'd been angry.

Liane. How many times he'd told himself he was free of her memory forever. Now he knew he'd been deceiving himself, and he felt a surge of fury at this intruder who had brought the past to life once more.

His fingers tightened, and he jerked her closer, so that the length of her pliant body, her long thighs, her full breasts were touching him. He breathed in the scent of her, and it stirred his senses, filled him with an overpowering need. Della and the other village wenches smelled of sweat and cooking grease. This girl's skin, her hair, gave off a delicate, flowery fragrance.

Kristy Sinclair. A Scottish name. Was she from Scotland? No, she came from a more distant land. Otherwise she'd not have spoken so freely of fortune-telling; it was strictly forbidden, for it carried the taint of witchcraft.

She turned her head away, and her hair brushed lightly against his face, stirring an unexpected desire within him. He wanted to press his face to the curve of her throat, to feel the waves of tawny hair against his cheek. To cup her breasts, to stroke and tease her nipples until they hardened under his fingers. To strip off her jacket and breeches, her silk shirt, to lift her onto the bed. . . .

Why did this girl arouse him so? He had taken hold of her only to keep her from escaping; but her scent, the touch of her softly curved body, had sent a pulsating heat coursing through him. He'd been without a woman for too long. He drew a deep breath, and managed to regain his self-possession.

"No more of your senseless chatter." His voice turned harsh. "I'll have the truth out of you, right now!" He had shaken off the Lord Protector's troopers back on the cliffs; but danger came in many shapes, and this tawny-haired, amber-eyed girl could be dangerous.

"You lied about Prescott. He wouldn't have given my chamber to a stranger."

"Mrs. Ainsworth rented the room to me. I explained about my accident. She phoned for the tow truck to take my car to the garage."

Phoned? Tow truck? She was still trying to confuse him with meaningless words.

"When Morag came to help me unpack, she found the scrying mirror—"

Diana Haviland

"You must be out of your wits to speak of such forbidden practices to a stranger."

Kristy stared up at the man's stern expression and said softly, "But you're not a stranger. I saw your face in the scrying mirror. And even before that."

Before that, her dreams had linked them together. All those nights when he had come to her across time and space. . . .

Quickly his hand covered her mouth; she winced as his powerful fingers tightened on her jaw. He forced her against the bedpost, pinioning her with the weight of his body. She struggled to free herself, writhing against him.

He took his hand from her mouth but his eyes never left hers. "Who sent you here, Mistress Sinclair? That is what you call yourself, isn't it?"

"Shall I show you my passport, my driver's license and credit cards to prove who I am?"

His baffled stare told her that she was using words he did not understand. And now, swiftly, inexorably, her indignation started to give way to a growing fear. Was it only Jared Ramsey she was afraid of? No, it was something far more terrifying: a glimpse of a dark force that could sweep her up and carry her beyond the boundaries of reality. This man might be her captor, her enemy, but she found herself clutching at his arm instinctively, drawing reassurance from its warmth, its hard, solid strength beneath her fingers.

As if sensing her terror, he spoke in a quiet, measured tone. "I'm not going to harm you, so long as you give me the truth." She nodded her assent. "Were you sent by one of the Lord Protector's magistrates?"

The Lord Protector. She had taken a course in English history back at college; now she struggled to remember what few facts she had managed to retain. The Lord Protector. Oliver Cromwell. He'd led his Puritan forces against one of the Stuart kings. Charles I? But that had been centuries ago.

"Speak up! Who sent you to spy on me?" She tried to fix

her whirling thoughts on Jared's questions, to frame a plausible answer.

"I'm not a spy. Marisol sent me." She could scarcely get the words out; a tight band of fear gripped her throat.

"Marisol?" She saw the suspicion in his searching gaze. "Who is this Marisol you speak of?"

"Marisol's not a person. It's a corporation. They opened branches in London and Paris a couple of years ago. And now there's a new one in Manchester."

Was it really possible that he didn't know the widely advertised name of the corporation she represented, that he didn't begin to understand what she was talking about?

Or was he was playing some sort of outrageous game for his own devious purpose? Yes, that had to be it. But why would he do such a thing? And what about those men who'd come here with him, driving the heavily laden wagons; and what of Prescott, who called himself the landlord of the Rowan Tree? What possible reason would all these strangers have for joining with Jared in this bizarre charade? Were they, too, determined to shake her belief her own sanity?

Careful, Kristy. If you start thinking like that, maybe you're really losing it.

She stiffened as she heard a knock on the door. A young girl entered the room, carrying a pitcher, a thick cloth, and a grey-white ball that might be some kind of homemade soap. "Uncle said you'd be wantin' to wash up, sir." The girl gave Kristy a startled glance.

She set the pitcher down on the washing stand near the bed, poured the water into a tin basin, and placed the cloth and soap beside it. "Thanks, Morag." He gave the girl a brief, dismissive nod, and she started for the door.

"Wait, Morag." Kristy's taut voice reflected her inner turmoil. "What's going on here? You've got to tell me!"

Then her breath caught in her throat, and she could not go on. Her eyes widened in stark disbelief.

Morag's hair had changed color from flaxen to light brown.

35

And it was no longer cut short; from under a starched white cap, two thick braids fell to her waist. She was shorter and plumper, and her homespun cotton dress, with its square white collar, covered her from her throat to her ankles.

The girl returned Kristy's searching gaze and her pale blue eyes rounded in surprise and disapproval. Was she shocked at the sight of a female in breeches? But she'd seen Kristy in this same burgundy pantsuit only a few hours ago. . . .

No! Not this Morag.

This Morag.

Mrs. Ainsworth's daughter had been a different girl. A girl from another century, from Kristy's own time.

This Morag was Master Prescott's niece. She belonged to another time. Oliver Cromwell's time. Jared's time.

God help me. I'm the stranger here. An exile in a century long past.

Until this moment, she had forced herself to hold on to the rapidly fading hope that these bewildering illusions were being caused by her accident; that the impact of the car against the rocky incline had caused some kind of shock to her senses. But she could no longer cling to that hope.

Morag was saying, "Your supper's waitin' downstairs, sir."

"Bring it up here," Jared ordered. "I will dine with Mistress Sinclair."

Would Morag recognize her name? No, not this Morag. She curtsied to Jared, cast another uneasy look at Kristy, then hurried from the room, her light brown braids swaying across her back.

Jared strode to the washing stand, took off his doublet and shirt, then tossed them both on the bed. Kristy's face went hot as she remembered that last dream about him: She'd been chained to the rock, the night wind tugging at her thin shift, the iron bands cutting into her wrists and ankles. He'd leaned close to her.

Touch me. Hold me. Her own shameless words came back to her now. And it was as if she could feel again the heat, the pressure of his hands, cupping her breasts. She'd strained at her bonds, her body arching upward, taut with her all-consuming need.

Now he was here in this room with her. But how could that be? What unknown force had drawn her back to him across the boundless reaches of time and space? She did not know, could not begin to understand.

She could only stand there, her gaze fixed on his broad shoulders, his powerfully muscled chest with its scattering of dark hair. And, as in the dream, her turbulent desires began to awaken, to stir inside her again.

If Jared was aware of her emotions, he gave no sign; instead, he began scrubbing himself vigorously. The soap was different from any she'd ever seen, but it made enough lather to serve its purpose. Drops of water clung to his thick dark hair and ran down his face and chest.

She wanted to push the damp hair away from his face, to stroke the muscles of his arms and chest, to feel the wet heat of him, under her fingers. Somehow she forced back the traitorous urge. Instead, she fixed her thoughts on those tormenting questions about this man who had intruded on her dreams.

Who was Jared Ramsey? Why had he come to the Rowan Tree tonight? He'd talked to Prescott of a long journey, of being trailed by Cromwell's soldiers and escaping out on the cliffs. Whatever business he was mixed up in, it was surely unlawful. Yet Prescott had addressed him as "my lord."

Jared had begun drying himself when the door opened again to reveal, not Morag, but a big, burly man in a knitted cap, leather vest and breeches. "You'd better come down to the stables, Jared," he said. "I been over the tally sheet twice. We're six crates short, by my count. There's a dozen casks of geneva missing, too. Prescott swears he don't know nothin' about it."

"Mind your tongue, Dermot." Jared nodded in Kristy's direction.

The man's gaze swerved, and he fixed her with a long, unabashed stare. "Morag wasn't lyin'," he said. "This wench is wearin' breeches!" He grinned. "She's a fine-lookin' piece, all the same." His light ginger-colored brows drew together in a puzzled frown. "Who is she? Not a village doxy, I'll be bound."

Jared pulled on his shirt and doublet. "She calls herself Kristy Sinclair."

"And how did she get up to your bedchamber without Morag catchin' sight of her? Or Prescott, either. He takes his oath he didn't see her at all. She didn't just come flying in through the window."

Jared silenced him with a gesture. "Mistress Sinclair has some explaining to do. I'll find out the truth about her before the night's over." He started for the door. "But first, I'll see to our cargo, and start those wagons on their way."

He turned a hard emerald stare on Kristy. "You will wait here for me." It was a command from a man who expected his orders to be obeyed without question.

After he and Dermot had left the room, she remained motionless, staring at the closed door. Where did Jared Ramsey think she might go running off to? What refuge could she hope to find in Glenrowan? Or in the alien world that lay beyond it?

Wave after wave of icy panic swept through her. She wrapped her arms around herself, but she couldn't drive away the bone-deep chill that possessed her.

Outside the courtyard of the inn lay the moors. The highways marked on her map would not have been built yet; there'd be rough wagon tracks, rocky cliffs. Her only escape lay forward in time. But how could she even begin to try to return to her own century? She shut her eyes, pressed her fingers to her temples and tried to focus her thoughts.

The scrying mirror. It had sent her back here. Maybe somewhere in the depths of the opaque black surface lay the power to carry her forward again, across the vastness of time and space. But where was the mirror now?

She'd been sitting opposite Morag at the round table with its two candles, when the mirror had slipped from her hand. The table had stood near the window. She knelt down and ran her hands over the planked floor, her heart thudding against her chest.

Then she touched something hard. The curved ebony handle. Her fingers closed around it. She stood up, and looked into the dark oval. Only the black surface, empty as it had been when she'd first seen it. How could she draw on the power that had lain buried somewhere deep inside her all these years?

Lost in thought, she stiffened as the door creaked open. Morag carried in a laden tray. Another Morag from another century, Kristy reminded herself. Even so, was there a chance that this girl could help her? She had to find out. What other hope was there? She crossed the room and confronted the girl.

There was no time to choose her words with care. "When did you first see me, Morag?" she demanded.

The girl gave her a wary look. "When I came up to bring Master Ramsey the water, you were here with him."

Kristy grasped the girl's arm. "But before that! I came to the inn this afternoon. Don't you remember?"

The girl shook her head. "I never saw you before tonight. My uncle questioned the cook, the hostlers. They never set eyes on you." Morag pulled free from Kristy's grip, and set down the tray. "Please, Mistress. I'm needed in the taproom." Her voice shook, and she twisted the coarse fabric of her skirt between her fingers.

She's afraid of me. Scared out of her wits.

Mrs. Ainsworth's daughter hadn't been afraid. If only she could get through to that other Morag. "Please—help me! If not for you, none of this would have happened. All your talk about the full moon—and drawing down the—Wiccan power? The goddess—you called her Aradia.''

"It's a lie! I don't know about such evil creatures!''

"But the mirror—''

"I know nothing of any mirror!'' The girl retreated to the door and flung it open. Jared stood blocking her way, his arm outstretched.

"What's all this screeching about?'' he demanded. "I heard you two going at it like a pair of angry cats.''

"It's her, Master Ramsey. She's wicked, tellin' those lies about me!''

Kristy thrust out the mirror, the one link between the past and the future. "Look at this, Morag! The scrying mirror—''

"Keep it away from me!''

"You do recognize it.''

"It's a witch's tool.'' Her gaze skittered from the mirror to Kristy's face and her voice rose, shrill with terror. "May the Lord protect me. You—'' She pointed an accusing finger at Kristy. "You are a witch! A lost soul! A servant of Satan!''

Morag was shaking, but fear lent her speed. With one swift movement, she slipped under Jared's outstretched arm and ran down the shadowy hall.

Jared shut the door and locked it. His eyes probed Kristy's. Then he said, "I'll have to take you with me.''

"Take me—where?''

"Out of Glenrowan. That foolish wench will rouse the village. This inn will be swarming with Cromwell's troopers by dawn.'' He threw his cape over his shoulders and put on his wide-brimmed hat.

"I'm the one Morag accused, not you,'' she reminded him.

His lips curved in a sardonic smile, but his eyes were cold. "She found you in my bedchamber. I've no intention of swinging from the gallows along with you.''

"The gallows?''

"Or burned at the stake, more likely.''

She flinched from the terrifying images his words conjured

up. It was as if she could already smell the acrid smoke and feel the searing heat of the flames. She took a step back, stumbled over her carry-on and clutched at a bedpost to keep from falling. He tossed her canvas bag on the bed. "What's in here?"

"A flashlight, extra batteries. A Walkman and—"

"More witches' tools?"

Surely this hard-eyed, self-possessed man couldn't believe in such superstitions. "You're talking nonsense," she began. But she felt an icy touch, deep within her. Witches. Had she ever believed in witches? How could she know what she had believed during those early, lost years?

Why can't I remember about my mother, Aunt Vera?

It's a blessing that you can't. Don't speak of her ever again.

Jared's voice pulled her back to their immediate danger. "Give that to me." He seized the mirror and shoved it into the bag. "How do you lock this?" he demanded. He didn't know what the zipper was for. It hadn't been invented yet, not in his time.

His time. And it will be mine, too. Unless I can get back where I belong.

He picked up the carry-on then strode to the wall beside the bed. He lifted the lantern from its hook then pressed on a knot in the wood. The heavy oak wall panels swung open. "Follow me."

She wanted to protest, but his driving need to escape had communicated itself to her. He held the lantern high. Its wavering light revealed a flight of stone steps. With her eyes fixed on his back, she started after him, down into the waiting shadows.

Chapter Three

As Kristy followed Jared down the narrow stone stairway, the chill, damp air enveloped her. The dim lantern light flickered across the walls, but she could see only a few feet ahead.

She fought the urge to turn and run back up to the bedchamber. Even if Jared would let her retreat, she would not dare to. Not with the memory of Morag's strident, accusing voice echoing in her mind.

. . . Witch . . . lost soul . . . servant of Satan . . .

At the bottom of the stairs, she felt rough stones scrape against her shoes and she hesitated.

"Come along and be quick about it! We've got to get as many miles as we can between us and Glenrowan before dawn." There was no mistaking his driving urgency.

She remembered what he'd said about the punishment for witchcraft. The gallows or the stake. A shudder ran through her body.

She caught a brief flicker of compassion in his eyes. "It's cold down here," he said. He took off his heavy cloak and put it around her. Let him think it was only the penetrating cold of the stones that was making her shiver.

As he fastened the metal clasp, his fingertips brushed her throat, her chin. His touch sent a surge of warmth flowing through her body.

They started down the narrow passage. Because his cloak was too long for her, she had to hold it up to keep it from dragging on the damp stones. Once, when she stumbled over the hem, he caught her arm to steady her. She walked as quickly as she could, trying to match her pace to his long-legged stride.

They must have covered at least a mile before she caught sight of another flight of steps, steeper than those going down from her room back at the inn. He led the way to the top, then set down the carry-on and handed her the lantern.

"Hold it high as you can," he ordered. By the dim, wavering light, she could just make out the square of a wooden trapdoor overhead.

Now she remembered the high-intensity flashlight in her carry-on. Before she could offer to find it for him, he had already set his shoulder against the heavy boards. The door began to lift, its hinges screeching. He grasped the rough wood with both hands and swung the door open.

She followed him into a wide space, bounded on three sides with broken stone walls. She looked upward, then cried out as she caught sight of a winged figure hovering in the darkness overhead. In one hand it grasped a flaming sword.

Jared put his arm around her shoulders. The heat that radiated from his powerful body enveloped her. "Easy, Mistress Sinclair. This was once the chapel of St. Edmund's Abbey. Cromwell's soldiers destroyed it."

Drawing reassurance from his nearness, from the hard strength of his encircling arm, she let herself relax against him. And now she realized that the figure with the flaming sword was only part of a shattered window: an angel made of colored glass. One of its wings and pieces of its white robe had been knocked out.

The last faint rays of moonlight slanted though the open spaces of the roof and touched the shards of glass scattered about the floor. A raw, penetrating wind tugged at her cloak, and lashed her tawny hair against her cheek. Looking about her, she saw that one of the stone walls had been smashed in; the massive oak doors hung loose from their broken hinges.

"Now you can rest for awhile," Jared told her. He found a seat in a pew that somehow had been left intact, and drew her down beside him; then he stretched out his long legs. "As soon as Dermot gets here, we'll be moving on."

"Moving on where?" she interrupted.

"The Rowan Tree's only one of my stops. Some of my wagons are already on their way to London. Others are going east, across the Pennines. But my route lies north to the Scottish border. You'll travel with me."

"And what makes you think I'll go anywhere with you?"

"You'll do as I say, Mistress Sinclair." He spoke with quiet authority.

Indignation shot through her. "Not until you answer a few questions."

She remembered his arrival at the inn, the brief conversation between him and Prescott in the downstairs hall. "First I want to know just why the landlord was afraid he'd be arrested for giving you shelter. Your wagons—what goods do they carry?"

His jade eyes narrowed. "I've already risked my neck bringing you this far. If you prove troublesome now, I'll leave you here to deal with Cromwell's troopers on your own."

"I can take care of myself." But even as she spoke, she suspected that her voice betrayed her lack of confidence.

"As you please, my lady. Try talking your way out of a charge of witchcraft. You won't succeed."

"Surely none of Cromwell's officers will believe Morag's foolish talk."

"It's you who are the fool. Morag's certainly been spreading the word about the witch she saw at the inn. By now, the villagers of Glenrowan have raised the hue and cry. When the news reaches the garrison, Cromwell's troopers will move out. They'll be scouring every mile of these moors, searching for you." His mouth tightened. "What possessed you to push your damned witch's mirror in Morag's face?"

Somehow, she had to make him understand. "It seemed the only way at the time," she began. "As soon as I saw Morag—this Morag—I knew she wasn't Mrs. Ainsworth's daughter. Her hair was a different color. And her clothes—that cap and apron—were all wrong. But the other Morag knew how to use the mirror. I hoped this one might know, too."

She tried to ignore his incredulous frown, as she hurried on, the words tumbling out. "The mirror brought me here. I'm sure of it. And so I thought it might take me back to my own time."

"Your own time," he repeated.

"The future—the twentieth century." She searched his face, seeking some trace of understanding, finding only cool detachment. "You don't believe me, do you?"

"Either you've escaped the guards at Bedlam, or you're trying to deceive me with your gibberish, for some purpose of your own."

"I'm no lunatic! And my only purpose is to return to—"

"This is the year 1654, Mistress Sinclair," he interrupted. "And no one, not even a witch, has the power to travel through time."

His hand shot out, and his fingers started to close on her arm, but before he could get a firm grip, she jerked away. The metal clasp at the collar of the cloak flipped open and the heavy garment slid off her shoulders.

He didn't believe her. Why should he? Just yesterday she'd

have denied the possibility of time travel. Yet now she had to make him accept the truth. She'd never be able to survive in his time, or get back to her own, without his help. But how . . . ?

"My carry-on."

"Your what?"

She gestured toward the canvas bag at his feet. "Back at the inn, you tried to close it, remember? But you didn't know how."

"And just what does that prove?"

"It proves that you never saw a zipper before. Because they haven't been invented yet."

"Or because you've come to England from another country." A smile touched his lips. "But I already knew that much from your peculiar accent."

"*My* peculiar accent!"

"I'm told that the artisans of Araby and Cathay have invented many curious devices—some of them most remarkable."

He prodded the bag with his booted foot, lifted it onto the bench, and studied the zipper carefully. Then he jerked at the metal loop on the end and pulled the bag open. "A clever invention, I agree. But it doesn't confirm the truth of your fantastic claim. What other proof can you offer?"

Without waiting for her answer, he thrust his hand inside the bag. He pulled out a bit of black lace and satin. One of her bras.

"Put that back!" Her cheeks burned and her voice shook with indignation.

He ignored her protest. He studied the shape of the cups, tugged lightly at the straps, then ran his fingers over the tiny metal hooks. His gaze shifted to the swell of her breasts, under her closely fitted jacket.

"I'll admit I've never seen such an enticing female garment before." He laughed softly as he rubbed the delicate fabric

46

between his thumb and forefinger. "What other wonders do you have to show me?"

Darts of fire flickered through her.

The dream stirred in the depth of her memory. Vivid, over-powering, it engulfed her senses. The torchlight, the unholy laughter of the masked figures surrounding her. And then Jared, leaning over her. Feral green eyes locked with hers.

Destroyer or rescuer?

Her body straining upward from the flat rock to which she was chained . . . his hands on her breasts . . . her thighs parting. . . .

No!

That was her dream. He didn't know, couldn't know, anything about it.

Drawing on all her inner strength, she thrust the dream away.

"What else do you have to show me?"

What proof that she had come from another time?

She had to convince him, beyond a doubt, that she spoke the truth. But how? She reached inside, and her hand closed around a hard oblong shape. She lifted it out. Her tape machine.

Had she left a tape in it? She couldn't remember. Take a chance, then. She pressed the switch.

A man's voice, deep and resonant, filled the chapel, echoing from the damp, moss-grown stone walls. Jared, his imperturbable calm shaken at last, leaned forward to catch the words of the song. They were seductive, yet eerie.

. . . *the power of the music of the night. . . .*

The hairs on the back of his neck lifted. His mouth went dry. Icy sweat sprang out on the skin of his back and trickled down his spine.

Fantastic. Unbelievable. Yet he could not deny the evidence of his own senses. Here in the chapel of St. Edmund's Abbey, a man's voice singing, accompanied by the harmony of unseen, unfamiliar instruments. And coming from a box small enough for this fey, amber-eyed girl to hold in the palm of her hand.

He watched as she pressed a button on the side of the object. The voice, the music vanished. Now he could hear only the first whisper of the dawn wind, the rustling of the dead leaves on the stone floor.

"It's called 'The Music of the Night.' " Her voice was calm, even casual. "The Phantom sings it when he . . ."

"Enough!" He drew a deep breath and forced himself to speak more quietly. "One of your witches' chants, I suppose." His linen shirt, damp with sweat, clung to his back. "You may be a witch, as Morag said you were. But you'll never make me believe you traveled here from the future." He tried to speak with all the conviction he could muster.

She only smiled, her amber eyes glowing with triumph. "Then suppose you explain where the music came from, Master Ramsey."

There was an explanation, he told himself. There had to be. Before he could even try to find it, he was brought up short by the distant creak of wagon wheels, the clopping of horses' hooves.

"I was expecting only Dermot to seek me here," he said. "But there are others with him. At least two wagons. Maybe more."

He got to his feet and pulled her up beside him. Once more, he was in control. "You will not display any of your witches' tools or boast of your powers." He pushed the carry-on back under the bench with his booted foot.

His followers were a rough lot: soldiers who had fought for the Stuart cause, and had narrowly escaped hanging; tinkers, peddlers, horse thieves who knew every road and crag on the moors. Until now, he had exerted an iron control over them. At his command, they had sailed across the North Sea in the teeth of the roughest storms. They had evaded Cromwell's well-armed troopers and had laughed about their exploits afterwards.

But witchcraft. That was another matter. These moors were still marked by the standing stones, the flat granite slabs that had served as sacrificial altars to the ancient gods. Circles of blackened heather still marked where the Beltane fires had burned on countless May eves. And would burn again, while decent folks kept their doors locked, their shutters bolted.

The wagons were here now. He heard the drivers' voices as they drew to a halt outside the abbey. Kristy moved closer to him. The slight pressure of her slender body, the fragrance of her tawny hair, stirred his senses. Looking down, he caught the flicker of uneasiness in her amber eyes.

His hand cupped her chin. He tilted her face upward. "Keep silent until I give you leave to speak." He threw his cloak over her shoulders again, and arranged the heavy folds close about her. "Don't let them catch a glimpse of that outfit you're wearing. The law forbids a female to wear a man's attire."

She had no chance to discuss the matter, for already she heard the whinnying of the horses, the stamping of their hooves, the voices of Jared's men.

His arm went around her shoulders. "If luck's with us, I may be able to save both our skins."

Kristy nodded. A moment later, she saw three men push open the sagging oak doors and come striding into the chapel. She looked them over in the first grey light of dawn.

The only one she recognized was the burly Dermot. His light blue eyes rested on her and his shaggy brows drew together in a disapproving frown, but he remained silent

A tall, wiry man, his face disfigured by smallpox scars, spoke out. "We always leave our doxies behind when we're moving freight. That's *your* orders, Master Ramsey."

"Guard your tongue. Mistress Sinclair's no doxy." Jared spoke quietly, but she heard the warning edge to his tone.

"Who is she, then? And where'd you find her?" asked the pock-marked man.

"That's no concern of yours, Owen." Jared took a step forward. "Unless you choose to make it so."

Owen eyed Jared uneasily. "But you, yourself, always said a wench could make a heap o' trouble in our sort o' business. As for this one, she's likely to be more dangerous then a whole wagonload o' the ordinary sort." He turned to his companion, a skinny, balding man in a leather jerkin. "Ain't that so, Nehemiah?"

The balding man nodded. "That's the truth, Master Ramsey. There's been talk about her already."

"Go on," Jared said.

But Nehemiah lapsed into silence. Owen hesitated, then swallowed hard. "We split up when we left Glenrowan, same as we always do. Nehemiah an' me was drivin' along the stretch of road that skirts Ashfield. We figured the townsfolk would be abed, it bein' after midnight."

"But they was all millin' about High Street," Nehemiah broke in. "Gabbin' like a flock o' geese, they was. Talkin' about a stranger—" He lowered his voice slightly. "A witch who came out of nowhere. They were sayin' that nobody saw how she got inside the Rowan Tree. Not Prescott, nor his niece. None o' the servants, neither. But there she was, in yer bedchamber, Master Ramsey."

Jared's hand closed around Kristy's. Remembering his warning, she kept silent.

"And that proves she's a witch." There was no mistaking the mockery in Jared's tone.

"A witch has ways o' makin' herself invisible," said Owen.

"Everybody knows that," Nehemiah said. "She speaks a spell an' puts fennel seeds in her shoes, an' you can't see her. Not even if she's standin' right next to you."

"Enough!" Jared silenced him. "And what have you to say, Dermot? Are you in fear of this maid, too?" But before

Dermot could answer, he went on: "You're not, and with good reason. You know as well as I do that Mistress Sinclair's no witch. She's only a reckless young lady who fled her home to escape a forced marriage with an unwanted suitor."

"She told you that?" Owen asked. "You let yourself be cozened by this wench you never saw before?"

"She's no stranger to me. I've known her since she was in short skirts. Her father's estate lies a few miles from Cragsmore. When we came ashore at Whitby I caught sight of her. The foolish wench was outside a tavern, talking with a sailor, seeking passage for Holland."

Although Owen looked somewhat subdued, his voice still held a touch of disbelief. "How'd she get into the Rowan Tree then? Without anybody seein' her?"

"I kept the rest of you busy while Dermot smuggled her up the back stairway and into my chamber," Jared said. "She traveled with us, hidden in Dermot's wagon.

"An' what was the need for keepin' the wench hidden?" Nehemiah demanded.

"To spare her reputation. Mistress Sinclair's no common village wench. She's a squire's daughter. Once the word of her escapade spread about the countryside, she'd have lost all hope of making a suitable marriage."

Kristy kept her eyes lowered to hide her surprise. Jared Ramsey was clever, quick-witted—and an accomplished liar.

How could she trust her safety to such a man? She reminded herself that she had little choice.

"You mean the wench was hidden in your wagon all the way from Whitby, and none of us the wiser?" Owen demanded of Dermot.

She tensed, fearing that Dermot might deny Jared's explanation. But when she glanced up, she caught the swift look that passed between Jared and Dermot.

"You doubt Master Ramsey's word?" Dermot's huge hand closed into a fist.

"I never said that," Owen protested. "But whether she be

51

a witch or not, it's still a risk lettin' her travel along with us. We'll have the Lord Protector's troopers on our trail in no time. An' half o' Yorkshire, besides.''

"That's the truth," said Nehemiah. "You did enough, bringin' her this far. Let her make her own way back to her father's estate."

"That's my decision, not yours," Jared reminded him. "You and Dermot will take one of the wagons to Exmoor. And you, Owen, will drive east across the Pennines."

"And the squire's daughter, what of her?" asked Dermot.

"She rides north, with me."

The heavily laden wagon, sturdy canvas tied down over the freight, creaked and jolted along the dirt road. Kristy sat close beside Jared on the narrow seat, her feet propped against her carry-on.

Low grey clouds darkened the eastern sky, down to the horizon. By mid-morning a heavy rain started to fall, turning the dirt track to mud. A rising wind drove in from the west, with only a few gnarled trees and rocky crags to break its force.

Jared watched as Kristy drew the cloak around her, obviously grateful for the thick folds that shielded her body. But the cloak gave no protection against the icy drops that stung her face, dripped from her cheeks, and drenched her hair.

Jared's doublet and wide-sleeved linen shirt were already soaked. Rain collected in the wide brim of his high-crowned hat, and streamed down, obscuring his view. With an impatient gesture, he pulled off the hat and tossed it down on the seat. His eyes remained fixed on the track ahead. From time to time he cracked the whip over the horse's back. It plodded on at a steady gait.

"That was a near thing, back at the abbey," he remarked. "Lucky for both of us that Owen and Nehemiah believed my tale."

"You're a most convincing liar."

He shrugged, ignoring the irony in her voice. "It's a necessary skill in my trade."

"And just what is your trade?"

"That doesn't concern you."

"It's against the law, I'm sure of that."

She turned to glance at the canvas-covered freight behind them. "What goods are we carrying?"

When he did not answer, she persisted. "Since you've forced me to travel with you, I have a right to know what I'm letting myself in for."

"You're bound to find out soon enough. We're smugglers, my men and I."

Smugglers. She stiffened and drew away from him.

In her own time, smuggling meant the Columbian drug cartels, with their illicit cocaine shipments. Or criminals who sold weapons of death and destruction to terrorists. Frightening images flashed through her mind. TV accounts of raids on crack houses. Newspaper photos of the World Trade Center bombing. The shattered shell of the Federal Building in Oklahoma City.

"We travel between the east coast—Whitby or Robin Hood's Bay—and Holland. We never lack customers eager to buy our duty-free tobacco. Our Brabant lace to trim milady's gown. Tea and geneva."

"Geneva?"

He grinned. "Certainly. It's becoming a most popular tipple. In London, a cask of geneva will always find a ready market."

Geneva . . . gin.

She relaxed a little. Although his trade surely was unlawful, it did not seem all that bad.

"The Scots favor their own native brew," he went on. "There's little demand for geneva north of the border."

He broke off abruptly, his eyes fixed on a rocky hill in the distance. A group of men were clambering over the top of the jagged rise, and making their way across the moor. They were heading straight for the wagon.

She saw his lips tighten, felt the tension that flowed from him like a tangible force.

"Jared, what's wrong? Those men—do you think they're looking for us?"

"Likely they are."

"Can't you make the horse go faster?"

"That would be unwise," he said. Instead, he jerked on the reins. The wagon came to an abrupt halt, throwing her against him. She clutched at his arm, but he drew away.

He reached down under the seat and when he straightened up again, she saw a knife in his hand. Surely he wasn't going to try to fight off the mob single-handed.

Before she could try to reason with him, he was unfastening the cloak. He pulled it off her, tossed it aside. He gave her a swift, appraising glance. "It might work," he said softly.

He seized her ankle. "Jared—what are you doing?" She tried to twist free from his grip, but it was useless. With one quick movement he slashed at the burgundy wool of her pants, and tore it away. Her leg was bared up to the knee.

"Now, the other." Too shocked to protest, she raised her other leg. Again he cut away the wet fabric.

"Your shoes. Take them off."

Her hands shook as she obeyed. He shoved the shoes under the carry-on. He pulled off her opaque burgundy knee-highs, the ones she'd chosen to match her Marisol pantsuit.

He thrust his fingers into her hair, then pushed the wet strands down over her forehead and across her cheeks.

The mob, twenty or more, were closer now. One of them raised his arm and shouted, but his words were carried off on the wind.

"Get down and go around to the back of the wagon."

"You'll have to help me. The seat's too high—"

"Get down, Kristy." He gave her a slight shove. "Now."

He had saved her with his quick-witted response once before. She'd have to trust him to do so again.

Somehow she managed to scramble down from the seat. She staggered, then regained her balance. Her bare feet sank ankle-deep into the mud.

She glared up at him through the pelting rain. "Get behind the wagon," he ordered. "Tug at the ropes that tie down the canvas. Fumble with the knots as if you're trying to open them."

"But why? Can't you tell me—"

"Keep your back to the crowd. No matter what happens, don't turn around."

The urgency in his voice silenced her. Mud splashed her naked legs. The force of the wind left her gasping for breath. Doggedly she kept going.

Now she was behind the wagon. She reached up and began to pull at the ropes. They scraped the skin of her hands. A carefully manicured fingernail broke off at the quick.

Although she dared not turn to look at the crowd, she heard the rumble of their voices. They were surrounding the wagon.

"What brings the lot of you out in such a storm?" Jared called to them.

She pressed her face against the wet canvas.

"We're bound on the Lord Protector's business," one of them replied.

"Are you, indeed?" She caught a touch of irony in Jared's tone. "You don't look like a regiment of dragoons to me."

The same man spoke again. "It's every man's duty to join the hue and cry when there's evil abroad." The man must be their leader. A self-important bully, by the sound of him.

"If you mean to rid this land of evil, it's quite a task you've set yourselves."

"Alas, 'tis all too true," said another. "Unholy creatures are lurking everywhere. Yet every righteous man must do what he can."

"And what unholy creatures do you seek hereabouts?"

"We seek a witch," said another. Kristy* pressed herself harder against the canvas.

"She appeared last night in Glenrowan."

"Then vanished into the darkness."

"She had a raven perched on her shoulder."

"Not a raven—a black dog, ye fool."

Now a dozen voices were raised, arguing, contradicting one another.

"These are fearful tidings, indeed!" Jared managed to sound suitably impressed. "What does she look like, this witch?"

"We'll ask the questions," the mob's leader interrupted. "Why do you linger in this rain when you have a horse and wagon to carry you to the nearest inn?"

"My worthless apprentice did not tie down the canvas properly at our last stop. My goods were getting soaked. This time he'll do a better job, if he knows what's good for him."

"You'd best go and see for yourself, master," came a voice from the crowd. "Else your freight'll be soaked, if it isn't already."

Kristy felt the wagon jar, then heard the squelching of Jared's leather boots pulling against the mud with every step. She didn't dare turn her head.

Jared was beside her now. "Hurry up, you lazy bag of bones!" His big hand shoved hard against her shoulder. Her bare feet slid out from under her, and she fell face down in the mud. She ignored her first instinct, to scramble to her feet. He'd warned her that the crowd mustn't see her from the front.

Jared bent over her and pushed her head deeper into the mud. No doubt he considered this a necessary part of the charade. All the same, she couldn't control her indignation at his rough treatment.

"Clumsy, witless young fool," he shouted. "I've a good mind to take the whip to you."

She heard the crowd rumble its approval.

"That's the way, master!"

"These apprentices need discipline."

"Skin the hide from his back!"

They were moving closer, shouting their encouragement, urging Jared on. Kristy went rigid as she remembered the horsewhip, set in its metal holder. Her stomach muscles clenched. Under her soaking-wet shirt, she felt the skin on her back start to prickle.

There was no way she would submit to such brutal treatment, not without a struggle. Her body tensed, as she prepared to leap to her feet.

"The whelp will pay for his carelessness," Jared said. "But not until I've reached the next inn, and stowed my goods safely."

Kristy went limp with relief.

"And what goods do you carry?" She recognized the leader's harsh voice.

"That's no concern of yours," Jared told him.

"Maybe we'll make it our concern."

Jared's laughter mocked him. "You'd sooner linger here, interfering with an honest merchant, than go seeking the witch. Is that it?"

"I fear no witch on earth or in hell!" the leader shouted.

"Thou shalt not suffer a witch to live!" cried another.

She heard the men encouraging one another, eager to prove their devotion to duty. Their voices receded, as they went slogging away from the wagon to take up the pursuit.

She started to rise. "Not yet," Jared warned. "Not until that mob's out of sight."

Chapter Four

Jared bent down and helped Kristy to her feet. The pelting rain had given way to a light drizzle. Peering across the moor, she saw that the witch-hunters had started on their way again, squelching through the mud, caught up in the thrill of the chase. She watched them climb over the rocky ledge, then disappear from view.

"You made a most convincing apprentice boy." Jared put his arm around her waist.

"If you mean that as a compliment, I'm in no mood to appreciate it. I'm soaking wet and filthy." She wiped the mud from her lips with the back of her hand.

Before she could do anything more to rid herself of the clinging mask, he lifted her into his arms, carried her to the front of the wagon, and set her down on the seat.

Her eyes rested briefly on the whip, set in its holder. "Would you really have beaten me?"

"Certainly," he said, "if it had proved necessary."

The cool callousness of his reply filled her with anger. She took a deep breath and when she spoke again, her voice was carefully controlled. "What stopped you?"

He shrugged. "There was no need. I'd already convinced the crowd that you'd get your punishment soon enough."

"Otherwise, you'd have slashed my back to ribbons to save your precious freight?"

He reached into a leather pouch that hung from the side of the wagon, pulled out a strip of cloth, and started to wipe the mud from her face and hair. "If I hadn't managed to get rid of that mob, they'd have dragged us both off to the district magistrate. He'd have confiscated my freight."

"Because it was smuggled cargo?" she asked. "But how could he have known that?"

A brief, ironic smile touched his lips. "The magistrate would not have charged us with the lesser crime of smuggling, not when he could have taken far greater credit for having captured a witch—and her companion."

"But your freight—"

"Surely you haven't forgotten Cromwell's edict. A witch's goods and chattel are to be confiscated by the local magistrate."

Forgotten? How could she have forgotten the edict, when she'd never known it to begin with?

"I'd have been condemned for aiding you in your unholy practices," he went on.

She shuddered inwardly. What other brutal, senseless laws would she have to deal with before she could escape from this alien century? How could she possibly hope to survive long enough to return to her own time?

She was a hunted fugitive, with only Jared Ramsey to help her. For now, she was completely dependent on him.

He went on wiping away the mud, his hand moving over her forehead, her cheeks, her throat. And even now, against all common sense, she felt an unexpected reassurance at his touch.

Only reassurance, and nothing more? How would she respond if he were to caress her as he had in her dream?

Think about something, anything else.

She seized upon the first distraction that came to mind.

"That cloth—it smells peculiar."

"It smells like horse," he told her. "That's what it's for, to rub down horses."

She swallowed her indignation and forced herself to keep silent.

His eyes moved over her body. "You're shivering," he remarked.

Although the rain had stopped, a fierce east wind blew across the barren moorland. She'd been drenched and now her clothes clung to her body like an icy sheath.

She reached for his cloak, but he grasped her arm. "Not yet, Kristy. You'll have to change first. Do you have any garments in your bag—besides that flimsy bit of silk and lace you showed me back in the abbey?"

What else had she packed? She tried to remember. It seemed like a century since she'd stood in her bedroom, back in her New York apartment, preparing for her flight. More than three centuries, she reminded herself.

"I think there's a nightgown."

"A night rail?"

"Whatever." She wasn't about to quibble over his choice of words when she had all she could do to keep her teeth from chattering.

"Get out of those wet clothes, all of them."

She stiffened with indignation. "I'll do no such thing."

His dark brows shot up. "A modest witch?" His lips curved in a faint smile. "You've no scruples about dancing naked in the light of the full moon. Sky-clad, isn't that what witches call it?"

"How should I know? I've told you, I'm not a witch— How can you possibly think—"

He ignored her outburst. "Here, take the cloth." He pushed it into her hand. "Climb under the canvas back there. Strip, rub yourself dry, and put on your night rail. Then wrap yourself in my cloak. Otherwise you'll be seized with the ague before we reach the Scottish border.''

Ague? Whatever that was, it didn't sound good.

He lifted the canvas and she crawled underneath it. A moment later, he pushed her carry-on after her. Although there was little space among the casks and crates, she somehow managed to struggle out of the ragged remains of her clothing.

She rubbed the horse cloth hard over her breasts, her belly and thighs. What wouldn't she give for a steaming shower right now, with a cake of her own scented soap and a plastic bottle of shampoo. Had she packed them in the bag?

She opened it and groped around inside. Her fingers brushed against something small and hard. Her flashlight. She switched it on, and found her nightdress.

She set down the flashlight long enough to pull the sheer blue nylon gown over her head. Too bad she hadn't thought to pack a heavy flannel gown instead. The kind Aunt Vera had made her wear.

But how could she have known she'd find herself out here, driving across the windswept moor in a jolting wagon, pelted by rain, covered with mud?

"Hand me your wet clothes."

She started slightly at his brusque command, then carefully lifted a corner of the canvas.

He turned to take the tattered clothes from her, then stopped short and stared in disbelief at the unearthly glow that illuminated her face and turned her eyes deep amber. He could not look away.

That gown, sheer as cobwebs. Heat surged through him at the sight. Had she been naked, her body could not have been more enticing than it was now, sheathed in filmy blue folds.

He drew a harsh breath, as he felt the tightening in his groin. Damn! Was he a callow boy, to be overpowered by physical urgency?

He tried to look away, to fix his eyes on the road ahead, on the rocky ledge in the distance. But his treacherous body had a will of its own. Driven by his inexorable need, he started to reach out for her. He wanted to push aside the flimsy gown. To lay bare the soft, tawny triangle at the apex of her thighs.

To feel its humid heat under his fingers. To caress her, stroke her, until she opened herself to him willingly. To bury himself deep in the hot, moist center of her.

What held him back?

The light.

The light that didn't flicker in the wind, as a candle flame would have done. The light, infinitely brighter than a thousand candles. That small, silvery object in her hand—that was the source of the light. But how had she created it?

His hot, pulsating response to her lush femininity gave way to an even more primitive instinct. Fear of the unknown.

Who—what—was she, this tawny-haired, amber-eyed stranger? Even as he sought an answer, he saw her finger move slightly; the light disappeared.

Quickly he snatched her wet clothes away, and thrust his cloak at her. "Here, cover yourself with this."

He might have demanded that she tell him where that light had come from. He didn't. He wasn't sure he wanted to know.

Besides, this was no time for questions. Although she had stopped shivering, and there was even a faint touch of color in her cheeks, he could sense her exhaustion. Witch or no witch, she needed rest. Her lids were beginning to close. Whatever her occult powers might be, they were contained in the body of a mortal woman.

With an abrupt movement, he pulled the canvas back in place. "You'd better get some sleep," he told her.

She mumbled a response but he didn't catch the words; she sounded half-asleep even now.

He picked up the reins. The horse shook its head, whinnied,

and plodded forward. The wagon creaked and lurched its way on across the moors.

They had to keep moving north, to put as many miles as possible between themselves and this part of Yorkshire. They'd been lucky during that encounter with the witch-hunters. They might not be so lucky a second time.

It hadn't been luck alone that had saved them. He glanced briefly over his shoulder, at the canvas shelter where Kristy slept.

The girl had courage, he'd say that for her. Even under the threat of the lash, she'd remained motionless, lying back there facedown in the mud. One glimpse of her soft red mouth, her slender neck and firm, jutting breasts, and the charade would have been over.

Suppose the mob had demanded that she should be flogged, then and there. Would he really have taken the whip to her, to convince them that she was a lazy apprentice boy?

The very thought filled him with repugnance. Yet why should he feel that way? Apprentices and servants were whipped when they displeased their masters. Children, girls as well as boys, were beaten by their parents for the smallest misdeeds.

Surely it would have been better to have used the lash on Kristy than to see her charged with witchcraft and sentenced to the flames or the hangman's rope.

But was she a witch?

His dark brows drew together with his baffled frown. She'd shown the scrying mirror to Morag without a moment's hesitation. Wouldn't a witch have behaved more cautiously?

And she hadn't known the penalty for practicing witchcraft. Even after he'd told her, he wasn't sure she believed him.

What about her fantastic claim that she'd traveled here from another time?

No! He didn't believe that. His mouth clamped together in a hard, tight line. No sane man could believe it. Yet the tools she carried with her were unknown to him. That music she'd evoked from the box, back in the abbey. The radiant light she could control with a flick of her finger.

Why the devil had he brought her with him from Glenrowan? What was the bond that had joined his destiny to that of the tawny-haired, amber-eyed girl?

Kristy woke with a start, her muscles stiff and cramped. Her body was curled up on a hard surface that kept jouncing and swaying beneath her. Baffled by her unfamiliar surroundings, she stirred, reached out and felt the folds of the heavy woolen cloak wrapped around her. It smelled of salt, of horse and leather.

A jumble of frightening images crowded in on her, invading her consciousness, overwhelming her.

She recalled Morag's shrill, accusing voice; the long trek with Jared down the damp stone tunnel leading away from the inn; the first glimpse of the ruined abbey, with its menacing angel. She thought of Jared's men, quarreling over what was to be done with her, and the witch-hunters surrounding the wagon.

And always beside her was Jared Ramsey.

She raised herself on one arm, pushed aside the canvas, and squinted into the sunlight. The sky was blue and cloudless once more—as it had been that day she'd left Manchester to drive northeast to Leeds.

For an instant, she remembered the unearthly mist, and the figure of the dark-haired, silver-eyed woman in the road. She forced the image to the back of her mind.

"Jared!" She leaned forward and called out his name as if it would somehow serve as a talisman to dispel the forces of darkness.

"Good morrow to you, Mistress Kristy." His voice, casual and friendly, reassured her. "High time you were awake."

She clambered out from under her canvas shelter and he shifted to make room for her on the seat beside him. "How long did I sleep?"

"Right through the afternoon, and all night, too."

"And you were driving all that time?"

"I stopped now and then to rest and water the horse. And I borrowed some hay for the beast from a farm along the way."

"You borrowed it?"

"The horse needs food to keep going."

"So do I."

He grinned. "I won't let you starve," he assured her. "But before you break your fast, I suppose you'll want to get tidied up a bit."

He stopped the wagon and got down, helped her from the seat, then jerked his head in the direction of a high stand of jagged rocks beside the road. "You'll find a waterfall over there, and a stream."

The pebbles on the road cut into her bare feet. "My shoes," she said. He reached up and retrieved them from under the seat. She had to rest a hand on his shoulder for balance as she slipped them on.

"And my bag."

He handed down the carry-on. "Will there be anything else, your ladyship?"

She ignored his sarcasm and started for the rocks. "You'll have all the privacy you need," he called after her.

She kept going across the stretch of ground, thick with the stalks of dry heather and bracken, then circled behind the towering rocks.

The stream and the high waterfall glittered in the morning sunlight. She opened her bag; a search revealed a cake of soap in its plastic box. Marisol's own signature brand, scented with fern and lavender.

Kneeling beside the fast-running stream, she cupped her hands and scooped up the crystal water. Trying to ignore the icy cold, she made a thick lather and washed away the lingering traces of mud. She soaped and rinsed her hair, combing the suds through its tangled strands with her fingers.

Too bad she hadn't packed a towel; she'd have to dry herself with that smelly horsecloth instead. Nevertheless, when she returned to the wagon wearing her nightgown with Jared's cape over it, she felt thoroughly refreshed.

Jared helped her back onto the seat and picked up the reins. She put a restraining hand on his arm. "You said you wouldn't let me starve," she reminded him.

He grinned. "I made do with bread and cheese last night, while you slept. I saved some for you."

He unhooked a leather pouch from the side of the wagon. "Your breakfast, Mistress Kristy."

He passed her the remains of a round loaf and a hunk of cheese. "This should hold you until we reach Braethorn," he told her.

"Braethorn?"

"It's a market town, some twenty miles north. I've a bit of business there."

"Smuggler's business, I suppose."

He didn't deny it. "But before we get to Braethorn, you'll need a change of clothes." His green eyes held a hint of amusement. "That bit of blue cobweb you use for a night rail won't do at all."

"I'll keep your cloak on over it."

"We can't take the risk." His eyes, his voice, were somber now. "There'll be horse and cattle traders at Braethorn. Peddlers and tinkers, too. Any one of them might be carrying word about the witch of Glenrowan. The Witch of the Dark Mirror."

"You do have a way with words, Jared Ramsey."

He laughed softly. "It's only one of my many talents." Then he pressed her hand and she felt reassured by his touch. "Once we cross the Scottish border, you'll be safer."

"Don't the Scots believe in witches?"

"They do. But I doubt they'll have heard about you that far north."

She swallowed hard, hesitated, then took the plunge. "And you, Jared? Do you believe in witches, too?"

He didn't answer at once. In the taut silence, she was conscious of the creak of the wagon wheels, the clopping of the horse's hooves.

When he spoke, he chose his words carefully. "Every village has an old crone who uses herbs and spells to ease a woman through a difficult childbirth—to brew a potion that will break a fever. Or even to get a cow that's gone dry to give milk again."

"But if witches do only good, why are they feared so?"

"Most do good. But not all. There are those who choose the left-hand path. They use their power to do harm."

"And Morag thought I was one of those."

"You showed her the dark mirror."

The mirror. Always it came back to the mirror.

She shifted uneasily on the wagon seat. It hadn't been chance that had made her buy the mirror. It hadn't been the persuasive saleslady at The Magick Caldron. Or Liz, either.

It had been some power hidden in the depths the mirror itself. It had been the feel of it in her hand, as if it belonged there. As if it had been lying in the darkness, waiting for her, all these years.

"Jared, look at me." She gripped his arm. "Do you think I'm a witch who's chosen the—left-hand path?"

His eyes met hers for an instant; then he turned away.

"Do you?"

"I don't know what to think, damn it!"

"Jared—"

He leaned over the side of the wagon, reached into the leather pouch again. "You said you were hungry. Eat, then—and slake your thirst with this." He took out an earthenware jug.

Although her appetite had lost its edge, she obeyed. The bread was hard and coarse. The flavor of the cheese was strong, unfamiliar. He pulled the cork from the jug and handed it to her.

She took a swallow, then coughed and sputtered. "What is this stuff?"

"Geneva. It'll warm you."

She took another sip and felt the heat move through her, down to the pit of her stomach, to the tips of her fingers and toes.

Her eyes watered and she coughed again.

"Not used to strong drink, are you?"

"I've never drunk gin straight—with my breakfast."

"Gin?"

"That's what it's called in my time."

"Your time!" He glared at her, then picked up the reins. The horse broke into a brisk trot. "If you can't talk sense, keep still!"

But she refused to be silenced. "Is it really that you don't believe me? Or are you afraid to admit you do?"

His voice shook with barely leashed fury. "Hold your tongue! I've saddled myself with a wench who's being hunted the length and breadth of Yorkshire, from Kilnsey Crag to Westerdale. I've had to deceive my own men, and stand off a band of witch-hunters. But I'm damned if I'll put up with your mad prattle about traveling through time."

"Then set me down right here, Jared Ramsey. Be rid of me and my 'mad prattle,' once and for all."

"Don't tempt me."

At his words, the practical side of her nature took command. She bit down hard on her lower lip to force back the tide of angry words. She dared not antagonize Jared. He was her only hope of survival, here in this alien time, on this desolate stretch of countryside.

She lapsed into silence. But as the wagon went jouncing on, she asked herself if she was concerned only with her own safety. Seated close beside Jared, she sensed the powerful bond between them, the inexorable force that had drawn them together across the gulf of time and space.

Now that she had found him, she knew with bone-deep certainty that he was part of her. He always had been. His green eyes, his hard slash of a mouth—how many nights had she awakened, her body aching for his, gripped by the fierce need to be possessed by him? How many times had she dreamt of giving herself to him with a passion that matched his own.

It was passion that was no dream, but stark reality.

She had caught the naked hunger in his look, when he'd seen her in the beam of the flashlight. He'd been stirred to the depths of his being, his senses aflame. Why hadn't he taken her? What had held him back?

"We'll stop here at the inn." His voice broke in on her thoughts. She realized that they had covered a considerable distance since early morning. Where there had been only moorland stretching out around them, now she saw hills, softly rounded. She caught a glimpse of a broad river sparkling in the sunlight between copses of pines.

To one side of the road, she caught sight of a rambling stone building. Wind and rain had scoured the wooden sign beside the door. She could barely make out a rough likeness of a pair of roosters, and the faded lettering. THE FIGHTING COCKS.

"I know the landlord here."

The inn had a desolate, sinister look about it. "Surely he can't attract many travelers in such a lonely spot," she said.

Jared grinned. "Rufus Dunstan does well enough in his own way." He drew rein, climbed down, and helped her to the ground. Then he went around to the back of the wagon, pulled the canvas aside, and lifted down four wooden casks.

He crossed the inn's yard, but before he could reach the door, it swung open to reveal a hulking man in a soiled shirt and leather breeches.

"Master Ramsey!" he shouted. "Yer a welcome sight, that

ye are. If ye'd taken a few more nights gettin' here, my guests would've had to slake their thirst with well water."

His gaze moved past Jared and rested first on the casks, then on Kristy. "Not travelin' alone this time, I see."

Jared motioned to Kristy, who followed him into a low-ceilinged taproom with smoke-blackened beams.

Dunstan motioned to a skinny, ragged boy who was cleaning out the fireplace grate. "Let that wait. Go bring in Master Ramsey's casks, an' be quick about it."

The boy hurried outside.

"Is Sally about the place?" Jared asked.

Dunstan gave a harsh bark of laughter. "So ye need more'n one female to pleasure you." Kristy flinched at the implication, but remained silent. The landlord sauntered to the foot of a narrow flight of stairs. "Sally! Get yer lazy arse down here an' give Master Ramsey a proper welcome."

Kristy heard quick footsteps on the stairs and looking up, she saw a full-figured girl whose ample breasts were scarcely covered by her low-cut blouse. Dark chestnut hair fell around her shoulders in an untidy mane.

Her brown eyes lit up at the sight of Jared; then her glance shifted to Kristy, and her brows drew together in a puzzled frown. "Since when've ye been dealin' in that sort of goods, Master Ramsey?"

"The wench is not for sale. I've no doubt you're able to take care of all Rufus's guests yourself."

"An' keep 'em comin' back for more," Sally said, with a toss of her head. But she slanted an uneasy glance at Kristy. "What did ye bring 'er 'ere for, then?"

"Mistress Sinclair needs a proper dress. If you've got one to spare, I'll pay you a shilling for it."

"A proper dress? Is the wench naked under that cloak then?"

"She might as well be," said Jared. "Speak up, Sally. Do you have a dress to sell?"

"Only what I'm wearin'."

"What about that homespun dress ye was wearin' when ye came to work here?" Rufus broke in.

"Plain as an old sack it is," said Sally.

"So much the better," Jared told her. "Take Mistress Sinclair upstairs and let her change clothes."

"Open yer cloak, girl. Let's see how yer built. Maybe my dress won't fit ye."

"Upstairs, both of you." Sally obviously recognized Jared's brusque tone of command, for she turned without another word, and motioned to Kristy to follow her.

She led Kristy up to a small, shabby room, with an untidy bed, a sagging chair and a scarred wooden chest. She opened the lid of the chest, rummaged around, pulled out a crumpled grey garment and tossed it onto the bed.

"It'll make ye look a proper fright," she said with a touch of satisfaction. "Squire used to make all his maidservants wear 'em. Frozen-faced psalm-singin' Puritan, he was. Used to preach at us for an hour every night after dinner an' twice on Sundays." She gave a scornful laugh. "But after his wife was abed, he'd come sneakin' up to my room for a quick tumble."

Kristy turned away and examined the coarse garment with its frayed white collar and wrist-length sleeves.

"Why does Master Ramsey want his wench dressed like this?" Sally asked. "He's no Puritan. But I expect ye know that already."

"I know nothing about Jared's taste in women!"

"Ye tellin' me he's been travelin' with ye an' hasn't laid a hand on ye yet?"

Jealousy clawed at Kristy's insides. This buxom, chestnut-haired girl sounded as if she knew all about Jared's ways with women. Determined to hide her turbulent feelings, Kristy said only, "I suppose I should wear a white cap with this." She remembered the one Morag—the other Morag—had worn after the Rowan Tree had undergone its transformation.

Sally shrugged, rummaged in the chest again, and came up with a dingy white cap, a frayed petticoat and a pair of woolen stockings. "I'll throw these in an' no extra charge," she said with derisive smile. "I'd have thought Jared Ramsey would want his whore decked out in silk an' lace."

Unable to restrain herself another minute, Kristy confronted the other girl. "I'm not his whore! What right have you to imagine—"

"Just goin' along for the ride, are ye? Where'd he find ye, anyway? Ye don't talk like a Yorkshire woman."

Caught off guard, she remembered Jared's explanation to his men, back at the abbey. "I come from Holland," she said. A few more weeks with Jared and she'd be as glib a liar as he was.

"Holland, is it?" Sally gave her a malicious little smile. "If ye followed him across the sea, hopin' for a wedding ring, ye won't get one from him."

"I never considered the possibility." That, at least, was true enough.

"An' neither did he," Sally told her. "His lordship ain't about to give his fine name to the likes of you."

Kristy ignored the implied insult. "His Lordship! Jared's a common smuggler."

"He's a smuggler, that's for sure—but he's no commoner."

Sally moved closer and lowered her voice. "Jared Ramsey is a nobleman, the fifth earl of Ravenswyck. Fought for the king in the wars, he did. He chose the wrong side, an' that cost him his great estate an' the highborn lady he was betrothed to."

"But he'll get his property back when Prince Charles returns and claims the throne."

"An' what makes you think the prince'll ever come back?" Sally gave her an uneasy look. "Do ye claim to read the future?"

There it was again—the same look of superstitious fear

72

she'd seen in Morag's eyes. How could she tell Sally that she knew what would happen because she had come here from the future? That she'd learned about the Restoration in her college history course. Charles Stuart would return to claim the throne after the death of Cromwell. He would banish the dark, repressive Puritan reign and win the love and loyalty of his subjects.

But all that lay years ahead. Right now, Cromwell still lived and ruled with an iron hand.

"I know nothing of the future. I was only repeating a bit of gossip I chanced to hear, back in Amsterdam."

Although Sally seemed to be satisfied, Kristy could not be sure. She warned herself that she would have to choose her every word with the greatest care.

Otherwise, she might still be condemned as a witch. And Jared along with her.

Chapter Five

The last wisps of fog had blown away and sunlight gilded the peaked roofs and cobbled streets of Braethorn when Jared drove his wagon through the town gate and drew rein beside the south wall of the crowded market square. Kristy saw that a row of wagons already stood there; a few were covered with canvas as Jared's was; others were open, so that Kristy could get a glimpse of their wares: crates of squawking chickens and geese, baskets laden with codfish and eels, with vegetables, and with freshly-baked bread.

She watched the gathering crowd coming from every direction; there were men on horseback, families in wagons and on foot, all of them converging on the cobblestone square. The women wore black, or drab shades of brown and grey; their high-collared, long-sleeved bodices did nothing to enhance the appearance of even the prettiest. The little girls wore the same prim clothing.

"Shall I wait in the wagon?" Kristy asked.

Jared shook his head. "You'll come with me. This is as

good a place as any to find out if you'll be accepted as a woman of—''

"A woman of your time," she finished for him. "That is what you were going to say, isn't it?"

"Something like that."

"I can't blame you for having doubted that I was telling you the truth. It didn't seem possible to me, either. Not at first. Traveling through time goes against all common sense. And when I couldn't deny it to myself any longer, I was frightened out of my wits."

"All the same, you've managed to put up a bold front. Back there, with those witch-hunters, you showed more self-control than most women would have done."

She caught a gleam of reluctant approval in his green eyes. He took her hand, the touch of his fingers sending a tide of warmth coursing through her. "We've made it this far, haven't we? And I'll get you across the border into Scotland. Trust me, Kristy."

"I do." Although the words came unbidden, she realized that they were true. How was it possible? He was a smuggler, a practiced liar, yet she trusted him.

He took his cloak off her shoulders and pushed it under the canvas. "It's a man's garment," he reminded her. "It could draw the wrong kind of attention." He looked her over and smiled with satisfaction. "That's better. Now you look like all these other women."

"Thanks a lot," she retorted, with a faint smile. "They look as drab as a flock of crows."

"Maybe so. But they're dressed like proper Puritan females," he assured her. He helped her down from the wagon, and they joined the crowd heading for the square. Men in loose smocks and mud-spattered shoes drove their sheep and cattle before them. One sturdy, red-cheeked woman tugged on a rope she had fastened around a pig. The beast tugged back with equal determination, squealing all the while. It gave a sudden lunge in Kristy's direction, then bumped hard against her legs, nearly knocking her off balance. Jared steadied her with his arm.

"Your pardon, mistress," said the woman.

Kristy opened her mouth to speak, then felt the warning pressure of Jared's hand on hers.

"No harm done, goodwife," he said. Kristy only smiled and nodded. Although her dress and cap helped her to blend in with the crowd, Jared evidently feared that her accent might set her apart. Better to keep silent.

He took her arm and led the way past the cattle pen to the rows of stalls beyond. She saw that their wares were strictly practical: wooden buckets and spoons, iron cooking pots, piles of turnips and potatoes, baskets of eggs, slabs of butter laid out on cabbage leaves. A butcher and a housewife haggled over the price of a joint of mutton. Only one stall-keeper displayed more frivolous goods: gold-colored earrings, strings of carved wooden beads, a red shawl embroidered with flowers.

A young girl, her hair hidden by her starched cap, paused for a moment to gaze longingly at the brightly colored wares but a heavyset, grey-haired man caught her by the arm. "For shame, Charity! You'll not deck yourself out like a trollop while you live under my roof."

"I was only looking, father." But her eyes were wistful as she turned away.

"How do you expect find any buyers for those laces and silks of yours in this crowd?" asked Kristy.

He grinned and spoke in an undertone. "Even the Lord Protector hasn't been able to stamp out all female vanity. Plenty of frivolous young ladies still adorn themselves in the privacy of their own homes. Right here in Braethorn, I already have a merchant waiting for such goods."

He stopped before a stall far larger than the rest; its roof and sides were hung with sturdy canvas. Kristy breathed deeply; her mouth watered at the tempting odors of baking meats, warm bread and cinnamon.

"Now we'll have that hot dinner I promised you," he said. "Mother Jenkins keeps the best cookshop in the Braethorn market."

A few minutes later they were seated at a small table. A serving girl had already put down a roast goose on a wooden platter, a bowl of potatoes, a dish of apples and raisins spiced with cinnamon and topped with thick cream, a loaf of freshly baked bread and an earthenware crock of butter. Jared heaped Kristy's plate with slices of goose, the skin glistening golden brown; a thick slab of bread; and a couple of potatoes with a scoop of butter, before he served himself. As he watched her enjoying her meal, he smiled. "I was right, wasn't I?"

"It's delicious." She sighed, "But when I think of all the cholesterol—"

"What's that?"

"Never mind," she said, as she savored the crisp skin and tender meat from the breast of the bird.

He filled her pewter tankard, then his own, with dark brown ale. "You've a hearty appetite for such a slender lass," he remarked.

"If you think I eat this way in my own time—" A shadow fell across the table; she looked up at a short, stout man whose dark suit, although somber, was well-cut and of good woolen cloth. He wore a high-crowned hat with a square pewter buckle in front.

"Master Ramsey," he said with a smile. "Welcome back to Braethorn." He gave Kristy a curious, sidelong glance.

Jared stood up quickly. "Mistress Sinclair, may I present Master Thomas Hutchinson, a leading merchant of this town."

Kristy, still uneasy about her speech, inclined her head. "Master Hutchinson," she said softly. She held her breath, waiting for Jared to invent some explanation for her presence here. But he only said: "Finish your meal, Mistress Sinclair. Take all the time you like. This gentleman and I have business to discuss."

Hutchinson made a quick bow in her direction; then he and Jared left the cookshop together. They shouldered a path through the growing crowd drawn by Mother Jenkins's good cooking.

On her own now, she felt a twinge of uneasiness. A woman alone here might draw attention. Suppose someone should speak to her? Her appetite vanished, but she kept her eyes cast down and made a pretense of eating, picking at the apple and raisin pudding, pushing it around on her plate. How long would it take for Jared to strike a bargain with Master Hutchinson, and unload his smuggled goods? No matter. She would stay here until Jared returned.

But even now, the cookshop was getting more mobbed by the minute, as farmers and their families came jostling in, along with teamsters and cattle drovers. The plump young serving girl who had waited on her and Jared made her way through the crowd to Kristy's table. "Will there be something more you're wanting, mistress?"

Reluctantly, Kristy shook her head, knowing she wouldn't be able to swallow another bite. The girl frowned, as well she might, with all those other customers waiting to be seated. Kristy hesitated, racking her brain for an reason to delay, then pointed at the remains of the goose, the bread and potatoes.

"It's a shame to let such good food go to waste," she began, playing for time. Tense as she was, she felt a brief, incongruous urge to laugh. What would the serving girl say if she asked for a doggie bag? Luckily, she didn't have to.

"The gentleman paid the reckoning on his way out," the girl told her. "I'll wrap up the rest of this, and you can take it with you."

And what would she do to occupy her time after she left the cookshop? Out in the crowd, without Jared to cover for her, could she really hope to blend in with the others?

She'd find out soon enough, for now the young serving girl was back, carrying a crude woven basket and a coarse cloth. Quickly, expertly, the girl cleared the table, wrapped the remains of the meal, and placed it in the basket.

Kristy smiled her thanks, stood up, and headed for the entrance. Should she return to the safety of the wagon? No, not yet. Jared hadn't asked her to come along when he'd gone off with Master Hutchinson probably because the respectable Braethorn merchant preferred to transact his illegal business with the smuggler in privacy.

All right, then. She'd walk about the nearest stalls, pretend to examine the goods, while she kept an eye out for Jared to return. *Keep moving. Look interested and keep your mouth shut.* Her glance flicked over a basket of eels, a display of tin plates and iron pots, a row of spicy-smelling gingerbread cakes.

She started at a deep, booming noise close by. She turned around quickly; then, peering through a gap in the crowd, she saw a shabbily dressed man standing beside a small cart. A bony horse grazed nearby. On the cart stood a large wooden box with a bright red and green striped curtain draped across the front. A tall, gangling boy kept beating away on a drum to attract the crowd.

The man scuttled around behind the cart, and a moment later, she saw the curtain move aside. A couple of crudely painted figures popped up on the small makeshift stage.

"What's that, Mama?" asked a small, round-eyed boy close by.

" 'Tis—why I do believe 'tis a Punch and Judy," said the gaunt woman who held his hand.

"What's that?"

"A puppet show, dearie." Her long, narrow face, under the starched cap, took on a wistful look. "I saw one when I was no older than you. Long ago, it was. In the reign of his Majesty, King Charles, poor, martyred soul—" She broke off abruptly and her hand flew to her lips. She glanced around anxiously, as if afraid someone might have overheard her.

"Can we go see it, Mama?"

Diana Haviland

"Your father might not think such mummery fit for decent folk."

"But he's all the way over in the cow pen," the boy said.

The woman sighed. "And he'll not be back 'til he gets every shilling he can for our old Bess. A hard bargainer, he is." She gazed longingly in the direction of the puppet theater. "All right, then, dearie." She led the boy to a wooden bench set in front of the stage for the children; then she took her place behind him, eyes fixed on the stage.

Others in the crowd hesitated, then they, too, approached the cart, their eyes bright with anticipation. Kristy joined them, relieved that she'd found a way to pass the time until Jared returned for her.

She couldn't understand much of the dialogue, only that Punch and Judy were quarreling. Punch struck Judy on the head with a flat paddle and she shrieked loudly, then disappeared beneath the stage. A moment later a brown and white dog with enormous teeth popped up, barking fiercely as he went after Punch and seized him by the seat of his pants. The audience roared with laughter, faces flushed, eyes aglow. This probably was a rare treat for them, Kristy thought; they certainly were making the most of it.

But not all of them had been caught up in the spirit of fun. From nearby, Kristy heard a woman call out, "Shameful! That's what it is! The law forbids such idle mummery!"

Others, of like opinion, joined in.

"We'll see such as them capering about a maypole on the green, next we know!"

"Not likely. Look there!"

"'Tis Constable Grimes."

"He'll soon put a stop to these lewd carryings-on."

The curtains jerked closed. The puppeteer scurried to hitch the swayback horse to the cart. The boy dropped his drum and ran to help his master. But they were too late. The constable and his two burly helpers seized them.

"I arrest both of you in the name of the Lord Protector!"

the constable bellowed. His big, meaty hand tightened on the puppeteer's shoulder. The boy writhed in the grip of the constable's men. Even from where she stood, Kristy saw that his face had gone chalk white.

"Now they'll get what they deserve," said the woman who stood beside Kristy.

"What's going to happen to them?" Kristy asked.

"Why, what do you suppose? The puppet master's on his way to the pillory. And the boy along with him."

"The pillory?"

"That's what I said." She grinned with relish. "They'll be fastened in good and tight, neck and wrists. Pelted with rotten fruit and dead cats, if they're lucky."

"Lucky?" Kristy repeated.

"Rocks—that's what they deserve."

"Likely they'll be branded as well," said another woman. "Constable Grimes knows his duty."

Kristy's insides clenched in a hard knot. Her cheeks went hot. Seized with indignation, she forgot the need for caution. "They're going to be punished just for giving a puppet show?"

" 'Tis the law."

"The law!" Kristy's voice shook with indignation. "What sort of law would punish a man for giving pleasure to children?"

"You dare to question the Lord Protector's justice?" The man who had challenged her was looking her up and down. "Never saw you here before. Where do you come from?"

"Not Braethorn, surely."

"Maybe she's one of them who're hopin' for young Prince Charles to come over from France an' take back his father's throne."

Those nearest to Kristy had shifted their attention from the puppeteer and the boy to her. As they began to move closer, her indignation gave way to fear. Some eyed her with casual curiosity, but others looked openly hostile.

Why had she been foolish enough to speak out without thinking? If Jared had been here, he'd have silenced her.

He should have come back by now. The sun was setting behind the pointed roofs of the houses near the market square. Merchants started to pack up their wares, and take down their makeshift stalls.

"Have mercy, sir—I beg you!" The crowd parted as the constable and his men dragged the puppeteer and his helper along. "Please, sir, we meant no harm," the man cried out. He tried to break free from the constable, but he was no match for the big, muscular man. "Let us go—we'll never show ourselves in your town again."

The constable answered with a harsh laugh. "And where will you go, once we've put our mark on your face for all to see?"

"At least turn the boy loose," the puppeteer pleaded.

"He's not too young to know the law."

"Well said!" someone shouted.

Kristy felt a stab of pity for the puppeteer and the boy, but she realized that she, too, was in danger. If the punishment for giving a show was so brutal, what would they do to a stranger suspected of being a Royalist sympathizer?

Her heart thudded against her ribs; she struggled even to draw a deep breath, but somehow she managed to keep her wits about her. The crowd had lost interest in her, for now. This might be her only chance to get away. Back to Jared.

Swiftly, she darted behind a stall, then looked about, trying to get her bearings. Jared had left his wagon against the wall near the town gate. But which way was that?

A farmer plodded past her, driving his cows before him. Maybe he'd be heading for the gate, to make his way home before darkness fell. Cautiously she stepped out from behind the stall and followed the farmer and his herd. With the basket on her arm, her prim cap on her head, her eyes cast down, she looked no different from the other women around her.

There it was, the archway over the town gate. And the

wagons. But so many of them. Jared—where was he? Anxiously she peered around.

Her legs went weak, and she gave a heartfelt sigh of relief. Jared's height, his wide shoulders, set him apart from the other men nearby. She forced herself to keep moving at a sedate pace.

The farmer drove his cows through the gate. She stepped to one side, her back against the wall, then wheeled around and headed for Jared.

The two men were talking amiably, while Master Hutchinson's helpers finished loading his cart. She hurried to Jared and clutched his arm. If he sensed her agitation, he gave no sign. He greeted her with an easy smile.

"Master Hutchinson and I have nearly finished our business. Here, let me help you up on the wagon."

He lifted her to the seat and when she was settled, he shook hands with the merchant, who nodded politely to Kristy. If the man was curious about her, or if he wondered why she was traveling with Jared, he gave no sign of it. "A safe journey to you both," he said. "I look forward to your next visit to Braethorn." He turned and strode off into the deepening twilight.

Jared climbed up beside Kristy, cracked his whip, and the wagon rolled forward, through the town gate.

She moved closer to him, seeking reassurance from his nearness. He must have sensed her tension. "What's wrong, Kristy?"

"A puppeteer and a boy were arrested."

Jared nodded. "We saw them dragged off to the pillory," he said.

"Are they really going to be branded?" She gave a shudder of revulsion.

"On the cheek," Jared said. "With the letters "L" and "V" for lewd vagabond."

"Just for giving a show, making those children laugh, and their parents, too?"

"It's one of Cromwell's laws. No public entertainment, live actors or puppets. No dancing around the maypole on the village green. No Yule log for the Christmas hearth. The puppeteer and the boy knew the risk they were taking." His green eyes searched her face. "But that's not all that's troubling you, is it?"

She looked away.

"Tell me what's wrong, Kristy."

"I didn't know about those laws," she began. "I spoke without thinking."

"Why doesn't that surprise me?" There was no mistaking the irony in his tone. "You launched a public protest, I suppose. With half the townsfolk for your audience."

"It wasn't like that! I only said—"

"What did you say?"

She glared at him, her anger rising. "I said it wasn't right, punishing them that way. Do you think it's right?"

He ignored her question. "What happened then?"

"They all stared at me, they crowded around me. Somebody asked me where I was from, then somebody else said I had no right to challenge the Lord Protector's law. A man said I was one of those who wanted to see the young prince restored to his father's throne." She paused to catch her breath. "Are there many who do?"

Jared gave a tight smile. "Enough of us to keep Cromwell on his guard."

"You're one of them. You fought against Cromwell. Sally said you did. And you lost your estate."

"I'll get it back."

And the girl you would have married?

Would he get her back, too? She decided not to mention that.

He gripped her arm and his face darkened. "What else did you tell the crowd?"

"What else?" Then she understood. "You think I was

84

foolish enough to say I'm being hunted as a witch? That I'd have risked my life, and yours?''

''Who knows? You're even more unpredictable and impulsive than most females.''

Somehow, she managed to choke back a furious retort. She turned her head away and lapsed into silence.

They drove along at a steady pace, while the evening shadows lengthened around them. Gradually, the crowd on the main road began to thin out. Jared turned the wagon onto a narrow wagon track that led into a woods. He glanced down at the basket beside her. ''What's in there?''

''The remains of the goose and some bread. I had the serving girl wrap it for us.''

''That showed some forethought.''

He brought the wagon to a stop. Oaks and elms rose thick around them; silver rays from the rising moon slanted down through the branches.

''There's a stream close by. We'll stay here for the night,'' he said. ''We can both do with a sound sleep. But first we'll dine.''

He held out the basket and opened the cloth, but she shook her head. ''I'm not hungry.''

He helped himself to a portion of the goose and a piece of bread. ''There's more than enough here for both of us,'' he said.

''I couldn't eat, not now.''

''Because of that puppeteer in the marketplace? You can't let that put you off your food,'' he said.

''It certainly hasn't spoiled your appetite. But then I suppose you're indifferent to such brutality.''

He stiffened, and she longed to call back her thoughtless words. ''No decent man is indifferent to cruelty or injustice,'' he said evenly. ''But tell me, Kristy. The time and place you come from—is your world so much better than mine? Surely those who break the law are punished. Or does no one break the law?''

She thought of the newspaper headlines, the TV news. Murder, rape, child abuse. "My time's not better, or worse," she admitted. "Only different."

"I can well believe that," he said. With a swift turn of his body, he got down from the wagon.

"Where are you going?"

"I have to unhitch the horse, and lead him to the stream."

"Jared, please wait."

"You're safe enough here," he told her, his tone surprisingly gentle. "Get into the back of the wagon and bed down."

There was more room, now that some of the crates and casks were gone. She took off her white cap, undid her hair and let it fall around her shoulders. Then she stretched out on Jared's cloak. But although she closed her eyes, sleep would not come. After a time, she heard Jared leading the horse back from the stream. He got into the wagon, lifted the canvas and crawled in beside her.

She turned on her side to look at him.

"I thought you'd be asleep by now," he said. He reached out and put his arm around her. "You're not going to lie awake all night, brooding about what happened back in Braethorn, are you?"

And when she did not answer, he went on. "It won't be easy, I know. But in time, you'll learn our ways. You'll know when to speak, and when to remain silent."

A shiver ran through her. "You speak as if you don't believe there's a way for me to return to my own time—as if you think I'll be here for the rest of my life."

"Forgive me, Kristy." She warmed to the comforting tone. "It's only natural you'll be wanting to get back to your family." He paused, then added, "Your husband, your children, perhaps."

"I'm not married."

"But you're of marriageable age—"

"I'm only twenty-five."

"And still unwed? Surely, with your fair face and your other charms, you must have been sought after by more than one man."

"There was a man who wanted to marry me."

Brian. Handsome, caring, successful. "When he asked me to set the date, I knew I couldn't go through with it."

"Your parents allowed you to break off your betrothal?"

"I have no parents."

"And the rest of your family, what about them?"

"There's no one." That wasn't quite true, she thought. "Aunt Vera, my mother's sister took me in when I was six. But only because she believed it was her duty. After I left her home, I wrote. She never answered. . . ."

Her voice broke. Furious with herself for her weakness, she set her jaw hard, He put his arm around her and held her against him. "You're not alone now," he said softly. "I'm here. Cry if you want to."

Her voice was muffled against his shoulder. "I never cry."

"With all you've been through, you have nothing to be ashamed of. Just let go."

"I can't!"

Jared pulled back slightly, as though that disturbed him. Then he drew her closer.

He stroked his palm along her back. Kristy felt the tight knot inside her chest begin to loose itself. She reached out for him, burrowing into the heat of his body, drawing comfort, reassurance from his nearness.

His mouth brushed hers. He parted her lips and his tongue slid inside, touching, teasing, savoring.

She sensed the change in him. His protective instinct was swiftly giving way to the more primitive, male need for complete possession. His arms tightened around her. Quickly, deftly, he opened the top buttons of her bodice. His fingers moved inside, cupping her breast.

His hunger awoke an answering need within her. She was engulfed in a sweet-hot tide of longing. A fiery tide that grew and swelled, that lifted her and swept her along. She reached out and stroked his hair, his shoulders, the hard muscles of his back. This—this was what she wanted, too. What she had wanted all this time. . . .

She moved against him, her thighs molding themselves against his. And felt his hardness, bold and urgent, through the folds of her skirt. Let him push the skirt aside, or tear it from her. Let him bare her body, invade her, possess her.

But now, with one violent movement, shocking and unexpected, he pulled himself free of her clinging arms. He raised himself, looked down at her face, then pushed her away.

What had he seen, to change him so suddenly, so completely? He had wanted her—she *knew* he had wanted her. He still did.

"No!" The word tore itself from his throat, like the cry of a man in pain. His body shook with the urgency of his need. Yet he was moving from her, withdrawing as far as he could in the narrow confines of the wagon.

"Jared—What have I done?"

"Go to sleep."

As if she could sleep now.

Once before, when he'd seen her in that blue wisp of a nightgown, he had reached out to her with passion, then drawn away. And now, as before, he turned from her, leaving her baffled, frustrated.

He lay motionless, his back to her. What kind of a man was he? How was it possible that he could be asleep so soon? She watched him a few moments longer, confusion, humiliation, desire, all warred within her. Then, with every muscle tight, her hands clenched into fists at her sides, she closed her eyes.

Jared forced himself to breathe deeply, evenly, to try to ignore the hunger she had aroused in him. Kristy. . . . the delicate scent of her hair, brushing his cheek. The silken heat of her breast, cupped in his hand. Her nipple hardening under his touch.

I never cry.

Even as she had spoken the words, they had stirred a half-forgotten memory. He'd pushed it aside, but now it came back to taunt him.

Ravenswyck, his home. The ruddy light from the kitchen hearth casting shadows on the stone walls. Evening in an autumn long gone by. The old cook with her bent body and cracked voice, talking to the serving wenches.

''—there are many ways to know a witch, be she ever so careful.''

And the wenches leaning forward, lips parted, frightened yet fascinated by the ancient lore. A small boy, seated in a corner, took it all in.

''Tie a witch, hand and foot, and toss her in a stream, and she'll float.'' The boy's warm square of ginger cake was forgotten, halfway to his lips.

''. . . A witch has no tears to shed, like any mortal woman. Ah, she'll shriek and rant, that she will, or curse a body. But a witch can't cry.''

Foolish, senseless talk, Jared told himself. An ignorant old woman, weaving fantastic tales to impress a couple of silly wenches. Kristy was lying here only a few feet from him. His mind's eye saw her so clearly: tawny hair, amber eyes, body rounded, yielding, giving. Kristy, brave and warm and passionate. But the disturbing thought remained.

A witch can't cry.

Chapter Six

"You see those towers on the hill beyond the woods?" Jared pointed with his whip. "That's Lachlan Hall. It was built in the last years of Queen Elizabeth's reign."

During the past three days, as they had journeyed steadily northward from Braethorn, Kristy had felt mounting bewilderment at Jared's behavior. He might have been a tour guide, she thought: courteous but impersonal, pointing out the landmarks and commenting on their history.

Surely, he hadn't forgotten the swift surge of passion that had drawn them together that night they had camped outside Braethorn. Yet each time she had tried to break through the barrier between them, he had refused to respond. So far, she had forced herself to play by his unspoken rules.

Last night at sunset, when the wagon had rumbled across the ancient fifteen-arched bridge, he had explained that the Tweed River below marked the boundary between England and Scotland. She had felt a brief reassurance, remembering what he'd told her: Once they'd crossed into Scotland, she'd be safe; the Yorkshire witch-hunters, for all their fanatical determination, would not carry their pursuit across the border.

But her relief was short-lived. How could she forget that, whether in England or Scotland, she was still trapped in the past, without the slightest idea of how she might return to her own time?

While Jared went on speaking of Lachlan Hall, her thoughts moved far away. Had her disappearance created a stir among her friends, back in New York? Surely Liz would be frantic by now. She'd be making calls, leaving messages, seeking information. And she must have contacted Ted Ferguson, the head of Kristy's department at Marisol's Madison Avenue headquarters.

Ted would be worried, too; he knew it wasn't like her to go off on an important assignment, then disappear without sending an explanation. Maybe he'd already notified the NYPD.

That brief report, faxed from Manchester, was the last word he'd had from her. Had he contacted their Manchester office?

She remembered the Toyota she'd rented for her drive north. Had the Yorkshire police traced the car as far as Glenrowan? Had they questioned Mrs. Ainsworth at the Rowan Tree? Much good that would have done.

She could imagine the landlady's protestations. "Yes, sir. A Miss Sinclair did check in. Said she'd been in an accident. No, I don't know what became of her. She disappeared that same night. And she left all her luggage behind, too."

No, not all her luggage, Kristy reminded herself. The carry-on had traveled back in time with her. But how was that possible? She'd fallen with one arm flung across it, when she'd plunged into darkness. Maybe the physical contact with her body had carried it along. She shook her head in utter bewilderment. How could she hope to explain what had happened to her? It made no sense at all.

Or did it? Was there an unknown force that had sent her back to this particular place and time, that had brought her face to face with Jared? They were meant to be together, she was sure of it. Had he, too, sensed this invisible yet powerful link between them?

Twice he had reached out to her, his green eyes hot with passion; yet twice he had recoiled. That evening they'd camped outside Braethorn, she, too, been aroused, her body yearning to meld with his. But she'd felt more than a physical need. All these years she'd felt an aching loneliness, a sense of being an outsider. And she knew that only Jared could change that. They belonged together.

Had he, too, sensed the bond between them? If so, he'd given her no sign.

She realized he was speaking to her again, in that same impersonal way. "Lachlan Hall is considered one of the finest estates in the Borders. It was designed and built by Sir Andrew's grandfather in 1590. The six crested towers and those fine mullioned windows are much admired. They have a saying around here: 'Lachlan Hall, more glass than wall.' "

"Jared! Put away the damn guidebook!"

He turned to stare at her, and his dark brows shot up in surprise.

"I don't care about the history of Lachlan Hall. I don't want a rundown on Sir Andrew's ancestors, or their taste in architecture." Her eyes locked with his. "It's you I want to know about. I want answers, now!"

She could see she'd startled him. But the Marisol staff wouldn't have been surprised by her. They'd heard her assert herself during many a heated discussion on company policy. That was one reason she'd advanced through the ranks so quickly.

Jared never had seen her like this, and he was caught off-guard. "You know too much about me already," he muttered.

"Not really. You've told me you're a smuggler, that's all. But I want to know more." She reached out and put a hand on his arm. Her tone softened. "You risked your neck to get me out of Glenrowan. You lied to your own men to protect me. Why?''

He turned his head away. They were approaching a thick woods, and he fixed his eyes on the narrow, rutted path that led into it. "I've told you, I fought against Cromwell in the war. I despise him, and all he stands for. I'd have helped anyone who was being pursued by Cromwell's followers.''

She eyed him with disbelief. "Anyone? If I'd been a man, you'd have helped me to escape, lied for me, stood off that mob of witch-hunters? You're sure you didn't treat me differently because I'm a woman?''

"If you're seeking flattery, then, yes, I find you desirable.'' His lips curved in a reluctant smile.

He was trying to keep her at a distance, to hide his deeper feelings. But she wouldn't let him—not this time. "You haven't forgotten that evening after the Braethorn fair.''

She saw his hands tighten on the reins, but he didn't answer.

"You wanted me—you were ready to take me right there in the back of the wagon. What stopped you?''

She heard his sharp, indrawn breath. "You certainly don't mince words, do you? Is it the custom for a woman of your time to speak to a man so freely?''

"Sally spoke boldly enough, back there at the Fighting Cocks,'' she reminded him.

"Sally's a tavern slut. You're not.''

"What am I, then?'' she challenged him. "What do you see when you look at me, Jared Ramsey?''

"I wish I knew!'' He turned his head, and his eyes searched hers. The barrier he'd raised between them, with his cool, impersonal talk, was falling away. "The first night I saw you, I was drawn to you in a way I can't explain. I've never felt that way about any other woman.''

"Not even the lady you were betrothed to?''

His green eyes went dark and smoky with anger; his lips

clamped together. Had she gone too far, probed too deeply, touching hidden places inside him?

He tugged on the reins; the wagon jerked to a stop.

"How the devil could you know about Liane?"

"Not through any witch's spell, if that's what you're thinking," she retorted. Although the barely restrained fury in his voice frightened her, she would not back down now. "It was Sally who told me. She said you were a nobleman, that you fought on the king's side, and that was why you lost your estate and your highborn lady."

"Sally should learn to hold her tongue."

"She meant no harm."

He glowered at her in moody silence. Then he said, "I suppose you won't be satisfied until you know the rest. After the king was executed, I escaped to Holland along with young Prince Charles and some of his followers."

"Why did you come back?"

"To get to Liane, and take her to Holland with me. I returned to Yorkshire in secret, aboard a smuggling ship. We docked at Whitby, and I went on to Cragsmore. That's a small village near Ravenswyck, my family's estate. I sought out the vicar, an old man, loyal to our cause. It was he who told me."

His wide shoulders hunched forward, and he stared into the green depths of the woods. It was as if he'd forgotten she was there beside him. "Cromwell had already given Ravenswyck to Sir Roger Fairfax, one of his most devoted supporters."

"And Liane?"

His voice was heavy with self-mockery. "She'd married Sir Roger Fairfax. She was the mistress of Ravenswyck."

"But she was engaged—betrothed—to you."

"When the king was executed, and it was plain that our cause was lost, her father went over to Cromwell's side. He had Liane's betrothal to me set aside, so she could marry Fairfax."

"And she agreed?"

"Why not? Better to be the lady of Ravenswyck than the wife of a penniless fugitive." He spoke with feigned indifference but Kristy saw the pain in his eyes. "I went back to Whitby and joined the smugglers who'd brought me over from Holland. In time, I became their leader."

"You never tried to see Liane again?"

"To what purpose? She had all she wanted. Fairfax had become a man of importance. Wealthy, influential. No doubt she was content with her new life, for as long as it lasted." He looked away, his voice husky. "She was killed in a riding accident, the year after her marriage."

Kristy felt a surge of pity, not only for Jared, but for the girl she'd never known. Perhaps she had betrayed her promise willingly, or maybe she'd yielded under pressure from her father. Whatever her reason, she'd left Jared bitter and cynical, unwilling to trust another woman.

Before she could speak again, he brought the whip down on the horse's back, and the startled beast broke into a trot; the wagon went speeding through the woods, swaying from side to side, tilting dangerously. She gripped the seat to steady herself, and ducked her head to avoid being struck across the face by a low-hanging branch.

She breathed a sigh of relief when they emerged from the woods, onto a broad path that curved across a spacious park. He pulled at the reins, and the horse slowed its pace.

Although she'd said she had no interest in Lachlan Hall, she was impressed and fascinated by the regal house and its surroundings. Deer grazed beneath the great, ancient oaks. A quail led her brood across the grass. In the distance, six tall grey towers stood out against the sky. Pale spring sunlight glinted from the large mullioned windows.

She half-expected a party of knights in armor to come riding out to meet them. Instead, as they approached the stone stairs leading to the massive front door, a grey-haired man of middle height, in a velvet coat and doeskin britches, came striding out to welcome them. "That is Sir Andrew Lachlan," Jared told Kristy. While the servants hurried forward to take care of the horse and wagon, their host escorted them into the house.

Inside the great entrance hall, Jared introduced Kristy to Sir Andrew. As a manservant helped her off with the cape, she dropped her gaze to the floor, suddenly self-conscious. Sally's shapeless grey dress and frayed white cap had looked all right at the Braethorn market; here in the hall, with its tapestried walls, her clothes were out of place.

But Sir Andrew bowed over her hand, as if she'd been a great lady. "Welcome to my home, Mistress Sinclair." He gave her a warm smile. "No doubt you're weary after your journey." He motioned and a serving girl stepped forward.

"Show Mistress Sinclair up to the Blue Chamber, Polly," he said. "See that she has all she needs for her comfort." And to Kristy: "Your trunks will be brought to you, as soon as they're unloaded."

Kristy threw Jared an uncertain glance. "Mistress Sinclair has no trunks," he told their host. "She brought only one small bag with her. We left Yorkshire in rather a hurry."

Sir Andrew smiled. "As you so often do, Jared."

He turned to Kristy. "Polly will provide you with whatever garments you'll require. And you'll have ample time to rest and refresh yourself before you change for dinner."

Kristy still hesitated to speak, then told herself that she'd have to, sooner or later. "Thank you, Sir Andrew."

Should she curtsy? She'd never curtsied to anyone in her life, and she wasn't sure she could manage it properly; instead, she inclined her head, then turned and followed Polly across the entrance hall, under a gallery supported by classical columns, and up a flight of wide stairs.

The Blue Chamber must have taken its name from the magnificent bed curtains: heavy blue velvet embroidered with gold. A large, ornately carved chest stood at the foot of the bed. "It belonged to the master's daughter," Polly told her.

"Those dresses inside would be too small for her now, though. Married, she is, and mother of two strapping lads. There's many fine garments packed away in there, your ladyship."

"It's Miss—Mistress Sinclair," Kristy said quickly.

Her carry-on had already been brought upstairs and placed beside the chest. But this time, she knew better than to let Polly, or any of the other servants, examine its contents. "Will you help me choose a suitable dress?" she asked.

"That I will, Mistress Sinclair. But first, perhaps you'll be wanting to wash away the dust of the road. Shall I have a tub brought up for you?"

After bathing in icy streams, it sounded like heaven. After her bath Polly helped her to dress. She stifled her surprise when the maidservant laced her into a busk—a short, tight, boned corset. Polly mustn't suspect that she'd never even seen such a garment before, let alone worn one.

It was early evening when Kristy, wearing a pale yellow silk dress with a low-cut bodice and a full skirt, her feet in pointy-toed slippers, entered the great dining hall. Jared and Sir Andrew were deep in conversation, but they broke off at once and got to their feet; his lordship escorted her to the long mahogany table, where silver candelabra cast their light on the polished surface.

Jared's lips parted at the sight of her; she caught the gleam of admiration in his eyes. Had the elegant silk dress changed her so much? The tightly laced busk set off her slender waist, and pushed up her breasts so that the low-cut bodice emphasized their curves.

Polly had brushed Kristy's freshly-washed hair until it glowed like molten bronze, then parted it in the center and carefully arranged it in waves that fell to her shoulders.

She had waited until the maid had left the room before opening her carry-on; even then, she had hesitated about putting on her makeup. Did a lady of this century—a respectable lady—wear lipstick? Eyeshadow? She had compromised by applying only a light touch of each.

"Kristy Sinclair." Sir Andrew was saying. "A fine Scottish name, for a lovely Scottish lass."

"But I'm not—"

She caught Jared's warning glance. He and Sir Andrew were obviously good friends; but even so, she'd be willing to bet Jared hadn't told his lordship the circumstances of their meeting at the Rowan Tree; surely he hadn't said she'd come here from another century.

"Mistress Sinclair has been living abroad," Jared told their host.

That's the understatement of the year, she thought.

"But her parents were Scottish," he added.

Maybe Jared was right about that. Her father might have been of Scottish descent. Whenever she thought about her parents—her father, whose name she didn't know; her mother, whose face she could not remember—she felt a painful surge of loneliness.

Aunt Vera, her mother's sister, had never married; Sinclair was her maiden name. Why was Kristy's last name Sinclair, too? Because she was illegitimate. That must be the reason. Maybe that was why her aunt had disliked her so much.

Kristy started as she noticed that Sir Andrew was looking at her with concern. "Is something amiss, my dear?" he asked.

Again, it was Jared who spoke, before she had to invent a suitable explanation. "We've traveled a long way, and under difficult conditions," he said. "But a few glasses of your fine Burgundy wine and one of your excellent dinners will soon restore her."

The dinner *was* excellent: roast pheasant, venison, ham and veal pie, and baked salmon "caught only this morning in the Teviot," as Sir Andrew told her. Dessert was a rich concoction called a gooseberry fool, with berries, thick cream and sugar. Although she could only eat a part of each course, she was soon sated. The men finished a couple of bottles of wine between them, but after her second glass, her eyelids started to grow heavy.

"Perhaps you should retire early," Jared suggested. "Sir Andrew and I have much business to discuss."

"I'm sure you do," she said with a touch of irony. Smuggler's business, no doubt.

The bed with its down comforter was a welcome change from the boards in the back of the wagon. Kristy had left her blue nylon nightgown packed away with the rest of the contents of the carry-on. She wore, instead, an embroidered linen gown with long sleeves and a high neck, provided by Polly.

Polly brought a round iron pan filled with hot coals, and ran it over the sheets. "You'll sleep warm and sound tonight, mistress," she said. She stirred up the fire in the hearth, and left a single candle burning atop a chest of drawers before she left the room.

Yet, although Kristy should have fallen asleep at once, she couldn't. She shifted about restlessly, her muscles tense. If only Jared were here beside her. Even when they had shared the back of the wagon, and he had slept as far from her as possible, his presence had been reassuring.

What were he and Sir Andrew talking about down there in the dining hall all this time? And why had Jared felt it necessary to come all the way to Scotland to dispose of the rest of his goods? Surely there must have been plenty of customers back in England, eager to buy all the duty-free merchandise he carried in the wagon.

She turned on her side, so that she faced the casement window. The candlelight flickered over the leaded glass. She closed her eyes, but still she couldn't sleep. From outside, she caught the small noises of the night. The cry of a hawk, hunting for its prey: some small furry animal, crouching in the grass—a rabbit, maybe. The night wind rustled in the trees, and a single branch tapped against the pane.

Diana Haviland

Or was it a branch? No, it was too loud, too insistent. There was a urgency in the sound, as if someone were trying to attract her attention.

She sat up, her body taut, then looked toward the window. It was open, that was all; the two frames were tapping against each other. Polly must have forgotten to fasten the latch.

She felt an brief reluctance to leave the safety of the bed. *Don't be silly. Would you rather lie awake all night?*

She took a deep breath, pushed back the comforter and thrust her feet into the deerskin slippers Polly had left there for her. She started for the window, then stopped short. A thick fog swirled out there. It must be rising from the river nearby, the Teviot. Long, wispy tendrils came reaching in around the open casement. Fog, from the river.

Her heart speeded up, and she had to struggle to draw breath. This was no ordinary grey river fog. It was red-tinted, shot with whirling sparks. Like the fog that had enveloped her car, that afternoon back in Yorkshire.

Her hand went to her lips to stifle a cry. She turned, ran across the room and flung open the door to the hall.

"Kristy!" Jared had climbed the wide stone stairs. He stopped on the landing, stared at her in surprise, then hurried to her side. "What are you doing out here at this hour?"

"The fog." She forced the words past the tightness that gripped her throat. "It's coming through the window—into my room. Fasten the lock—please."

He put a reassuring arm around her shoulders and led her back inside her chamber. "The fog." Her voice was unsteady. He strode to the window, and she followed close behind him.

"The lock's fastened tight, Kristy. And I see no fog."

"But I saw it."

He drew her close to him; she relaxed, feeling the warmth of his body, inhaling his familiar scent.

"You were dreaming. Look for yourself."

She stared past him, her lips parting in disbelief. The fog was gone. Moonlight streamed in through the window. And

100

the latch was fastened securely. "It seemed so real," she said.

"Dreams sometimes do." He stroked her hair, his voice soft and comforting. Then he lifted her, cradled her against him, carried her to the bed. But when he set her down she clung to his arm.

"Don't leave me."

"Kristy, there's nothing to be afraid of."

"Stay with me, tonight."

"No!" He sounded like a man in pain. "You think I can lie here beside you all night, and not touch you?"

"You've done it before . . . back in the wagon. . . ."

"But not this time. If I stay with you tonight, no power in heaven or hell will keep me from taking you."

"Take me, then."

He looked down at her in wonder and disbelief. "You're not saying this because you're afraid to be alone, surely?"

She shook her head. "I'm not afraid anymore," she said. "I want you. As you want me." She spoke without shame or pretense. Such emotions had nothing to do with her and Jared.

A fierce heat surged through him. His loins ached with the need to possess her. How easy it would be to say yes.

And how dangerous, for both of them. Yes, he wanted her—he'd wanted her since he'd first seen her. But there was no place in his life for a deep, lasting attachment to any woman. Certainly not a woman like her, from another time and place, a woman whose powers he could not begin to fathom. If he took her, it would be no brief, pleasurable interlude for him.

Even as he tried to warn himself of the consequences, his need overpowered his reason. He lowered himself to the bed, and drew her against him. He buried his face in her tawny hair, inhaled its fragrance. He brushed the soft waves back from her face and stroked her cheek, the satin softness of her throat. His fingers moved to the buttons at the collar of her linen gown. One by one, he opened them. Then his hand slid inside, to cup her breast.

He felt her nipple harden under his touch. Her swift response told him she wanted him. He bent his head to take her nipple between his lips. He suckled at the rosy peak, laving it with his tongue. Her hands were reaching for him, tangling in his hair, stroking his shoulders.

He heard her wordless cry of protest as he let her go and moved away to take off his clothes. Then he was with her again. He drew her night rail over her head and tossed it to the floor. He climbed into bed beside her.

His gaze moved over her, lingering on the swell of her breasts, the curve of her hips. But now it was not enough only to look at her. Reaching out, he traced each curve, each hollow. His hand rested on her belly, then moved downward, to stroke the soft tawny triangle at the apex of her thighs. He cupped her mound and felt her move upward, pressing against his hand. Slowly, he parted her with his fingers, felt the warm moisture under his fingers, inhaled her woman's scent.

He wanted to take her. He would have entered her, buried his hardness deep inside her. But he held back, controlling his own need.

Her lips moved, shaping his name. She put her arms around him, and her body arched upward. She saw his eyes glow deep green.

Her hands moved over his shoulders, down the length of his back. She'd never made love with a man before, yet now her instincts guided her. Her fingers stroked the flesh at the base of his spine, and she heard him groan softly. She pressed herself against his hot, hard arousal.

He raised himself above her, and thrust into her. A stab of pain caught her unaware and she gave a wordless cry.

"Kristy. . . ." She heard the surprise in his voice, felt him drawing out. But the pain swiftly ebbed away, and she reached out, her hands pressing his hard buttocks, urging him back inside her. She closed herself around him, hot and wet.

He began to move, each stroke long and lingering. She caught the rhythm, moving with him, locking her legs around him. She heard him cry out, and felt the spasm that ran through his body. She clung to him, losing herself in him, becoming one with him.

Gradually, her breathing grew slow and even, as she lay in his embrace. The loneliness that had been a part of her ever since she could remember was gone now. She had found the fulfillment she'd been seeking. They belonged to one another, now and forever. . . .

In the first light of dawn, Jared moved away from her slowly, reluctantly. He got out of bed, then stood gazing down at her, with wonder. How young she looked, her lashes resting on her cheeks, her lips parted, her tawny hair loose and tousled around her face. The white mounds of her breasts rose and fell with her even breathing.

He'd been the first with her, yet she had given herself to him with an overwhelming passion. She'd shared not only her soft, enticing body, but all of herself.

He lingered there, beside the bed, unable to turn away. His eyes searched her sleeping face, seeking answers to the questions that had tormented him since their first meeting.

Who was she? What was she? Strange she might be, gifted with unfathomable powers; but there was no evil in her—he would swear to that. All his doubts, his misgivings fell away.

Yet even now, bound together as they were, he could not forget that he was held by other ties. He had pledged his honor, his loyalty to the cause of the prince now in exile across the sea.

He moved away from the bed. Kristy shifted, and a smile curved her soft, red lips. It took all his willpower to keep from going back to her, embracing her again. Quickly, he dressed and left the room, closing the door behind him.

Chapter Seven

Kristy awoke and stretched, with a sigh of deep contentment. She reached out her hand, seeking the warmth of Jared's body, but he was no longer beside her. She sat up and saw the sunlight streaming in through the window.

Probably Jared had returned to his own room before dawn, to shield her from the scandalous gossip of the servants. But why had he left in silence, without waking her?

She heard a light knock on the door, and Polly came in. Seeing the maid's round-eyed stare, Kristy realized that she was naked, her breasts exposed, her nightgown lying on the floor beside the bed. Her cheeks went hot and she pulled the comforter up to her chin.

Had Polly caught sight of the discarded nightgown, the rumpled pillow where Jared had lain? "I hope you slept well, Mistress Sinclair," she said with a smile, then added, "Lord Ramsey rode out early with the master."

At the mention of Jared's name, the flush on Kristy's cheeks deepened; a wave of heat spread down the length of her body. But Polly was already bustling about her duties, opening the lid of the carved chest, laying out fresh clothes: a linen underskirt, an embroidered shift, a busk, silk stockings, satin garters, pointy-toed black leather shoes. She held up a light woolen dress of striped cinnamon and yellow. "Will you wear this today?" Kristy gave a nod of approval. Surely the maid knew what was suitable for morning wear better than she.

Polly's eyes widened with surprise when Kristy asked for a bath. How often did they bathe here, Kristy wondered. What with the lack of plumbing and central heating, maybe a daily bath was considered a luxury.

After a moment's hesitation, Polly said, "As you wish, mistress," and went to heap fresh coals on the hearth. She pulled the embroidered bell cord; shortly after, two menservants carried in the tin tub Kristy had used last night, set it down in front of the fireplace, then hurried out again for buckets of hot water. Kristy glanced at the now-familiar greyish-white ball Polly held out to her, then shifted her gaze to her carry-on, where her own soap, in its plastic dish, was packed away. She was about to ask the maid to take it out, but she stopped herself in time.

"I'll bathe and dress myself," she said.

Again, the maid looked surprised; she bobbed in a curtsy, then started for the door. "Breakfast is laid out in the small dining chamber downstairs. When you're ready, you've only to ring and I'll show you the way."

Kristy waited until the sound of Polly's footsteps died away, then rose and took her scented soap from her carry-on. She zipped the bag shut and shoved it under the bed before she got into the tub. Although she couldn't stretch out full length in the small tub, the steaming water felt good. Running her hands down along her body, she sighed with sensuous pleasure; her lips curved in a smile as she thought about last night. She touched her nipples and seemed to feel Jared's fingers again, flicking, stroking them until they peaked, hard

105

and tingling. She cupped the rounds of her breasts in her hands; they felt fuller, heavier than before. Slowly she laved them, and remembered the warm moisture of Jared's tongue tracing patterns on the surface of her skin.

She soaped her belly, her thighs. Spreading her knees, she felt a slight, stinging sensation, and caught her breath, as she relived that brief moment of pain when he'd first thrust into her. Pain that had swiftly given way to the most intense pleasure she'd ever known.

How many young women of her own time still were virgins at twenty-five? She'd never confided that secret to any of her friends, not even to Liz. Some of the men she'd gone out with had been baffled; a few had been angered by her refusal to have sex, had accused her of being frigid. Even Brian had teased her, had called her his Snow Maiden; but he'd accepted her refusal to sleep with him before they were married.

She wasn't cold or indifferent to passion—she never had been. But she was different, somehow, from other women; she'd always sensed that. Not only because she'd remained a virgin until now. Different in other, more subtle ways that she, herself, did not understand.

Even now, warmed as she was with the memory of Jared's loving, she felt a faint stir of uneasiness. She looked over at the bed, underneath which the carry-on lay, and remembered the scrying mirror. Though it was tucked away in its velvet bag, and buried under her nylon nightgown and the tape player, it was as if the mirror lay in wait for her; she feared that it radiated a sinister aura.

But that made no sense. Why should she fear it now? It had served its purpose; its power had carried her back to this time and place so that she could find Jared. Last night, he had taught her what it meant to love and be loved.

Or had she been sent here for another reason? Were there other unknown powers that still lay hidden in the depths of the dark mirror? In spite of the steaming hot water, she shivered.

Hastily she finished bathing, got out of the tub and dried herself. She put her soap back in its plastic case, and returned it to the carry-on, then she started getting dressed. There was no way she could lace up the busk without Polly's help; she hoped the dress would fit her waist without it. She pulled on the stockings and garters, then the shift; panty hose were much more convenient. Did she have another pair left? It didn't matter, because she'd have to get used to wearing stockings and garters. She'd soon learn to dress like a woman of this time, to talk and act like one. It wouldn't be easy, but she'd manage.

What was she thinking of? She wasn't going to stay here. All right, so she hadn't found a way to return to her own time, not yet.

And if she did, then what? A sense of desolation swept through her. If she returned to the twentieth century, to the life she'd known there, what about Jared? He couldn't go with her. And she wouldn't let herself think about leaving him, not after last night.

Why did she want to return to her own time? She had no warm, loving family waiting for her, no husband or child, no lover. Liz was there, and her other friends. Her coworkers at Marisol. Macavity, round and furry. She thought what it would be like if she never saw them again. Certainly she'd miss them.

But to leave Jared, never to see him again . . . Never to lie enfolded in his arms, to feel the heat, the hardness of his lean, strong body pressed against hers, to breathe in his now-familiar male scent. Never to hear his voice again, warm and comforting, or deep and husky with passion. No! She couldn't leave him.

She pressed her fingers to her temples, as if to still her whirling thoughts. Then she finished dressing. The striped gown was only a little tight in the waist. She brushed her hair and parted it in the center, trying to arrange it as Polly had done last night.

She tugged at the bell cord, and Polly came to show her the way downstairs, along a hall hung with tapestries, to the chamber where breakfast was laid out on the sideboard. The "small dining chamber" was a lot larger than any pricey New York studio apartment. And breakfast, although not as lavish and varied as last night's dinner, was more than ample: covered platters of fresh eggs, bacon, ham, kippers, oat cakes, a crock of butter, a jar of honey. A big pot of steaming tea with a pitcher of heavy cream beside it.

I'll need a whole week of workouts at the health club when I get back. . . .

She felt a sinking sensation. She thought of her health club, with its Olympic-sized pool, its array of exercise machines. Girls in leotards and tights, stair-stepping, lifting weights, sipping fruit juice, or spooning low-fat yogurt. And outside, the city, with its gridlocked traffic, buses, cabs, stretch limos, the jostling crowds.

That's my time, my place. It's where I belong.

But if she returned, she'd be without Jared. Confused, shaken, she set down her cup and looked about her, torn between two worlds, struggling to get her bearings.

"Mistress Sinclair—is anything amiss? Would there be something you're wanting?" Polly's soft voice startled her.

Jared. I want Jared. I always have—even before I met him. I always will.

She shook her head, then forced a smile. "When do you expect Lord Ramsey and Sir Andrew to return?"

"The master left word they would be back by this afternoon. Maybe you'd like to take a stroll to pass the time. The weather's turned mild, the mist is gone."

Wrapped in a woolen cape Polly had found for her, she left the house and walked slowly along the broad path that curved across the green sweep of the lawn. A hawk wheeled and dipped overhead. The pale spring sunlight streamed down; a light breeze stirred her hair.

A grazing deer raised its head; it stared at her with soft,

dark eyes, then went bounding across the grass and up the steep rise leading to the woods where it disappeared among the trees.

She hesitated, then followed. Maybe she'd find a high rock ledge where she could wait to catch a glimpse of Jared and Sir Andrew on their way back.

Yesterday, when Jared had driven the wagon through the woods at top speed, she'd scarcely noticed her surroundings; it had been all she could do to keep her balance on the seat. But now she saw that the path he had taken branched off into others, far narrower, half-hidden by waist-high ferns. She turned aside to follow one of those.

She walked only a little way before she felt a change. The enchantment of the ancient forest enveloped her. The song of the larks, the cries of the starlings, came to her, along with the rustling of small, unseen animals deep in the undergrowth. The branches of the great oaks were beginning to bud; the tall ferns brushed her cape. Towering dark green pines shut out the pale rays of sunlight; their spicy fragrance mingled with odors of herbs and loam.

She kept going, peering into the darkness around her, until she caught sight of a high rocky ledge. Its flattened top looked broad enough to stand on. Surely it must be past noon now. Jared and Sir Andrew would be returning soon; she'd be able to see them from up there.

She started to climb, but her borrowed shoes kept sinking into the slippery carpet of the last year's rotting leaves. The ferns pulled at her cape and her long skirt, and she pushed them aside impatiently.

Abruptly she stopped and raised her head, like an animal scenting danger. Something was not right. Unnatural. The birds fell silent; she could no longer hear the rustling sounds of the small creatures moving in the underbrush. A growing uneasiness gripped her, and she forced it away. Keep going, she told herself. Get to the top of the ledge. Wait there for Jared.

But she could scarcely see the ledge now; gauzy veils of mist were drifting around it. The mist was getting heavier, thickening into a red-tinted fog, shot through with whirling sparks.

Keep moving. Don't stop. The fog hasn't reached the top—not yet. Her breathing speeded up. Her bodice felt too tight. But she forced herself to go forward. She almost reached the base of the ledge.

A figure blocked her way.

It was a woman, silver-eyed and red-lipped, her hood flung back, her black hair falling around her face. "Kristy." Her voice was soft, low-pitched.

Kristy felt as if an iron band had tightened around her throat. Her skin prickled with fear. "Who are you?"

"I am Gwyneth Trefoil."

Kristy gripped her hands together, as she fought to keep back the rising tide of panic. "I've seen you before. Back on the road to Glenrowan."

"I was waiting there for you," she said, with the hint of a smile. Kristy's heart stopped, then lurched against her ribs.

"Who are you?"

"I've told you my name." The silver eyes glinted with amusement.

"I want to know more."

"You want to know why I followed you across the miles from Yorkshire to Scotland."

Not only across the miles—across the years, too. Kristy stared at the woman in disbelief. Gwyneth Trefoil had also traveled across time.

The woman's red lips parted in a smile. "I was sent to find you."

"Why?"

"Because you are needed by our coven."

"Your coven?" She recognized the word. A meeting of witches.

Jared had said of witches, "There are those who choose

the left-hand path. They use their power to do harm.''

''You're a witch.'' Kristy said.

Gwyneth laughed softly. ''Don't look so frightened, Kristy. You are one of us. You, too, possess a witch's gift of power, though you don't know how to use it yet.''

''No! It's not true!''

''You are sure?'' The low-pitched voice mocked her. ''But how can you be? How much do you know about yourself, Kristy Sinclair?''

An icy shudder ran through Kristy's body. She tried to turn her face away, so Gwyneth would not see her fear. The woman's silver eyes held hers. ''Those early years of your life—you can't remember anything about them. You know nothing of your mother, do you? Who she was? What she was?''

''Do you? But how could you?'' Her fear didn't matter now. It gave way before her urgent need to find the answers to the questions that had tormented her for so long.

''I know,'' said Gwyneth.

''Then tell me.''

''Not yet. You will learn about your mother at the Sabbat on Beltane Eve. You will join our coven, you will take your place among us. Then you will discover what great power you possess.''

''I have no such power!''

''Then how did you use the mirror to travel here from your own time?''

Kristy shook her head in bewilderment. ''I don't know— I'm not sure. It just happened.'' In spite of her growing confusion, she managed to keep her voice steady. ''I want to know about my mother. Aunt Vera never would tell me. I have a right to know.''

''And you shall,'' Gwyneth assured her. ''On Beltane Eve, when you come to join us.''

A wave of revulsion swept over Kristy. Dizziness blurred her sight, and set the trees spinning. Somehow she found the strength to cry out, "No! I won't come. You can't force me."

"I won't have to use force. You'll join us of your own free will."

"No!" She remembered last night: the fog that had swirled outside her window and crept into her room. It had seemed real, until Jared had come to her. His arms had held her, and the fog, the sense of impending evil, had disappeared. "Jared will keep me safe. He loves me."

The silver eyes narrowed with contempt. "Your Jared is only a man. He's not for you. At the Sabbat you will offer yourself up to the coven master." Kristy thought she heard a touch of envy in the other woman's voice. "There are ways of passion unknown to Lord Ramsey, or any mortal man. Only the coven master can teach them to you."

"Jared's the only man I'll ever want. As for your coven master—whoever he is—"

"I serve him. We all do. His power is without limit. It was he who commanded me to send you to Glenrowan."

"I came there by accident—I smashed up my car in the fog."

"It was no accident. I brought the fog. I obeyed the master's command. As you will, on Beltane Eve."

"I don't know what you're talking about. I never even heard of Beltane Eve."

"Beltane Eve falls on the last night in April. It is one of our four great Sabbats." Gwyneth spoke patiently, like a teacher instructing a gifted but unwilling student. "No doubt this still seems strange to you. Believe me, Kristy, you already possess great power. As the high priestess, I, myself, will teach you how to use it."

From a distance, Kristy heard the pounding of hooves. Jared, returning with Sir Andrew? Let it be Jared. At the thought of him, she felt a new strength surging through her. She was able to break the hold of that silver gaze, to turn away.

"Wait!" Gwyneth's voice stopped her. "You asked me

about your mother. You've always wanted to know about her, haven't you?'' She flung back her cloak. ''Look at this.'' She touched a silver chain around her neck; it held a star that lay between her full breasts. A five-pointed star. ''This is the pentacle,'' Gwyneth said. ''Remember . . . you do remember. . . .''

Kristy fixed her eyes on the pentacle with growing recognition. A five-pointed star. Where had she seen it before? Slowly, a memory took shape. She saw a summer afternoon, a green meadow speckled with daisies and buttercups, and herself, a little girl now, the sun warm on her skin. She was looking up into the face of a woman with long, tawny blond hair and hazel eyes. The woman wore a yellow cotton dress. The sunlight caught the gleam of a chain around the woman's neck, and the five-pointed star. She hummed softly, and rocked Kristy in her arms.

''Mama,'' Kristy heard herself call out in a child's high-pitched voice. She tried to hold on to the memory. ''Mama, stay—don't leave me. . . .'' But it was no use. The image faded and was gone. Kristy felt a sense of unbearable loss.

''You don't need your mother. You have us, now. You belong with us.'' Gwyneth reached out her hand.

Kristy drew back. Even the thought of being touched by those long white fingers repulsed her.

The sound of the hoofbeats grew louder. Gwyneth pulled her cloak about her, drew the hood up over her dark hair, then turned away slowly. ''Beltane Eve, Kristy. You will come to us on Beltane Eve.''

''But my mother—she loved me. I know she did, now. Why did she leave me?''

Gwyneth didn't answer. She slipped away into the shadows of the pines and was gone. Kristy stood motionless, still dazed by her vision. Never before had she been able to remember her mother. A loving smile, arms to hold her, a soft voice humming a lullaby. But what about the pentacle? Why had her mother worn a silver pentacle like Gwyneth's?

Still gripped by lingering fear, she lifted her long skirt and started to run, slipping on the fallen leaves, stumbling over rocks and broken branches, moving toward the wide path, toward the pounding of hooves.

Emerging from the thick undergrowth, she caught sight of Jared, mounted on a grey stallion. He rode at a brisk canter, with Sir Andrew a few paces behind him. Heedless of danger, driven by her need to reach Jared, she pushed aside the clinging ferns, and ran out onto the path. Jared's horse reared up, hooves flailing. By sheer strength and expert horsemanship, he brought the startled animal under control. "Kristy!"

She tried to speak but no sound came. Her skin felt damp; a trickle of perspiration slid down her back. Jared reached down his hand to her; she grasped it and he swung her up in front of him. "What the devil were you doing, wandering about in the woods?" She heard the anger in his voice, but she didn't mind; it was only his reaction to her brush with danger, moments ago.

She leaned back, rested against his chest, hard and heavily-muscled; his breath warmed her cheek. She inhaled his scent and felt the tension going out of her. Jared was solid, real.

But Gwyneth Trefoil was real, too.

And how could she hope to explain the fleeting glimpse of her mother? That had surely been an illusion. Her mother, wearing a pentacle like Gwyneth's.

They rode out of the woods, with Jared leading the way, Sir Andrew following. Down the slope to the lawn where the deer grazed and hawks swooped and wheeled overhead. The path was wider, and Sir Andrew could ride beside her and Jared. She looked about her, at the broad sweep of grass, the imposing facade of Lachlan Hall, bathed in afternoon sunlight; all was as it had been an hour ago.

A sweating hostler, with bits of straw clinging to his boots, hurried up to meet them. "The new mare's goin' to drop her foal early, master," he told Sir Andrew. "A brave one, she is, but she's havin' a hard time of it."

"I'll come and have a look at her," said Sir Andrew.

He stayed in the saddle; Jared drew rein and dismounted, then helped Kristy down. Sir Andrew looked at her closely. "Your cloak's damp, lass, and your shoes are muddied. Jared, you'd best take Mistress Sinclair into the house. I'll join you as soon as I can." Sir Andrew went off with the hostler, who led Jared's horse along.

Jared paused to search her face; he reached out and brushed a twig from her hair. "You haven't told me what you were doing in the woods. It's not wise to go wandering about in unfamiliar country alone."

"I know that now," she said softly.

He cupped her chin in his hand. "What's wrong, Kristy? Have you been seeing that fog again?"

Her voice was unsteady. "I wish that were all."

"Tell me."

He stroked her cheek. She drew reassurance from his voice, the touch of his fingers. She threw her arms around him, pressing her face against his shoulder. "Hold me. Don't let me go."

"You're safe with me, love. Come inside."

"Not yet—the sun's warm. It'll dry my cape. And I'm not afraid, now you're here."

He led her to a stone bench and drew her down beside him. "You looked scared out of your wits, when you came running from the woods. What happened there, Kristy?"

"I met a woman."

"A servant, or a villager, I suppose."

She shook her head.

He made an impatient gesture. "A gypsy? Sir Andrew sometimes lets them camp on his land."

"No, she wasn't a gypsy. She said her name was—Gwyneth Trefoil."

When she spoke the woman's name, she saw his body stiffen. "Gwyneth Trefoil." She heard the revulsion in his voice.

"You know her?" she asked.

"I've heard of her." His green eyes narrowed. "But I didn't know she and her coven had spread so far."

"It's true then, what she said—she's the high priestess of a coven. A witch of the left-hand path."

"That's what they say of her, back in Yorkshire." He paused, his face somber. "Kristy, why did you go to the woods to seek her out?"

"I didn't! I went there to try to find a high place, where I could see you when you rode back. It was Gwyneth who came to me."

"Why? What has she to do with you?"

Kristy went cold inside. Only last night, she and Jared had been as close as a man and woman could be. For the first time, she'd known what it was not to be lonely, an outsider. Now her instincts warned to her to keep silent. But she couldn't. There must be no secrets between her and Jared.

"She said I was like her. That I had certain powers. That she and her coven would teach me how to use them."

"And you believe her?"

"I don't know what to believe. Jared, I've always known I was different. I couldn't remember anything that happened to me before I was six. I felt a kind of emptiness—as if I'd lost a part of myself."

He put his arm around her shoulders, and spoke more gently now. "And when you were six, what happened to you then?"

"I'm not sure. I remember I was alone and it was night. I was standing on a road near a big, old-fashioned kind of house, with trees around it. I don't know who left me there. Later I found out it was my Aunt Vera's house—she's my mother's sister. She took me in, and gave me a home, but she never loved me. She always said she felt it was her duty to raise me. I asked her about my mother, but she never would tell me anything. She said it was better that I shouldn't know."

"And you never were able to find out?"

"Not until today. Gwyneth showed my mother to me."

"You mean she told you about her."

"No. She showed me. I don't know how, but for a moment, I saw my mother. I heard her, singing to me. And I saw myself—only I was a little girl. And Jared—" she hesitated, fearing his response, then forced herself to go on. "My mother wore a pentacle on a silver chain around her neck. Like the one Gwyneth was wearing." She gripped his arm. "I think I can guess how this must seem to you, but it's true."

"What more did Gwyneth tell you?"

"She said I was to come to the Sabbat on Beltane Eve. That I would come, of my own free will. I told her I wouldn't go, but she only laughed. She said I was one of them. That the coven master would teach me—" Kristy felt her insides tighten. *The master will teach you the ways of passion unknown to any mortal man.* She struggled to blot out the obscene images engendered by Gwyneth's words. "Jared, who is the coven master? Do you know?"

He jerked his arm away. His eyes glinted like ice on a winter lake. "Why should you ask? You told her you weren't going." He searched her face, his eyes wary.

"I'm not. I don't want to. But she said I would find out more about my mother, and myself, if I went to the Sabbat on Beltane Eve."

"And you believed her?"

"I don't know what I believe. I know I'm different. How else could I have used the mirror to bring myself here?"

"And now you want to discover how to use your other powers, is that it?"

"I only want to know about my mother. Who she was—why she deserted me."

"Or maybe you want to use that damn mirror to take you to your own time." His voice shook with anger. "No doubt the coven master can teach you how."

"No! I don't want to return to my time, not without you."

Chapter Eight

"Even if I could find a way to return to my own time, I wouldn't leave you. Not after last night." Kristy reached out to him, but he stiffened and drew away.

"It would have been better for both of us, if I hadn't stayed the night with you." She caught the harsh accusation in his voice, and sensed that it was directed against himself. "I shouldn't have taken you."

"You didn't take me. I asked you to stay with me, remember? I wanted you—I was more than willing. I was quite shameless." She gave him a teasing smile, but there was no answering glint of amusement in his eyes.

"You were a virgin. How could you have known—"

She started to speak, but he didn't give her the chance. "I've no doubt you had a fairly good notion of what happens between male and female. Any of our country-bred wenches knows as much. But did you know what loving would mean? How it would change us both?"

"I knew you, Jared." She spoke with quiet assurance.

"Even before that first night we met at the Rowan Tree, I knew you." She wanted to tell him about the dream that had tormented her, arousing her desire for a man she'd never met. But some deep-seated instinct warned her not to speak of the dream, not yet.

She hadn't forgotten the revulsion in his eyes, the anger in his voice, when he'd learned of her meeting with Gwyneth. She searched his face, and felt a sudden uneasiness. Had he believed her when she'd said she hadn't gone seeking Gwyneth, that the silver-eyed sorceress had come in search of her? He already had reason to believe she possessed certain supernatural powers; if she spoke of the dream, that would only serve to convince him.

She remained silent, looking up at him, her eyes holding his. He moved closer and drew her against him; his arm went around her shoulders, his warm breath fanned her cheek. His embrace tightened. "Even before I touched you, I knew how it would be. I knew I couldn't make love with you, then turn and walk away."

His words, the tenderness in his voice, sent a tide of joy surging through her, but it swiftly ebbed away. She saw the tension in his face, the hard lines bracketing his mouth.

"I don't want to leave you." She caught the torment in his voice.

"But why should you? Now we've found each other—"

"How can I make you understand? I have other loyalties. Long before I met you, I gave my word."

"To another woman?"

He shook his head, stood up abruptly, and held out his hand to her. She rose to face him, her eyes searching his.

"My life, my honor are pledged to a cause," he told her. If a man of her own time had spoken that way, she'd have thought him pompous or affected. But those same words, coming from Jared, carried deep, unshakable conviction.

Hot indignation surged through her. "You're a smuggler. You call that a cause?"

119

His lips curved in a brief, ironic smile. "Certainly not. Smuggling's a way to earn a handsome profit, nothing more."

She searched her mind for some other explanation. "Then is it your loyalty to your men?"

"No, my dearest. Except for Dermot, perhaps. We fought against Cromwell's forces together. But as for the rest of my men, they are neither better nor worse than all those other smugglers who sail out of Whitby or Robin Hood's Bay."

"Then what is it that means so much to you—more than I do?" She tilted back her head and searched his face. "Tell me, Jared. I'll try to understand."

"It's no concern of yours," His voice was gentle, but implacable. "I can tell you only that, once this cargo's been disposed of, my men and I will be setting sail again."

She felt a swift, sinking sensation in the pit of her stomach. "Take me with you."

"Kristy, my love, it's not possible."

He took her arm and she let him lead her along the path beneath the towering oaks, to the great house, then on up the wide steps. He stopped before the massive door, and turned to look down at her with such deep tenderness and longing that she felt herself go weak.

He brushed a lock of hair back from her brow, then stroked the curve of her cheek. "This morning at dawn, I stood beside the bed and watched you as you lay sleeping. Sweet Jesú, how I wanted to stay there with you. To lie down beside you, to make love with you again. I wanted to tell you I'd keep you with me, always. But even then, I knew it would be wrong."

"Jared, why? This cause you speak of—even if it's dangerous—"

"Believe me, it is."

She took his hand and her fingers tightened around his. "I don't care."

"But I do. How can I lead you into danger for a cause that can mean nothing to you?"

"We've faced danger together before," she reminded him. "Out there on the moors, with the witch-hunters chasing after us. And again, at the Braethorn market—" She went on quickly, "I know I nearly got us into trouble, talking against Cromwell the way I did. But I promise it won't happen again. I'll learn to think before I say a single word—"

"You, my bold, impulsive Kristy? I suppose you'd try." His lips curved in a brief smile, but it was quickly gone. "And as for your courage, I don't question that, my love. You might not be afraid. But I'd be afraid for you. With a woman to protect, a man grows overcautious. He'll hesitate to take risks, even when it's necessary."

Before she could protest, he went on. "When I left you at dawn to ride out with Sir Andrew, I had already started making plans. You must stay here, under his protection."

He'd made plans for her—just like that! It was all she could do to choke back an indignant protest. Maybe he was behaving as he'd been trained to do. He was a man of his time, after all. And a woman of his time probably would expect him to take charge without consulting her. "How long do you want me to stay here?" How was it possible for her to sound so calm, when she was seething inside?

"As long as necessary."

"A month? Six months?" He didn't answer.

"Sir Andrew's a gracious host," she went on. "He's been kind and considerate. And I don't doubt he'd be able to protect me. But he's a stranger—they're all strangers to me here."

Although the facade of Lachlan Hall was bathed in sunlight, she shivered, as if she'd been brushed by an icy wind. He was heading into danger. Whatever his cause might be, he'd be risking his life. Suppose he didn't come back at all?

Only last night, the loneliness that had been a part of her for so long had been swept aside; she had been one with him. How could he talk of leaving her now? Again she wanted to tell him of her dream—again she held back. She raised her

121

eyes to his, willing him to understand, to share her conviction. "We were meant to be together."

He pulled her against him and his lips claimed hers in a long, lingering kiss. His tongue, hot and seeking, plunged between her parted lips. She reached up and thrust her fingers into his thick, dark hair. She pressed herself against him, and gave herself up to the tide of passion that surged through her. When at last he raised his head, she clung to him. The trees, the grass, the sky were spinning around her. Then, as if from far away, she heard him saying, "Before I cross the sea I've got to go back to Yorkshire, to join my men. It's not safe for you there."

She steadied herself, resting a hand on his arm. "Why not? The witch-hunters must have stopped looking for me by now."

"Perhaps they have." His voice went harsh. "I don't want you to be anywhere near Glenrowan. Not with Beltane so close."

She stared at him reproachfully. "How can you think I'd go to the Sabbat?" She gripped his arms. "You know me better than that—or you should. Nothing, no one, can force me to join Gwyneth and her coven against my will." She stopped short, touched by uncertainty. What was it Gwyneth had said?

I won't have to use force. You'll join us of your own free will.

Her grip tightened on his arms, her fingers pressing against the rock-hard muscles. As if he alone could protect her from the evil that threatened. "Gwyneth said she caused the accident that sent me to Glenrowan. That she was following the orders of the coven master—whoever he may be. Jared, I don't understand any of it. Why do they need me at their Sabbat? What can I possibly have that they want so badly?"

"Power," he said. His eyes were somber. "A coven draws on the combined power of all its followers. It thrives and grows, feeding on such power. They believe they can call up a storm with their obscene rituals, and drive a mighty fleet of ships against a rockbound shore. It's said the witches take credit for having raised the storm that drove back the Spanish Armada, in Queen Elizabeth's time. They seek to increase their power, to gather enough force to change the fate of nations.''

"I don't believe any of that! Raising storms! Destroying the Spanish ships! You don't believe it either. Do you?'' He was a man of his time, yes—but he had a native shrewdness, a keen intelligence.

"It doesn't matter what I believe.'' His voice was bleak, remote. "Gwyneth Trefoil and her master must be convinced that you possess great power. Else why would that damned witch have traveled all the way from Yorkshire to seek you out here?''

"They can believe whatever they want to. I know I have no such power.'' But even as she spoke, she felt a uneasy stirring of doubt.

How was it possible that the sight of Gwyneth's pentacle had swept aside the veil that had shrouded her memory so long? For the first time, she had seen into the darkness; she'd caught a glimpse of those lost years . . . of her mother.

She recalled her mother, gentle and loving, holding her, humming a lullaby; but the woman had worn a pentacle, a five-pointed star on a silver chain around her neck. Kristy struggled to push away the terrifying suspicion that rose from deep inside her. If her mother really had been a witch—one of Gwyneth's kind—had she, herself, inherited a power that had lain dormant all these years?

Was she, too, a witch of the left-hand path?

No! It wasn't possible. She would have known long ago. She would have caught some hint, some warning.

What about Aunt Vera, who had refused to speak of her mother, or show her even a single picture? All at once she remembered those blank spaces in the family photo album. Had there been pictures of her mother, removed, destroyed?

And the others back in Hillsboro, the adults who'd shunned her, who'd refused to let their children play with her.

She'd always suspected she was illegitimate. No big deal in a city of any size. But Hillsboro was a small town; its people had been strait-laced, judgmental. Maybe they were different now, more understanding, more tolerant. She didn't know, because she'd never gone back.

Suppose Aunt Vera had another reason for treating her so coldly, for not telling her about her mother. Suppose the others in town had shared her aunt's dislike because they, too, were afraid of her. Had they also guessed the truth?

What truth?

She struggled hard against her growing suspicion, but it was no use. Even after she'd left Hillsboro, during her years in college and later, when she'd been living in New York, working for Marisol, leading an active, successful life—even then, there'd been other hints, other warnings.

The dream that had come to her, night after night. Glaring torches; masked faces; shrill, unholy laughter.

The mirror with its curved ebony handle, its dark surface. The saleswoman in The Magick Caldron had said that it was for her, that only she could use it.

A shiver ran through her. "Time we went inside," Jared said. But he did not take her arm again; he made no attempt to touch her as they entered the tapestried hall together.

If Sir Andrew sensed the tension between Kristy and Jared at dinner that night, he pretended to ignore it. As the lavish meal was set before them, and the tall candles flickered, Kristy could make only a pretense of enjoying her food. Their host filled the long, uneasy lapses in the conversation with talk of his daughter's coming visit.

"Fiona and her husband will be here in May, along with their three bairns. We'll have a ball, as we always do, to celebrate their visit." He gave Kristy a warm smile, his eyes twinkling under his thick, grey brows. "Our Border gentry will come from miles around. You'll get acquainted with plenty of young people like yourself. No doubt you'll enjoy the music and the dancing.''

"I'll be looking forward to it," Kristy assured him, while wondering what sort of dances were popular here in Scotland in this century. But it didn't matter, she reminded herself, because she wouldn't be at Lachlan Hall in May—not if she could help it. She'd be far away in Holland or maybe France, with Jared. He was determined to leave her here, but she'd convince him to take her along.

She started as she realized that now Sir Andrew was no longer talking of the ball. He was telling her and Jared about the foal born that day.

"I'll take you down to the stables to see him tomorrow morning, Mistress Sinclair," he said. "And afterward, perhaps you'd enjoy a good, bracing ride. We've a fine mare named Tansy, a spirited beast, but suitable for a young lady."

"I'm afraid I don't ride," Kristy said.

Sir Andrew's brows shot up in surprise. Probably all young ladies here on the Border were taught to ride early on, Kristy thought, as she searched for a suitable explanation. Before she could find one, Jared said, "This is as good a time as any for Mistress Sinclair to learn. But perhaps she should start with a more tractable mount."

"Araminta will be most suitable, then," said Sir Andrew. He turned to Kristy. "In a few months you'll be ready to test Tansy's mettle."

Again, Jared and Sir Andrew between them had settled the matter for her. She stifled her indignation, and gave her host her most dazzling smile. "I should so like to see the new foal. Must I wait until tomorrow? Please, can we go to the stables tonight?" She didn't have any intentions of going up to bed as she had last night, leaving Jared and Sir Andrew to talk of masculine affairs until all hours. She had plans of her own.

"The grass is wet now," Sir Andrew said, with a doubtful glance at her flowered silk gown.

"I'll change to something more suitable," she said quickly.

"As you wish," her host conceded.

"I won't be long," she assured them. Before he or Jared could object, she was already out of her chair and crossing the dining hall.

When she returned, she was wearing a plain blue woolen dress and a matching cloak and sturdy leather shoes. Although Polly had looked startled by her announcement that she would visit the stables that night, the maid had lost no time in finding the simple but becoming outfit.

A manservant, carrying a lantern, led the way to the stable. A crescent moon rode high in the night sky, touching the edges of the few scudding clouds with silver. Holding her skirt high to keep it from brushing against the damp grass, Kristy slid her other hand through Jared's arm. Although she felt a touch of guilt, she quickly pushed the feeling away. They mustn't be parted, not now; she would use whatever means might be necessary to get him to change his mind.

The servant pushed open the stable door, and Sir Andrew led the way inside. Kristy looked around the large, well-constructed brick building. The sleeping foal was nestled close beside its mother; a smile touched Kristy's lips at the sight. The mare raised her head and whinnied softly as she looked at her visitors with dark, mild eyes. Sir Andrew spoke to the animal, his tone reassuring. A couple of stablehands, big, burly men, came over to join them. Sir Andrew led the way to a nearby stall, where he pointed to a russet mare. "This is Araminta," he said to Kristy. "You'll find her gentle as a lamb."

Kristy felt a twinge of regret. It would have been pleasant to remain at Lachlan Hall, to learn to ride and to savor the beauty of spring, up here on the border. And she would have been safe here. But she didn't care about her safety, not if it meant that she and Jared would be far apart.

Jared and Kristy left the stable together and started back to the house, while Sir Andrew stayed behind, deep in discussion with his stablehands over the possible purchase of a gelding from a nearby estate. Outside the stable, Jared dismissed the manservant and carried the lantern himself. The moon rode high overhead; from a nearby tree, Kristy heard the hoot of an owl and glanced up to see a pair of round yellow eyes.

"Careful," Jared warned, his hand tightening on her arm. "That's Shadow Glen down there." He held the lantern higher, and the light flickered over the thick stand of pines below.

Kristy inhaled deeply. "Such a wonderful, spicy smell," she said.

"Not only from the trees. There's a thick carpet of last year's pine needles under the trees," he said. "Their scent is finer than any perfume from France, to my way of thinking." She moved closer to him, and was enveloped in the warmth that radiated from his tall, powerful body.

"Jared. Let's not go back to the house right away," she said softly. "Take me down into the glen. Look, there's a path, and you can lead the way."

She caught the swift glint of passion in the sea-green depths of his eyes. She reached up and brushed her fingertips along his cheek, the hard line of his jaw, then slid her hand under his shirt and stroked his hair-roughened chest. "The pine needles will make a soft bed."

"It's turning cooler now," he said, but his voice was deep and husky.

"We'll keep each other warm enough." The first touch of his body on hers would send the heat coiling through her. "Take me down, Jared."

His fierce, inward struggle was reflected in his eyes; she felt his muscles tighten beneath her fingers. She found his flat male nipple; at her touch, she heard the quick intake of his breath. The ways of loving were still new to her; yet, guided by instinct, she was learning quickly.

127

He drew her hand from inside his shirt, turned it palm upward, then circled his tongue over the sensitive flesh, slowly, sensuously. She made a soft sound deep in her throat, as desire stirred within her.

He set down the lantern and drew her close against him. Even through her skirt and petticoat, she felt the pressure of his steely thighs. And the urgent hardness of his arousal. Her legs began to tremble; she went lightheaded.

He bent his head; his tongue flicked at her lips; his teeth caught her lower lip, nibbling, teasing. His arms tightened, and she molded her body to his. She parted her lips, and his tongue plunged between them.

The need she'd aroused in him was engulfing her, too. She couldn't think, couldn't plan any longer. She pressed tighter against him, moving her body slowly, sensuously, against his hardness.

With a fierce, swift movement, he drew away. Startled, shaken, she stared up at him. Her lips tingled; her breasts, their nipples taut, ached for his touch. His chest rose and fell with his quick breathing. "No, love." His voice shook, but she saw the determination in his eyes. He picked up the lantern. "We're going back to the house. Now."

In the Blue Chamber, warmed by the fire crackling in the wide hearth, Polly helped Kristy to undress and put on a fresh linen nightgown with a high collar and long sleeves. "Shall I brush your hair, mistress?" she offered.

"I'd like that." Kristy was still shaken to the depths of her being by Jared's abrupt refusal to give in to his passion, and hers; her body ached with unsatisfied need. She knew that she'd find it impossible to sleep right now.

"Such beautiful hair you have, mistress." Polly drew out the tortoise-shell combs that held the thick tawny waves back from Kristy's face, set them down on the dressing table, and then picked up a silver-mounted brush. "Like the fine, rich silk Lord Ramsey carries from over the sea, it is." She smiled. "I'll do it up for you, on the night of the ball."

"The ball?" Her embrace with Jared, the warmth of his kisses, back there at the glen, had wiped everything else from her mind.

"It won't be for a month, yet. Not until Mistress Fiona comes to visit with her husband, the laird, Ian Macneil—a great, strapping Highlander, he is. And their three bairns. Each year in spring they come and the master gives a ball for the gentry hereabouts."

As she went on brushing Kristy's hair, she smiled, her blue eyes sparkling. "You'll have no lack of partners, all vying to dance with you, mistress."

Kristy made no response. The maid set down the brush. "I might have guessed—it's Lord Ramsey you want, and no other."

Before Kristy could speak, she went on, " 'Tis the same with me and Ben—he's my young man. There's plenty of others who want to walk out with me, but I want none of them." She flushed. "Beggin' your pardon, mistress, for speaking out so bold."

"But you're right, Polly. For me, it's Jared—Lord Ramsey—and no other."

The girl's brow furrowed. "But Mistress Sinclair, you must know—his lordship will be leaving soon. A wanderer, he is. Always moving on—across the Border, down the north of England. And then over the sea."

"I know that. This time, I'm going with him."

"You are?" Kristy heard the misgivings in the girl's voice, "But every woman—and surely a highbred young lady like yourself—needs a man who'll settle down. One who's able to give her a safe home, where she can raise her bairns."

Bairns. A child . . . Jared's child. Not until this moment had she even considered the possibility. But as Polly spoke, she knew, with bone-deep certainty, that she wanted to bear his child.

Until now, she'd thought it would be enough to be close

to him. To lie beside him in the night, and feel the rise and fall of his chest beneath her head, to make love with him. To follow where he led. But for her child, she wanted more—a home, a secure haven, filled with love. The kind of home she'd never had.

"Jared told me that he had a home, once," she said softly.

"Aye, Mistress, so he did. Ravenswyck." Polly spoke the name with awe. "And it was no ordinary home, that I can tell you, but a castle." Seeing the surprise in Kristy's face, she went on, "Didn't you know that?"

It was strange to think of Jared as Lord Ramsey. And as for a castle—the idea was alien to her. Castles belonged in those fairy-tale books she'd brought home from the library until Aunt Vera had forbidden her to fill her head with "such far-fetched nonsense."

Master Prescott had called him Lord Ramsey, that night at the Rowan Tree, and Jared had silenced him harshly. She guessed he used his title only here in Scotland, with Sir Andrew and his trusted servants.

"One day, he'll get Ravenswyck back," Kristy said. "He must."

"Not until the young prince returns from over the water, and takes his place on the throne," said Polly. "Though there's them that calls him by his rightful title, King Charles, already." Her blue eyes sparkled as she picked up the brush and resumed her task. "They care nothing about the threats of the Lord Protector and his army. I heard Sir Andrew tell Mistress Fiona's husband that the governor of the Castle at Pontefract melted down his own gold ring and struck a coin with the name of the second Charles upon it."

Polly's voice rang with pride. "The first of its kind, it was—but I'm thinkin' it'll not be the last."

Then she stopped short and averted her eyes, as if she feared she'd said too much. "I'm always letting my tongue run away with me."

"It's all right," Kristy assured her. "I'm sure Prince Charles will return. It will happen, one day, you'll see."

"It must! With fine, brave men like Lord Ramsey, and my master risking their lives for the cause."

Kristy caught her breath; she understood now. The restoration of the Stuart monarchy—that was the cause Jared had spoken of.

"Did Sir Andrew fight against Cromwell, too?" she asked.

"Not on the battlefield. But he played his part, for all that. After the battle of Dunbar—a terrible time it was—Lachlan Hall sheltered many a brave man who'd otherwise have been caught and hanged by the Lord Protector's troopers. Mistress Fiona cared for those who'd been wounded. And Sir Andrew helped them to escape into the Highlands, or across the sea."

"He must have been devoted to his cause, to have taken such risks," Kristy said.

"So he was. There'd have been a great reward for anyone who betrayed him. But none of us spoke a word about it. Not the house servants like me, nor his tenants. We guarded the secret well."

So that was how Sir Andrew had managed to keep possession of Lachlan Hall. "But Ravenswyck went to a man called Roger Fairfax," Kristy said.

The man who had married the girl Jared had been betrothed to. "I wonder what sort of man he is, this Roger Fairfax?" she asked.

"A stern man, they say. Hard as flint—one of them Puritans that think a bit of pleasure's a sin. And he's stricter even than most. He was no more than a squire, so Sir Andrew says. He got his title and Ravenswyck from the Lord Protector."

Polly put aside the hairbrush, went to the bed and laid out a flannel robe, then started to turn down the covers. "I'm still wide awake," Kristy said.

"Could be you're feeling spring in the air. Makes a body

restless-like.'' She gave Kristy an knowing smile, then started for the door. ''Good night, mistress.''

Then she paused and said softly, ''His chamber is across the hall and two doors down.''

Before Kristy could reply, the maid slipped out the door and closed it behind her.

Across the hall and two doors down. Jared, too, would be lying awake, restless and aching with unsatisfied need. She was sure of it. She stood motionless in the moonlight that streamed through the windows. Then she ran her fingers lightly over her body. Through the linen nightgown, she felt the pulsing heat of her breasts, her belly and thighs.

Back at the glen, he'd held himself in check. He'd mastered his need for her.

Could he do so again? Or was there a way to break through his resistance? A smile touched her lips. She remembered how Jared had stared at her, when he'd seen her in the back of the wagon, wearing her blue nylon gown. Quickly she unbuttoned the long-sleeved linen nightgown, then pulled it off.

Naked, she knelt beside the bed, took out the carry-on. Quickly, she found the blue gown, put it on. It clung to her breasts and swirled down over her hips and thighs. But there was no way she could go out of her room dressed like this. She thrust her feet into the deerskin slippers Polly had set out for her and put on the flannel robe.

She picked up the candle from beside the bed, crossed the room and opened the door. The hall was deserted, lit only by a few torches set in their sconces along the wall.

With a quick, light step, she started for Jared's chamber.

Chapter Nine

The manservant laid Jared's cloak carefully over the back of the chair. "Cleaned and well-brushed, it is, your lordship." The man bent and helped Jared off with his boots. "These'll be well-buffed and outside your door when you rise, sir."

"And you've ordered the hostlers to have my horse hitched to the wagon an hour before sunrise, Ogilvie?"

"That I have, sir. And there'll be a basket of provisions for the journey. A fine tasty ham, a haunch of venison, a dozen beef pasties and plenty of bannocks. And a keg of the master's best whiskey, too."

He opened the door of Jared's chamber, then paused on the threshold. "But before your lordship starts on such a journey, would you not wish to break your fast with some good hot fare? Cook will be only too pleased to prepare a spread and have it waiting for you, as early as you wish."

Jared shook his head. "That won't be necessary. I mean to be on my way by dawn."

"As you please, my lord." The man bowed. "A good night

to you, then.'' He closed the door behind him.

Jared stripped off his doublet, unbuttoned his linen shirt, then tossed them aside. He wouldn't be able to fall asleep, not yet. He put on a thick woolen robe, thrust his feet into elkskin slippers, sat down in a high-backed chair beside the fire, and poured himself a goblet of wine. Staring moodily into the leaping flames, he drank slowly.

It was high time he was on his way. If all had gone according to plan, his men would be waiting for him in Whitby, their goods already disposed of; he'd divide the profits among them, as always. Then they'd board a ship and cross the North Sea to Holland again.

Inside the lining of his doublet, safe in a waterproof packet, lay certain documents to be delivered to Prince Charles. It would be a risky business, but if he should be waylaid in Holland by the Lord Protector's spies, Dermot knew what to do; he was to take over and carry out the mission. As for the other men, they knew nothing; this would be only another smuggling expedition for them.

And what about Kristy? Should he have told her that he was leaving tomorrow? As he drained his goblet, and set it down on the table beside him, he tried to ignore a twinge of remorse. He'd be away from Lachlan Hall before she awoke tomorrow morning.

No need to feel guilty. He'd made all the necessary arrangements with Sir Andrew. She would be comfortable here, safe and cared for. Their host would see to it that she kept occupied.

She'd start her riding lessons and before long, she'd be cantering across the rolling green hills of the estate, her cheeks aglow, savoring the heady scents of spring here on the Border. Then, in mid-May, she'd be dancing at the Lachlan ball, decked out in a fine, new gown. She'd meet the local gentry; no doubt, they would beseige her with invitations to visit them. She wouldn't have time to feel lonely.

But to leave her like this, to disappear without a word of

farewell? He refilled his goblet, then fixed his gaze on the fire once more. It would be easier for her this way, he told himself.

But he'd never been good at self-deception, and now his mouth twisted in a sardonic smile. Had he been thinking only of her feelings, when he'd decided to drive away before dawn, leaving Sir Andrew to tell her that he had gone?

Suppose he changed his plans, delayed his departure—and went to her tomorrow to say good bye. He knew what would happen. She only had to reach out her slender white arms to him, her topaz eyes glowing with passion, her soft red lips parted for his kiss . . . and he would not be able to leave her.

It had taken all his willpower to turn away from her, back there at the glen. He'd wanted to take her down into those shadowy depths, to lie with her on the thick, soft carpet of pine needles. Even now, the thought of the ecstasy they might have shared sent heat flaring up inside him. His loins tightened with the urgency of his need.

Then why not take her with him, as far as the harbor at Whitby? He imagined how it would be, making love with her under the shelter of the canvas in the back of the wagon. To know again the joy of holding her slender, enticing body in his arms, tasting her lips, feeling her breasts against his chest, her hands stroking his shoulders. Sheathing himself deep within her, satisfying his desire—and hers.

Once they reached the harbor at Whitby, it would be easy enough to hire a coach to bring her back here to Lachlan Hall. But until then, why not share a few more nights with her?

Why not? Because the longer they were together, the deeper the pain he'd feel when the time came to leave her. She was already a part of him. She always would be.

He hadn't wanted this to happen, hadn't planned it. He'd fought against his hunger for her as long as he could, to no avail. And now, in spite of his need, he had to leave her. He dared not delay their parting any longer, otherwise he'd be endangering his mission.

He shifted uneasily in the chair, and refilled his goblet yet again. But he knew the wine would not drive away the doubts that had tormented him from their first meeting. Suppose he took her to Whitby, then sent her on her way back here to Scotland. What if she left the coach the first time the driver stopped to change horses along the road? What if she made her way across the moors on foot, back to Glenrowan?

No! She wouldn't do that.

But how could he be sure?

She might return to seek out that silver-eyed witch, Gwyneth Trefoil. Would she? Sweet Jesu! Was it possible she was already planning to join in the Beltane Sabbat?

His insides lurched with revulsion. Kristy wasn't a witch, dammit! Not Gwyneth's kind of witch. She could not possibly have chosen the left-hand path, could not willingly give herself over to those obscene, unholy rites. Not his Kristy, with her clean, satin-skinned body, her fragrant hair, her warm golden eyes.

His Kristy?

What the devil made him think of her that way? Even after all this time together, what did he know about her? He set down his goblet with a force that scarred the top of the table. The goblet overturned, and a few drops of wine spilled on the thick wolfskin rug that lay in front of the hearth.

His muscles went rigid; his mouth tightened. What kind of woman was Kristy Sinclair? She claimed she had traveled through time and, reluctantly, he'd come to believe her. She carried strange tools he'd never seen or even heard of before.

With the flick of her finger, she had caused the broken walls of the ruined abbey to resonate with the voice of an invisible man, singing an eerie ballad, accompanied by the music of unseen instruments. She had sent a brilliant, unwavering beam of light across the windswept darkness of the moors. She had carried the scrying mirror with her, and had claimed she'd seen visions reflected in its dark surface—mystical visions no one else could see. A fey creature, she was, like no other woman he'd ever known.

And he'd let himself fall in love with her. Now it was up to him to guard her from harm. How could he bear to think of her out there on the moors on Beltane Eve, when all decent, God-fearing folk stayed behind their bolted doors, with their windows tightly shuttered? Kristy, taking part in arcane rituals, among the grotesque, wind-scoured stones, with Gwyneth and her followers. Worshipping the coven master, whoever—whatever—he might be.

His eyes narrowed as he stared into the fire. Where had he heard of those unholy rites? Sometime in the faraway past. . . .

And all at once, those half-forgotten memories were coming back to him: memories of the servants' talk he'd overheard, back at Ravenswyck. A small boy, he'd been, sitting motionless on a bench in the shadowy corner of the firelit kitchen that was pungent with the smells of cooking food and dried herbs. He hadn't wanted to draw attention to himself as he listened avidly to Nan Mulgrave, the old cook, and the maids who clustered around her. He held his breath as he heard the tales of the Sabbats out on the moors; of the witches—withered crones, some of them, but others young and fair. Then the cook had told the maids about the coven master.

"The Horned Man, some call him." Even now, he could hear her creaky voice and see her face, wrinkled like a dried apple. "There's them that say he be not a man at all, but a fearsome beast. 'Tis the head of a beast, he has—stag's horns, and a forked tail. And there be thick, black fur growing all over his body. And great claws instead of a man's hands. Yet 'tis said he choses a mortal woman and lies with her on the night of the Sabbat."

The boy had spent enough time hanging about the stables to have formed a fairly clear notion of what the cook meant by that. The maids, although round-eyed with fear, were eager to hear more. But Kate, a flaxen-haired, big-bosomed girl, and bolder than the rest, had given a shrill giggle. "Beast or no, he must have the pizzle of a man, else how could he couple with a woman?"

"A man's pizzle!" The cook had stopped stirring the pot; she cackled with unholy glee. "Nay—'tis far bigger than any man's. And the feel of it—icy-cold it be, inside a woman."

"And how would you be knowing that?" Kate had asked. "Mayhap you lay with the Horned Man yourself, Nan Mulgrave—at a Sabbat night many years ago."

The cook, her eyes burning with indignation, had turned on her, brandishing a ladle. "Hold your tongue, girl! Or I'll fetch you a blow you'll not soon forget."

A light tapping at the door of Jared's bedchamber brought him back to the present; to the high-ceilinged room, with its tapestry-hung walls and the wolfskin rug at his feet. He heard the tapping again, louder this time.

The door swung open and he drew in his breath at the sight of Kristy, the shining waves of her hair loose about her face, a candle in her hand. She wore a modest, long-sleeved robe buttoned to her chin.

"Have you had another nightmare?" he asked.

The robe did not quite conceal her graceful movements as she walked over to the hearth and paused there, her slippered feet deep in the wolfskin pelts.

He rose from his chair and came over to her. "Was it the fog again, creeping in through your window? The fog seen by no one but you?" He tried to speak lightly, but he could not keep the hard edge from his tone.

"I saw no fog tonight."

"Why aren't you sound asleep in your bed, then?"

"I'm not ready to go to bed." She glanced at his goblet, lying on its side. "And neither are you, it seems." She reached out her hand to him, then drew it back as if she were uncertain he would welcome her touch. "I needed to be with you. Is that so strange? I thought—I hoped—you'd want me, too.''

This was the moment he'd hoped to avoid, but perhaps it would be better to tell her his plans and get it over with. ''Kristy—it's as well you should know now. I'm leaving here tomorrow, before dawn.'' His hands closed lightly on her shoulders; but he fought the impulse to draw her to him.

He saw the warm color drain from her face. She set her jaw, and pressed her lips together.

''You knew I'd be going away,'' he reminded her.

''But not so soon. And not like this, without even waiting long enough to say goodbye.'' He caught a flicker of anger in the depths of her eyes. ''I suppose you and Sir Andrew had it all worked out between you. You'd be long gone, leaving him to tell me you'd left.''

''I thought it would be better this way.''

''Better for me—or for you?''

Her amber eyes held a challenge; he wanted to look away, but he couldn't. ''For both of us, I suppose.''

''You were afraid I'd make a scene, is that it? You thought I'd cry—that I'd cling to you and beg you to take me along?'' He sensed the effort it was costing her, to keep her emotions under control.

''You told me once that you never cry. As for begging, it's not your way. You have too much pride for that.''

''Then why didn't you come to me tonight and tell me you were leaving?''

''Because I didn't trust myself.'' It wasn't easy for him to make such a confession. ''I was afraid that if I saw you, if we made love again, there'd be no need for you to ask to go along. I wouldn't have been able to leave without you.''

''And having a woman along—that would have interfered with your mission. You and Sir Andrew both fought for the Royalist cause, each in your own way. And you haven't given up the fight—you never will.'' Her golden eyes held a touch of mockery. ''You needn't look so surprised. Polly told me a little about it—and I could guess the rest. There's some kind of conspiracy, on both sides of the Border, to overthrow Cromwell and restore Prince Charles to the Stuart throne.''

His eyes darkened with anger. "That foolish wench! She had no right to let her tongue run away with her."

"She knew I wouldn't betray you. But you, Jared—you don't trust me—you don't believe I'd keep your secret."

"I don't know what to believe any longer." His voice was harsh, tormented. "I only know I want you more than I've ever wanted any other woman."

"Even Liane? You must have loved her once—you were going to marry her."

Although the words came unbidden, she wasn't sorry she'd spoken. What had he felt for his lost love?

"Liane was a gentlewoman, beautiful, and well-bred. We'd grown up together, both our families favored the match." His jaw tightened. "The war changed all that."

"If it hadn't been for the war, you'd have married her. And even now, you haven't forgiven her for marrying another man, have you? Maybe it's because of her that you don't trust any woman. Not even me."

He groaned, deep in his throat. "I want to trust you—to take you with me. But I can't."

His hands dropped from her shoulders and he stepped away from her. "We've said our farewells now. Go back to your chamber."

She made no move to obey, but stood looking up at him. Then, with her eyes fixed on his, she started to unbutton her robe. Slowly she drew it from her shoulders and let it fall to the rug.

His mouth went dry and he felt the blood start to pound in his temples. Her body was sheathed in her enticing blue gown, sheer as cobweb; it was the same one she'd worn that night in the back of his wagon. This time she wasn't holding that strange instrument—a flashlight, she'd called it—but the glow of the firelight behind her revealed every sensuous curve, every shadowed hollow of her body.

His gaze moved over her flesh through the fabric, devouring her high, rounded breasts, with their rosy nipples . . . the swell of her hips . . . her long legs . . . the darkness at the apex of her thighs. He went hard, his manhood swelled, his loins tightened.

With one swift movement he seized her wrist, thrust her hand inside his robe and pressed it against his hardness. The warmth of her touch sent ripples of fire surging through his body. "You planned this, didn't you? You meant to set me burning for you. To make me forget all else."

"Jared, no!"

He ignored her protest. "You meant to bind me to you. To keep me from leaving here without you."

Kristy flinched under his gaze. She tried to draw her hand away, but he held it against his arousal. She felt him swelling beneath her fingers. She struggled to draw breath, to speak—to make him understand.

"Maybe it's true. Maybe I hoped it would happen that way, back there at the glen. And was it so wrong of me—wanting to be with you? Wanting us to be together, always." Tears stung her eyelids but she blinked them back. "But that's not what you want, is it?" She raised her chin, held her head high. Somehow she kept her gaze steady, her voice unwavering. "All right, you can leave without me. I won't try to stop you."

"I'm leaving, but not yet. We have one more night left. Don't we?"

He let go of her wrist, then tore off his robe and tossed it aside. Her startled gaze dropped to the proud thrust of his manhood, straining against his tight-fitting doeskin breeches. She raised her eyes to his heavily-muscled chest, with its sprinkling of dark hair—to his wide shoulders.

He moved closer, his green eyes narrowed, smoky with

desire. She caught the heady male scent of his body. He reached out, cupped her breast; then, bending his head, he caught the nipple between his lips. He was suckling her through the sheer covering of her gown. She moaned softly, gripped his shoulders, then threw back her head and gave herself up to the fiery sensations coursing through her.

His mouth moved downward. With one lithe movement, he dropped to his knees. He pressed his face against the soft flesh of her belly, then went lower still. He moved his lips against her soft center. She gasped, feeling the heat, the moisture deep within her.

She pulled off her nightgown and threw it aside, aching to feel his mouth against her—with nothing between them. His gaze caressed her, ravished her. Still kneeling, he drew her down to him. The thick wolfskin was soft and warm beneath her back, her buttocks. He drew away only long enough to strip off his breeches.

She held out her arms to him and he stretched himself beside her, his hardness pressing against her thigh. She stroked his hair, his neck, then ran her hands over his shoulders.

He moved his palm over her soft woman's mound, slowly, sensuously. Now he was parting her, seeking—finding—the hard bud of her womanhood. He took it between his fingers. She arched against his hand, wordlessly pleading for release.

With one swift movement, he was above her. She parted her legs to him, aching for the first thrust of possession. But he held back, sliding the length of his arousal against her soft, wet flesh. Driven by her overpowering need, she reached out and pressed her fingers against his buttocks, drawing him to her.

He thrust deep into her, but stayed motionless, looking down into her eyes. She started to rotate her hips, and he was moving now, slowly at first, then faster. She matched her rhythm to his, her hips rising with each thrust. She wrapped her legs around him, gripping his lean hips, drawing him deeper still.

She felt herself starting to throb now, caught up in the rising spiral of ecstasy. He gave a cry of triumph, as he spilled himself inside her.

She lay close beside him, her head against his chest, drowsy and utterly fulfilled. The firelight played over the length of his body. Slowly, reluctantly, he moved away, but only to lift her from the wolfskin rug and carry her to the wide, curtained bed. He set her down and climbed in beside her, drawing the heavy blankets over both of them. Cradled in his arms once more, she sighed and drifted off to sleep.

When Kristy opened her eyes, she saw the grey light of dawn filtering in through the windows. For a moment, she lay motionless, afraid to turn her head. Had he left without her? As she moved, she felt his warmth against her. She raised herself, resting her weight on her arm, and looked down at him.

His eyes were closed, his dark hair tangled across his forehead. His chest rose and fell with his even breathing. She smiled, as she remembered the wonder of their night together.

But her smile quickly faded. The morning light was growing brighter, and Jared shifted in his sleep. She didn't want him to wake up, not yet. She hadn't forgotten her promise—she wouldn't try to persuade him to take her with him. Her throat tightened. How could she let him go?

Sleep a little longer, love. Only a little longer. . . .

But a heavy log cracked in the fireplace, and his eyes opened. He sat up and reached out to her, and stroked her hair, the curve of her bare shoulder.

He feathered light kisses over her forehead, her cheek, her throat. He caressed her back, his fingers moving down along her spine. Delicious sensations stirred inside her.

From outside the window came the sounds of early morning: the harsh cry of a starling, the grating call of a grouse, the shrill barking of a hound. Then she tensed as she caught the familiar creak of wagon wheels. With an abrupt movement, he pushed aside the blanket and swung his legs over the side of the bed.

"Your wagon?" Her voice was steady. She'd given Jared her word to let him go when the time came. She wouldn't break her promise, no matter what it cost her.

"I told the servants I'd be making an early start."

She nodded, and got out of bed. Her blue nightgown lay near the fireplace, along with her robe and slippers. "I'd better get back to my own bed, before one of the servants comes in and sees me."

She crossed the room and bent to pick up her nightgown. With a few swift strides, he was at her side, his hand gripping her arm. "There'll be no servants in here. I told them I wouldn't be needing them this morning."

"But what about your clothes—your breakfast—"

"My cloak's been cleaned. It's over there on the chair. My boots will be outside the door." He grinned. "Ogilvie assured me there'd be a basket of food in the wagon. Enough provisions to feed a troop of dragoons." He looked down at her, his green eyes tender and reassuring. "Certainly enough for the two of us."

The two of us.

Her heart soared at his look, his words. "Are you sure? I promised last night—"

"I remember. And I should keep you to that promise, leave you here with Lachlan. He pulled her to him, holding her so close that his hair-roughened chest rubbed against her bare breasts. "But I can't. Kristy, you're coming with me."

The first rays of sunlight slanted across the park and glittered over the tall windows of Lachlan Hall. When Kristy came out, Jared and Sir Andrew already were standing beside the wagon, deep in conversation.

Polly, although she'd been startled by Kristy's sudden

144

change of plans, had helped her into the woolen gown and cape she'd worn to the stable the night before. Now the maid, holding the canvas carry-on, followed her down the curving steps.

Kristy caught only a few words of the men's conversation. "... better to leave her at Whitby," Sir Andrew was saying.

"... unwise for her to return here by public coach ... I have my reasons—"

As soon as the men caught sight of Kristy, they fell silent. Although Sir Andrew obviously had been questioning Jared's decision to take her along, he quickly concealed his feelings. He greeted her with a bow and a smile, but she felt a lingering tension in the air.

Anxious to break the uneasy silence, she said, "I hope you don't mind my borrowing your daughter's clothes. They're warm and—practical for a long journey. I'll send them back as soon as I can manage it."

"There is no need, Mistress Sinclair. I'm sure my daughter would wish you to keep them." Although he spoke with his usual courtesy, she caught an undertone of disapproval in his voice; or was it uneasiness? Was he afraid she'd be a burden to Jared, that she would interfere with his carrying out his mission?

As the wagon moved away from the lawn into the misty woods, Kristy turned and kept her gaze fixed on Lachlan Hall. She and Jared had made love here for the first time. He'd taught her the magic, the soaring splendor of a man and a woman joining in body and spirit. She might not return again, but she would never forget the glorious fulfillment she'd known here.

She kept looking back until the towering oaks pressed in on both sides, their massive trunks and dark branches shutting out the last glimpse of the great stone mansion. Then she moved closer to him, and fixed her eyes on the narrow path ahead. The early morning dew trickled down from the twigs, leaving drops on her cape and gown. She brushed them off, and smoothed the folds of her skirt. Her borrowed leather shoes, with their square pewter buckles, were a bit too tight, but she'd manage.

"Considering how little time I gave you to dress, you've made a sensible choice," he said. "These garments are of good cut and fabric, but plain enough so you'll pass for a well-to-do Puritan lady—the wife of a prosperous merchant, perhaps." He grinned, and gave her a nod of approval.

She smiled back at him. "And what goods do you deal in, Master Ramsey?"

"Luxury items from abroad. Surely a sensible wife should know that much about her husband's business."

Her husband. If only that were true. A merchant and his wife, sharing their placid days, lying close together, night after night, in their own bed.

"I'll do my best to play my part," she assured him. "I won't do anything to attract suspicion." She laid her hand on his arm. "I heard some of what Sir Andrew was saying. He didn't want you to take me along."

"Only because he's afraid your being with me will make it more difficult for me to do what I must."

"More dangerous, that's what you mean, isn't it?" Her fingers tightened on the hard muscles of his forearm. "I'll be careful, I promise. I've already learned how to dress properly. I'll learn to speak as other woman do, in your—"

"In my time," he finished for her.

They were coming out of the woods now; turning onto the wide rutted road that led south. He brought the wagon to a halt. "You still haven't found a way to return to your own time, have you?"

She shook her head. "I'm beginning to think there is no way."

He gave her a long, direct look. "Would you return there, if you could?"

"Not if it meant being separated from you."

"But to be exiled forever from the time you were born in, the world you've always known. Surely that won't be easy."

She was silent for a moment, her eyes fixed on the road, and the Tweed River glittering in the the distance. "I'll miss my friends. Especially Liz. And Macavity—"

She felt the muscles of his arm tighten under her hand. "Macavity?" His straight, dark brows drew together. "Who the hell is Macavity? That man you were bethrothed to?"

She tried to hold back her laughter, but she couldn't. "Macavity's my cat—a big marmalade tomcat."

"That's a peculiar name for a cat." But even as he spoke his lips twitched and now he, too, was laughing. He put his arm around her and drew to him.

If only it always could be like this for them, she thought wistfully. Laughing together in the sunshine of a fresh-scented spring morning.

The moment was over too soon. "There's so much I don't know about your other life," he said. His eyes were troubled.

"What does it matter? We're together now," she said. "That's all I care about."

"Kristy, my love." His arm tightened around her shoulders, and his lips, warm and caressing, brushed her cheek. Then, reluctantly, he let her go. "We'd best be moving along. I want to cross the river before dark." He flicked the reins and the wagon started forward again, jouncing over the ruts in the road.

So much he didn't know about her. So much she did not know about herself. And never would know. She thought of Gwyneth Trefoil, and felt as if an icy wind had touched her.

Jared was taking her away, to Whitby and then across the North Sea. Away from Gwyneth and the moors. On the night of the Beltane Sabbat, she'd be far off in Holland with him.

She'd never have a chance to discover the truth about those early, lost years. The truth about her mother. About herself.

Chapter Ten

The wagon rattled over the wide stone bridge spanning the Tweed River, then Jared turned onto a rutted track that stretched upward into the Cheviot Hills. As they traveled south, he kept the horse moving at a steady trot. Although he scarcely spoke to her, Kristy sensed the tension that gripped him.

The sun was dropping behind the hills in a blaze of crimson and gold, when he drew to a halt to make way for a stoop-shouldered, sandy-haired shepherd in a homespun smock, who was waiting to herd his flock across to the meadow on the far side.

"Thanks to you, master," the man called out, as he and his brown-and-white dog drove the black-faced sheep into the meadow. The dog moved around the flock, nipping gently at an occasional straggler. "You'll find few inns hereabouts," he remarked. "If you and your lady would do us the honor to spend the night at our cottage, you would be most welcome."

He gave them a broad, gap-toothed grin. "My Meg is a good cook, though I do say so myself, and what with our cottage so far from town, she'd enjoy a bit of female company."

"That's a generous offer, and we'd be pleased to accept," said Jared, "but we're expected at the home of our friends, and we're already late." He pointed in the direction of a deep ravine that ran down between two steep, conical hills. "Their house lies that way."

"A safe journey then, to you and your lady." The shepherd turned away, and started moving his flock across the meadow, heading for home.

Jared flicked the reins, and the wagon went jouncing down a rocky path into the shifting blue-grey shadows of the ravine. Kristy looked at him reproachfully. "You never said a word about spending the night with friends. Who are they?"

Though he stared straight ahead, and did not answer, she understood. "You lied to the shepherd, didn't you?" He shrugged, and remained silent. "Why did you refuse him?"

"We have no time to delay." He spoke in a hard, clipped voice, and still did not look at her, as he guided the wagon down the steep, narrow road.

"It was because of me, wasn't it?" They'd traveled only this short distance, and already she was proving to be a burden to him. "You were afraid I'd arouse the man's suspicions—or his wife's."

He reached for her hand. "Easy, love. You've done remarkably well so far. But you still have so much to learn. If we'd spent the night at the shepherd's cottage, and his wife had sat down for a cozy chat with you, it's possible you'd have betrayed yourself. What do you know of ordinary household matters here? I thought it better not to take any unnecessary risks."

He'd acted sensibly—she couldn't deny it—yet she still was troubled. Maybe he was beginning to regret he hadn't left her behind at Lachlan Hall.

Diana Haviland

"We'll drive only a little farther, and then we'll stop for the night." He turned to her with a teasing smile. "Maybe we won't sleep in a proper bed tonight, but I'll see to it you're warm and comfortable back there, under the canvas."

She caught the glint in his eyes, and she felt a sweet-hot anticipation stirring inside her. When she moved closer to him, he put his arm around her shoulders. He leaned over and his mouth brushed her cheek.

"Keep your mind on your driving," she admonished him. But he'd already awakened her senses with the touch of his lips. A delicious shiver went through her as she thought of the night ahead.

A room in a shepherd's cottage, a velvet-curtained bed in Lachlan Hall—or a blanket under the canvas in the back of the wagon. What did it matter, so long as Jared lay close beside her?

Her lips curved in a sensuous smile. Tonight she'd show him that he'd made the right choice, the only possible choice, in taking her along.

They crossed the Cheviot Hills, pale green with the new spring grass; then they drove through Northumberland, and down into Yorkshire. He turned the wagon east, heading toward the coast; soon she breathed the fresh salt scent of the sea, mingled with the rich loamy smell of damp earth, the tang of moss. If only they could linger here for a little while, she thought wistfully. But Jared kept the horse to the same steady pace.

On every side, the moors were stirring, coming alive with promises of spring. The branches of oaks and ash trees, bare and grey only a few weeks before, flaunted their gauzy green haze of new leaves.

Late one afternoon she watched a flock of plump grouse feeding on fresh, young shoots; they took flight with their clacking cries, as the wagon came rumbling toward them.

"Jared, look—there's a village up ahead. Maybe there's an inn where we can stop."

"There is. But we're not stopping."

Why must he be so stubborn? "Can't we even drive through it?"

"We'll keep to this track, and drive around it." The line of his jaw had gone hard.

She leaned forward for a closer look at the thatch-roofed cottages, and the few shops with their painted signboards swinging over the doors. "But it'll be quicker if we drive through the village—"

"Cragsmore, that's its name. And we're going past it as quickly as we can." He speeded up the horse with a flick of his whip. Baffled by his response to her simple request, she lapsed into uneasy silence.

They had left Cragsmore nearly a mile behind when he drew the wagon to a halt and pointed upward. "Look there," he said. Her eyes widened as she caught sight of the great stone parapet set high on the rocky ledge overlooking the sea.

She gazed in awe at the massive towers looming dark against the orange and scarlet of the sunset sky.

"Ravenswyck." She heard the exhaltation that resonated in his voice as he spoke the name; but she caught an undertone of deep resentment, too.

"Ravenswyck. That's your home."

"It was my home." She saw the desolation in his eyes, and her throat constricted. She longed to draw his head down against her shoulder, to stroke his hair, to murmur endearments. But she stopped herself in time. Jared was not a child to be comforted with caresses; he was a proud man, a warrior still fighting for his cause.

"It will be yours again." She spoke with quiet conviction.

"It will. But not so long as Cromwell rules England." He cracked the whip and the horse broke into a steady trot.

Silence stretched between them, until she could stand it no longer. She rested her hand on his arm. "You thought you

151

might have been recognized back there in Cragsmore—that's why you wouldn't stop."

He nodded. "I was eighteen when I left home to fight for the king." His mouth twisted in an ironic smile. "A fine figure of a man, I thought myself that day. I wore a plumed hat and a velvet cloak, and carried my father's sword. I rode the finest stallion in our stables, another parting gift from my father." The smile vanished. "Maybe no one in Cragsmore would have recognized me now, but I couldn't take the risk."

She thought of Jared, a high-spirited young man in a plumed hat, riding off to war. Eager to fight for his king, sure of victory. And now he was a smuggler, a homeless outcast. Though he hadn't traveled to another century, as she had, he, too, was an exile.

We're two of a kind.

His mouth was a hard, tight slash, his tanned skin drawn taut across his cheekbones. If she couldn't comfort him, perhaps she might distract him.

"After we've gone a little farther, why don't we stop and have our dinner."

"You haven't lost your hearty appetite," he said. His smile was a little forced, but his eyes no longer held the remote look that troubled her so.

"There's a wood with a stream, a few miles ahead," he said. "We'll stop there for the night. I'll build a fire, and we'll have the ham, sizzling hot."

The firelight flickered over the trees surrounding the clearing where they had stopped for the night. From close by, she heard the water rushing over the rocks. Jared had contrived a spit out of two pieces of metal, driven into the ground, and another between them, to hold the ham. Now he spread a thick blanket over last year's dry leaves. Kristy settled herself, smoothing the folds of her skirt.

"This is the best picnic I've ever had," she said, with a smile.

"The best—what?"

Once more she was reminded of the gulf that stretched between them. There was so much she didn't know about his time, so much about her century that was unfamiliar to him. "A picnic's a meal you eat outdoors. You bring a blanket and a basket of food." Back in Hillsboro, she and Aunt Vera had gone to the Fourth of July picnics, but they'd always kept apart from the crowd.

She pushed the memory to the back of her mind.

The delicious smell of ham made her mouth water. Jared laid a thick slice on one of the pewter plates, handed it to her, then took another for himself.

"If this isn't enough to satisfy your ferocious appetite, we'll have a couple of those beef pasties." He gave her a teasing smile. "And there are plenty of the bannocks—"

He broke off and turned to peer into the darkness of the nearby thicket, his eyes alert and wary.

"Jared, what—"

"Be still."

Now she heard the noises, too: the snap of a twig, the crunch of footsteps on dried leaves, a whining sound that did not come from any human throat. With one swift, lithe movement, he was on his feet. She saw his hand go to his boot, and she drew in her breath as she caught the glint of firelight along the steel blade of his knife.

At the edge of the thicket, two dark figures stood watching them. "Come over here where I can see you," Jared ordered.

A man and woman slowly shuffled forward. The man was short and thin; his threadbare jacket was too big for him, and his breeches were worn at the knees. The woman's lank black hair fell around her gaunt face; she wore a soiled green skirt, torn at the hem, and clutched a ragged crimson shawl around her shoulders. They stared first at Jared, then at the ham on the spit over the fire.

"Please, master, we don't mean no harm. Lafe Bulmer's my name. He jerked his head in the direction of his companion. "This be my woman, Tess." A dog, its ribs showing through its brown-and-white fur, moved cautiously toward the fire.

"Get back, you," said the man. The animal looked wistfully at the meat, then whined softly and moved off.

"What were you doing, skulking about in these woods? Poachers, are you?"

"Poachers! You think we'd be stealin' game on Lord Fairfax's land? A man'd be daft to take such a risk. It's a tinker I am—when I can find work."

"Jared—they're hungry," Kristy said softly, but he didn't turn to look at her. His hard gaze was fixed on Lafe Bulmer, and he still gripped the handle of his knife.

"If you're a tinker, where are the tools of your trade?"

"Back in my cart behind those trees, master."

"And your horse?"

"We got no horse," the woman said. "We had an ol' donkey, but we sold it to a knacker for the price of its hide. Since then, Lafe and me have been pullin' the cart."

She stared longingly at the ham on Kristy's plate, swallowed hard; then fumbled in the pocket of her bedraggled skirt and pulled out a coin. "This be all we have left, sir— would it buy us a bit o' that meat?"

Jared did not answer at once. His gaze moved over the pair. Then he spoke quietly. "Come here to the fire. We've enough to spare." He gave the woman a brief smile. "Put away your coin, Tess."

The couple came nearer; then, after a moment, the dog followed them. "You be uncommon kind, master," said Tess. "If you got a pan or a skillet that needs mending, my Lafe's a good tinker."

"A good tinker can always earn a few coins in any village in Yorkshire," Jared said.

"Not these days he can't," Lafe told him. "An' not back there in Cragsmore. He's lucky if he can get out o' that cursed place with a whole skin."

He squatted down, rummaged quickly among the pieces of tree bark scattered about the fire, then selected a couple of flat slabs. He brushed the dirt off, handed one to Tess, and kept the other for himself.

"Sit down, both of you," Jared said. They obeyed instantly, staring at him with avid eyes, as he cut off two thick slices of ham and laid them on the improvised plates. Then he tossed a bit of meat to the dog, who pounced on it, swallowed it, and sat close by, its gaze fixed hopefully on its new benefactor.

The tinker and his woman devoured the ham, tearing at it ravenously. Grease dripped down the woman's chin; she wiped it away with a corner of her shawl. Kristy averted her eyes. Under other circumstances, she would have felt disgust at their crude manners, but now her throat constricted with pity.

"Tain't often we meet gentlefolk who be kind like you, master," said Lafe. "Sure you got no job I can do?"

Jared shook his head, then cut off another slab of meat for each of them. "But what about the good wives of Cragsmore? Surely they have plenty of knives to be sharpened, and skillets in need of mending."

"We didn't dare stay long enough to find out," said Lafe. "Not with him up there in Ravenswyck. Travelin' the roads like we do, we've learned to smell trouble right off. An' that one—he's nothin' but trouble to folk like us."

"Sir Roger Fairfax?"

The tinker nodded. "Aye, that's his name. Damn him, an' curse the day the Lord Protector sent him here. A cruel one, is Lord Fairfax. Why his own servants, an' his villagers go in fear of him. He's even worse with strangers like us."

"Guard your tongue, man," Tess pleaded. "For the love o' heaven, say no more." She gave Jared a fearful glance. "Don't pay him no mind, sir—he don't mean half he says."

Kristy heard the naked fear in the woman's voice, and she understood. Jared had said they could pass for a prosperous

155

merchant and his wife; as such, they might be loyal supporters of the Lord Protector. Anyone who spoke a word against Cromwell had ample reason to be afraid. She remembered how the crowd had turned against her, when she'd defended the puppeteer back at the Braethorn marketplace.

But Lafe ignored Tess's warning, his resentment overcoming the need for caution. "Time was, a travelin' tinker could make a fair livin' in most any village in Yorkshire," he said. "Mayhap we didn't find the villagers over-friendly—us bein' strangers, an' all. But I done good work. I earned my handful of coins. Now Tess an' me, we be starvin'. If it hadn't been for you, master—"

Kristy, who had remained silent so far, now spoke impulsively. "There are plenty of beef pasties in the wagon. And bannocks, too."

She stopped short, gave Jared an uneasy glance. But she caught the brief flicker of amusement in his eyes. Then it was gone, and he spoke as soberly as any Puritan spouse.

"We've enough to go around, my dear. Your charitable nature does you credit." He was playing up the role of the respectable merchant to the utmost, and enjoying it.

As she started for the wagon, she heard the tinker say, "Your lady's not one for talkin' overmuch, if you'll pardon my sayin' so."

"Most females talk when they would do better to remain silent. And much of what they say is frivolous nonsense, to my way of thinking. As for me, I have trained Mistress—Singleton well. She learns quickly." Jared spoke solemnly, but he was teasing her, and she knew it.

Her lips twitched, but she managed to keep from laughing. Later, when they were alone, she'd find a way to get back at him.

Mistress Singleton, he'd called her. Even while he was enjoying himself at her expense, he hadn't been off his guard—he hadn't mentioned his name, or hers. She lowered her eyes demurely, then went on to the wagon.

"Don't try to lift the keg of whiskey," he called to her. "It's too heavy for one so frail as you, my dear." He hurried to her side to help her.

When Lafe and Tess had swallowed the last crumbs of the pasties and the flat oat cakes the Scots called bannocks, Jared filled the pewter mugs with whiskey, and handed them around. "Drink hearty," he said. "Say what you will, there's nothing like good Scottish whiskey to prevent an attack of the ague."

"That's the truth, sir," said the tinker. "It warms a man right though." Lafe drained his cup, with a sigh of satisfaction. "Never tasted such fine spirits, Master Singleton."

"Have another," said Jared. "And you, too, Tess." Again the tinker gulped down this whiskey; again, Jared refilled his cup. Kristy gave Jared a sharp glance, sure that he was not acting only out of generosity.

After the tinker had drained his mug for the fourth time, he wiped his mouth on his sleeve, leaned his back against a tree and grinned.

"Traveling about as you do, you must know a good deal about the north of Yorkshire," Jared remarked. "As for me, I've driven through Cragsmore, but that was years ago. I know little about it—or about Lord Fairfax." Although his tone was casual, Kristy guessed his purpose. He wanted to discover all he could about the man who now was master of Ravenswyck.

"His Lordship be a flinty-hearted man, without a spark of pity in him," said the tinker.

"Be still, Lafe." But this time there was less urgency in Tess's warning. Her speech was slurred; she'd matched the tinker drink for drink.

"You needn't fear to speak your mind with me," Jared said, still in the same casual tone. "You were telling me of Cragsmore. I suppose there have been many changes since the wars."

"An' not for the better. A right sorry place it be, these days."

Jared reached out to stir up the fire. "How has it changed?"

"Time was, the castle belonged to the Ramseys. Fine gentry, they were. An' they kept to the old customs. May Day revels, with a ribboned maypole standin' out on the green in Cragsmore, an' the lads and girls dancin' around it, all decked out in their finery.

"But Christmas, that was best of all. There'd be a Yule log in the Great Hall, and gifts for the servants an' the tenants. Even folk like us found a warm place in one of the outbuildings, to shelter us from the snow. An' meat an' drink, too." He turned to Tess. "Ale an' mutton—remember, lass?"

The woman's gaunt features softened. "An' her ladyship, a gentle, warm-hearted soul she were," she said. "She gave out good lengths o' homespun for presents. Gave 'em to the servants. An' the villagers." She shook her head. "Long ago, that were—before the war. Lady Ramsey's gone now. An' his lordship."

They were talking about Jared's parents, and Kristy looked over at him. She saw no trace of emotion reflected in his eyes. The firelight played over his hard, tanned face; she could only guess what it cost him to maintain a look of casual interest as he listened.

"They had a son," the tinker interrupted. "But he went off to fight for the king."

"What became of him?" Jared asked.

"Some say he was killed in battle—but there are them that believe he escaped over the sea."

"Did you ever see him?"

"Only once, an' that was from far off. Tall he was, with black hair. Sat his horse like a prince, he did."

"An' he had an eye for the wenches, so they say," Tess remarked, with a grin.

Kristy, who was still sipping her first mug of whiskey,

choked, coughed, then glanced at Jared again. But he kept his
eyes fixed on the tinker and his woman.

"That were no more than human, him bein' a healthy,
high-spirited young gentleman," said Lafe. "But Lord Fairfax, he's different."

"In what way?" Jared was determined to find out all he
could about the new master of Ravenswyck, and conditions
in the village.

"He don't take a dram o' whisky, nor even a cup o' ale,"
said Lafe. "He's stopped the landlord from servin' strong
drink at the village inn. Right strict Puritan he be."

"Strict!" Tess interrupted. "Downright unnatural, that's
what he is. He don't lie with the wenches—not them in the
castle or the village lasses, neither." She lowered her voice.
"He takes his pleasure in other ways."

"And what might they be?" asked Jared.

"He had a man flogged—fifty lashes—just for gettin'
drunk out on the green. An' he ordered the village whore
whipped through the streets at the back of a cart an' driven
out to starve on the moors." Her eyes hardened. "He won't
allow no vagabonds into Cragsmore. We found that out fast
enough, an' we got ourselves out o' there."

"But you and Lafe aren't vagabonds," Kristy broke in.
"You have a trade."

"Mayhap his lordship don't see it that way," said Lafe.
He stretched, got to his feet and motioned to Tess. "Even out
here in these woods, we ain't safe. We'd best be movin' on."

They started off, with their dog trailing behind them. But
before they disappeared into the darkness, Lafe stopped and
said, "We'll not forget your kindness, master—nor your
lady's, neither."

When Kristy woke in the first grey light of dawn, warm and
drowsy after a night of loving, she reached out for Jared, but
he no longer lay beside her. She pushed aside the canvas flap
and saw that he was already hitching up the horse. "You can

wash over there in the stream, but don't dally.''

"We're not going to have breakfast here?''

He shook his head. "We'll have a couple of bannocks on the road. If we keep up a steady pace, we should reach the Fighting Cocks by noon.''

"Do we have to stop there again? There must be a more comfortable inn along our way.''

"I know of several,'' he said. "But that's where Dermot is to meet us.'' He lifted her down from the wagon and she headed for the stream. It would be icy cold, like all these moorland streams.

She thought longingly of the tile and glass shower in her apartment, back in New York. All the hot water she wanted, at the turn of a knob. Of her microwave, her blow-dryer, her electric coffee maker. The early morning weather report on TV. Of Macavity, rubbing up against her ankles, demanding his breakfast. . . .

She forced the memories to the back of her mind. Jared was anxious to get started, and she mustn't keep him waiting.

It was nearly noon when Jared drove the wagon across a swaying wooden bridge, and turned onto a narrow moorland track that wound its way between the high, jagged rocks. Since he and Kristy had set out at dawn, he'd been lost in his own grim thoughts, and had discouraged her attempts at conversation. She must have sensed his mood, for she'd kept silent until now.

"Did you get the information you wanted from Lafe and Tess?'' she asked.

"I wish I could have found out more.''

"What do you think will become of them now?''

He shrugged. "Not all Puritans are as harsh as Fairfax. Maybe their trade will pick up as they move farther south, beyond his jurisdiction. Otherwise, they may one day be forced to turn to poaching after all.''

"But that's so unfair.'' Her amber eyes burned with indig-

Thrill to the most sensual, adventure-filled Romances on the market today...

FROM  LOVE SPELL BOOKS

As a home subscriber to the Love Spell Romance Book Club, you'll enjoy the best in today's BRAND-NEW Time Travel, Futuristic, Legendary Lovers, Perfect Heroes and other genre romance fiction. For five years, Love Spell has brought you the award-winning, high-quality authors you know and love to read. Each Love Spell romance will sweep you away to a world of high adventure...and intimate romance. Discover for yourself all the passion and excitement millions of readers thrill to each and every month.

Save $5.00 Each Time You Buy!

Every other month, the Love Spell Romance Book Club brings you four brand-new titles from Love Spell Books. EACH PACKAGE WILL SAVE YOU AT LEAST $5.00 FROM THE BOOK-STORE PRICE! And you'll never miss a new title with our convenient home delivery service.

Here's how we do it: Each package will carry a FREE 10-DAY EXAMINATION privilege. At the end of that time, if you decide to keep your books, simply pay the low invoice price of $17.96, no shipping or handling charges added. HOME DELIVERY IS ALWAYS FREE. With today's top romance novels selling for $5.99 and higher, our price SAVES YOU AT LEAST $5.00 with each shipment.

AND YOUR FIRST TWO-BOOK SHIP-MENT IS TOTALLY FREE!

IT'S A BARGAIN YOU CAN'T BEAT! A SUPER $11.48 Value!

Love Spell ✦ A Division of Dorchester Publishing Co., Inc.

Get Two Books Totally
F R E E —
An $11.48 Value!

▼ Tear Here and Mail Your FREE Book Card Today! ▼

PLEASE RUSH
MY TWO FREE
BOOKS TO ME
RIGHT AWAY!

Love Spell Romance Book Club
P.O. Box 6613
Edison, NJ 08818-6613

AFFIX
STAMP
HERE

nation. "They're not vagabonds—they're decent people, willing to work for a living. Lord Fairfax had no right to drive them from the village."

"Roger Fairfax is the chief magistrate of the district. It's his prerogative to enforce the law here in North Yorkshire."

"But how could Cromwell give such a man the power of life and death over all those people?"

"That's enough, Kristy. I'd have thought by now you'd have better sense than to speak out against the Lord Protector."

"There's no one to overhear me," she said. He gave her a hard, warning look. "You needn't worry. I know enough to be careful when we're among people."

He fell silent again, but his thoughts gave him no peace. Fairfax and Liane. Liane, Lady Fairfax.

Had her shrewd, domineering father forced her into the marriage? What sort of life could she have led as Fairfax's wife? Her exhalted station as chatelaine of Ravenswyck had brought her wealth and luxury; no doubt she and her husband had entertained the highest Yorkshire gentry. The Lord Protector, himself, may have honored them with a visit.

But what of the nights when they were alone; when she had lain beside Fairfax, in the wide, curtained bed? Could a man like Fairfax have shown any trace of tenderness or consideration to his bride?

Downright unnatural, that's what he is. He takes his pleasure in other ways. Jared went cold inside, as he remembered what Tess had said.

He no longer loved Liane; perhaps he never really had. Certainly not as he loved Kristy. Even so, it angered him to think of the gently bred girl he'd once known, married to a man like Roger Fairfax. All these years, he'd been unable to forgive Liane for having broken her promise to him. Now, for the first time, he found himself thinking, not of himself, but of the girl he would have married, if not for the war. He could remember her, not with bitterness, but with affection and pity.

Defeated in the wars, exiled from his home, he'd built a shell of hard indifference around himself. He'd turned to the smuggler's trade, and done well at it. His only loyalty had been to the Stuart cause.

Until a girl with amber eyes and tawny hair—a brave, outspoken, impulsive girl—had taught him to feel love again.

Chapter Eleven

They passed through a cleft between the rolling green hills and moved around a bend in the river. The horse strained against the traces, and the wagon swayed and creaked as it lumbered up the steep path.

When they reached the top, Kristy felt a surge of depression, for even now, in the full flush of spring, this particular stretch of the Yorkshire moors, with its covering of last year's blackened heather and its few stunted elms and oaks, had a forlorn look about it. A flock of rooks wheeled and screeched overhead. A raw, salt-scented breeze blew in from the east; she shivered and drew her cape more closely about her.

"Look," Jared said, pointing with his whip at the rambling stone structure; it looked dark and even a little menacing, silhouetted against the grey sky. "There's the Fighting Cocks. Once we're inside we'll have a fire to warm you, and a good dinner."

"I can hardly wait," she said.

She could draw up no enthusiasm for a second stay at Rufus Dunstan's tavern. The rambling stone building didn't look at all inviting, up there on its barren, windswept stretch of land.

"I've found it to be a safe meeting place for men in our trade," he said. "And others who make their livelihood outside the law. Rufus Dunstan keeps his eyes and ears open. Somehow, he always gets word when Cromwell's troopers are in these parts, and he gives his guests ample warning. As for any foolhardy exciseman who invades the Fighting Cocks to search the stable or pry around in the outbuildings or under the floorboards for smuggled goods, he soon discovers his mistake. If the man values his hide, he takes a bribe from Dunstan and goes on his way."

Jared reached over and pressed her hand. "Don't look so downcast, Kristy. Perhaps we won't have to spend the night here."

Rufus Dunstan caught sight of the familiar wagon jouncing over the moor and hurried out to greet them.

"Welcome, Master Ramsey," he called in his booming voice. His eyes went over Kristy and he grinned. "Ye've done well by yer lady—she looks fair an' flourishin' in 'er new clothes." He wiped his hands on the front of his soiled shirt. "Yer friend, Master Burgess, got here two days ago," he added.

"Dermot?" she asked Jared, and he nodded. She gave a heartfelt sigh of relief; she would much rather sleep in the back of the wagon than to spend even a single night here.

"Miles!" the landlord bellowed. She recognized the skinny boy who came running from around the back of the tavern. "Unhitch Master Ramsey's horse, an' be quick about it, ye lazy bag o' bones."

"See to it the horse is well rubbed down, fed and watered, lad," Jared said. He tossed a coin to the boy, then swung himself to the ground and helped Kristy down.

Together they crossed the yard, then followed Rufus Dun-

stan under the faded signboard and into the low-ceilinged taproom with its blackened beams. The small windows were
tightly closed, and so thick with grime and cobwebs that
Kristy wondered if they'd ever been cleaned since the tavern
first opened for business.

Although there were no other guests here now, the taproom
must have been crowded last night, for it still stank of spilled
liquor and unwashed bodies. A lean, scruffy cat brushed
against her skirt.

The landlord paused at the bar long enough to pick up a
couple of pewter tankards, then led them to a door at the rear.
"We still got plenty of that good Holland geneva ye
brought—will that be to your liking?" he asked Jared. "Or
would you rather have ale?"

He opened the door to a small room, where Dermot sat
waiting. "You sure took your time, Jared. I was startin' to
wonder if you'd been set upon by Cromwell's troopers—"

Then he saw Kristy, and his smile faded; his shaggy,
ginger-colored brows drew together in a perplexed frown. He
set down his tankard and pushed his chair back from the
scarred table.

Kristy flinched under his hard stare. Dermot, like Jared,
had fought for the king. He, too, was still devoted to the
Royalist cause. Would he try to talk Jared out of taking her
along?

She didn't doubt Jared's love for her, not after all those
nights of passion and tenderness they'd shared. But how could
she be sure he would keep his word, if Dermot persuaded him
that he'd be risking the success of his mission?

Surely the landlord must have sensed the tension between
Jared and his friend, but he chose to ignore it. "What's it to
be then, for you an' yer lady, Master Ramsey? Will ye share
that cask of ale with Master Burgess?"

"The ale will do," said Jared.

"Now, as for dinner, we got a fine, fat piece o' beef turnin' on the spit. Eel an' onion pies, too. An' them eels was fresh caught yesterday."

"Later." Jared spoke brusquely, and the landlord left the room.

He helped Kristy off with her cape, then drew out a chair for her. As soon as he had seated himself beside her, Dermot launched into his tirade.

"Have ye taken leave of yer senses, man? What made ye keep the wench with ye all this time? An' bring her here? Ye said ye were goin' to take her back to her father."

"I could hardly have done that, since Mistress Sinclair has no family in England."

Or anywhere else, she thought—except for Aunt Vera, who'd been openly relieved to see her leave Hillsboro. During her years at Ohio State, and later, in New York, she hadn't once had a call from her aunt. Her letters, her Christmas cards had gone unanswered.

A wave of desolation threatened to engulf her, as it had so often done in the past, but she turned to Jared, and was comforted by his nearness. So long as he was with her, she would never feel such loneliness again.

"I knew all along ye hadn't met her at Whitby, like ye told us," Dermot went on. "An' it's for sure she didn't travel to Glenrowan hidden in my wagon. But the rest of yer tale, about her bein' a squire's daughter, an' how ye was taken' her back to her father's house, secret-like, t' save her reputation—I believed that much."

He gave Jared a reproachful glance. "There wasn't a word of truth in it, was there?"

"Not a word. But it was the most likely explanation I could invent for the rest of them at such short notice," he said. "With Owen and Nehemiah clamoring to leave her there in the abbey, and the witch-hunters on our trail like a pack of hounds, you'll have to admit I had little choice. The fact is, I never saw Kristy before she appeared in my chamber at the Rowan Tree."

"An' a strange sight she was." Dermot paused and looked her over. "At least ye made her get rid of them outlandish breeches. She can pass for a lady now."

Kristy thought she saw a brief flicker of sympathy in Dermot's pale blue eyes. " 'Tis a pity she's got no kin to take care of her. But I don't doubt she'll be able to fend for herself."

"She'll have no need to," Jared said. "I'm taking her with us."

"The hell ye say! Have ye lost yer wits, man?" He slammed his tankard down on the table and glared at Jared. "Ye can't be foolhardy enough t' saddle yerself with a wench like her."

Every muscle in her body tensed. This was what she had feared from the moment they'd come in here. Why hadn't Jared spoken out in her defense? She didn't want to cause a rift between him and his friend, but she could think of no reasonable way to explain her situation to the outraged Dermot, to make him understand why she had to go to Holland with Jared. If she told him the truth, he'd never believe it—and who could blame him?

"It's not like ye to let a wench addle yer senses," said Dermot. "Not even one as good-lookin' as her." He leaned forward, resting his thick, muscular forearms on the table.

"Stop an' think it over, Jared. What do ye really know about her? If she ain't from Yorkshire, then where the devil did she come from? An' I won't swallow none o' yer cock an' bull tales—not this time."

Kristy glanced anxiously at Jared. How was he going to get out of this? He paused long enough to pour himself a tankard of ale, and fill the other for her.

"She comes from far away," he said calmly.

She realized she'd been holding her breath; now she gave a sigh of relief. Thank heaven he hadn't even tried to tell Dermot just how far she'd really traveled.

"I figured out that much for myself. I ain't never heard

nobody talk like her before—not in Holland, nor France neither. Her looks would tempt any man. She's got a fair face
an' a fine shape. An' a nice, ladylike way about her, too. But
ye better stop an' think this over. We got danger aplenty
waitin' across the sea. We can't take her along, I tell ye.''

He didn't answer Dermot; instead he turned to her. ''Drink
your ale, Kristy.''

She took a sip and although it was too bitter for her taste,
it helped to quench her thirst. She glanced at Jared uneasily.
Why didn't he speak out? He could have reminded Dermot
that he was in command; that his decision was law. Or had
he already changed his mind about taking her with him?

Dermot spoke quietly. ''Look here, Jared, I'll follow ye
through the gates o' hell, if ye say the word. Ye know that.
But what about them others? What'll they do when they find
out you're set on bringin' her along?''

''They'll obey my orders, as they always have.''

Jared Ramsey, fifth earl of Ravenswyck, thought Kristy.
Did his calm self-assurance come from generations of aris-
tocratic ancestors? Or was it a part of his own unique character?

''Maybe they would obey ye, if she was an ordinary female,'' Dermot conceded. ''But ye haven't forgotten what
they were sayin' back there at the abbey, have ye? About her
bein' a witch. They're used to dodgin' troopers and excisemen—part o' the smugglin' trade, that is. They'll risk a term
in jail or a floggin', if they're caught. They'll even take a
chance on bein' transported t' the Indies t' work like slaves
in the cane fields.''

He thrust out his heavy jaw, and fixed his pale eyes on
Jared. ''But they're not about t' have a crowd o' witch-
hunters chasin' after them. An' who can blame them? Have
ye forgotten that Lord Fairfax is the magistrate here?''

''I haven't forgotten.''

''Then ye know that anyone suspected of witchcraft—an
ol' crone who talks to her pet cat, a wench whose herb poul-

tice fails to cure a farmer's sick cow—they ain't got a chance if Fairfax gets hold of 'em.''

He took a swig of ale, as if to rid his mouth of an evil taste. "For them that don't confess right away, he's got plenty o' ways t' persuade them. Bad as ol' Matthew Hopkins, he is.''

"Matthew Hopkins—who is he?'' Kristy asked.

"Ye must come from far off, like Jared said, if ye've never heard of Hopkins. Witchfinder General, the bastard called himself.''

"Matthew Hopkins is dead,'' Jared reminded him.

"But Roger Fairfax is alive, an' he's out t' hunt down every witch in Yorkshire. The men ain't willin' to risk the gallows or the stake just so ye can keep yer lady with ye.''

"Are the witch-hunters still looking for her?'' Jared interrupted.

Dermot shrugged. "I suppose the hue an' cry has eased off some. But if Mistress Sinclair stays here in Yorkshire—if she's seen anywhere near Glenrowan—the chase'll be on again.''

"I intend to keep Kristy far away from Glenrowan. I'll take her down the coast to Whitby.''

"Ye'd do better to leave her right here 'til we get back from over the sea. It'll be safer for her, an' for us.''

Jared refilled his tankard, but he left the ale untouched, while he looked at Dermot thoughtfully. His friend was shrewd and practical; his suggestion made sense.

He thought about the documents he carried inside his doublet; the information had been gathered slowly, painstakingly, by men and women throughout the country who'd worked and planned for the restoration of Prince Charles. He himself was one of those chosen to keep the lines of communication open between the Royalists and their monarch. He hadn't any right to allow his love for Kristy to make him forget his oath of loyalty to the Stuart cause.

How could he leave her alone, defenseless, in a time and place that were still unfamiliar to her? But she wouldn't be alone. She'd have Rufus Dunstan to guard her. He'd see to that before he left. She would be safe here at the Fighting Cocks until he could come back for her.

Or would she?

Gwyneth Trefoil might come here to the tavern, seeking her. That was a groundless fear, he told himself. How could Gwyneth possibly know where she was?

And yet the silver-eyed witch had followed them across the border into Scotland; she'd contrived to meet Kristy in the woods near Lachlan Hall. The Fighting Cocks was so much closer to Glenrowan.

"What about it, Jared? I know Dunstan's a shifty customer, but he'll guard the wench for ye if ye make it worth his while."

Rufus Dunstan could guard her against any ordinary danger; he and the gang of ruffians who crowded his taproom every night had proved themselves a match for Cromwell's troopers or unwary excisemen. But Gwyneth and her coven were different. Who could guess what unholy powers they possessed?

"She can't stay here," Jared said carefully. "There are certain reasons why she must be out of England as soon as possible." He reached out and his hand closed around Kristy's. "She goes with me."

His words, his touch, sent fresh courage flowing through Kristy. Then the door creaked open and she turned to see Sally, her thick mane of chestnut hair falling about her shoulders, her worn, low-necked blouse revealing the curves of her ample breasts.

Her dark eyes moved over Kristy, taking in every detail of her dress and the cape that lay over the back of her chair; then her gaze came to rest on Jared and she gave him a wide smile, her teeth gleaming white in contrast with her olive skin.

"Master wants to know, are ye ready for yer dinner yet? If that beef stays on the spit much longer, it won't be fit to eat."

"We'll take that chance," he said. "Mistress Sinclair's had a long journey. She needs time to refresh herself. Take her upstairs, fetch hot water and a washball for her. And see to whatever else she requires."

That was a tactful way of putting it, Kristy thought. With the ale she'd been drinking, her most immediate need was for a privy or a chamber pot.

"As you wish, Master Ramsey." Sally gave him a provocative look from under her long lashes. "Come along, Mistress." Kristy rose and followed her out, through the taproom, up the narrow stairs and into a small chamber, dusty and sparsely furnished, but reasonably clean.

But she froze when she caught sight of her carry-on standing beside the bed. "There was no need to fetch that bag from the wagon," she said. "We're not staying the night."

Sally tossed her head. "Miles must've brought it up. Whenever Master Ramsey came here before, he bedded down for the night."

She caught the taunting undertone in girl's seemingly casual remark. Had he taken Sally to his bed, when he'd stopped here alone? Don't think think about it, she told herself.

"Chamber pot's under the bed. I'll get the hot water." She sauntered out of the room, her full hips swaying under her faded skirt.

While the girl was gone, Kristy used the chamber pot, and put it back in its place. Sally came back a few minutes later, carrying a chipped pitcher and a basin, a piece of coarse cloth for a towel, Kristy supposed, and the now familiar greyish-white washball.

Kristy laid her cape carefully over the only chair in the room, and Sally eyed the blue dress once more; it was simple enough, but of good wool and becoming. "Master Ramsey's done well by ye," she said. She didn't even bother to try to hide the envy in her voice.

Kristy stiffened. "Jared didn't give me these clothes. The dress and cape were a gift from—another gentleman."

"Ye must be mighty free with yer favors, fer all yer fine airs."

Kristy bit back an indignant retort; it wouldn't be wise to make an enemy of the girl. But Sally stayed there watching her, until Kristy, unable to stand her scrutiny any longer, said, "You must have a great many duties. Please don't let me delay you."

The girl shrugged, then turned and left the room. "Damn!" Kristy muttered as she struggled with the small buttons down the back of her bodice. She could have used a little help, but not from Sally; she couldn't deal with the girl's hostility.

She stripped down to her shift, then looked at the washball with distaste. Since Miles had brought her carry-on here, she might as well use her own lavender and fern scented soap. She found it and took it out, along with her toothbrush and paste.

She brushed her teeth, then bent over the basin and lathered her face, neck and arms. Would she ever enjoy a real shower again? She had taken all those small conveniences for granted back in her own time—her hair dryer, her stereo, her VCR, her microwave. Here they would be considered amazing luxuries. Or tools of Satan.

She would learn to do without them. Already she'd gotten used to bathing in icy streams—well, almost, and to jouncing over rutted roads in all kinds of weather.

None of that was important, so long as Jared was with her. So long as she could spend the nights in his arms, enveloped in his warmth, opening herself to the first thrust of his arousal. Tightening around him, sheathing him deep inside her. Rising higher and higher, carried on a tide of boundless ecstasy. . . . Until that shattering instant when they became as one.

Dermot didn't want her to come along on this expedition, and she couldn't blame him; but she knew, with bone-deep certainty, that she and Jared mustn't be separated. If they were

parted now, how could she be sure she'd ever see him again?
He was bound on a dangerous mission. Suppose he should
be captured; suppose he never came back? She would be
stranded here alone.

"Ye ain't used the washball. What's that yer washin'
with?"

Lost in her thoughts, she hadn't heard the door open. Now
she whirled around, water dripping from her neck and arms,
soapsuds stinging her eyes. How long had Sally been standing
behind her, watching her? "Whatever it is, it smells good."

The girl's gaze shifted to the open carry-on beside the bed.
"Ye were carrying it in yer bag, weren't ye? Let's see what
else ye got in there."

Kristy blinked and groped for the coarse towel; she tried
to wipe away the suds, but it was too late. Sally, quick and
inquisitive as a cat, was already crouching beside the bag,
peering inside. "Did all this stuff come from Holland?"

"Holland?" Kristy repeated.

"Ain't that where ye said ye came from?"

Before she could answer, Sally's hand already had closed
around the folds of the blue nightgown; her full, red lips
parted in awe. "I never seen nothin' like this." She slid her
other hand beneath the delicate fabric. "It's so fine I can see
right through it."

Kristy's heart speeded up and her mouth went dry. "Don't
touch that—put it back!" But even as she spoke, she realized
her mistake; for Sally's dark eyes narrowed with resentment.

"So I'm not good enough t' touch yer precious things, is
that it?"

"I didn't say that." But the girl already had tossed aside
the gown and was rummaging deeper into the canvas bag.

"An' what might this be?" She pulled out the flashlight
and held it up. Kristy didn't dare try to get it away from her;
in the struggle, Sally might accidentally press the switch and
flood the dimly-lit room with a powerful beam of light.

"It's nothing valuable—it's only a—paperweight," she

said. Then, seeing Sally's blank stare, she stumbled on. "It's for keeping papers in place on a desk."

But it was plain that the barmaid knew little about papers of any kind; probably she couldn't even read or write. She shrugged, dropped the flashlight back in the bag, and dug deeper.

Desperate to put an end to the girl's search without arousing her suspicions, Kristy forced a smile. "I have something in there you might like. Let me show you."

She opened her cosmetic case and took out a small plastic tube of Marisol's scented hand lotion; she twisted off the cap.

"What might that be?" Sally eyed the tube suspiciously.

"It's hand cream—with the same scent as the soap I was using. You rub it on your hands to make them smooth and soft."

"I'd like that," said the girl, setting aside her hostility for the moment. "The way I got t' work around here, my hands get rough, 'specially in winter," she confided. "An' no matter how much I wash 'em, they still smell like bacon grease or ale."

"Hold out your hands," said Kristy.

She squeezed a dab of the cream into Sally's cupped palms. "Now, rub your hands together as if you were washing them."

Intrigued, Sally obeyed. "Mmm—that feels good. It smells sweet, too—like flowers."

"You can keep it," Kristy said. All right, so she was bribing the girl. So what? While Sally was savoring the scent of the cream, Kristy bent down to close the zipper.

But Sally gripped her wrist. "Not so fast. Why are you givin' a gift t' me?" Again, her hostility surfaced.

"I thought it would please you. And I can get more in Holland," Kristy said.

"So he's taken' ye with him over the sea." The dark eyes narrowed with resentment. "He ain't never taken any o' his other wenches along. He must think yer somethin' special."

Kristy ignored the taunt, twisted her hand free and reached for the bag, but Sally intercepted her. "Let's see what else ye got in here." She grasped one of the handles.

Kristy tried to pull it out of her hands, but the girl didn't let go. The bag turned over. Its contents scattered across the floor.

Kristy tried to gather them up, but Sally shoved her aside. "Let's see what other frippery he gave ye, to pay for yer favors. Here now—what've ye got in this little velvet bag?" Kristy froze. The girl had found the bag that held the scrying mirror. She remembered Morag's hysterical accusations when she'd caught sight of it.

Icy fear welled up inside Kristy and she fought for breath. Then her voice rose to a shriek. "Give it back!"

But Sally had already opened the strings, while fending her off with the other hand. Kristy fought back with all her strength, driven by her fear for herself—and Jared, too. "It's mine! Let go of it!"

"Kristy! What the devil's going on in there?" The door swung wide and Jared stood confronting them.

"The boy brought up the carry-on—Sally saw it—she wanted to know what was inside. I tried to stop her—"

"Be still." She obeyed instantly, frightened by the cold glitter in his eyes. He'd never spoken to her in such a tone; nor had he looked at her this way before. She'd sensed his capacity for violence; but he'd always kept it under control in dealing with her.

He wrenched the velvet bag from Sally's hand and shoved it back in the carry-on. "Get downstairs, girl. Now!" Sally went scurrying from the room.

"It wasn't my fault," Kristy said. "The carry-on was standing beside the bed when we came in. Sally saw it and she—"

"She knew how to open the zipper—even though she'd never seen one before? How clever of her."

She was stung by his sarcasm; her fear gave way to hot

indignation. "All right, so I opened it to get my own soap. Was that such a crime? Then she came in and started poking around inside. I gave her a tube of hand cream but it wasn't enough to satisfy her."

"That's obvious." His voice was low, but implacable. He got down beside her; together they retrieved the scattered contents of the bag and put them back inside. He zipped the bag shut, picked it up and strode to the door. "Get yourself dressed and go downstairs. Don't just stand there. Get moving."

But after he strode out of the room, she started to shake all over, and the floor seemed to tilt under her feet. She'd promised to be careful; she'd sworn she wouldn't be a burden to him; and now, before they'd even reached the coast, she'd already put them both in mortal danger. A sickening feeling of self-reproach welled up inside her.

But she couldn't let herself fall apart, not now. Sally hadn't seen the scrying mirror, only the bag. Summoning up every shred of willpower, Kristy drew a steadying breath, reached for the coarse towel, and finished drying herself. Her knees still shook as she put on her dress, and she dealt with the small buttons as best she could. Her comb was in the carry-on, but she managed to smooth her hair with her fingers, then threw her cape over her arm. She hurried from the room, her tight, pointy-toed shoes clattering on the narrow stairway.

With the coming of evening, the taproom was no longer deserted; in the yellow light of the overhead lantern, she saw a small group of men drinking at the bar. They were a rough-looking lot, unshaven and noisy. They stopped talking and stared at her with open curiosity, but she ignored them and kept her eyes fixed straight ahead. She had to get back to Jared, and make him understand she wasn't to blame for what had happened upstairs.

She pushed open the door to the small back room. But only Dermot was inside, seated at the table, drinking ale and munching on the eel pie the landlord had praised so highly.

176

"Jared's gone to talk with Rufus Dunstan," he told her. "Don't just stand there, starin' like a scared rabbit—take a seat and help yerself."

She was grateful to sit down, for her knees felt like jelly. He cut off a wedge of pie, slapped it on a pewter plate, and shoved it in front of her. She hadn't eaten since morning, but she made no move to touch it.

"What's goin' on?" he demanded. "Jared was lookin' fit to kill." He peered at her more closely. "You're pale as skim milk—an' shaky-like. Eat yer pie. The rest o' the food's on its way."

"I'm not hungry."

"What's amiss with ye? Has Sally been givin' ye a bad time?"

"She can't stand the sight of me."

"I thought as much. It ain't yer fault. It's on account of Jared. She's always been fond of him. An' now, what with him bringin' ye back here, it's no wonder she's jealous. Not that he gives a rap for her, nor ever did."

He leaned toward her and lowered his voice. "Jared ain't cared much for any female. Not since that highborn wench broke off their betrothal and married Fairfax instead." He looked ill at ease, as if he were not accustomed to discussing such matters. "But he does care about ye. Fact is, he loves ye. I can tell." She heard the foreboding in his voice. "Better for all of us, if he didn't."

"You're afraid my coming with Jared will put him in greater danger."

"Somethin' like that."

"Because you think my being here in Yorkshire could start another witch hunt?"

He shifted awkwardly in his chair. "Like as not it could."

"Dermot, do you believe I'm a witch?"

"I don't know what t' believe about ye, an' that's a fact. But I do know what happens to them that's charged with

177

witchcraft. I ain't forgotten Matthew Hopkins. Nobody in these parts ever will.''

"You spoke of him before. Who was he?"

"They called him the Witchfinder General, an' a real terror he was. He went travelin' about, and wherever he stopped, folks paid him to rid their town of witches. Maybe some they accused were guilty, but it's said a lot of 'em weren't. All the same, he got them to confess they'd made a pact with the devil.''

"But why would anyone admit she was a witch, if she wasn't?"

"By the time he was finished questioning them, some of 'em had gone out o' their minds. They'd have confessed to anything." His thick features hardened. "He'd strip a female naked an' if he found the smallest mark on her body, a wen or a mole, he'd call it the devil's mark. Some he tied up, hand an' foot, and tossed into a river. If they floated, it meant they'd made a pact with the devil.''

"And what if they sank?"

"Then they were declared innocent, much good it did 'em. An' he had other ways—worse ways—'' He stopped himself, and cleared his throat. "But ye don't want to hear about 'em, Mistress Sinclair. He could get a child to give evidence against his own mother—a husband to swear his wife was a witch.''

Kristy felt the blood drain from her face; an icy tide moved through her veins. She set her jaw to keep her teeth from chattering.

"Hopkins has been dead these past ten years, but there're plenty o' others like him. And ye've been under suspicion since that night in the Rowan Tree, when ye went waving that mirror around an' Morag cried out against ye. What could've possessed ye t' do such a daft thing?"

"I shouldn't have shown her the mirror, but how was I to know any better? I'd only got here from my own—'' She stopped herself. "My own country. I knew nothing about witches then."

Dermot's shaggy brows shot up in astonishment. "Yer own country? And where might that be?" Before she could find a plausible answer, he went on. "Don't be tellin' me ye come from Holland, 'cause they got their own way o' dealin' with witches there."

"No—not Holland."

She wanted to tell him the truth, but how could she? Her own country was still only a handful of settlements: Massachusetts, Virginia. . . .

She was still trying to find a convincing explanation when Jared walked in.

Chapter Twelve

Jared seated himself beside her and pushed her carry-on under his chair. She searched his face, hoping to catch some hint of his mood. She still hadn't recovered from the look of icy rage he'd turned on her, when he'd walked into the room upstairs and found Sally going through the contents of the canvas bag. But although she studied his hard, tanned features, and tried to probe the depths of his green eyes, her scrutiny told her nothing. She repressed a sigh; she'd already discovered that he could conceal all traces of emotion when it suited him.

"If ye ain't from Holland, what part of the Netherlands did ye come from?"

Reluctantly, she turned her attention back to Dermot; he was still determined to get an answer from her. He wouldn't give up until he had satisfied his curiosity. She threw Jared a pleading glance.

"It's no great mystery," said Jared, with a careless shrug. "Kristy came across the western sea from New Amsterdam."

"New Amsterdam? Then why didn't she say so, the first time I asked her?"

"No doubt she had her reasons." Jared slanted a quick smile in her direction. Maybe he still hadn't gotten over his anger, but he was quick to help her out of a tight spot with a plausible lie.

Only he wasn't really lying, not this time. After all, New York had been called New Amsterdam in the seventeenth century, when it had been owned by the Dutch.

But still Dermot wasn't completely satisfied. "I suppose she had t' leave there in a hurry," he said. "It seems like our Kristy has a way o' gettin' herself into trouble wherever she goes."

Although she wanted to protest, she forced herself to keep silent. She could just imagine the look on Dermot's face if she tried to convince him she'd come from the future, or that she'd been drawn back through time by the power hidden in the depths of the scrying mirror—a dark force that she, herself, did not understand.

It took a moment before she realized that he'd called her Kristy. *Our Kristy.* Was it possible that, in spite of his objection to taking her along on the voyage, he was beginning to like her? It certainly would help to have him on her side, for Jared trusted him and respected his judgment.

"An' just what sort o' uproar did ye start over there in New Amsterdam?" Dermot asked. "Did ye go around showin' off that witch's mirror in the public square?"

She stiffened with indignation, but before she could defend herself, he went on. "From what I know of those Dutchmen, they're an open-minded lot. They're Calvinists, most o' them, but they give refuge to some o' the other sects—Huguenots, Mennonites, Unitarians. All the same, I'll wager they wouldn't welcome a witch into one of their colonies."

"Let it go," Jared cut in. "We've had enough talk of Kristy's past. Have you forgotten this voyage is not going to

181

be a pleasure trip? We've got far more pressing matters to discuss before we set out for the coast.''

''But we'll have plenty o' time to talk over our business on the way to Whitby.''

''We won't be traveling together,'' Jared said. ''You'll drive your own wagon, while Kristy and I share the other. We'll start out before dawn. And we'll go by separate routes. I'll give you one set of—the documents we spoke about—and I'll carry the other set.'' He paused and his gaze locked with Dermot's. ''One of us is bound to get through.''

Get through. Kristy didn't like the sound of that. It was the same as saying that he or Dermot might be intercepted, either here in Yorkshire or later, in the Netherlands. What was in those documents and where were they to go? They had something to do with the Royalist cause, that much she was sure of.

''But you're still set on takin' her along, instead of leavin' her here with Rufus Dunstan. It seems t' me that's a good enough reason she should tell us more about herself before we join up with the others.''

''I know all I need to know about her,'' Jared said quietly. His words were meant for her, as well as Dermot. He might deplore her impulsive behavior, but he loved her too much to leave her here.

''That's as may be, but after what happened at the Rowan Tree, I still think—'' Dermot lapsed into silence as the door swung open and Sally came in, balancing a heavily laden tray on one arm.

Kristy fixed her gaze on the table, unwilling to meet the other girl's eyes. No doubt she was still wondering why Kristy had tried to keep her from looking through the carry-on, why Jared had wrenched the velvet bag from her hand and turned her out of the room. There was no way that Sally could have guessed the truth; even so, her presence made Kristy anxious.

The nylon nightgown and the tube of Marisol hand cream

had aroused Sally's curiousity, but it wasn't likely that she had traveled beyond the borders of Yorkshire. Maybe she'd assumed that such exotic luxuries were considered commonplace in the far-flung ports where Jared went to buy his trade goods.

What about the flashlight? It had been sheer luck that she hadn't flipped on the switch accidentally. It must have looked like nothing more than a small oblong of shiny metal to her; she'd put it aside without showing any real interest.

Kristy's thoughts went racing on. Thank heaven the girl hadn't seen the scrying mirror. Or had she? She'd opened the strings on the velvet bag, but she couldn't possibly have had time to get even a glimpse of the mirror, before Jared had interrupted her. Still Kristy shifted uneasily in her chair, as the girl lingered to stare at her with unnerving intensity. Like Macavity, watching a bird outside on the windowsill.

"Put down our dinner, Sally. And get yourself back to the bar," Jared said.

She quickly set down the large wooden trencher that held the roast beef, crisp and golden brown, swimming in its own drippings, and an array of covered pewter dishes and earthenware bowls; then she left the room.

Jared served Kristy first, then himself. After carving the meat, he lifted the cover from one of the dishes. "Roasted oysters in wine sauce. Try some of these, Kristy, they're good." Another dish held pickled eggs; there was also a bowl of apple and ginger chutney, a dessert of quinces in a heavy syrup, a wheel of cheddar cheese, and a loaf of dark bread.

"There's one thing I know about Kristy—she has a hearty appetite for such a slender female," he told Dermot with a grin.

She wouldn't stay slender unless she started watching her calories, but right now, she was too hungry to care. And the food proved to be surprisingly good—better than she'd expected, considering the shabby surroundings. Whatever amenities the Fighting Cocks might lack, Rufus Dunstan had found himself a skilled cook.

"If we're travelin' by different routes, we ought to talk about our cargo here and now," Dermot said. "I suppose we'll be carryin' spirits, same as usual."

"French brandy, if we can get it. And I had no trouble finding buyers for the geneva. There's a merchant in Braethorn who would have gladly taken twice as many kegs as I could sell him."

"So would a certain Puritan preacher near Mowbray. He takes it strictly for medicinal purposes, ye understand. He told me he needed t' strengthen his voice an' get him through two long sermons in one day."

Jared grinned. "I'd wager the congregation could have used a swig of geneva, too. Sitting still through two sermons in a drafty meetinghouse is enough to freeze the—feet off any man."

"So you figure on bringin' over a bigger shipment o' geneva on this voyage?"

"I do, if Master Van Hooten will agree to a reasonable price."

"Van Hooten drives a hard bargain," said Dermot.

"He's no different from the rest of these Amsterdam merchants that way." Jared helped himself to another serving of oysters. "I'll make the best deal I can. As for spices, our customers have been clamoring for more."

"It's not easy t' make a profit on pepper," said Dermot. "Not as long as they ship it in their own vessels from their own islands, along with their cloves, nutmeg an' cinnamon. An' they charge us ten times what it cost them. Bleedin' highway robbery, that's what it is."

"We can't do much about it," Jared reminded him. "Not as long as the Netherlands holds the monopoly in the East Indies." He looked past Dermot, and spoke with absolute conviction. "One day when we're rid of Cromwell, and a Stuart king sits on the throne again, we'll break the Dutch hold on trade. In the meantime, we'll at least make it possible for our customers to get all the spices they want, duty-free.''

Dermot nodded, then cut himself another thick, juicy slab of the beef. ''Now, as to them laces,'' he went on. ''I figure what with Cromwell's laws about dress gettin' stricter by the day, maybe we shouldn't carry as much of the Brabant or the Mechlin on this run.''

''I don't agree,'' said Jared. ''It's been my experience that, when a lady has to choose between her feminine vanity and the law, her vanity will win out every time.''

''But that don't make sense. If she can't deck herself out in a fancy gown an' show herself off at one o' them balls, why would she want t' buy the lace?''

''She'll want it to trim her night rail, of course. So she can display her charms in the bedchamber for the pleasure of her husband.'' Jared smiled at Kristy. ''Don't you agree?''

''Yes, I suppose so,'' she said, absently.

All this talk about the details of the coming voyage meant little to her. While he and Dermot finished their meal with generous wedges of cheese and thick-sliced bread, and went on with their plans, she leaned back in her chair and let herself relax. She was sated with the heavy meal, comforted by Jared's assurance that he still trusted her enough to take her along.

Her gaze drifted to the small window on one side of the room. There was little for her to see through the grimy pane— only the dark stretch of the moors. A strong east wind had sprung up, bringing a driving rain. As she listened to the steady rhythm of the drops pelting against the glass, and the creaking of the chains that held the signboard outside, her eyelids began to close. Her thoughts slid away.

She thought about her talk with Dermot, before Jared had joined them; she couldn't forget what he'd told her about the brutality of Matthew Hopkins, Witchfinder General. Innocent women tortured into confessing—children made to give evidence against their own parents—husbands against their wives. And Dermot had stopped himself from describing the most revolting details about the Witchfinder General.

Had Cromwell given Hopkins that bizarre title, or had he taken it for himself?

Witchfinder General. The words seemed to resonate through the hidden places in her mind.

In her own time, such a title would have sounded ridiculous; sensible adults didn't believe in witches. A witch was a spooky character in a child's storybook. *Snow White . . . Hansel and Gretel. . . .*

She'd seen one of the many TV reruns of *The Wizard of Oz*. She remembered a witch with a weird green face and a pointy black hat, who had pursued Dorothy and her friends. But there'd been a good witch, too. She'd worn a pink dress and had fluffy yellow curls. Glinda, the good witch of the North. "Only bad witches are ugly," Glinda had said.

But Gwyneth was beautiful, with her silver eyes, her red lips and lustrous black hair. And Gwyneth was real.

Kristy shook her head as she struggled to bring some kind of order out of her tangled memories.

Those storybook witches were fantastic creatures, invented to entertain small children. To frighten them a little, perhaps—though not too much.

And yet . . . such stories weren't new. They'd come down from the distant past, when adults believed in the existence of witches and feared their power. She tried to push such disturbing thoughts away, to fix her attention on the men's conversation.

Jared was saying something about a ship. "We'll get Captain Harrison's lugger, if she's in port. Otherwise, we'll use Captain Fletcher's *Marianne*. She's a sturdy vessel with a good-sized cargo hold."

"A few more profitable runs and we might think about buyin' a vessel o' our own," Dermot suggested.

"We'd have to find a trustworthy crew, who can be

counted on not to inform to the excisemen. I'll give it some thought.''

''How big a crew do you think we'd need? The sea can get rough sudden-like, even this time o' year.''

She tried to keep her mind focused on this talk of ships and crews, but it was no use. Again she remembered Matthew Hopkins. Jared had said Hopkins was dead; but Dermot had said that there were others like him. She hadn't forgotten the witch-hunters who had pursued her and Jared across the moors. . . .

Why would Gwyneth—why would anyone—risk such terrible punishment? Were they trying to escape the monotony of life under the reign of the Lord Protector? Did they seek some kind of forbidden sexual pleasures unknown to ordinary mortals?

She remembered what Gwyneth had said, back in the woods near Lachlan Hall. *There are ways of passion unknown to Lord Ramsey, or any mortal man. . . .* Gwyneth had spoken of the coven master, who would initiate her into these secret rites. The thought filled her with revulsion.

But Gwyneth and her kind lusted for power, too. Witches of the left-hand path. They weren't content to win the thanks of the villagers by brewing herbs to cure a fever or make a cow gone dry give milk again.

They wanted much more. They sought to raise up a storm or turn a tide. They didn't work with nature, but used it, distorted it, for their own selfish ends. Their hunger for power knew no bounds. They even sought to change the fate of nations to serve their own ends.

Whatever passions drove them, there was no way they could force her to join them. She tried to draw reassurance from the thought. Before Beltane Eve, she and Jared would be out of England, across the sea. And once their Sabbat had passed, the danger would be over. She'd be safe.

Or would she?

Beltane wasn't the only Sabbat. It was one of the four great

Sabbats of the witches' year. There was the festival of Samhain, too. And Brigantia and. . . .

How did she know these alien names? Where had she first heard them?

Wave upon wave of terror went coursing through her. Her heart began to hammer against her ribs. She gripped the edge of the table so hard that the wood bit into her palms. Think, Kristy. There's got to be a logical explanation.

Maybe there'd been a few books about witchcraft in the Hillsboro Public Library, but she doubted it. Or perhaps she'd come across a collection of such books in the library at Ohio State. But she'd never opened one of them—that much, she was sure of.

The Magick Caldron. She'd noticed a shelf of books on witchcraft at the shop, but she'd passed them by, and wandered around the place, waiting for Liz to finish her shopping.

All right, then—how did she know the names of the witches' Sabbats? Why were they coming back to her now?

Samhain, when the veil between life and death was drawn aside. Brigantia, festival of the Triple Goddess, Brigit. Place a white candle to the left of the sacred cauldron, a green candle to the right.

And Lughnasadh—that was a festival held in August. She was overwhelmed by a swift, shockingly vivid impression: incense drifting in the air . . . ivy . . . yellow and orange candles . . . a sword lying across the foot of an table draped in scarlet.

No, not a table. An altar. And a man's large hands reaching for her.

A convulsive shudder shook her body, and she cried out.

"Kristy, what's wrong?" Jared's voice came through to her. It brought her back to the small room, the scarred oak table still spread with the remains of their meal. She felt dizzy and shaken.

She realized that he was staring at her, waiting for an answer.

"I was remembering—" Her throat tightened so that she couldn't go on.

"Tell me, Kristy." He searched her face, his eyes filled with concern. She felt the warmth of his hand as it covered hers, his touch driving out the darkness. "What made you cry out like that?"

"It was nothing, really," she improvised. "I thought maybe—I might have left something behind in that room upstairs."

If Jared suspected she was hiding the truth from him, he gave no sign. "Is that all?" he asked with a reassuring smile. "Then you've no need to worry. The mirror and the rest of your possessions are safe inside your bag. I made certain of that."

"Ye'd do better to get rid of the mirror," Dermot interrupted. "Take my advice, Jared. Once we're out to sea, throw the accursed thing overboard, and be done with it."

And why not? She hadn't wanted to buy the mirror. She'd tried to leave it behind in her apartment. From the first time she'd touched it, she'd sensed its power. Yes, it had brought her here to Jared. But it had put her into danger, too—it had sent her fleeing for her life . . . Even so, she knew she could not bring herself to part with it. Not yet. . . .

"He can't do that! He mustn't! Dermot, I have to keep the mirror with me."

"What the devil do you want with it?" he demanded. "Hasn't it already made enough trouble for ye—an' for Jared, too?"

"It hasn't served its purpose, not yet."

His pale blue eyes glinted with rising indignation. "An' what purpose might that be?"

"I don't know," she admitted.

He struck his huge fist on the table. "You're not makin' sense, girl.

"The mirror belongs to Kristy," Jared said, with cold finality. "Let her do with it as she pleases."

*   *   *

It was past midnight when they left the Fighting Cocks. "See ye both in Whitby." Dermot drove his wagon down the slope and then into a deep ravine, where it was lost to view. The rain had stopped, but the air was raw, the night wind penetrating. Clouds hid the moon; only the lantern hanging on the side of Jared's wagon lit their way.

They sat close together, but he did not speak or even turn to look at her. Hesitantly, she reached out and put a hand on his arm. "I'm sorry about what happened back at the tavern. I'll be more careful from now on, I promise."

"At any rate, you didn't give Sally that flashlight for a gift. Or the box that makes music—the tape player."

"I'm not a complete idiot."

His voice softened. "You're not an idiot at all. But you are still too impulsive."

He paused and looked ahead into the darkness. The wind rustled through the dried heather and the shrill cry of a hawk echoed across the moors. A small furry creature ran across the path and scuttled into the shadow of the rocks.

"I suppose I was once like you," he said. "Acting on impulse. Too trusting for my own good."

That must have been before he'd gone riding off to fight for the king, she thought. His next words confirmed her guess.

"If not for the war, I'd have lived out my life at Ravenswyck, only visiting London now and then. I never cared much for the formalities of the court, or its intrigues. I would have overseen my estate, listening to the complaints of the villagers and settling their disputes. I'd have taught my sons to ride, to hunt."

"Your sons and Liane's," she said softly.

She threw him a quick glance, trying to read his expression by the wavering yellow light of the swaying lantern overhead.

"Are you jealous of Liane?" He put his arm around her, and drew her close. His lips brushed her cheek. "Kristy . . . my sweet Kristy. There's no need for you to be jealous."

He went on, with quiet intensity. "I won't deny the shock, the anger I felt, when I came back and found she'd married Fairfax. I never believed I could forgive her."

"And now?"

"Finding you, loving you, has changed all that." She sensed that such words did not come easily from a man like him. He'd learned to hide his emotions, so that he would not leave himself vulnerable to any woman ever again.

He had shared his most intimate feelings with her. If only she could be equally open with him. But how could she share all of herself with him, when there was so much that was buried in her past?

He kissed her cheek, the sensitive spot at the angle of her jaw, the curve of her throat. His mouth claimed hers, and desire welled up inside her, driving out the last traces of doubt. Her lips parted and she gave herself up to the sensations of the moment. His questing tongue, exploring her mouth; her own, coming up to meet it. She reached up to stroke his hair, his powerful neck and shoulders.

He raised his head long enough to say, "If we go on like this, we'll end up with the wagon overturned in a ditch." He moved the wagon over to the side of the road, drew rein, and took her in his arms again. His hands, swift in their seeking, slid under her cape to cup her breasts, his fingers caressing the softly swelling mounds. Desire stirred inside her, hot and urgent.

"We shouldn't—we've got to get to—Whitby—" She protested between kisses.

His breath was hot against her cheek, his voice deep and unsteady. "We'll get there soon enough."

Even as he got down to tether the horse to a wind-twisted tree, she was already getting into the back of the wagon. And now he was beside her, spreading out his cloak for them to lie on.

"This isn't like the beds at Lachlan Hall," she said.

He laughed softly. "Does that trouble you, my love?" He

191

moved his palms over her breasts, tantalizing her until her nipples went hard. "If it does, we can wait until we get to Amsterdam." He took a nipple between his fingers, tugged at it gently. "They have plenty of excellent inns there, rooms with thick feather beds and curtains and—"

She reached up, put her arms around him, and silenced him with her kiss. Her hand moved down to stroke his shoulders, his chest, to find the hard swell of his arousal. She heard the sharp intake of his breath. "Shameless wench . . ."

"Shameless," she agreed, her fingers moving, pressing.

Then she took her hand away, and rolled over on her stomach. "The buttons—I can't reach them—"

Driven by his own need, his fingers worked quickly, undoing the small buttons, sliding the dress down around her waist. She raised herself and wriggled out of it. "If I'm shameless, you taught me . . ."

She buried her face in his cloak, and breathed in the scent of him. A shiver of pleasure ran through her, as his hands moved down along her back. He stroked the sensitive spot at the base of her spine. He slid his hands under her shift, cupped her bare bottom and squeezed the rounds of her buttocks.

He slid off her garters, then drew down her stockings. "Turn over."

She moved over onto her back and now his hand slipped under her shift, to stroke the insides of her thighs. Unable to conceal her aching need, she parted her legs and his fingers slid between them. He tugged lightly at the damp, tawny curls. He took her moist bud between his thumb and forefingers, and rubbed it gently.

He took his hand away, and she couldn't hold back her cry of protest. She felt the wagon sway as he moved about, stripping off his own clothes.

He stretched out beside her, and took first one nipple, then the other, between his lips, suckling her through the thin cambric. But even that fragile barrier was too much; he slid the shift over her head and cast it aside.

His mouth moved from her breasts, his tongue tracing a line of wet heat along her skin, sending ripples of desire through every nerve of her body. Ripples that grew and con- verged at last, deep in the center of her being.

He pressed his face against her smooth, flat stomach. She scarcely recognized her own voice. "Good . . . so good. . . ."

But it wasn't enough. She wanted, needed more . . .

She thrust her fingers into his hair and drew his head down. His mouth was hot and seeking, his tongue flicked the hard peak of her womanhood, and she gasped with pleasure.

She raised her hips and arched her body. He moved up and knelt between her thighs. With a long, slow thrust, he buried himself in her sheath. As a rhythmic throbbing began inside her, her hands gripped his shoulders, and her head fell back, her lips parted.

And now they were rising together, moving upward in a dizzying spiral, higher and higher still . . . the throbbing inside her grew faster. His thrusts came deeper, and she cried out as he carried her with him to the peak of fulfillment.

Dawn laid a slash of crimson above the dark grey horizon as they took up their journey again. She sat close beside him, her head resting on his shoulder; she was filled with drowsy contentment. If only they could go on like this, just the two of them, side by side, moving along the narrow path across the moors. Free as gypsies, exploring the roads, stopping when they chose, then moving on.

But even now, she caught the sharp tang of the wind from the sea, and she knew they were approaching their destina- tion. Soon they'd reach Whitby, where his men were waiting. He'd be caught up in his preparations for the voyage.

Now, while they still had time to themselves, she felt a need to speak; to tell him that her memories, hidden away so long, were starting to come back to her. Not all at once, but in brief flashes. She wanted to tell him what she'd glimpsed back at the tavern—and the words she'd remembered. The names of the witches' Sabbats.

But she was afraid to share those memories, even with him. Whatever had happened to her during those early years of her life, it must have been terrifying. That had to explain why she'd put it out of her mind, burying it so deep that it had lain all these years in utter darkness.

She wanted to speak out, to keep nothing from him. But even now, she was afraid of how he might respond. He had put aside his doubts about her, had let himself love her completely.

She dared not risk losing his love.

Chapter Thirteen

It was close to sunset when they reached Whitby, and Kristy leaned forward to get a closer look at the small fishing village that lay between the mouth of the River Esk and the North Sea. The small, red-roofed cottages clung to the side of a slope, huddled together as if for protection from the buffeting of the sea wind. Overlooking the port stood the ruins of a sandstone abbey. On either side, a row of towering cliffs loomed dark against the crimson sky.

Her spirits plummeted as she realized that their brief, magic interlude had come to an end. Even now, Jared's men would be gathering here, and he would be absorbed with his preparations for the voyage to Amsterdam. But she reminded herself that at least he was taking her with him, and once they were aboard the ship, perhaps they would be able to share a private cabin.

At the edge of the fishing village, he drew the wagon to a stop in front of a small stone inn whose painted sign bore a name, Mariner's Rest. It looked far more welcoming than

Rufus Dunstan's tavern. A plume of smoke rose from the chimney, and there were freshly painted flower boxes at the windows.

"Will we be staying here?" she asked hopefully.

He shook his head. "We're only stopping long enough to leave the horse and wagon in the stable. Then we'll go the rest of the way on foot." He gave her an encouraging smile. "It'll be a long climb down the cliffs, but it's not dangerous if you know the way."

She looked up at him uneasily. "There's nothing to fear," he said. "I've made the descent before."

"But I thought Dermot and the others would be meeting us here in the village." She wriggled her cramped toes inside her too-tight, borrowed shoes, and wished she had packed her Nikes in her carry-on, along with a pair of heavy jeans. But then, she hadn't expected to go clambering down the side of a cliff. "Just where is this meeting place of yours?"

"You'll find out soon enough," he told her. "I'll admit it's not as comfortable as the Mariner's Rest, and the food's not nearly as good, but we'll have all the privacy we need."

He drove around to the stableyard behind the inn; there he helped her to the ground, then took the carry-on down from the seat. "Ezekiel!" he called out. The hostler, a bowlegged man with a weather-beaten face, hurried into the cobblestone yard, stared at Kristy for a moment with open curiousity, then turned to Jared.

"Welcome, Master Ramsey. We've been expectin' ye all this past fortnight." He took the reins and led the horse into the dimly lit stable. "Dermot Burgess got here two days ago," he went on. "Owen Purdy, too. Young Tom Wagstaffe an' Nehemiah Gill." As he spoke, he was already unhitching the horse. "An' the rest of 'em have been comin' in all day. They bought themselves two kegs of our best ale, two of brandy, an' a dozen bottles of port wine."

He gave Jared a gap-toothed grin. "I guess that'll keep

them warm enough while they wait for ye. By now half of 'em will be drunk as fishes.''

"I don't doubt it," Jared interrupted. "No matter, so long as they sober up before it's time to set sail. Which of the luggers is in port?"

"Let's see now." The hostler scratched his head. There's the *Maid o' Scarborough,* the *Lettie Brewster*—but she'll need repairs before she can put out t' sea again—an' there's the *Marianne.*"

He paused and gave Kristy another appraising glance. "If the lady'll be stayin' here at the inn tonight, she can have a room all to herself, an' it won't take no time at all t' make up a fresh bed." He looked at the carry-on. "Is that all the baggage she's got? I'll get one o' the lads t' tote it inside."

"That won't be necessary," said Jared. "The lady's not spending the night here. She's coming with me."

The hostler's jaw dropped. "Yer takin' her down there with ye, sir? Beggin' yer pardon, but some o' yer men've been drinkin' fer two days, an'—"

"She'll come to no harm," said Jared.

"Just as ye say, Master Ramsey." Still, he sounded dubious.

Jared tossed the hostler a coin, took Kristy's arm, and led her from the stable, across the courtyard and down a narrow passage that led out onto the cliffs.

Remembering her first encounter with Jared's men, the night she'd fled from Glenrowan, Kristy wasn't looking forward to another meeting with them. "Why don't we walk through the village while it's still light?" she suggested.

"We're not here to enjoy the sights," he reminded her. "My men are waiting to collect their shares. When I've seen to that, I'll go down to the harbor and have a talk with Captain Fletcher, the master of the *Marianne.*"

He guided her along a rutted path that edged the top of the cliffs. Gorse bushes rustled in the wind, and a few twisted trees stretched their bare branches toward the sea.

"The *Marianne* is a sturdy vessel, and well-suited to our purpose, with plenty of cargo space," he went on. "And she's armed with six four-pounders."

"This ship carries guns?"

"Cannon," he corrected her. "Certainly she does. And Fletcher's found himself an experienced gunner's mate—Barnaby Corbett. The man got his training in His Majesty's navy, but I doubt we'll have need for his skill. The revenue men hereabout aren't likely to meddle with us, not if they have any good sense."

"It's their job to intercept smuggled cargo, isn't it?"

"The people of these villages up and down the coast—Whitby, Robin Hood's Bay, Scarborough—make a good part of their living out of the trade. Revenue men aren't given a warm welcome hereabouts."

She would have questioned him further, but it was all she could do to catch her breath and keep going; with the coming on of evening, the wind was growing stronger. It pulled at the folds of her cape, and tossed her hair about her face, lashing the loose strands against her cheeks.

Gulls and curlews wheeled and screamed overhead, and from far below, she could hear the surge of the waves against the rocks. "This is where we start climbing down," he said, as he led her to the edge.

She held back. "Where is this meeting place of yours?"

"These cliffs are honeycombed with caves," he told her. "Dermot came upon this one a few years ago. It's got a wide outer chamber and half a dozen deep passages leading in all directions."

"Where do they go?"

"Some of them open out onto the moors. And the longest one leads straight to the church crypt at Robin Hood's Bay."

The sun had slipped below the horizon now, leaving a fading glow of orange and gold; the steep side of the cliff already was swathed in shadows. "Wait, Jared—let me have the bag.'' She tried to take it from him, but he kept a firm grip on the handle.

''We can use my flashlight,'' she said impatiently.

''And risk having someone catch sight of that glaring beam? When will you learn to think before you go leaping into some foolish action?''

''I am thinking!'' she retorted, her voice shaking with indignation. ''I'm thinking that I'd rather not leap over the side of a cliff in the dark and break my neck. And as for the light, who's going to see it all the way out here? One of those gulls?''

''There are sailors on the fishing boats down there in the harbor. And villagers coming home to their dinner. We'll manage well enough without your flashlight.''

His hand closed around hers. ''Your fingers are like icicles.'' He held her hand against his cheek, and his voice was softer now. ''You've nothing to fear, I promise you. Just keep hold of my hand and don't look down. Ready?''

''As ready as I'll ever be.'' She watched him, her heart hammering against her ribs, as he stretched one booted leg, then the other, over the edge of the cliff. Her mouth went dry, and she stood frozen to the spot for a moment, before she could summon up the courage to follow him.

She had thought the wind had been strong before; now it struck at her with a stunning force that drove the breath from her body. It seemed to her like a mortal enemy, bent on tearing her away from the side of the cliff and sending her crashing down to the rocks below.

''There's a path that leads all the way down to the beach.''

''That's good.'' She did all she could to avoid catching her foot in the hem of her skirt. In spite of his warning, she couldn't keep from looking down into the shifting shadows. That was a mistake. Her stomach lurched and she fought against the sudden vertigo that threatened to engulf her.

''At least you might have—brought along the lantern— from the wagon.''

"Even the lantern throws enough light to draw attention. In our trade, we don't take needless risks."

"You said the revenue agents wouldn't interfere with smugglers."

"I said they wouldn't be likely to trouble us." She caught the edge of impatience in his voice. "But there's always the chance we'll meet with a foolhardy exciseman who's willing to risk his neck out of a sense of duty—or because he hopes for a promotion."

She decided to ask no more questions. Otherwise, he might start to regret that he'd taken her along.

Something reached out and caught at her skirt, like a skeletal hand. It was only the branch of a leafless, stunted bush, growing out of the side of the cliff. She pulled free and kept going.

She thought longingly of Lachlan Hall. She could have been safe there right now, with Sir Andrew to protect her. With his servants to carry up hot water for her bath. Polly's cheerful chatter. A warm bed with a down comforter and heavy velvet curtains to keep out the drafts. But Jared wouldn't have been there to share her bed.

She'd wanted to be with him; now she'd have to take the discomforts of the journey, and whatever risks might lie ahead. She held on tightly to his hand and she didn't look down again.

The rising wind grew stronger with every step; it went through her woolen cape and gown. Then she stepped on a small rock, and felt her ankle twist painfully. She couldn't hold back a cry of pain.

"Are you all right?" Jared asked.

"It's not a sprain," she said, between clenched teeth. They went on down the path, Jared's movements lithe and easy. They were close to the foot of the cliff when she caught the first faint, ruddy glow coming from an opening in the side. She heard the rise and fall of the men's deep voices coming from within.

"That wasn't as bad as you feared, was it?"

Without waiting for her answer, he led her through the mouth of the cave, and into a wide rocky chamber. The men had built a large fire. She blinked as she tried to get used to the ruddy light. Then she looked over the group, and her heart sank; they were a rough-looking lot, and all of them were armed: Some wore swords; others carried knives thrust into their belts. One carried a seaman's steel cutlass.

She recognized Dermot first, then Owen Purdy, who gripped a nearly empty bottle in his fist; his pock-marked face was flushed from the heat of the fire and the wine he'd been drinking. And there was Nehemiah Gill, chomping a hunk of bread and drinking from a tankard. She didn't know the names of the rest, but she remembered a few of their faces. She supposed there were about forty of them.

A barrel-chested, bearded man in a yellow jerkin was bellowing out a song.

We brought brandy for the squire,
An' laces for his daughter.

The others grinned as they struck their tankards against the rocks.

A fair young wench was she,
With tits big as melons—

The song echoed through the low-ceilinged chamber and down along the passages beyond. But it came to an abrupt stop when Owen caught sight of Jared, inside the mouth of the cave. "Here's Master Ramsey."

Then his face darkened. Still clutching his bottle, he got to his feet. "So ye didn't bring the wench back home t' her father, like ye said ye would." His small eyes were dark with resentment. "An' do ye mean to take her along t' Amsterdam, t' warm yer bed?"

Jared didn't answer him, but spoke to Dermot instead. "Take Kristy into the passage over there."

Dermot set down his tankard, got to his feet, and went quickly to her side. "Come along, lass," he said. He took her

201

bag from Jared; then he led her to a narrow opening on the right side of the main chamber. She stopped just inside the entrance, her eyes fixed on the men around the fire. She went taut with a sense of impending danger. There was no way Jared could avoid a confrontation with his men now. And she was the cause of it.

"Ye ain't answered my question, Master Ramsey," Owen persisted. "Ye figurin' on takin' her across the sea? We got a right t' know."

"Mistress Sinclair is coming along," Jared said brusquely. "She'll sail aboard the *Marianne* with the rest of us. Now that you've satisfied your curiosity, let's get down to business. We've had a profitable venture. Now it's time to distribute the shares."

"That's what we been waitin' for," said one of the men with a grin; he picked up a large wooden chest and set it upon a broad rocky ledge near the fire. Jared reached into his cloak, took out a key, and opened the chest. Even from where she stood, Kristy saw the coins glittering in the ruddy glow, as they emptied the loot they each carried into the common coffer.

"I know how I'll spend my share once we get to Amersterdam," said one of them. "Mistress Juliana's place—that's where I'm headin' for."

The others laughed and jostled one another, all talking at once, as they crowded around the chest.

"Ye'll have plenty o' company at Juliana's. I'll get me a fine, fat whore with yellow hair."

"It's a red-haired wench for me. Never tupped a redhead that wasn't hotter than a pistol."

"Yellow hair or red, it don't matter t' me. All cats are grey in the dark."

Owen's voice, loud and belligerent, rose above the rest. "But we ain't aboard the lugger yet."

One by one, the others fell silent and glanced at him uneasily, all except for the bearded man who'd been singing the bawdy ballad. "What's that supposed t' mean?" he demanded. "We'll be under sail tomorrow. Then it's off to Amsterdam an'—"

"I'm thinkin' we may not live t' see Amsterdam at all," Owen cut in. "Not if we take Ramsey's woman with us. Are the rest o' ye willin' t' risk yer skins, so he can pleasure himself with Mistress Sinclair?"

A tall, fair-haired young man in a wine-stained doublet got to his feet and swayed unsteadily, clutching at an empty bottle. "I'm ready to risk it, if Master Ramsey'll give us each a share of the wench, along with our share of the loot. A real beauty, she is."

Kristy caught her breath, and felt the warning pressure of Dermot's hand on her arm. "Easy, lass," he said softly. "That young fool don't know what he's sayin'. He's been drinkin' steady since he got here. You stay quiet an' keep out o' sight."

He left her and strode back into the main chamber, where he took his place at Jared's side. He planted himself with his thick legs set apart. His huge hand rested on the handle of his knife. "Guard yer tongue, Tom, if ye want t' keep it in yer head," he said.

"I only spoke in jest, Dermot. I meant no harm—" The young man turned to Jared. "Only a jest, Master Ramsey—"

Jared's hand shot out and gripped Tom's shoulder. He propelled the young man forward with such force that he stumbled and nearly fell on his face. "Get outside and stay there until the wind clears your head. I'll give you a lesson in manners, when you've sobered up."

Tom staggered to the mouth of the cave and disappeared into the darkness. Jared turned and looked over the others, his eyes moving slowly from one face to another.

"As for the rest of you, understand this. Mistress Sinclair is under my protection. Any man who lays hands on her or treats her with the least disrespect, won't live to reach Amsterdam.''

''Ye needn't have no fear on that score,'' Owen said. ''No man in his right mind would want to lie with one o' her kind!''

''And what kind might that be?'' Jared's voice was deceptively quiet, but no man could fail to hear the threat that lay beneath his words.

''A witch, that what she is! We've got t' get rid o' her before she brings disaster on us all.''

Emboldened by the other man's accusation, Nehemiah spoke out. ''It's the truth. We shouldn't ought t' let a witch set foot aboard our ship.''

From where she stood, her body flattened against the rough, damp wall, her muscles rigid with fear, she watched Jared's face in the firelight. His feral green eyes narrowed to slits; his tall, lean body was poised for swift action. Like a jungle beast, ready to pounce on its prey. But when he spoke, his voice was quiet and controlled. ''I am master here. I give the orders. Does any man among you question my right to do so?''

''We ain't questionin' yer right, Master Ramsey—not when it comes t' runnin' the trade an' dividin' up the shares an' suchlike,'' Nehemiah conceded. ''It's that wench we're talkin' about. The village folk must've had good reason t' drive her out o' Glenrowan.''

Tension crackled through the chamber, as the rest of the men raised their voices in support of Owen and Nehemiah.

''Prescott's niece says Mistress Sinclair carries witch's tools with her. She tried t' cast an evil spell on Morag—frightened the maid near out o' her wits, she did.''

''An' we saw the mobs huntin' her as far off as Kirkham an' Ampleforth. But they never caught a glimpse o' her.''

''I'll not set foot on the deck o' the *Marianne*, not with a witch aboard. An' so I tell ye.''

''Nor I, neither. A witch knows how t' call up the winds

and turn the tides. She'll get her coven t' send a storm that'll smash the vessel to bits.''

"We'll run aground before we're out of Whitby harbor. What good's our gold, if we're lyin' at the bottom of the sea?''

"Somebody ought t' tell Captain Fletcher about her. He'll not take her aboard once he finds out—''

"Enough!''

Jared's voice, deep and powerful, resonated through the rocky chamber; it echoed from the walls and penetrated the passage where Kristy waited. One after another, the men fell silent.

"I'll tell Captain Fletcher all about Mistress Sinclair, when I meet with him tonight,'' Jared told them. "He's got too much good sense to be carried away by such foolish rumors.''

But Owen wasn't about to back down. "Fletcher can risk his ship and crew, if he pleases,'' he said. "As for me, I won't board the *Marianne* until you get rid of the girl.''

"And what about you, Nehemiah?'' Jared asked.

The man shuffled his feet uneasily, and refused to meet Jared's hard stare. "I figure I'll go along with Owen.''

"As you wish. I want no man to follow me against his will,'' said Jared. He paused, then added, "Take your shares, both of you, and leave. At once.''

"Now wait a bit, Master Ramsey,'' Nehemiah began, but Jared cut him off.

"Take your shares, I said, and that's an end to it.'' He strode the wooden chest, reached inside, and counted out a heap of coins. "This is your share, Nehemiah. Be sure it's all there.''

"And you, Owen. Here's what is owed to you.''

The tense silence that followed was broken only by the clink of coins, the crackling of the fire, the soughing of the sea wind outside the mouth of the cave.

"You gave me my fair share, Master Ramsey. Down t' the last farthin', same as ever,'' Nehemiah said. "Ye've always treated us right. If ye could only see reason, an' change yer mind about takin' the wench along—''

"Get out, you and Owen. Be gone from Whitby within the hour."

Owen threw him a baleful glance, then stalked out, with Nehemiah trailing after him. After their footsteps had died away, Jared looked around at the others. "Any man who wants to follow those two, speak up now. You're free to take your shares and go with them."

Peering from the narrow entrance to the side passage, Kristy held her breath as she watched their faces. The squat, bearded man was first to break the silence. "I'll sail with ye, Master Ramsey. T' hell with all this natterin' about witches an' spells an' such. There'll be good hard cash t' be made on this next voyage. That's all I care about."

"Caleb's right," said another. "Since we been followin' ye, we've always made a handsome profit."

"An' with them two gone, there'll be more for the rest of us!"

The tension flowed out of her, and she let herself slump against the wall, limp with relief. She heard the rumble of praise from the others, the protestations of loyalty to Jared. The lewd remarks and harsh laughter as they talked of their coming visit to the bawdy houses of Amsterdam. One by one, the rest of the men came forward to collect their shares, then seated themselves near the fire and started drinking again.

Warmth welled up inside her, as her eyes rested on Jared. If she'd ever doubted his devotion to her, she never would again. He had risked everything for her—his smuggling trade, the private cause to which he'd pledged himself, his life itself.

He came into the passage, carrying a pile of driftwood. "You'll need your own fire to keep off the damp," he said. He dropped to his haunches, and arranged the wood, then set it ablaze; the flames leaped up, casting shadows on the rocky walls.

Then he got to his feet, and his arms went around her. She pressed herself against him, resting her head against his chest. "You're shaking, love," he said, and drew her closer. "There's no need for you to be afraid any longer. The danger's past."

"If it hadn't been for my coming along, there'd have been no danger. And you wouldn't have lost two of your men."

"It's no great loss," he said. "Owen was always a malcontent, and Nehemiah followed his lead. We're better off without them."

"And what about Tom Wagstaffe?"

Jared shrugged. "A young fool, the worse for drink. He's scarcely eighteen and wanting to show off his prowess with women. He'll ask your pardon, once he's sobered up."

He let her go only long enough to take off his cloak and spread it on the ground near the fire. Then he drew her down beside him. "It'll be best if you spend the night in here," he said. "But I'll see to it you have more comfortable quarters when we sail tomorrow."

"I wish we could sail right now."

He cupped her face between his hands and looked down at her, his eyes alert. "Kristy, what's troubling you now."

She wanted to say she was only cold and hungry; or that she hadn't yet recovered from the tension she'd felt during the conflict between him and his men. She tried to look away, but she couldn't.

"I can't forget what Owen said about me—that I'm a witch—that I'll bring disaster on you and your men."

"To hell with Owen. Put all that out of your mind."

She hesitated, then forced the words past the tightness in her throat. "I only wish I could. But suppose it's true, what then?"

"You're not a witch. If you were, you'd have known it always. Even in your own time."

"It's not that simple," she said slowly, choosing her words

207

with care. "I can't remember my early years. I've told you that."

"But you said remembered your mother."

"Only after I met Gwyneth Trefoil in the woods near Lachlan Hall that day."

"I'll make sure you don't meet her again."

"That's why you're taking me away from England, isn't it?"

"Only until Beltane's passed."

She gripped his arm. "What if I'm not safe, even then? There are other Sabbats. I didn't know their names, but now I do."

"What are you trying to say?"

"That I'm starting to remember. And without Gwyneth anywhere near me. That night at the Fighting Cocks. We'd finished dinner. You and Dermot were talking about the voyage. I was so sleepy, I started to drift off."

"Go on."

"I'd been thinking about Beltane. I thought you wanted to get me out of Yorkshire before Beltane Eve. And then I knew it would be no use. I started to remember that there would be other Sabbats. Four great Sabbats each year. And Jared, I knew their names."

"Kristy, stop it! You fell asleep, you were dreaming."

"That's not possible. Don't you see? I'd never heard them before and yet I knew them. Samhain, Brigantia—"

"You heard someone speak the names."

"But you've been with me since I came back here into your time."

"That afternoon you were alone in the woods with Gwyneth. She must have told you then."

"She only spoke of Beltane. She didn't name any of the other Sabbats. I'll swear to that."

"Then maybe you heard one of the villagers speaking about the Sabbats, at the Braethorn fair. Or maybe Polly filled your head with such idle chatter, back at Lachlan Hall."

"No one spoke of witchcraft or Sabbats at the fair—not to me. And Polly didn't either."

"You're sure?"

She hesitated, as she tried to remember all that she and Polly had talked about.

"When I was a small boy back in Ravenswyck," he went on, "I used to sit in the kitchen, and listen to our old cook. She nearly frightened the kitchen maids out of their wits with her tales of witches and demons. She frightened me, too." But his smile was forced, and she felt the tension in him. "No doubt Polly was trying to scare you with her talk of Sabbats and sorcery."

"Polly was talkative," she admitted. "But she never said a word about the Sabbats. I'd have remembered."

"Then you heard of them in your own time."

"No, Jared. People in my time—the sort of people I knew—didn't believe in witchcraft."

"But there must have been those who did. Otherwise, how did you come by the scrying mirror? You said you brought it with you when you traveled back in time."

His question caught her by surprise, but she rallied quickly. "I found it in a shop, The Magick Caldron."

"And this shop? It sold other such witches' tools?"

"I suppose so. But I—"

"Then that proves it. There must have been those who believed in the witchcraft in your time."

"I suppose so."

She'd occasionally seen the headlines in the supermarket tabloids, while she was waiting at the checkout counter. Revolting stuff about weird cults—Satanists and animal sacrifices. You read about such far-out practices, or heard about them on TV, and then put them from your mind.

"Kristy, why did you buy that mirror?"

"I don't know. It was as if I couldn't leave the shop without it." She reached out and clung to him, cold with foreboding. "Jared, suppose there was a—a force that made me

Diana Haviland

buy the mirror. Suppose that same force—power—call it what you want to—suppose it brought me back here for a purpose.''

''Even if that were so, the mirror has already served its purpose. It brought you to me.'' He stroked her hair, his voice soothing. ''Kristy, my love, I don't claim to understand all this. And you don't, either. Maybe we never will. I only know we're together now. And nothing will ever separate us again.''

She heard footsteps approaching; then Dermot coughed and cleared his thoat to let them know they were no longer alone. Reluctantly, she drew away from Jared.

''It's time for us to leave, Jared,'' he said. ''Fletcher's waitin'.''

''You stay here with Kristy, and make sure she's not—disturbed.''

''She'll be safe with me,'' Dermot said. He went back into the main chamber, and Jared took her in his arms again. ''You'll have nothing to fear with Dermot here to guard you,'' he assured her. ''I'll come back as soon as I can.''

''Let me come with you.''

''I'm late for my meeting with Fletcher as it is.''

And she would only delay him longer, she thought.

She raised her face for his kiss. His mouth covered hers, his tongue tracing the shape of her lips.

Heavy footsteps echoed across the rocky floor as Dermot returned with a bottle of wine and a basket of food. ''There's salted fish in here, bread an' cheese, too. Nothin' fancy but it'll hold ye 'til mornin'.''

''When you've finished your meal, wrap yourself in the cloak and go to sleep,'' Jared said. She went with him to the opening of the passage, and stood looking after him as he crossed the main chamber, then disappeared into the darkness.

Dermot set down the basket. ''Eat hearty, lass. Ye'll be needin' yer strength for the voyage tomorrow.'' Although she had little appetite, she broke off a bit of cheese and a piece of bread.

"Try one o' them salted kippers. That's the way." He gave her a reassuring grin. "I'll bed down here." He stretched himself out across the entrance.

"But you can't sleep on the bare ground," she protested.

"It won't be the first time." He shoved her bag under his head. "This makes a good pillow." A few minutes later, she heard him snoring softly.

She withdrew to the far end of the passage. After she'd finished eating, she drank a cup of wine, then another. She lay down on Jared's cloak, wrapped it around her, and buried her face in the folds. It still held the warmth of his body, his familiar scent, mingled with the tang of salt.

The long climb down the cliff had left her exhausted; the wine had relaxed her. She kicked off her shoes with a sigh of relief, and let herself drift into darkness.

Chapter Fourteen

It was not yet dawn when Jared returned from his meeting with Captain Fletcher. The fire in the center of the main chamber had burned down to a heap of glowing embers, and the men lay sprawled around it, among the empty bottles and kegs.

He picked his way among them, as he moved on to the passage; Dermot lay sleeping, his body blocking the entrance, his head pillowed on Kristy's canvas bag. At the sound of Jared's approach, he stirred, opened his eyes, and was on his feet, his heavily muscled body poised for action, his hand going to the handle of his knife.

"You won't be needing that," Jared said, with a grin. Dermot stepped to one side.

"Did you strike a good bargain with Fletcher for our passage?" he asked.

"That I did." He drew a sword from its scabbard and held it out for Dermot's inspection. "And I bought this from one of his crew, a native of Cordova."

"A fine Spanish blade, an' no mistake," Dermot said, with a nod of approval. "Ye think ye'll be needin' it on this trip?"

"With those documents I'm carrying, I'll take no chances. The Lord Protector has a network of spies from Amsterdam to Paris."

He broke off as he heard a sound from the back of the cave, where Kristy lay sleeping. "I reckon she's havin' another nightmare, poor lass," Dermot said softly. "I heard her cry out like that before, but I didn't want t' wake her."

Jared went to her quickly. He stood looking down at her for a moment; then, as she cried out again, he eased himself to the ground beside her. In the flickering light from the fire, he saw that she was tossing restlessly from side to side, her hair tangled about her face. She had twisted the cloak around her, so that now it bound her arms to her sides. He loosened the heavy woolen folds that held her arms immobile, then began stroking her hair back from her forehead. The tawny strands were damp with perspiration.

At his touch, she cried out again; her eyes flew open, wide with fear. Then as she came fully awake, she recognized him. "Jared—hold me." He raised her up and drew her head against his shoulder. Her fingers gripped the sleeve of his shirt. "Don't leave me."

"I'm right here. You're safe with me, love. No one will harm you." He spoke as he might have done if he'd been soothing a frightened child. His hand moved to the back of her neck, stroking, caressing. He felt the tension gradually draining from her body. She reached up and put her arms around him. He kissed her cheek, then her lips.

"Guess ye won't be needin' me around here no more," Dermot said. He left the passage and returned to the main chamber.

Jared lay down beside her on the cloak and drew her against him. The pressure of her soft breasts, her long, tapering thighs, the scent of her hair, stirred his hunger; but he restrained himself. He contented himself with stroking her, until her eyes closed again. Even then, encircled by his arms, she stirred uneasily from time to time.

"No—don't—" he heard her say. "I won't—you can't force me—" She was in the throes of another frightening dream. He drew her closer and spoke her name, softly, reassuringly. She relaxed and lapsed into a peaceful sleep.

He'd never known her to be troubled by nightmares before. Except for that time at Lachlan Hall, when she'd dreamed of a fog creeping in through a window that had been tightly locked.

Maybe she'd been more frightened by the climb down the side of the cliff than she'd wanted to admit. And then there'd been the clash between him and his men, their accusations of witchcraft.

Or was her nightmare caused by some other, more deep-seated fears? Earlier that night, she had spoken to him about those memories she couldn't account for. She'd insisted that, although no one ever had told her the names of the witches' Sabbats, she'd known them. But how was that possible? What childhood terrors lay buried in that dark place far back in her past?

Anger flared up in him, and with it an unfamiliar sense of his own helplessness. He had no doubt he could protect her from whatever physical dangers they might encounter, but how could he free her from these nameless, deep-rooted fears?

He stared moodily at the last red embers of the fire. Though it was not yet dawn, already he heard the men starting to move about. Gently he withdrew from her clinging arms. She made a wordless sound of protest, but she did not awaken. He got to his feet and headed for the main chamber. He swore as he nearly tripped over the canvas bag Dermot had used for a pillow.

Then he paused, dropped down on his haunches and opened the zipper. Maybe he'd discovered a way to help Kristy rid herself of her fears, after all. . . .

*   *   *

"We got t' get movin'," Dermot called to him.

He stamped out the fire. Then he went back to Kristy and shook her shoulder lightly. "Wake up, love. It's time to leave now." She blinked, stretched, then smiled up at him. He helped her to her feet. But when she caught sight of him buckling on his sword, her smile faded and her eyes widened uneasily.

"I told you this wasn't going to be a pleasure trip," he reminded her, as he threw his cloak over his shoulders. "If you're having second thoughts about coming along, it's too late to change your mind now."

"I haven't changed my mind," she assured him. She raised her face, her lips parted for his kiss. She put her arms around his neck, and his mouth claimed hers. For a long moment, they clung together.

Then slowly, reluctantly, he let her go. He took her arm, picked up her bag, and led her out of the passage, then on across the main chamber. At the mouth of the cave, she stopped and filled her lungs with the fresh salty breeze. They started down the windswept beach toward the sea. A row of small wooden boats bobbed up and down at the shoreline.

The rising sun sent a glittering path over the smooth grey expanse of the sea, and gilded the sails of the *Marianne*, a trim craft with its two masts and running bowsprit. Although the lugger was a small vessel, designed for carrying cargo, he'd persuaded the captain to give him a private cabin. "I'm traveling with a lady this time," he'd explained.

He looked down at her and a smile touched his lips. Last night he'd contented himself with holding her, soothing her. Now he wanted more. He was impatient to be alone with her again, as they had been when they'd traveled the roads in his wagon. As soon as they boarded the lugger, he would take her to their cabin and lock the door. He couldn't wait to pull off her prim white cap. To draw her tawny hair down around her face. To undo the buttons of her gown and carry her to the bunk. His body was already throbbing with his need for her.

He brushed his lips across her cheek. "Look, Kristy—that's our ship out there," he said. "We'll row out to her in one of those small boats, and then we'll sail with the morning tide."

"How long will we be staying in Amsterdam?" she asked.

He shrugged. "That depends on how much time it takes me to find a cargo."

And to carry out his other, more important enterprise: to arrange a private meeting with England's future king. The reports he carried in his doublet must be delivered directly to Charles Stuart. He hoped the information they contained would convince his sovereign that, although many Englishmen already were growing restive under the harsh Puritan rule, it was not yet time for him to return and claim his throne.

Cromwell's power had already started to wane. The ordinary Englishman bitterly resented the Lord Protector's decrees of arrest without due process of law, and trial without jury. In cities and towns all over England, supporters of the Stuarts had been meeting in secret, and there were plenty of hotheaded men who were eager to go into battle. But the information gathered from Royalist sympathizers from Cornwall to Yorkshire had made it plain that their forces were not strong enough to defeat Cromwell's army—not yet.

He could only hope that Charles, who had grown to manhood since his escape from England four years ago, and had been a penniless exile in the courts of Europe ever since, would restrain his reckless spirit; that he would be persuaded to remain abroad a little longer, for if he were to return and make a landing on the shores of England too soon, the Stuart cause might be lost forever.

"We'll be gone for a month at least," he told her with a reassuring smile.

"You want me out of Yorkshire until Beltane Eve has passed. But what about the other Sabbats?"

"Forget them. They have nothing to do with you, not any longer."

"How can you be sure? Maybe it's because you've never spoken with Gwyneth Trefoil."

"And I hope I never do."

But she ignored his interruption, and went on, her voice taut with apprehension. "Gwyneth said the coven master has ordered her to bring me to him. She doesn't want to risk his anger—I know she's afraid of him."

"To hell with Gwyneth Trefoil and her master!" He stopped and drew her into the shadow cast by a great, jagged rock that loomed up out of the sand. He set down her bag, then turned her around to face him. "Once we're at sea, you'll forget her, Kristy. And these visions—these night-mares—you'll forget them, too."

"But you're wrong." She looked away. "Every time I see the scrying mirror, I'll remember that night at the Rowan Tree. How can I forget what I saw—"

"You saw my face, that's what you told me." He forced a smile. "Did I look so frightening to you?"

"That wasn't all." She hesitated, and then the words came rushing out. "I saw masked figures carrying torches . . . I heard the sound of their laughter on the wind—"

"Kristy, be still. I don't want to hear any more. Whatever you thought you saw in the mirror, whatever sounds you thought you heard—I promise you they're gone now. They'll never come back to frighten you again."

She gave him a searching look. "How can you be so sure?"

He drew a deep breath. She'd have to know sometime. He might as well tell her now, and get it over with. "The mirror's gone."

She glanced down at the bag at his feet. Quickly she raised her head and searched his face. The color drained from her cheeks and her amber eyes widened with disbelief.

"When you were still asleep, I took it out of your bag and

left it behind. Kristy, don't look at me that way. I did it for you."

Why didn't she speak? He'd rather she berated him, screamed at him, cursed him like a fishwife, than that she should go on staring at him with that fixed, accusing gaze.

"Maybe I had no right to take it without telling you. But it had some kind of hold over you. You told me as much last night. I suppose I might have waited until we were aboard the ship but—"

"But you were afraid to carry it aboard, weren't you?" Her voice shook with outrage. "You believe what Owen and the others said about me last night. That I have the power to raise a storm, turn a tide, to wreck a ship. Maybe you were afraid I'd sink the *Marianne*."

"Don't be ridiculous. I never said anything of the sort."

"You love me, and you don't want to believe I'm a witch. But deep down, you've never really been sure, have you?" Her eyes were filled with anguish. "Jared, where did you leave it?"

"Forget the mirror. And all the rest of it. Covens, Sabbats. Come with me, now, and leave all that behind."

"Where is the mirror now?"

It was as if she hadn't heard a word he'd said. Or maybe she just didn't care. His hands balled into fists, as he fought off the impulse to take hold of her and shake her until her teeth rattled. When he could bring himself to speak, his voice was quiet, his emotions under control. "I left your precious mirror in the passage where you slept last night. I took it out of your carry-on, and shoved it into a cleft in the rocks. Can't you understand I did it for you, Kristy?"

"But I've got to get it back!" A few of the men, on their way to the waiting boats, turned to stare at her. "I have to keep it with me, always."

"The hell you do!" He was no longer able to control the rage that came surging up in him. "I say you're well rid of it! It's brought you nothing but trouble. Have you forgotten what happened when you showed it to Morag? One look at it, and she sent those witch-hunters chasing after us.''

''I know, but—''

''And what about your run-in with Sally, back at the Fighting Cocks? It was sheer luck that I walked in before she caught sight of it. Otherwise she'd have raised the hue and cry, and we'd be running for our lives again.''

He kicked the bag deeper into the the shadow cast by the towering rock, as if he could get rid of his anger by venting it on an inanimate object. His hands gripped her shoulders and he drew her against him. Her face was chalk white, except for the hectic flush on her cheeks.

''Kristy, listen to me. Whatever power lies in that mirror, you've no need of it any longer, unless—'' A frightening suspicion stirred in his mind and would not be silenced. ''Unless you want to use it to return to your own time.''

''You know I don't, not without you. But I can't go out to the ship until I get the mirror back.''

''Come on, both of ye,'' Dermot called out to them as he strode past. ''There'll be time enough fer talkin' later. Right now, we got t' get t' the ship. Captain Fletcher sails with the tide.''

''You heard him.'' He seized her arm, but she twisted free. ''You're going to walk with me to the rowboat. Now. Otherwise, I'll carry you down there and toss you in. I'll tie you to the oarlock if I have to.''

''If you do, I'll never forgive you.''

He looked down at her, stunned by the quiet intensity in her voice. There was no doubt in his mind that she meant what she said. ''You left it in the passage.'' She intoned the words softly, as if she were under a hypnotic spell.

''And that's where it's going to stay, at least for now.'' His voice was tight with anger. ''The next big storm will send the tide in, and the waves will carry the accursed thing to the bottom of the sea.''

She gripped his arms. "You've got to come back with me, and help me find it."

He spoke with icy finality. "I'll be damned if I do."

"Then wait here for me."

She let go of his arms and whirled around. He tried to restrain her, but she seemed to be possessed by an unnatural strength. She pulled herself free and then she was running back up the beach, her cape billowing out behind her.

"Kristy!"

She did not look back, or even slow down.

He stood staring after her. His first doubts about her, the questions he'd forced himself to ignore, now assailed him once more. Had Owen and Nehemiah been right about her from the start?

"Where's she goin'?" Dermot was beside him, looking at him in confusion. "Don't she know we've got no time t' lose?"

But he didn't answer. He turned and stared out to sea, his eyes fixed on the lugger that lay waiting for him and his men. The sky was growing brighter and a few low-lying clouds already were edged with gold.

Rage surged through him. And a sickening sense of defeat. Was it possible she was so obsessed by her witch's mirror that she'd left him to go in search of it? Let her go, then. Her act of defiance, her total disregard of his wishes, confirmed his darkest suspicions.

Last night she'd recited the names of the witches' Sabbats, yet she had insisted she'd never heard them before. How had they come to her, then? And where had she found those other uncanny tools? She'd said she had carried them with her from her own time.

Her own time.

His jaw tightened, his muscles went rigid as he forced himself to confront the facts. Who but a witch had the power to travel through time? What other unknown powers did she possess, that were strong enough to send Gwyneth Trefoil in pursuit of her? She, herself, had told him the silver-eyed witch had tried to persuade her to join the coven.

Let her go then. Let her join Gwyneth and her coven. Let her give herself to the embraces of the coven master on Beltane Eve.

Then he had a sudden vision of her slender white body, her rounded breasts and long thighs, bared to the touch of another man. If the coven master could be called a man.

"No!" The sound of his own voice, harsh with revulsion, startled him. No matter how she'd infuriated him, he couldn't let her go. He couldn't let her give herself up to those unspeakable rites.

She had become a part of him. He would fight for her with all his strength. He'd take her away from here, by force if necessary.

He was vaguely aware that Dermot and some of the the others were staring at him, as if they thought he'd lost his wits. And maybe he had. He only knew he had to get to Kristy, now. He turned away from them and started up the beach toward the towering cliff.

"Halt! In the name of the Lord Protector! Halt, I say!"

A musket shot rang out, breaking the stillness of the early morning. The sound sent a flock of gulls soaring high into the air. He wheeled to the right, the direction from which the command had come. An officer on horseback drew his sword, and held it straight out at arm's length. At the signal, troopers with their muskets at the ready, bayonets flashing in the morning sun, came charging from the base of the cliff.

His own men, caught off guard, began to scatter, only to be driven back by a second detachment of troopers who ran at them from the other side, their boots kicking up the sand. He looked up to see yet another line of them, standing high atop the cliff. More shots rang out and two of his men toppled to the ground.

This maneuver had been carefully planned and carried out. They were trapped with the sea in front of them and the cliffs at their backs. Suspicion swiftly turned to certainty. He and his men had been betrayed.

"Take to the boats!" Jared shouted. But the troopers were already cutting them off from the shoreline.

He saw Caleb get off a single, well-aimed shot. It hit a trooper who cried out and fell backward. Dermot wrested a musket from the nearest trooper's hands, and turned it against him, lunging forward and driving the bayonet deep into the man's chest.

On every side, the rest of the smugglers were fighting with a ferocity born of desperation, but they were vastly outnumbered by Cromwell's battle-hardened soldiers.

Young Tom Wagstaffe lay sprawled on the sand, blood streaming from a wound in his throat.

The commanding officer, a wide-shouldered colonel, swiftly dismounted and advanced, sword in hand. Jared whipped his own sword from the scabbard, and prepared to meet his attacker. The colonel slashed at Jared, who parried with speed and agility.

Steel rang on steel. Jared quickly realized he'd come up against an experienced opponent. The officer thrust again.

Jared warded and countered. His blade slashed across the other man's chest, slicing through a leather doublet, drawing blood. Step by step Jared drove his enemy toward the sea.

"Jared! Behind you!"

He heard Dermot's warning shout an instant too late. The heavy stock of a musket caught him across the side of the head and sent him pitching face down in the sand.

He fought against the pull of the spinning whirlpool that was drawing him down . . . down . . . into its dark vortex. He braced himself with his arms and tried to stand up, but a heavy booted foot caught him in the ribs. He heard a voice from somewhere close by. "Run the bastard through and be done with it."

Instinctively, he struggled to rise. But even as he did so,

he knew it was no more than a futile attempt at survival. The trooper already had raised his bayonet.

"Stop!" The colonel's voice rang out. He strode across the sand and stood towering over his fallen prey. "You're Jared Ramsey. You lead this pack of renegades." He thrust the hilt of his sword under Jared's chin and forced his head back. "Look at me when I speak to you."

Jared looked up at the colonel, and pressed his lips together in a hard line. "That's him, Colonel Marsden, sir," said a young lieutenant. "He fits the description we got last night."

"It seems we caught ourselves a good haul this time. The colonel's voice rang out with grim satisfaction. "Lord Fairfax will want to deal with Ramsey himself. Take him to the barracks."

He turned. "You, lieutenant. Carry a message to Ravenswyck. No doubt his lordship will ride out as soon as he gets word of Ramsey's capture."

A couple of troopers wrenched Jared's arms behind him, and soon after, he felt a rope cutting into his wrists. "On your feet, Ramsey." Searing pain tore through his battered ribs as they dragged him toward the side of the cliff; his head throbbed from the blow of the musket butt.

Where was Kristy? He'd seen her running toward the cave. He could only hope she would stay out of sight until the troopers were gone.

But how long could she survive in hiding, and what would become of her, after they'd taken him away?

You're safe with me, love. No one will harm you.

The words he'd spoken to comfort her last night, now returned to mock him.

"If I were in his place," one of troopers said, "I'd sooner be shot here and now, rather than be turned over to Lord Fairfax."

"He's got to have a trial, before they hang him." The other man said, with a harsh laugh. "That's the law."

"With Fairfax actin' as both judge and jury, he don't stand

a chance.'' The troopers were passing close by the mouth of the cave now. Sand and pebbles scattered under their boots.

''You had a wench travelin' with you, Ramsey,'' one of them said. ''What's become of her?''

Jared kept his face impassive, while he sought an answer. Whenever he'd found himself in a tight place before, he'd been able to concoct a plausible lie. But now he hesitated. Kristy's freedom, her survival, might depend on his reply.

She was stubborn and impulsive, totally unpredictable. Maybe she was a witch. It didn't seem important, not now. He only knew that, against all reason, he still loved her. He'd promised to keep her from harm.

''I saw her, myself,'' said the other trooper. ''She was running across the beach, with her cape flying behind her. Blue it was.''

Although it went against all his instincts, he forced himself to laugh, then to speak with easy indifference. ''That one? She was only a common whore,'' he said. ''We all had a go at her.''

''That's not what I heard. Those two that came to the barracks last night—they said she was a witch.''

''Witch, my arse!'' Dermot spoke out scornfully, his deep voice echoing in the still morning air. ''Ye weak-brained Roundheads—yer no better'n a gaggle o' old women, seein' witches in every corner. Closing down taverns an' bawdy houses. But ye go sneakin' around, whorin' an' drinkin' on the sly. England'll soon be rid of ye—an' yer Lord Protector. That misbegotten son of a—''

Had Dermot lost his senses, baiting the troopers like that? Jared looked up in time to see one of them slam his fist into Dermot's face. Although his hands were tied behind him, Dermot fought back; he drove his massive shoulder into the trooper's chest. The man swayed, struggling to keep his balance, then toppled over the edge.

Jared saw his friend running along the curving path. He stared in stunned disbelief; surely he could not hope to escape. A trooper raised his musket, a shot cracked out, and Dermot fell forward. The trooper drew back his foot and kicked Dermot's prone body over the side of the cliff. "One less treasonous dog we'll have to take to the barracks." He spoke with indifference, and a moment later, they were moving on.

Through the red haze of helpless rage that swam before his eyes, Jared heard the other troopers talking. "We ought to ask Colonel Marsden what he wants to do about the woman."

"Why waste our time looking for a common slut? It's Ramsey his lordship wants."

"What so special about Ramsey?"

"That's not for the likes of us to ask. But with Fairfax taking charge of his case, he'd be better off if we'd shot him, along with that other one."

Chapter Fifteen

Kristy remained motionless, her body pressed tightly against the wall at the mouth of the cave. She had gone rigid with anger when she'd heard Jared tell his captors the woman he'd traveled with had been no more than a common whore, shared by him and his men; now she understood. He had spoken of her with contempt because he had been trying to protect her in the only way he could—trying to make sure the troopers would not go searching for her.

Her throat tightened as she remembered that they had parted in anger. Would that be his last memory of her? She could not face the possibility that she might never see him again.

But this separation wouldn't last forever. They'd be together again. He was strong and resourceful; he'd come through the wars unscathed; he'd escaped from England, along with the prince and a handful of other Royalists. He'd carried off dangerous smuggling expeditions, and had evaded Cromwell's excisemen every time. Surely he would find a way to escape from the troopers and come back to find her.

If he were in any condition to escape. A shudder ran through her. The troopers had said Lord Fairfax was coming to interrogate him. By the time his lordship had finished with him. . . .

Don't think about it. Don't think about Lafe, the tinker, and all he'd said of the new master of Ravenswyck. Think about something—anything—else.

What was happening in her own time? Think of the small, everyday stuff. What was Liz doing right now? Had she remembered to come up and feed Macavity every day; or had she taken the cat home to her own apartment? Who was covering for her at Marisol? Probably Nicole, her red-haired assistant. Nicole would manage well enough. She was capable and efficient. . . .

But it was no use. She could think only of that night in the woods near Ravenswyck. The words of the tinker and his wife came back, blotting out everything else, sending an icy tide of fear coursing through her.

Fairfax took a perverted pleasure in the ruthless exercise of his far-reaching power; he was a stern Puritan who showed his captives no mercy; he had them flogged and branded for even the most minor transgressions of Cromwell's rigid laws. She could imagine how Jared would fare at the hands of such a man.

She couldn't let the troopers take him away without taking her, too. If she confessed she was a witch, they would have to arrest her. They would take her along to the barracks. Although she shuddered at the thought, she told herself that was the only way she'd be able to stay with him for whatever time they had left. She lifted her skirt and ran toward the mouth of the cave.

When will you learn to stop and think before you go leaping into some foolish action?

Jared had said that last night, when they'd stood together at sunset at the top of the cliff. This time she would restrain her turbulent emotions; she would not give way to impulse.

If they took her to the barracks, she'd suffer the same harsh treatment as Jared and the others; Lord Fairfax wasn't likely to spare her because she was a woman.

She had to stay here in hiding, until she could find a way to help Jared escape. But what chance did she have? He and his men would be imprisoned at the barracks. What barracks—and how far away? Once he was inside, probably he would be placed under special guard until Lord Fairfax arrived. What could one woman, alone, unarmed, hope to do under such impossible circumstances?

There had to be a way to save him. She would find it.

She forced herself to remain still until she could no longer hear the voices of the troopers, or the sound of their heavy boots on the cliffside path. Then the strength drained out of her; she sat down on the floor of the cave and buried her face in her hands. Along with her fear for Jared came a sickening sensation of guilt.

Jared hadn't wanted to take her along, not at first. If only she'd listened to reason, and remained behind at Lachlan Hall, there'd have been no cause for the clash between Jared and his men last night. Owen and Nehemiah would not have gone off to inform on their comrades.

Jared had been captured because of her. Those men who lay dead down there on the beach—young Tom Wagstaffe and the others—she was to blame for that, too. Whatever happened to Jared at the hands of Lord Fairfax, she'd be responsible.

Jared had tried to reason with her; Sir Andrew had objected, too. But she'd been too stubborn to give in. And too much in love with Jared to be parted from him, even for a little while. Now she might have lost him forever.

"No!" She heard her own voice echo down along the depths of the cave, and the eerie sound startled her. A renewed strength coursed through her.

She wouldn't let him go, not after she had traveled through

the years to find him. He had banished the aching loneliness that had been a part of her life ever since she could remember. For the first time, she knew what it meant for a man and woman to be joined in body and spirit. With him she'd known a love beyond the narrow confines of time and space. A love beyond forever. They belonged together and no force on earth was strong enough to part them now.

She got to her feet and steadied herself against the wall, ignoring the shakiness in her legs. Yes, she'd find a way to free him; but she couldn't do it alone. And who could she turn to for help? Her mind went racing ahead, seeking an answer.

What about Rufus Dunstan? He had dealings with the smugglers; he held Cromwell's laws in contempt; and she was sure he could gather a force of reckless men who felt as he did. But he wouldn't lift a finger to help her unless she were able to pay him. Jared had told her that the landlord of the Fighting Cocks had no personal loyalty to anyone.

All right, then. Forget Dunstan. Jared had other friends, supporters of the Royalist cause. Once she got to the Border and told Andrew Lachlan what had happened, he surely would come to Jared's defense. He was a man of influence and power who could call on other Scotsmen who were loyal to the Stuarts. He would organize them, send them to mount an attack on the barracks, and set Jared free.

But the hope that surged up in her swiftly faded away. It would take too much time for her to reach the Border, and even more for Lachlan to gather a force of fighting men. How long before Jared was interrogated, brought to trial, and sentenced? Lord Fairfax was likely to act quickly, and without mercy.

Her heart sank as she remembered once again her parting with Jared, there on the beach. What had driven her to berate him, to turn her back on him and go running to the cave in search of the scrying mirror? What had she hoped to gain by retrieving it and keeping it with her?

Power. The mirror was a source of power. The power that had brought her to Jared. Was it possible that same power would save him, and bring him safely to her side?

Kristy paused to listen before she left the cave, but she heard only the sound of the waves and the cry of the gulls. She started down the path to the bottom of the cliff. Then, as she walked across the sand, she tried not to look at the bodies of the smugglers who had been shot down in their clash with Cromwell's men. The troopers must have carried off their own casualties to give them a proper burial.

She kept her eyes fixed to the jagged rock, where she'd stood talking with Jared only a few hours before; her carry-on still lay where he'd left it.

If she were to find the mirror in the depths of the cave, she would need the flashlight. Even if Jared had left his flint and tinder behind, she hadn't learned to use them to make a fire; she'd left that to him. She realized once more how difficult it would be for her to perform even the simplest tasks, here in this alien time. All these weeks, she had depended on Jared; now she would have to manage alone.

She saw sunlight glittering on a musket that lay half-buried in the sand—the bayonet was still in place, a long, wicked-looking blade. One of the troopers must have dropped it, as he fell. She bent and picked it up. It wasn't easy, carrying it under her arm while she lugged the bag in her free hand; but alone as she was, she might soon be needing some kind of weapon with which to defend herself. How, exactly, did you load a musket? She'd have to figure that that out later.

She went back inside the cave, laid the weapon down carefully, then unzipped the bag. She pushed aside her nightgown, her makeup case.

She kept on searching. A little leather sewing case, a gift from Liz. The small first aid kit she always packed. The tape player that had startled the wits out of Jared, when she'd turned it on back in the abbey.

The lacy bra Jared had discovered that same night. He'd been puzzled by it, but not for long. His green eyes had rested briefly on the swell of her breasts, under her jacket. *I've never seen such an enticing female garment before.*

Don't think about that, not now.

She gave a sigh of relief as her hand closed around the flashlight. She pressed the switch, then hurried through the main chamber to the passage where she'd slept last night. Slowly she moved the yellow beam over the damp, rocky walls, splotched with fungus. Her eyes darted from one spot to another.

Where had Jared left the mirror? He said he had shoved it into a cleft between the rocks.

But where? She clutched the flashlight tighter, and tried to fight down a wave of panic, as she moved the beam over the sides of the passage; she pointed it down at the floor. Her eyes lingered on a heap of charred driftwood: the remains of the fire Jared had built to keep her warm last night. Her throat tightened as she remembered how he'd held her in his arms, his hand stroking her hair, his voice soothing, comforting. . . . His touch, the warmth of his tall, powerful body close to hers, had driven away the last clinging strands of her nightmare. He'd been there for her when she needed him; now, she would have to manage on her own.

Desolation washed over her. She shook it off, set her jaw, and retraced her steps down the length of the passage, examining the rocky walls again. Find the mirror. Keep looking until you find it.

And what would she do with it when she found it?

Maybe it would be better to give up the search right now, to leave the cave. To get away from Whitby and try to make her way back to Lachlan Hall. Even if it were too late to help Jared, she was sure Sir Andrew would give her shelter in his home; although he hadn't wanted her to go along with Jared, and might blame her for what had happened, he would take care of her.

But she couldn't give up, not yet. She had to find a way to free Jared before Lord Fairfax arrived.

She stopped short. In her determination to retrieve the mirror, she hadn't stopped to ask herself just where they had taken Jared. The barracks—but there must be more than one barracks in the north of England. Here in a country ruled by Cromwell's martial law, there might be a dozen barracks in Yorkshire.

Panic raced through her, and the flashlight jerked in her unsteady grasp. The beam skittered over the dark rocky floor, then rested for a moment on a crumpled piece of cloth. She caught her breath as she recognized the velvet bag, with its drawstrings untied.

In his haste, Jared had pulled out the mirror, then tossed the bag aside. She ran to the section of wall closest to the spot where the bag lay. Inch by inch she moved the beam, steadying her wrist with her other hand. There it was, the curved ebony handle of the mirror, protruding from a deep cleft.

She restrained her impulse to wrench it out of its hiding place. Carefully, an inch at a time, she eased the mirror from between the jagged rocks, taking care not to crack or even scrape the smooth surface. She gave a sigh of relief, and thrust it back into the velvet bag; she fastened the strings, then slipped the bag into one of the large pockets inside her cape.

Even now, in broad daylight, it would be safer for her to climb up the steep side of the cliff if she left her carry-on behind, but she didn't want to part with it. The carry-on and its contents were her last links with her own time.

Although she was anxious to be on her way, she reminded herself that she'd need all her strength for whatever might lie ahead. In the main chamber, she found a bottle of brandy, a half-filled a keg of ale, and the leftovers from the men's supper: some broken pieces of cheese, a chunk of dark bread, a few dried fish.

Even after she'd brushed off as much of the sand as she

could, the stale food didn't look particularly appetizing. She picked up a piece of cheese. Her hand froze halfway to her mouth, as she heard a scuffling sound. It was coming from just outside the cave. An animal—a large one, by the sound of it. Did wolves still roam the north of England? Surely not in broad daylight.

She looked up at the towering figure of a man blocking the mouth of the cave. She saw that he was unsteady on his feet; he lurched toward her. She got up, prepared to run. If she couldn't get past him, she'd have to seek a hiding place in one of the passages deep in the cave.

"Kristy . . . it's me, lass. . . ."

Dermot. But he had been taken prisoner along with the others. His arms still were bound behind his back. How had he managed to escape?

He took a few more halting steps. Then she caught sight of a deep, jagged cut over his right eye. One side of his jaw was greenish blue, swollen to twice its normal size. His jerkin and shirt were torn and crusted with blood. He swayed forward and before she could catch him, he fell face down on the ground.

She dropped to her knees and she saw that the ropes were cutting deep into his wrists. She tugged at the knots but she couldn't get them open. She reached for the musket she'd retrieved on the beach. He turned his head. "Holy saints—where'd ye find that?

"Down on the beach. I'll have to use the tip of the bayonet to cut the ropes."

"Ye can't handle a weapon like that. You're apt t' slice off yer fingers instead." He thought for a moment. "Those Roundhead bastards took my knife—but they didn't look in my right boot. Ye'll find a smaller one in there."

She crouched down and tugged with all her strength; it wasn't easy but she managed. She pulled out the small, bone-handled knife and cut him loose. Then she turned him over on his back.

He flexed his numb wrists. "That's better, lass." His lips were cracked, but somehow he managed a smile. "Got anythin' t' drink?"

She raised his head and held a tankard of ale to his lips. She let him slake his thirst before she spoke.

"Dermot, tell me. How did you escape?"

His massive chest rose and fell; she realized it was an effort for him to speak. "I made a run for it. I got myself shot—I dropped down an' lay still. An' then one o' them pushed me off the edge of the cliff."

She stared in at him in disbelief. "But if you fell from all the way up there, how did you—"

"I ain't a ghost, if that's what you're thinkin', lass." he assured her. "I landed on a ledge, partway down. Reckon I must've passed out for awhile. When I came around the sun was beatin' down on me, fit t' roast me alive. Then I saw ye comin' up the path. I tried t' call out t' ye but I was that parched I couldn't make a sound. It took me awhile t' climb down here."

Hope flared within her. "And Jared? What about him? Did he get away?"

He gripped her hand tightly and spoke with unusual gentleness. "No, lass. They took him off t' the barracks. He must be there by now." He paused to take another swallow of ale. "An' him still carryin' them papers inside his doublet. He won't be able t' get them across the sea, not this time. That's why I risked my neck t' get away. Because of the papers—"

Was he delirious with fever? "Papers—what papers?"

"I'll tell ye all about that later. But first, there's work fer ye t' do. I hope ye're not the sort o' female who faints at the sight o' blood."

"If I were, I'd have passed out at the sight of you."

"Guess that's true enough. All right, then. First ye'll have to cut away my shirt. I think the bullet went clean through my shoulder, but ye'll have t' make sure."

She gripped the knife, set her teeth in her lower lip, and cut away the torn linen. Blood trickled from the wound in his massive shoulder.

"My tinderbox is inside my jerkin. Ye won't need t' light a big fire, just enough t' get the knife blade red-hot."

She understood, and her insides lurched. He wanted her to cauterize the wound, to sear his flesh with the knife. She flinched at the thought of inflicting such pain, but she knew she had no choice.

She found the tinderbox inside his leather jerkin, and set about her task. She'd seen Jared use such a box many times. The flint would strike sparks from the steel and they would ignite the tinder. It had looked easy when he'd done it, but she broke two of her fingernails before she could get it to work. Perspiration was trickling down her face by the time she got the driftwood to catch fire.

She would have to use the flashlight to get a good look at his injuries. When she switched it on, Dermot stared at the powerful beam in surprise. "Where the devil's that light comin' from?" he demanded. "Never saw anythin' like it."

"Just try to hold still and don't ask questions." She used the knife to cut a strip of cloth from her petticoat, folded it into a pad, soaked it in brandy, and washed away the blood.

"Waste o' good spirits," he said through gritted teeth. She could only hope that the bullet had passed through the flesh, that it wasn't lodged inside.

"Turn around," she said, and was somewhat reassured when she saw what must be the exit wound in his back.

"Ye ain't carryin' any o' them witch herbs, are ye?"

"Witch, my arse," she mimicked, hoping to distract him from the ordeal to come. She had no herbs, but she did have sterile gauze and adhesive in her first aid kit, and a tube of antiseptic gel. Once she had cauterized the wound and covered it, she hoped his own rugged strength would pull him through.

"Ye'd better give me a swig o' that brandy." He swallowed and handed back the bottle. "Right, lass," he said. He clenched his jaw, but she felt the muscles of his whole body jerk violently as she pressed the blade to his lacerated skin.

She'd expected him to lose consciousness, but he hadn't. He only sagged back, his eyes dazed with pain. When she opened her first aid kit, he scarcely glanced at its contents. "What's that you're doin'?"

"I'm putting on an antiseptic cream and sterile gauze," she said.

"Antiseptic?" he muttered. "Sterile?"

"They'll keep the wounds clean," she said. "That will help with the healing." This certainly was not the time to explain the discoveries of Pasteur and Lister—scientific advances that still lay far in the future. She used the knife to tear another strip of linen from her petticoat. She bound it around his shoulder and tied it tightly, to hold the bandages in place.

He stretched out on the rocky floor, and slept for a few hours; when he woke, she thought his color was a little better. Although he didn't look feverish, she gave him another tankard of ale.

"You'll have to stay here and rest for a few days," she said. "There isn't much food left. I'll try to get some in Whitby. Do you have any money?"

"Enough for my passage, an' here's some left over for you. But you ain't goin' near the village," he added sternly. "You're a stranger in these parts. There'd be too many folks askin' questions, 'specially after that battle on the beach this morning. You got t' be gettin' out o' here at dawn."

"But I can't leave you like this. Your wounds aren't healed yet. The dressings should be changed—"

"Now don't ye go worryin' about me," he interrupted with a reassuring grin. "I've been takin' care o' myself all these years. I'll stay in here an' rest up a few days an' then I'll go to find myself another ship t' take me across t' Amsterdam. Them papers got t' be given t'—" He broke off abruptly.

Her curiousity got the better of her. "You said you'd tell me about them, remember?"

He was silent for a moment, his brow furrowed. "All right, then. 'Tis best ye understand I'm not goin' off an' leavin' ye on your own without good cause. They're reports that was gathered from Royalists all over England. An' Scotland, as well."

"What kind of reports was Jared carrying?"

"Better ye don't know more than I already told ye, lass. They have got to be handed over t' the prince an' no one else. Jared had a second set made fer me, ye see. He figured it'd be better if each of us was carryin' one." His pale eyes went bleak. "The way it turned out, he was right."

"Are you saying that Jared has those papers with him now?" Her heart seemed to stop for an instant, then start again, lurching unsteadily against her chest. "Suppose they search him at the barracks?"

"They'll search him, that's for sure," Dermot said grimly. "If they haven't already."

"And then? Dermot, look at me. What's going to happen to Jared when they find those papers?"

"Kristy, lass, ye got t' listen t' me, an' do just what I say. Ye'll have t' go into hidin' at Lachlan Hall!" He thought for a moment. "First ye got t' get yerself t' the Fightin' Cocks."

He removed the bayonet from the musket. "Take the musket with ye. Wrap in a cloak; hide it, but ye may need it to protect yerself. Dunstan'll probably charge ye too much, but pay him what he asks—don't stop t' haggle. He'll put ye on a coach bound fer the Border. When ye get t' Lachlan Hall, tell Sir Andrew what happened to us here. He'll take care o' ye."

Kristy voice shook with indignation. "You're going to leave Jared locked in a cell, while you go off to the Continent? Is this cause of yours more important to you than his life?"

"I'm doin' what Jared would want me t' do."

"What will happen when Lord Fairfax sees those papers?"

This time he did not look away. "He'll be questioned, then charged with high treason."

"And then?"

"There's only one punishment for treason."

"Dermot, no! That mustn't happen. We won't let it happen. We've got to help him escape before Lord Fairfax gets there."

"Sweet Jesú! Ain't ye understood a word I been sayin'? There's nothin' more we can do for Jared."

"But if I can get to Sir Andrew in time, he can raise enough fighting men to attack the barracks."

He shook his head and gave her a pitying look. "Ye can't make such a journey in less than a week. An' if ye could, there still ain't no way Sir Andrew's men could take the barracks. Durin' the wars, the Royalists attacked Ashford more than once. They were always driven back. Ashford's stood off every seige since the days of Richard the Lionhearted. 'Tis the strongest fortress in all Yorkshire."

Dermot slept on and off for the rest of the day, and then through the night, with Kristy beside him. At dawn, he led her down a long, convoluted passage, stopping now and then to catch his breath.

He pointed to a rough oval of greyish light in the distance. "This passage opens out onto the moors," he told her. "I'm goin' t' leave ye here now. Wait for sunrise an' then get movin'. There always a few wagons headin' north. If you're lucky, maybe some farmer'll offer ye a ride. Get down at Old Ralph."

"Old Ralph? What's that?"

" 'Tis a stone cross that stands nine feet high, between Castleton an' Hutton-le-Hole. Ye'll go left from there. The Fightin' Cocks is about a mile further on."

He paused. "Time ye were gettin' started." He placed his big hands on her shoulders. "You're a fine lass, Kristy Sinclair. I'm glad you an' Jared found each other—even if it was only for a little while."

He bent down and kissed her, his stubble-roughened face scratching against her cheek. Then he turned and started back down the passage.

She stood looking after him until he was lost in the shadows. Then she picked up her belongings, heavier now with the weight of the musket, and moved toward the passage opening.

Chapter Sixteen

Jared stirred restlessly, then opened his eyes. He sat up and brushed away a few pieces of the filthy straw that covered the stone floor of his cell, and also served as his bed. He got to his feet, steadied himself against the wall for a moment; then he began pacing back and forth, trying to ignore the dull ache in his ribs, the pounding at the side of his skull.

How long had he been confined here in Ashford barracks? Two days—no, three. He had already started to measure the passage of time by the two scanty meals the guard shoved through the narrow slot in the iron door: a bowl of watery gruel in the morning, a rancid stew at night—and never enough of either. His meager ration of brackish water left him tormented by constant thirst.

He forced himself to keep moving to shake off the chill in this damp underground cell. He wore only his shirt, breeches and boots; they had taken away his cloak and doublet before they'd kicked him down the flight of steps and locked him in here. The sergeant who had confiscated his sword had hefted the weapon and grinned appreciatively. "It's a fine blade you have here, Ramsey. Too bad you won't have a chance to use it again."

But the loss of his sword was the least of his concerns. By now, one of the officers—perhaps Colonel Marsden, himself—must have discovered the dispatches hidden inside his doublet. There was no way they could trace the reports to their various sources, thankfully. He tried to find a measure of consolation in the knowledge that, although he was locked up here in Ashford, others still were free to go on working for the Stuart cause.

He quickened his pace, but here in this narrow space there was little room to move about; ten steps from left to right; twenty-two from the cell door to the rear wall. And whether he was pacing or lying on the straw and staring up at the ceiling, he could not escape the questions that tormented him ceaselessly.

Where was Kristy right now? Although the cave had offered her a temporary refuge, she couldn't stay hidden inside its passages much longer. Perhaps she'd already come out. If so, he didn't want to think of what might be happening to her; a defenseless young woman wandering across the moors would be fair game for the vagabonds, gypsies, itinerant day laborers who roamed the back roads of Yorkshire. His lips tightened to a thin, hard line, as he tried to shut out the ugly images that began to form in his mind.

He could only hope that somehow she'd be lucky enough to stay out of danger until she could find her way back to the Border. It would be a difficult journey, for she had no knowledge of the route. But if, somehow, she got to Lachlan Hall, he knew he could trust Sir Andrew to care for her.

Why the devil hadn't he left her there? Why? He gave a brief, self-mocking laugh, remembering how he'd put aside common sense and yielded to his emotions.

He stopped and stared at the wall, but he was seeing her now, as she had looked when she'd come to his bed chamber, the night before his departure from Sir Andrew's estate. Standing before him, her eyes on his, she had stripped off her robe, her movements slow and seductive. He'd been stirred to the depths of his being at the sight of her, the firelight bathing her body in an enticing golden glow, gilding each curve and hollow: flickering over the high, firm swells of her breasts, the sensuous curve of her hips; caressing the softness at the apex of her tapering thighs. Even now, his senses were stirred by the memory.

It had taken every ounce of self-restraint to keep from seizing her and throwing her down on the thick wolfskin rug before the hearth, from taking her then and there. But he'd held himself in check long enough to remind himself of the importance of the cause he'd sworn to uphold. He'd warned her that, no matter how deeply he loved her, he would go off alone when morning came.

Now, in the bleak confines of his cell, her words, brave and generous, came back to him. *All right, you can leave without me. I won't try to stop you.* She'd opened her arms to him; she'd given herself to him with all the fierce passion, all the warmth and tenderness of her nature. She had held nothing back.

Even so, he should have kept her to her promise; he should have left her in Sir Andrew's care and gone off alone. But at the last moment his determination had wavered and he'd surrendered to his overpowering need to keep her with him, no matter what the cost.

He'd risen from her side at dawn; had paused to look down at the oval of her face, shadowed by the heavy velvet bed-curtains, at her hair, falling around her shoulders, only half-concealing her pink-tipped breasts. She'd opened her eyes, and her gaze had locked with his.

She had not gone back on the promise she'd made the night before. She hadn't wept or pleaded or clung to him. She hadn't tried to persuade him to take her along.

The decision had been his. He hadn't been able to turn his

back on her and walk away. Perhaps, even after that night of loving, he still might have forced himself to go—if not for what she'd told him about her meeting with Gwyneth Trefoil, in the woods beyond Lachlan Hall.

Even now, he did not know what possible connection there could be between his beloved Kristy and the ruthless, silver-eyed witch. Perhaps Kristy had inherited certain uncanny powers from the mother she could not remember. He could not be sure. He only knew he had to get her out of England before Beltane Eve—far away the circles of ancient stones that dotted the moors. From Gwyneth and her coven.

He'd promised to take her across the sea to safety. But he'd failed her.

Just as he'd failed the cause to which he'd pledged his loyalty. The documents, gathered with infinite care, and at so great a risk, would not reach the exiled Stuart prince. Not in time to warn him against returning to England too soon. Charles was reckless, impatient. How much longer would he wait?

A hot tide of anger and frustration surged up inside Jared. He turned and slammed his fist into the stone wall, but the pain that went jolting up his arm did little to provide an outlet for his rage. He was imprisoned here in the fortress, with no means of escape. And Dermot was dead.

Dermot had fought beside him during the wars; he'd accompanied him to the Continent after the Royalist defeat. They'd returned to England together; they had shared the risks of the smuggler's trade; and had worked together, in secret, carrying on the struggle against the Lord Protector.

A Stuart would reclaim England's throne one day, but neither he nor Dermot would be there to witness the victory of their cause.

He drew a long breath, turned, and started his pacing again. He asked himself what had possessed Dermot to try to escape back there on the cliffs. Had he really hoped his desperate

gamble could possibly succeed? One chance in a million—
and his friend had taken it.

Jared tried to shut out the memory of Dermot, his arms still
bound behind him, running in a zigzag path, dodging the
troopers' bullets before he'd been struck down. *One less treasonous dog to take back to the barracks.*

He could only hope his friend had died quickly, even before they'd kicked him over the side of the cliff to the beach
below. Otherwise, the fall might have broken his back and
left him lying helpless before death claimed him.

He paced to the door, then back again. A rat scuttled across
his path and disappeared into a hole in the wall. From somewhere overhead, he heard the monotonous dripping of water.
Tormented by thirst, he'd already come to loathe the sound.

He wondered where the guards had taken those of his men
who had survived the battle? Probably they had been locked
up together; only he had merited the dubious distinction of a
solitary cell. How long would he remain here before Lord
Fairfax arrived to question him?

He went over a dozen plans of escape, and discarded each
one. Even if he could get out of his cell, he hadn't the
slightest idea where it was located, in this maze of ancient
underground passages.

He'd never been inside these walls before. Cromwell's
forces had captured the fortress in the early months of the
wars. They had put it to use as a barracks and a prison. In
the years that followed, the place had acquired a sinister reputation.

He had heard about the Royalist prisoners who'd been confined here before him. Some of them had died of their
wounds, or of jail fever; others had been beheaded out in the
courtyard, their severed heads fastened to the iron stakes high
up on the parapet: a grim warning to those who might want
to take up arms against the Lord Protector.

Not one prisoner had ever escaped.

* * *

When Kristy emerged from the narrow opening at the end of the passage, the sea mist already was rolling away. Looking to the east, she could see the tightly packed cottages of Whitby far off in the distance, their red-tiled roofs glowing in the spring sunlight, and the ruins of an ancient abbey standing on the steep hill above the village. She felt a touch of warmth in the breeze that swept in over the moors; it ruffled the fresh green shoots of bracken, and stirred the budding branches of a twisted oak tree. A hawk circled overhead, then flew off toward the sea.

She paused long enough to shake out her badly creased skirt and smooth the folds of her cape; then she pushed a few strands of her hair under her white cap, picked up her bag, and started down the path.

She reminded herself she must follow Dermot's advice, and avoid not only Whitby, but any of the other small villages she was likely to pass on her way north. She hadn't forgotten how the crowd in Braethorn had besieged her with questions, how quickly they had turned hostile when she hadn't been able to come up with right answers.

She gave a start as she caught the creak of wheels and the clopping of hooves close behind her. A woman's voice called out, "Have a care, lass. Stand aside."

As she turned quickly, she saw a sturdy, middle-aged woman in a black dress and russet cape that were somewhat the worse for wear; her round red face was framed by a starched white cap. When she stopped her donkey cart with a jerk on the reins, Kristy caught the pungent smell of fish. The woman peered down, her dark eyes alert. "Ye're not from Whitby or Robin Hood's Bay, are ye? Mayhap ye come from Scarborough."

"No, Mistress—"

"I'm Emmaline," she said briskly. "Where is yer home, then?"

Still shaken by all that had happened in the past few days, Kristy wasn't prepared with a ready answer. Desperately she searched her memory. "I live—in Braethorn." It was the first name that popped into her mind.

"Do ye, indeed?" The woman smiled and gestured toward the wooden barrels in the back of the cart. "I sometimes go as far as Braethorn market t' sell my dried kippers—but only when I'm carryin' a bigger load than this."

Emmaline was studying her more closely now, and she shifted uneasily under the woman's searching gaze. "What are ye doin' hereabouts?"

"I'm on my way to—" She broke off, torn by indecision. She was heading north to the Fighting Cocks, then on to the Border. It was what Jared would have wanted her to do.

"Speak up, lass."

All she had to do was to satisfy the woman's curiosity, and then start on her way again. Dermot had given her sensible advice; she'd be foolish not to follow it. But in the space of a single heartbeat, her common sense was swept aside by her emotions. As long as Jared was alive, as long as there was a chance of setting him free, she could not resign herself to losing him forever. She heard herself saying, "I'm going to the Ashford barracks."

But how? She had no plan for helping him to escape; all she had was the musket hidden in her carry-on—that and her stubborn refusal to surrender, no matter how great the odds.

First she had to find a way to the barracks as quickly as possible; then she would have to get inside. Dermot had said it was the strongest fortress in all of Yorkshire.

"Ashford's more than ten miles off." Emmaline's brisk voice jerked her back to the present. "What're ye doin' here on the coast?"

"I'm afraid I'm lost. It was after dark and I must have missed the turn in the road."

She caught a flicker of sympathy in the woman's eyes. "Have ye been walkin' all the way from Braethorn, without stoppin' fer the night?"

"I slept for a few hours along the way."

"Ye must've lain in a ditch, by the look of yer clothes." Kristy decided it would be better not to contradict her.

"And have ye eaten since ye left home?"

"I brought along some bread and cheese, and I found a spring to drink from."

"Ye still look a mite peckish t' me, lass." The woman broke off, her black eyes narrow with suspicion. "What's a young maid like yerself seekin' at a barracks full of them randy troopers? Ye don't look like a doxy—are ye new t' the trade?"

Kristy glared at her with indignation. "I'm not a—doxy!" But even as she spoke, she knew she'd have to think of a believable reason for her journey, and fast.

A brother stationed in the barracks . . . a family emergency. . . .

Before she could work out the details, Emmaline was already speaking. "Mayhap yer young man's a trooper, stationed at Ashford. Is that the way of it?"

Kristy gave a sigh of relief. "Yes—I'm going to see my young man—he's at Ashford."

That much, at least, was true. But what would Mistress Emmaline say if she discovered that Jared was not a trooper; that he was Royalist who had been plotting against the Lord Protector's government; that he had been arrested and was awaiting sentence? *There's only one punishment for treason.*

"An' did yer mother give ye leave t' go off by yerself t' see him?" she asked, disapprovingly. "Didn't she warn ye of the dangers ye might meet—a pretty girl like yerself alone on the moors?"

Kristy looked down. "She didn't know."

"You went runnin' off without even tellin' her where ye were goin'?"

"I was afraid to tell her. You see—"

"I believe I do." The woman looked her up and down.

Kristy took a quick step back. Why hadn't she thought to take off the blue cloak and hide it in her bag? No doubt

Emmaline already had heard about the clash between the smugglers and Cromwell's troopers, down there on the beach yesterday. All of Whitby must be gossiping about it by now.

And had they also heard rumors of the girl in the blue cape who had been seen running across the beach—the girl who'd been accused by Owen and Nehemiah of being a witch?

Her body tensed and she looked about quickly, ready to run for cover. She saw only the moorlands, stretching flat and barren on every side, with a few scrubby trees scattered about.

Maybe she could make a dash back to the cave. But if she did, Emmaline would raise the hue and cry, and the witch-hunters would be on the move. Dermot had not yet recovered from his wounds; he was in no condition to put up a fight; they'd be trapped and captured together.

She raised her head, met Emmaline's probing gaze, and forced a smile. "I must be on my way now."

"Just a minute, lass. There's no need fer ye to go skitterin' off like a scared rabbit." An understanding smile touched her wide mouth. "I can guess why yer in such haste t' reach the barracks."

But that was impossible! Until a few moments ago, Kristy, herself, had not known she'd be going to the barracks to try to help Jared escape.

The woman gave a self-satisfied nod, as if she was pleased with her powers of perception. "Yer young man was gettin' ready t' leave home and join his regiment, ain't that so? The night was warm and the moon was bright, and ye lay together under a hedge. He was hot an' horny, like all of 'em, and ye let him have his way with ye."

Kristy stared up at her and swallowed hard, unable to answer.

"An' now he's gone off an' left ye in pod."

"He—what?"

"Why, he popped ye an' pupped ye, an' now he's gone. Ain't that it?"

Although Kristy had never heard those peculiar words before, she had no doubt as to their meaning. This woman thought she was pregnant—and unmarried. Panic gripped her once more. Fornication might not be considered as serious a crime as witchcraft. It wasn't likely she'd be burned at the stake. But she was sure the Puritans wouldn't take a light view of her "sin." What humiliating punishment had they decreed for an unwed mother? Would she be whipped; or would she be confined in the town pillory, pelted with rotten fruit, and maybe a few rocks?

"So yer fine young soldier went on his way, without a thought o' the lass he'd left to bear his bairn. Ye're not the first t' make a such a mistake an' ye won't be the last."

"But Emmaline—you don't understand."

"Of course I do. Ye mightn't think it t' look at me, but I was young once, myself, an' good-lookin', with plenty o' lads runnin' after me, Ye're goin' t' the barracks t' try and talk him into marryin' ye."

She sensed that there was no way to convince Emmaline that she was mistaken. And why should she try? Others might condemn her, but this woman was more tolerant. And since she had leaped to the wrong conclusion, why not make the most of it?

Kristy fixed her eyes on the ground, as if she were too ashamed to look the older woman in the eye. "I know I did wrong, and I'm sorry. But if I can get to Ashford, I know he'll marry me. Please, Mistress Emmaline—it's a great favor to ask of a stranger—but if you could give me a ride there, I'd be most grateful."

Emmaline hesitated, then shook her head. "I wasn't fi-gurin' on goin' as far as the barracks. I can sell my fish much closer t' home, an' be back in Whitby before dark."

But she wasn't about to give up, not yet. There had to be a way to get Emmaline to change her mind. What about the small hoard of coins Dermot had given her? She had no idea how much they were worth. Enough to bribe one of Jared's guards, perhaps? But first, she had to get to the barracks.

"I can pay you," she said. She reached into the pocket of her cape and drew out one of the coins.

Emmaline snatched it from her hand and held it up in the sunlight. "A gold guinea! Ye're offerin' a guinea fer a ride t' Ashford?"

Wasn't it enough? Kristy wondered. Should she offer the woman another?

"Where'd ye get this?" Emmaline demanded.

"I earned it."

"Earned it, did ye? Tendin' the squire's sheep, I suppose. Or sellin' yer mother's butter an' eggs at the market? Do ye take me fer a fool? There ain't but one thing a pretty young girl has to sell, that'll earn her such wages—"

She broke off, and her gaze was fixed on Kristy's cloak. "So it was you them troopers were talkin' about! A girl in a blue cloak, runnin' across the beach like the devil himself was on her heels. I heard them makin' their jests about ye when they stopped t' water their horses at the Mariner's Rest."

All right, Kristy. Try talking your way out of this one!

"Ye let me think ye were a foolish little lass who'd made a mistake an' was goin' t' seek yer young man. But yer nothing more than a common trollop." Kristy stiffened with outrage under the woman's contemptuous gaze. "I guess ye know all the tricks o' the trade, don't ye? No doubt ye pleasured the whole lot of 'em, since they paid ye so well fer yer favors. An' now ye're off t' the barracks, t' sell yerself t' the troopers."

"That's not—Jared is the only one—" She choked back the rest, but it was already too late. Now there was no way Emmaline would take her to Ashford. She'd want nothing to do with a smuggler's mistress.

"Ye're Jared Ramsey's woman." There was awe in her voice, and perhaps a touch of envy. Kristy was at a loss to understand Emmaline's unexpected response.

"Don't ye know we all look up t' Master Ramsey here in

these parts? We'd have sent him warnin', if we'd had time. When we find the turncoats that informed on him—an' we will—it'll go hard with them, I can tell ye.''

Baffled by Emmaline's change of heart, she could only say, ''But Jared's a smuggler—''

''So he is—an' the best o' them! There's not a fishin' village along the coast that don't make good money from the smugglin' trade. Times ain't been easy, what with the Lord Protector's taxes weighin' us down. These past few years, Ramsey an' his men have kept plenty of us ordinary folks from starvin'. They pay well fer the hire o' their horses an' wagons; they keep the taverns doin' a lively business. They give our fishing captains and their crews good wages fer crossin' the water, bringin' their cargoes back an' forth.''

Emmaline slid the coin into the top of her bodice between her ample breasts, then reached down her hand to Kristy. ''Climb up here, girl.''

''Then you'll give me a ride to Ashford? Please, Mistress Emmaline—I've got to get there.''

''Then get yerself up an' be quick about it. We'll have time t' talk along the way.''

But Kristy glanced dubiously at the narrow seat; the woman's broad backside took up at least three-quarters of the space. ''Where will I put my bag?''

''It'll just fit between those two casks. Give it t' me.'' Kristy handed the carry-on to Emmaline, who shoved it between the casks of dried fish. ''Ye'd best give me yer cape, too. If I recognized it, there's others that might.'' Kristy obeyed, then scrambled onto the seat.

Emmaline brought down her switch on the donkey's back; it raised its head, gave a loud bray, then started along the path at a steady pace.

''Since we'll be travel' together, don't ye think ye might tell me yer name?''

''I'm Kristy Sinclair.'' She put a hand on the woman's arm.

251

"Please, Emmaline—you will take me to the barracks, won't you?"

Emmaline shook her head. "I'll get you away from here an' back home t' Braethorn. That's the best I can do."

"But that's not where my—I can't go back to Braethorn." There was no way she could tell Emmaline where her "home" was. "I've got to get to Jared."

"Holy saints, lass—ye must be daft if ye think ye can go strollin' past the sentry box and through the gates of Ashford."

"Don't they ever let civilians inside?"

"The troopers sneak a whore inside, now an' then, though it means a floggin' if they're caught. An' sometimes the colonel will send for a stonemason or a locksmith t' make repairs. An' peddlers t' carry in supplies. I've been let to bring my fish t' the commissary shed—that's out in the courtyard." She grinned. "No doubt I can talk the supply sergeant into buyin' a few barrels from me today."

Kristy's spirits shot up. "When you drive into the courtyard, take me with you."

"An' suppose I do? How's that goin' t' help ye?"

"Maybe I can bribe one of the guards to let me into the fortress."

Emmaline paused to consider the plan, then shook her head. "It's not every guard who'll take a bribe."

"I'm the one who'll be taking the risk," Kristy reminded her. "All you have to do is sell your fish and drive away. Once I'm inside I'll find my way to Jared's cell."

"Find yer way! If the guards catch ye skulkin' about, ye'll find yerself in a cell alongside his." Emmaline sighed and shook her head. "Like I told ye, we think a lot o' Master Ramsey hereabouts. I'd help him if I could, an' be proud t' do it. But there ain't a chance." Her dark eyes softened with pity. "Do ye love him so much that ye're willin' to get yerself arrested, on the chance ye might see him one last time before he swings from the gallows?"

"Jared isn't going to hang," Kristy said. "There's got to be a way to get him out of there."

By late afternoon, when they reached Ashford, the sunlight had disappeared. The tall stone fortress loomed up dark and sinister, against a pale grey sky. A burly young trooper, who wore an iron helmet and was armed with a pike, ordered her to halt. Emmaline jerked the mule to a stop in front of the sentry box. "No need t' be so stiff-necked with me, Colin, my lad." She gave him a teasing smile. "Can't ye smell them kippers there? Yer commissary sergeant said he'd be needin' a supply around this time."

"That's as may be, Mistress Emmaline, but I'm afraid ye picked the wrong day. I got my orders. No one goes in or out. Not today."

His eyes shifted to Kristy; he looked her over with keen interest; even the high-necked, long-sleeved dress could not conceal the fullness of her breasts, the curve of her waist. "Who's this lass you got with you?"

"I picked her up along the road." Emmaline kept her tone casual. "She was goin' home t' Braethorn an' as I was goin' the same way, I offered her a ride."

"Then ye'd best be gettin' on t' Braethorn, Mistress Emmaline. Because you ain't gettin' through the gates, not today."

"An' what's so special about today?"

The young man shrugged. "All I know is, Colonel Marsden's ordered the whole fortress closed up tight, right after his lordship's carriage drove through these gates."

"His lordship?"

The sentry glanced about, then lowered his voice. "Lord Fairfax of Ravenswyck. He got here about an hour ago, in a fine big coach with a black an' silver crest on the door. I hear he's come t' question the leader o' them smugglers they brought in from Whitby a couple o' days ago."

Kristy stifled a cry of dismay as she stared up at the fortress, its curving parapet black against the fading light. She went dizzy and for a moment she was afraid she might faint. She clasped her hands in her lap and dug her fingernails into her palms.

"An' why would his lordship make such a journey, just t' deal with a smuggler?" Emmaline asked. "The coast is swarmin' with them, as well ye know."

"That ain't fer a corporal like me t' question. I reckon I've said too much already, Emmaline. Sorry ye've made the trip for nothin'."

She shrugged. "If that's the way of it, I'd best be going on. I promised the lass I'd take her home safe. An' I might still find a few buyers in Braethorn."

She tugged on the reins and turned the cart around. As the donkey plodded down the road, the wind started to rise, sending heavy pewter-colored clouds scudding across the sky.

"Stop the cart! I'm getting down." Before Emmaline could speak, Kristy was already turning to tug at her carry-on, tightly wedged between two of the barrels.

"What're ye doin'?" Emmaline asked. "Ye heard what the sentry said. There's no way ye can get into the barracks— not now."

Kristy didn't take time to answer. She wrenched the bag free, lowered it to the ground, threw her cape around her shoulders and rose from the narrow seat.

"Here, now!" Emmaline called. "I said I'd take ye home t' Braethorn, an' I'll keep my word."

"Braethorn's not my home."

"I didn't think ye talked like a Yorkshire lass. Where did Ramsey find ye then? Did he bring ye across from Holland, maybe?"

"It doesn't matter. Because I can't go back, ever."

Emmaline gave her a troubled glance. "Then what do ye mean to do?"

Kristy was already out of the wagon. "I don't know— yet."

"Ye got t' get away from here. Ye can't do yer man any good, and ye're likely t' get yerself in a heap o' trouble. Jared Ramsey don't stand a chance—not with Lord Fairfax here t' deal with him."

Chapter Seventeen

Emmaline picked up the reins, but she didn't start the donkey moving on its way. Instead, she leaned forward on the seat, her dark eyes fixed on Kristy, her brow furrowed. "How can I just leave ye standin' here alone? Do ye even know where ye're goin' now, lass? Not back t' Ashford, surely."

Touched by the woman's concern, Kristy said, "I know better than that. I won't go back to the fortress, not until I've had time to work out another plan to get inside."

"An' in the meantime, I suppose ye'll go wanderin' around out here on these moors without food or drink, without a place t' rest. When yer strength's gone, no doubt ye'll lie down in a ditch an' starve. Saints above! If ye could look at yer face in a mirror, ye'd give yerself a proper fright, with yer skin pale as milk."

Kristy thought of the scrying mirror hidden away in her cape. Suppose she were to take it out right now—she wouldn't see a reflection of her face, she was sure of it. Maybe the surface might begin to stir, as it had before, like the waves of a midnight sea; maybe she could call up a vision of the future from its fathomless depths. Her future—and Jared's. She pushed the thought away, and fixed her thoughts on the present.

"Don't worry about me, Emmaline. I can take care of myself. I'll stop at the first inn I see along the road, and have my dinner. Maybe I'll ask the innkeeper to give me a room for the night."

The woman gave a sigh of relief. "Thank goodness ye have that much sense, at least. But when ye go inside an inn, ye'd best be careful. An' whatever ye do, don't go showin' them gold guineas around."

"I'll have to give the innkeeper a coin to pay for my food and lodging, won't I?"

"Wait a bit. Mayhap ye'll have no need t' stop at an inn, not fer awhile yet." Emmaline got up and balanced herself precariously; she reached for one of the smaller barrels, then, using a flat piece of iron, she pried the top off. She reached inside and took out a generous handful of dried kippers.

"These'll keep ye goin' fer now." She searched inside the capacious folds of her russet cape. "Take this, too. Ye'll need a bit o' bread to go with the fish." She wrapped the food in a clean rag and handed it down to Kristy. "As for me, I'll have my dinner soon as I get t' Braethorn."

"At Mother Jenkins' cookshop?" The words slipped out unbidden.

Emmaline's brows went up. "Ah, so ye do come from Braethorn after all."

"No, I don't—but Jared and I once stopped at the cookshop there." Her throat tightened at the memory of his laughter, the glint of amusement in his green eyes, as he'd teased about her hearty appetite.

"I thought we were friends, Kristy. Ain't ye goin' t' tell me where ye come from, even now?" Emmaline persisted.

A brief, ironic smile touched Kristy's lips. "You wouldn't

believe me if I did.'' She reached inside her cape and took out a coin.

''Put that away, lass,'' said Emmaline. ''Ye must come from far off, indeed, if ye don't know that other guinea ye gave me fer the ride would pay for a whole barrel of fish as well.''

Tears of gratitude stung Kristy's lids, but she blinked them back.

''Here, now—there's no need t' start blubberin'.''

''I won't—I never do.''

''Never?''

''I can't cry.'' But as she spoke, she realized how strange that must sound. All the same, it was true. Even as a little girl back in Hillsboro, when the other children had shunned her, or when her aunt had punished her, she had borne her unhappiness without shedding a single tear.

Don't cry, Kristy. Don't make a sound. We can't let them find us here.

A woman holding her close in the darkness, stroking her hair and whispering the warning with fierce urgency. My mother. But why was she so afraid? Who were the hunters? What would happen if we were caught?

Why can't I remember?

Emmaline's brisk, no-nonsense voice drove the shadowy memory away. ''Ye're a brave lass, Kristy Sinclair, an' no mistake. Ye don't give up easy. But ye got learn t' use yer common sense. Ye got t' let go, when ye know there's no hope o' gettin' yer way.''

''There is hope, as long as Jared's still alive.''

Emmaline sighed and shook her head. ''Then ye must do as yer heart tells ye, lass—an' may heaven help ye.'' She brought her switch down on the donkey's back.

Kristy stood staring after the cart as it jounced down the path, turned a bend in the road, and disappeared. Should she have listened to Emmaline's warnings, and admitted to herself that there was little chance of getting Jared out of the fortress?

She could have asked the woman to drive her away from Ashford and on to the Fighting Cocks. Rufus Dunstan would have pocketed her money, then hired a coach to take her to the Border.

But even if she had reached the safety of Lachlan Hall, she would have known no peace, for she'd have been tormented by thoughts of Jared, imprisoned at Ashford. Accused of treason, he'd be questioned, then sentenced by Lord Fairfax.

What had Dermot meant when he'd said Jared would be "questioned?" All at once, she understood; icy fear surged through her. Other Royalists were involved in the plot to restore Prince Charles to his throne, and Fairfax would stop at nothing to get their names. Terrifying images formed in her imagination.

How far would Fairfax go to force Jared to implicate the others?

She mustn't let herself think about it, not now. With bag in hand, she set out along a narrow path overgrown with gorse and bracken. Although she had no fixed destination she began memorizing the landmarks. She mustn't wander too far from the fortress; she might not be able to find her way back.

Yet, if she did return, what then? How could she hope to get inside the towering stone walls, or to find her way to Jared's cell? Even with Emmaline to help her, she hadn't been able to make it as far as the courtyard.

Emmaline had said the troopers sometimes smuggled a whore into the fortress. The young sentry had looked her over as if he liked what he saw; maybe if she went back there alone, he would help her to get inside.

But not today.

Her spirits plummeted. He had his orders. He'd refused to let Emmaline get into the courtyard to sell her fish to the commissary sergeant.

All right, she'd offer him a bribe, a large one. Six gold guineas should do it. But if his fear of punishment were greater than his greed, he might refuse. Or suppose he took the money, then turned her over to his commanding officer. Her insides started to churn. What was the punishment for helping a Royalist prisoner to escape from Ashford?

With her jaw set, her eyes fixed straight ahead, she plodded on. The bag seemed heavier with every step. The musket added to its weight, and her shoulder began to throb. Even when she stopped to shift the bag to her other hand, her thoughts went racing ahead.

Dermot had given her the musket to protect herself. Much good it would do her—she wasn't even sure how to load and fire it. But Jared knew. If she could get the weapon to Jared, if he could force his guard to unlock his cell. . . .

How could one man, even an experienced soldier like Jared, fight his way out of a fortress guarded by all those troopers? Even if he could free his men to fight beside him, the odds still would be overwhelming.

Keep moving, Kristy. There is a way. There has to be a way.

With the coming on of evening, the wind rose and a light rain began to fall. She looked about her, seeking a village or even a shepherd's solitary hut. But only the darkening moors lay ahead. Just as well, she thought. She'd have hesitated to offer an innkeeper or shepherd a gold coin in exchange for food and shelter. Emmaline had asked how she'd gotten hold of so much money; others might question her, too.

What would a decent innkeeper think about a girl who was wandering the moors alone, carrying a hoard of gold guineas? Her blue woolen gown, once suitable for a merchant's wife to wear, now was in a sorry state; the skirt was streaked with dirt, the hem was tattered. Her shoes were scuffed and one had lost its buckle. Would he think she was a thief, or maybe a trollop who'd been driven from her own village in disgrace?

She'd have to keep away from the respectable inns. But if she stopped at one of the other kind—like the Fighting Cocks—she could easily imagine how the rowdy, drunken customers would treat her.

She couldn't go on walking much longer. Her cape did little to protect her from the rain. She had lost her prim white cap along the way and now the wind lashed her hair across her face. She tugged the thick woolen hood of her cape up over her head. The wind pulled it off again.

She would have to find a place to stop for the night.

In her travels with Jared, she had learned it was best to camp close to a stream. She searched nearly half an hour more, before she heard the burbling of water. On the mossy bank, under a wind-scoured rock ledge whose flat top jutted out overhead, she dropped her bag and sank down with a heartfelt sigh.

Too hungry to wait any longer, she took out the rag-wrapped parcel Emmaline had given her. She munched the dried fish and bread, and saved a little to sustain her until she could find a place to get her next meal. The fish made her thirsty, and she had to leave her lair to drink from the stream.

The rain was heavier now. Although she quickened her pace, by the time she reached the sheltering ledge again, her shoes were soaked; her wet skirt and petticoat clung to her legs. She pushed her bag behind her head, wrapped her cape tightly around her body, pulled up the hood, and drifted off into an exhausted sleep.

When she woke, the rain had stopped. She crept out from the shelter of the ledge. How long had she slept? The sun was nearly overhead, but she felt chilled to the bone. She stood up and forced herself to stretch, ignoring the twinges in her stiff neck and shoulders. Time to get moving again.

As she walked, she kept looking for more landmarks to guide her. She mustn't get too far from Ashford. From Jared. Over to the right stood a great, ancient oak tree. And farther along the road, she caught sight of a stone cross. It wasn't Old Ralph, the stone cross Dermot had told her about; this one had been broken, and lay half-buried in the damp earth.

She went on another half hour or so, then stopped to finish

the remains of the dried fish and bread. This time there was no stream nearby, but a hollow in one of the larger rocks held a small pool of water from last night's rain. Tucking her skirt under her knees, she got down and drank from it.

As she started on her way again, she looked up and caught sight of an abbey, with the afternoon sunlight slanting through its shattered walls and broken windows. She thought the shape of the arches, the single tower, looked familiar. Had she passed it before? She shook her head. Cromwell's troopers, in their fanatical zeal, must have destroyed half the abbeys in Yorkshire, and left a trail of such ruins to mark their path.

It was close to sunset when she climbed a steep hill, and caught sight of a small village set in a hollow about a mile away. Her instinct warned her to avoid it. But she had eaten the last of the bread and fish, and although she wasn't hungry yet, she knew she would be before too long; besides, she couldn't spend another night sleeping out on the moors.

But she'd take as few risks as possible. Instead of having to cope with a curious landlord and his customers at a local inn, she might do better to stop at a cottage on the outskirts of the village.

Emmaline had befriended her. Wasn't there a chance she might find another kindly woman who'd overlook her disreputable appearance, and offer her food and shelter? She wouldn't show her money unless she had to; a shabby-looking stranger with so many coins surely would arouse suspicion. Instead, she'd ask if she could work for her food and her night's lodging.

Immediately, a host of objections raced through her mind. Suppose the woman agreed. What did she know about cooking over an open hearth? She'd never baked a loaf of bread in her life, not even in Aunt Vera's gas oven. Or suppose she were asked to milk a cow? To kill a chicken or skin a rabbit? Her insides lurched at the thought.

She wouldn't let herself think about that—not yet. First, she'd have to find a decent-looking cottage.

Walking more quickly, she drew near the village. How about that sturdy stone cottage over there? It was set apart from the others, with a herb garden on one side.

As she approached the door, her footsteps slowed. She felt a twinge of uneasiness. Although it wasn't evening yet, the two wooden shutters already had been closed and barred. When she knocked, softly at first, then harder, a dog started barking ferociously. A large, bad-tempered dog, by the sound of it.

"Down, Tad—down, I say! The woman's voice was taut with fear. Then Kristy heard her say, "Who do ye think could be abroad?"

"It don't matter," a man's deep, surly voice answered. "Just ye stay away from that door, Bessie. We're not lettin' nobody in here tonight."

"But it's not all that late yet."

Then why had they already barred the shutters?

"Please open the door," Kristy called.

"Simon, she sounds like a young lass. Could be she's lost her way."

"So much the worse for her."

"But we can't leave her out there t' fend fer herself! Not tonight!"

Encouraged by the woman's words, Kristy knocked again. The door stayed shut. Although she hadn't forgotten Emmaline's warning, she was getting more desperate by the minute. "I have money—I can pay well for a meal and a place to sleep."

"We don't want yer money! Be off, or I'll loose the dog on ye." Although the man's voice was harsh and threatening, she thought she sensed an underlying fear. What was frightening him so badly that he wouldn't even open the door a crack?

She turned away in defeat, and went on to the next cottage;

here, too, the shutters already had been closed and barred. This time, when she knocked, she heard only the low hum of voices; she could not make out the words.

"Open the door—please!" She heard the fear in her own voice. "I need shelter for the night. I can pay. . . ." But there was no answer, not even the sound of footsteps from within; the door stayed shut.

The breeze was rising now. It stirred the budding branches of the elms that arched across the path. Soon it would be dark. All right, so she'd have to go without dinner and spend another night outdoors.

Not tonight!

A mounting fear drove her on from one cottage to the next. In some of them, she heard the sound of muffled voices. In others, only silence. Not a single door opened in answer to her urgent knocking.

Closer to the center of the village now, she paused a moment before a blacksmith's shop. Like the cottages, it, too, was locked and barred. What if a traveler on horseback needed to have a horseshoe fixed? Could the blacksmith afford to turn business away by closing up so early in the evening? She hurried on, glancing briefly at the signs along the way: the saddler's shop, the wheelwright's—all of them were closed.

What were all the villagers afraid of? Had they heard rumors of a plague in a town nearby? Was a dangerous criminal on the loose, prowling the moors? Panic raced through her. She had to find shelter, fast.

She broke into a run, her bag jouncing against her leg. High Street cut through the center of the village; glancing from one side to the other, she thought the street looked familiar. But no, this wasn't Braethorn or Cragsmore—certainly not Whitby.

The last slanting rays of the sun were fading now, and the elms on either side of the street cast long shadows across her path. A rambling, two-story stone building, larger than those around it, loomed up before her. A painted signboard hung beside the heavy oak door. The village inn.

She ran up the wide drive, crossed the cobblestone courtyard, then stopped short. Her bag dropped from her hand. Here, too, every window was shuttered and barred.

All right, she'd try to forget about dinner. She'd go around to the stables, and if she could get inside, she'd sleep in the hayloft. At least it would be warm and dry.

The chains that held the sign creaked in the breeze. She looked up at the painted board and read the faded lettering.

THE ROWAN TREE.

And there beside the door stood the tree for which the inn had been named; it was tall and graceful, with smooth grey bark, and clusters of white blossoms.

But it wasn't possible. This couldn't be Glenrowan. Not the same village she'd first seen the day she'd been driving to Leeds. After the accident, she had walked across the moors and into Glenrowan, then up High Street to the inn.

She'd seen no blacksmith's shop that day, no saddle-maker's shop, no wheelwright. Instead, there'd been an auto repair shop, a small fish market, a greengrocer's. And the Rowan Tree. Mrs. Ainsworth's inn. She'd seen them right here along High Street. . . .

Three hundred years into the future.

Now she stood at the door of Master Prescott's inn. Although the inn was closed to travelers tonight, Prescott might be inside, behind those barred windows. And Morag, too. Prescott's niece. A short, plump girl with light-brown braids, prim white cap and apron. Morag, who had cried out with terror when she'd seen the scrying mirror—Morag, who had run downstairs and raised the hue and cry, setting the witch-hunters on Kristy's trail. Morag mustn't see her here tonight.

Run, Kristy! Run from here and keep on running!

But no other door had been opened to her, and none would be. Not tonight. A nameless evil was abroad on the moors tonight. It had driven the villagers into hiding behind the shuttered windows and bolted doors of their cottages.

She set her jaw and forced herself to stand still. She heard no sound from inside the inn. No stamping or whinnying of horses from the stable. She waited, feeling as if an iron band were clamped around her throat, growing tighter, choking off her breath. Still no sound, except for the creaking chains on the sign overhead. No hostler or servant came out to greet her.

She hesitated, then reached out and lifted the iron latch. The door swung open.

This one door in all Glenrowan stood unlocked tonight. If there were no overnight guests, no patrons in the taproom, she would take a chance and go inside.

What about Master Prescott and Morag? Suppose they were here? Although Prescott had not seen her face to face, his niece had.

Would Morag recognize her after so long?

Kristy reminded herself that her appearance had changed during the past months. Morag had seen her dressed in the burgundy pantsuit and tailored silk blouse that had marked her as an outsider. In the clothes given her by Andrew Lachlan, she might pass as a native of seventeenth-century Yorkshire. If she kept the hood of her cape close around her face, it was possible Morag mightn't recognize her at all.

She pushed the door open a little wider, then stepped inside the hallway. A dim lamp flickered overhead; by its wavering light she could make out her surroundings. The hall looked just as it had that night, after the mirror had sent her back in time. The night she'd stood on the upstairs landing, peering down at the tall, cloaked stranger whose wide-brimmed plumed hat had concealed his face.

Jared. Just the thought of him swept aside her fear and sent a new strength coursing through her. She'd climb the stairs and go inside one of the bedrooms. After she'd locked the door, she'd lie down and rest.

Later, if she still heard no sounds from outside, she'd go

down to the kitchen and fix herself a meal. Rest and food, that was what she needed. Surely by morning she'd have devised a scheme for getting Jared free.

Cautiously, she moved to the stairs. Still no sound from any part of the inn. She put a foot on the bottom step. How cold she was. Cold, and damp. As soon as she was upstairs, she'd build a fire. . . .

She raised her head and saw a grey mist swirling down the stairway like a living presence. A mist that, even as she stood staring, thickened into red-sparked fog. Swiftly, she wheeled around and ran for the front door.

She cried out as a hand touched her shoulder.

Gwyneth Trefoil. Her black hair spilled over her shoulders. Her crimson cape was flung back, and Kristy saw that her gown was crimson, too. It was belted at the waist with a silver sash. Kristy caught sight of the pentacle that hung from its chain; the five-pointed star gleamed against the whiteness of Gwyneth's full breasts. Her gaze locked with Kristy's and Kristy could not look away.

"You've kept us waiting. But you're here now, as we knew you would be."

"We?"

"The members of our coven. They're gathering now, out on the cliff, near the ring of standing stones. Tonight the fires will burn, to celebrate Beltane. The great Sabbat."

"I haven't come here to take part in your Sabbat. I don't want anything from you, or your coven."

"Are you sure? Suppose we were to teach you how to use your power to free Jared Ramsey."

"He wouldn't want his freedom—not that way!"

"And you? You have the power—a power greater than you can imagine. But you must learn to use it. We'll teach you."

"Get away! Let me go!"

"As you wish." She stepped aside and motioned Kristy through the door.

Outside there was no fog. The air felt clean and fresh against her face.

"But you must not go. Not yet." Gwyneth raised her arm and gestured toward the blossoming tree beside the door. "Look at the rowan tree. It was planted here to protect the inn from witches. Once it might have kept me from crossing Master Prescott's threshold. But now—"

She laughed softly. "Now I come and go as I please. My power is great—but not so great as yours. Touch the tree, Kristy. Now."

Kristy tried to speak but her throat was tight with fear. She could only shake her head.

"Strange, isn't it?" Gwyneth said. "You have the courage to go back to Ashford fortress. You're ready to risk your own life to save your lover. But you don't know how, do you?" Gwyneth's voice, her silver eyes, held a challenge that Kristy could not refuse. "Touch this rowan tree, and you will discover your power. Or are you too frightened to try?"

"I'm not afraid." Kristy reached out and brushed her fingertips along the smooth grey trunk. A stinging current shot into her hand, up her arm; it spread through every nerve of her body.

"Again," said Gwyneth.

Another, stronger shock went surging through her. She felt as if the earth were shifting beneath her feet. The tree was a living presence, and it had power, too . . . a power that might destroy her. Whose was the stronger? She had to know. She did not draw her hand away.

Although there was no wind, the branches of the tree began to sway. Then, even as she watched in disbelief, the delicate new leaves went sere and brown; a shower of white blossoms fell around her upturned face and caught in her hair. She brushed them away.

"You've felt the power, Kristy," she heard Gwyneth saying. "Your power. You can use it to free your lover from his cell, to take him far beyond the walls of Ashford. To call him to your side. But you don't know how, not yet.''

Gwyneth was lying—she had to be. Trying to trick Kristy into joining the coven for some unholy purpose of her own.

"You don't believe me," Gwyneth said softly. "Before the night is over, before the Beltane fires burn away, you will believe. Come, follow me.''

Chapter Eighteen

Kristy, still shaken by the discovery of her own power, followed Gwyneth back into the dimly lit hall, and on toward the stairs. When she started up the steps, she saw that the red-tinged fog still lingered there, its long grey tendrils moving down, writhing as if they were alive. Repulsed, she stopped, her hand grasping at the newel post for support.

"Come, Kristy. You've nothing to fear," Gwyneth assured her. "You'll not be harmed."

Still reluctant to go on, Kristy reached up and brushed a rowan blossom from her cheek. It lay in her palm, shriveled as if by an untimely winter frost. She had done that.

"Come along," Gwyneth urged. Kristy drew a long, steadying breath and forced herself to go on up the steps, into the swirling fog. She had expected that it would feel cold and stifling. Instead it caressed her, enfolded her, soft and seductive as a lover's touch. She moved through the fog to the top of the stairs.

"Prescott and his niece have locked themselves in the cellar with the other servants," said Gwyneth. "They'll stay down there until dawn."

Gwyneth led the way along the hallway, then opened the door to one of the bed chambers and went inside, but Kristy stopped on the threshold. She recognized this room with the low, oak-beamed ceiling, paneled walls, massive stone hearth, and wide, canopied bed.

"This chamber holds fond recollections for you, doesn't it?" asked Gwyneth. "Jared Ramsey first came to you here."

Kristy's throat tightened at the memory of Jared, striding into the room, tall and arrogant; tossing aside his cloak, standing over her, his green eyes dark with suspicion. Although he hadn't known what to believe about her, he'd taken her with him, out of reach of the witch-hunters. She remembered how he had led the way through the hidden door and down the stone steps behind it. He'd cared for her, comforted her, protected her. And taught her the meaning of love.

"You mustn't look so forlorn, Kristy. Jared will meet you again, here in this chamber. He'll kiss you, he'll hold you— he'll make love with you in that fine, soft bed." Then a hint of mockery flickered in the depths of her silver eyes. "If you still want him after tonight."

"I'll want Jared as long as I live. I love him." Kristy followed Gwyneth into the room, then turned to confront her. "I don't think you could understand what that means."

"Love." Gwyneth gave a slight shrug, then laughed softly. "Such a foolish weakness for one like you, Kristy. But you still know so little about your real self. You've not yet begun to fathom your hidden powers, your deepest, most secret desires. Soon you'll forget your feelings for Jared Ramsey. You'll know what you really want."

Kristy was silent for a moment. Before she would be completely free to love, she had to know all there was to know about herself. Although she was afraid to confide in Gwyneth, her instinct told her that only the silver-eyed witch held the key to her past; only she could answer the questions that had tormented Kristy since childhood.

"I need to know about my mother. My aunt would never speak of her. I only know her name—Ellen. I thought I saw her for a moment, that day in the woods near Lachlan Hall. Her hair was the same color as mine. She held me, she sang to me. I know she loved me." She hesitated, reluctant to go on. "She wore a pentacle on a chain around her neck. Was she—like you?"

"Ellen Sinclair was—will be—a witch of the left-hand path, a worshipper of the Horned One and the goddess, Aradia. But she was not as powerful as I am. As you might have been, if she hadn't interfered."

"I don't understand."

"She robbed you of your birthright," said Gwyneth. "She broke her oath, she left her coven. But it is not too late for you to reclaim your rightful heritage."

Gwyneth walked slowly to the hearth, where a few embers still glowed. She stirred them with the poker and the flames shot up. Shadows writhed over the paneled walls and across the low, beamed ceiling.

When Gwyneth started to speak in a soft monotone, Kristy felt her tension draining away. Her taut muscles relaxed, her limbs grew heavy. The flames danced before her half-closed eyes.

"You've always wondered about your mother," Gwyneth was saying. "Tonight you will have the answers to your questions. But you may not like what you discover."

"Tell me."

"Both her parents died before she was ten. Her older sister raised her."

"Aunt Vera. . . ."

Gwyneth nodded. "Ellen was a lonely child with a vivid imagination. An outsider. Your aunt had no fondness for children. But she fulfilled her duties. She provided Ellen food, clothing, a home."

Kristy felt a stir of pity, remembering her own love-starved childhood.

"Ellen was the prettiest girl in the village—its name is unfamiliar to me."

"Hillsboro," Kristy said.

"When your mother was fifteen, a naive, rebellious girl, she met a young man who was passing through—Hillsboro. She was drawn to him from their first meeting. But your aunt was strict, domineering. He had to meet your mother in secret.

"He told her of a settlement hidden deep in the mountains. It had been established by a man called Belenos. Free-spirited young people like her were flocking to join him. They could live there in their own way, escape the narrow rules of the outside world. They worshipped nature. From all he told her, your mother came to believe she could be happy there with him. She went away with him willingly."

"My mother joined a—kind of cult?"

"If that is what you choose to call it."

"And Aunt Vera let her go off with this young man?" That didn't sound like the stern woman who had raised her.

"Your aunt tried to stop her, but for the first time, your mother would not obey. She'd fallen in love with the young man. One spring night they slipped away together."

So that was why Aunt Vera had refused to speak of her mother, why she had ripped her photos from the family album.

"What happened to my mother in this—settlement?"

"You're sure you want to know?"

Kristy leaned forward, her eyes fixed on Gwyneth's face. "I want to know everything about my mother."

"You will see the rest for yourself. You've brought the scrying mirror with you?"

Kristy reached inside her cape and took out the velvet bag that held the mirror.

"You should put it outside, to draw down the light of the full moon," said Gwyneth. "But the moon has not yet risen."

"Then how can I use it?"

Gwyneth took the mirror from the velvet bag. She set it on the floor before the hearth. Then she lifted the chain from around her neck and held the pentacle above the dark oval.

Kristy watched the silver gleam reflected there. A star moving down . . . down . . . into a midnight sea. She felt as if she, too, were sinking deep beneath the surface of the mirror. She drifted on a dark tide that was drawing her away. . . .

Slowly, gradually, the darkness was beginning to lift. There was a light in the depths of the mirror. It grew brighter, touched with the soft glow of an autumn sunset.

She saw a girl with long, tawny-blond hair walking through a meadow hand-in-hand with a darkly handsome young man.

Was he my father?

Their sandaled feet scattered the fallen leaves of russet and gold. He stopped, put his hands on the girl's shoulders, and spoke to her softly, urgently.

She pulled away from him, her hazel eyes filled with revulsion. "No! I won't give Kristy to the coven! How can you ask me to do that?"

"We have no choice. It is the master's command. Remember, you promised to obey Belenos in all things. The night you were taken into the coven you gave your word—"

"I was fifteen. I didn't realize what I was doing."

"You swore your oath on the sacred names of Cernunnos—Rhiannon—Llyr—"

"Kristy hadn't even been born yet. How could I have known the master would want to use our child in that horrible way?"

"Why can't I make you understand? Kristy has been granted great powers. The master has said she must be trained to share those powers with the coven. In time, she will serve as our high priestess. But first she must be initiated. You will offer her up on the night of Samhain—"

"I won't take her to the Sabbat! You can't force me to—and neither can Belenos."

"You came here of your own free will!"

"I was lonely back in Hillsboro—I didn't belong. But I don't belong here, either. I wish I'd never listened to you— I wish I hadn't come—"

The mirror was beginning to darken. The autumn meadow was fading from view. Kristy bent closer and caught a glimpse of the girl breaking away from the young man, running through the heaps of fallen leaves. . . .

Now the oval was growing darker still. Kristy gripped the ebony handle so hard that the wood bruised her hand—as if she could bring back the vision by the sheer force of her will.

She started at the sound of Gwyneth's voice. "Do you want to see the rest?"

Cold with foreboding, Kristy did not know how to answer. Then she reminded herself that whatever she might discover, it had already happened in the past. Her past, hidden from her all these years.

"I have to see it all."

Again she caught the shimmer of silver across the mirror's opaque surface. Again the gleam of the star, sinking deep into the darkness. . . .

She saw an altar draped in red. On one side stood an iron incense burner; on the other, a tall red candle in an iron holder. A circle of worshippers in scarlet robes swayed back and forth, chanting.

And standing inside the circle, towering above the rest, a big, bearded man with deep-set black eyes. A man with the horns of a goat.

His huge hands, covered with thick, dark hair, were reaching for a little girl in a white shift. The child writhed and screamed in terror. From somewhere in the darkness came the shrill sound of a pipe, the beating of a drum.

The Horned Man was lifting her onto the altar. Bodies, gleaming with sweat and scented oil, swayed and writhed in a kind of dance. They moved around the altar, faster and faster. . . .

Diana Haviland

The frenzied dancers closed in around the altar. Hands were reaching for her, tearing at her shift, raking her flesh. The heavy smells of incense, oil, sweat—choking her. . . .

"Let her go!"

The little girl heard her mother cry out. She saw her mother spring out of the circle and get between her and the Horned Man. She quenched the flame with her hand, then knocked the candle and its holder to the ground, plunging the altar, the celebrants, into darkness.

Her mother was lifting her from the altar, carrying her away into the night. Hiding with her in a ditch beside the road, holding her tightly, while the crowd searched for them. Torches glowed in the night. Footsteps crackled through the dried leaves, close by.

Don't cry, Kristy . . . don't make a sound. They mustn't find us. We have to hide until they're gone. . . .

A jumble of images. She and her mother, traveling only by night. Sometimes on foot, with her mother carrying her. In the back of a big truck. Hiding from the light of day.

"My mother took me back to Hillsboro, didn't she? She left me in the dark, in front of Aunt Vera's house. I stood there and watched her running away. But I didn't cry. I didn't make a sound." Shattering grief swept through her, then numb desolation. "I never saw my mother again."

Her mother had loved her. Yet she'd run off and left her. How could she have done it?

Now she understood.

Kristy voice was low and unsteady. "She wanted the searchers to follow her. She was trying to draw them away from me. Did they—find her?"

Gwyneth spoke without a trace of emotion. "They found her."

Kristy drew a shaking breath. "And they killed her, didn't they?"

"She committed sacrilege. She broke her oath to the coven, and the master. She stole the offering from the altar."

276

"I was the—offering."

"They wanted to make use of your inborn gift. Belenos had already begun your initiation into the craft. But you never had the chance to discover the scope of your powers, to use them for the benefit of the coven. All because of your mother. Your foolish, frightened mother."

"You're wrong, Gwyneth. My mother was strong and brave. She saved me—she gave her life for me—"

She put up her hand. Her cheeks were wet with tears. Tears of love, tears of grief, for her mother. Now she was able to cry.

She set aside the mirror and got to her feet. "I want nothing to do with you or your coven. I don't need that kind of power."

But Gwyneth rose and stood confronting her. "Are you sure? Will you refuse us, even if it costs Jared Ramsey his life?"

Jared wouldn't want her to save him, not that way. But she couldn't let him go to his death, could she, if she had the power to set him free?

Gwyneth watched as if amused by Kristy's inward struggle. Then she said, "You will come to the cliff north of Glenrowan. We will wait for you there at moonrise, in the circle of standing stones."

She crossed the room, opened the chamber door, and started down the hall. The fog swirled up, closing around her, hiding her from view.

Kristy shut the door and returned to the hearth, where she stood staring into the fire. She wouldn't go to the Beltane Sabbat tonight. She would stay here in this room until the night was over. Then she'd slip away before Morag or her uncle could see her.

And what then? Where would she go—what would she do—without Jared?

She had tried to find a way to set him free, and she had failed. There was only one way to get him out of the fortress.

If she went to the Sabbat tonight, if she took part in the ceremony, the coven master would initiate her into the mysteries of witchcraft. She, like Gwyneth, would be a witch of the left-hand path.

Jared would never have to know what she'd done to save him. That would be her secret.

But he would question her. He'd keep on questioning her. She had never lied to him before. How long could she hope to keep the truth from him?

After he knew what she'd done, he'd never want to touch her, to look at her again. He'd leave her alone, to spend the rest of her life as an exile in this alien time.

She shut her eyes, but frightening images filled her mind. If he didn't break under questioning, if he didn't betray the other Royalist conspirators, Lord Fairfax would still order him to be executed. *Only one punishment for treason.* Dermot had said that. Unless she intervened, and quickly, Jared would die. Was it worth losing his love to save his life?

Before the moon rose over the circle of stones, out on the cliff, she would have to get to the coven, to take her place at the altar. She would have to give herself to the coven master, to obey his every command. She fought down the revulsion that threatened to overwhelm her.

She had to leave now, before she had time to reconsider. Quickly she moved past the hearth, where Gwyneth's fire was burning away. Down the steps she went, and out the front door of the inn.

She paused a moment, to glance at the leafless branches of the rowan tree, the white blossoms scattered on the ground. She had done that. How much more could she do, once she'd been initiated into the coven?

She pulled her blue cape around her and felt the weight of the mirror inside it.

In the darkness, she moved along High Street. Once she had left the outskirts of Glenrowan, she stood looking about her. Which way was north?

Far off in the distance, she caught the glow of a fire. Then another. And a third. The Beltane fires, blazing in the darkness, to guide the witches. By the time the fires had burned out and dawn rose over the moors, she, too, would be one of the coven.

Kristy crouched behind the outcropping of rocks close to the edge of the cliff. Her eyes were fixed on the three fires that had guided her. Then her gaze shifted, as the first of the dark figures appeared in the firelight. They had made the journey from every part of Yorkshire, to gather here for the Beltane Sabbat.

One by one, they thrust their torches into the fires, then held them aloft. She pressed her fist to her lips to stifle a cry of recognition, for these were the creatures she had seen in her dream.

Only now they as real as the salt-scented wind that blew in from the sea, or the waves surging against the base of the cliff. They were men and women, young and old, but their faces were completely hooded by their animal masks: a wolf, a weasel, a goat, a tusked boar. Their ankle-length tunics fluttered in the wind; some carried bundles or baskets.

Her insides tightened as she caught sight of the high stone slab that would serve as the altar. The members of the coven were entering the circle of standing stones.

She tried to crouch down lower still. Yet even as she did so, she asked herself why she should try to hide—to put off the inevitable confrontation? If she wanted to save Jared, she would have to show herself soon enough. She would violate her deepest instincts, to join them and take her part in their obscene rites. What would they expect of her?

They would join together to draw on her power. . . .

Her power.

That was what they wanted, Gwyneth and the others. But Gwyneth had told her it was an inborn gift. Suppose, even now, it was greater than she dared imagine?

They began laying out their tools—a sword, a cauldron, an iron brazier to hold the incense. No matter how great the force within her, she had not yet been trained to use it.

But no one had taught her to use the mirror. It had carried her back across the gulf of time, and had brought her to Jared.

A tremor shot through her, shaking her to the depths of her being. Her hands were trembling so that she could scarcely reach inside her cape. They were still unsteady when she opened the bag and drew out the mirror.

Gradually, she felt the tremors disappear. They gave way to a deep inner stillness, a clarity of mind such as she had never known before. She closed her fingers around the handle and held the dark oval upward to the light of the rising moon.

"Jared." Her lips shaped his name. And the great stone fortress where he was held prisoner began to take shape in the oval. She could make out the wide stone parapet, the great gates, the courtyard beyond. She concentrated on the vision before her. And summoned up all the love within her. "Jared, I need you. Come to me now."

Jared lay face down on the straw, his body throbbing, his face cut and streaked with dried blood. Twice he had been taken from his cell and brought before Lord Fairfax for questioning. At the orders of his lordship, the troopers had tried to force him to reveal the names of the other Royalist conspirators. Twice, he had endured their relentless brutality, and had remained silent. Today they'd left him alone in his cell.

But Lord Fairfax would question him again. He couldn't deceive himself—he knew that he, like every man—had a limit to his endurance. And even if he didn't break, if he kept silent to the end, what then?

The gallows, or the headsman's axe.

He closed his eyes and tried to fix his thoughts on Kristy. He remembered his last glimpse of her; she'd been running across the beach, her blue cape flaring out behind her.

Surely by now she had been forced to accept the truth—

that he wasn't coming back to her. She would have to do what she could to save herself. That meant getting as far from Whitby as possible. With Dermot gone, she had only one friend to turn to. Maybe she already was on her way north to the Border.

He didn't like the thought of her making such a journey alone. He could only trust that, in the time she'd traveled with him, she'd learned to be wary, to curb her impulsive nature. If a merchant offered her a place in his coach, or a farmer opened his house to her for a night, he could only hope she'd consider carefully before accepting.

Once she reached Lachlan Hall, she'd be safe. Lord Fairfax would never learn of Sir Andrew's part in the conspiracy. Not from him.

Forget Fairfax. Think about Kristy.

He shifted his aching body on the straw. The cell was quiet, except for the dripping of water somewhere overhead. Sweet Jesú, he was thirsty. His lips were cracked, his throat parched.

Kristy. Think about Kristy. Firm round breasts, softly curving hips, long, shapely legs. Her body entwined with his on the wolfskin rug in his chamber at Lachlan Hall. Kristy, in that outrageous costume she'd worn when he'd first seen her. Dark red breeches and jacket, like a man's. But no one could have mistaken her for a man, not for one moment.

His body tensed. He opened his eyes and raised himself on one arm. That sound. What was it? Not the dripping water, or the scuttling of a rat across the floor, not the thudding of the guard's booted feet along the stone corridor.

A grating noise from the direction of the heavy door. He was on his feet, staring at the metal oblong. It had begun to vibrate, only a little at first, then harder. Something was shaking the door, It shook in its frame, as if it were being attacked from the outside with a battering ram.

Had his men escaped from their cell? Not likely. And even if one of them had managed to steal a key from an unwary guard, if he'd let himself and the others out, they would have been stopped long before they could get hold of a musket or pike, let alone a battering ram.

He heard a sound like the crash of thunder. A screech of metal hinges. He barely managed to leap aside before the door fell inward. He stared into the empty, dimly lit corridor. Who had smashed in the door? What was happening here?

He heard a shout, then a volley of oaths. Heavy footsteps came pounding along the corridor. But the trooper who confronted him was thrown off guard; he stopped and stared in disbelief at the wreckage of the cell door. Before he had time to recover himself and call out for reinforcements, Jared smashed his fist into the trooper's jaw. The man toppled to the ground.

Jared bent down, took off the trooper's belt, and fastened it around his own waist. He drew the sword and held the point to the man's throat. "Where are my men?"

"The cell—up those stairs—end of the passage—" He silenced the man by knocking him unconscious with the sword's hilt.

He tore off the man's cloak and threw it around his shoulders. He'd attract less attention that way. Now he heard other troopers racing along the corridor. But he'd already started off for the cell that held the other smugglers.

As he ran, sword in hand, the trooper's cloak covering his own torn clothes, he thought he heard Kristy's voice. Her words echoed inside his head. "Jared—come to me."

Chapter Nineteen

Kristy caught a glimpse of Jared running down a dimly lit stone corridor, sword in hand. Even as she watched, his image began to waver; ripples spread over the surface of the mirror. It was starting to go dark.

Jared, come to me.

The oval went black.

No! It was too soon.

She'd only begun to explore her powers. She sensed that they were far greater than she had dared to hope. But she needed more time. Although she had destroyed the door and freed him from the confines of his cell, he was still locked inside the fortress.

With a muffled cry, she gazed at the black oval. Jared would have to do the rest. Unwilling to give way to despair, she tried to reassure herself. He was strong and resilient, a battle-hardened soldier. If any man could find a way to escape from Ashford, he could.

Trembling with exhaustion, she sank back against the trunk

of an oak. Its rough, twisted branches leaned out toward the edge of the cliff. A few of its gnarled roots rose above the ground to form deep hollows where the soil had been washed away. Her efforts had left her drained, but she couldn't give way. Not yet. She drew a deep breath, filling her lungs with the sea air.

The mirror. She couldn't leave it lying here in plain sight, yet she dared not take it with her. She put it back in its velvet bag, then tied the strings. Quickly, she looked about the moonlit clearing, then pushed the bag into the hollow under one of the thickest roots of the oak tree.

Jared, come to me. . . .

Her own words. But she knew that if he got out of the fortress—when he got out—he must not find her here at the Sabbat. She got to her feet, then walked out from behind the rocky ledge, her head held high, her hair tossed by the sea wind.

Step by step, she moved toward the circle of standing stones, where the masked worshippers were assembling. They thrust their torches into the fire, then held them aloft. She could see more of them hurrying across the moor, guided by the light of the fires, the flaming torches. From the darkness beyond the circle, she caught the slow, rhythmic beating of drums, the faint, eerie music of reed pipes.

Kristy moved through the space between two stones, then paused to look about her. She caught sight of a figure in a crimson robe, belted with a silver sash. Gwyneth, the High Priestess. From slits in her fox mask, her silver eyes gleamed. Gwyneth, a vixen with pointed ears and a sharp muzzle of sleek black fur.

The High Priestess took her place at the foot of the altar and began to set out a collection of pots and flasks; she arranged them in an elaborate pattern, naming their contents as she did so. "Loosestrife and laurel . . . moonwort and rue . . . vervain and yarrow. . . ."

A man whose features were hidden by a mask shaped like

the head of a bull rested his hand on the hilt of the ritual sword. "Here I place the athame, symbol of power," he said. Then he set down a whip with short, leather thongs. "Here I place the scourge, symbol of submission."

A woman with pendulous breasts, her own head concealed by that of a sow, tossed incense into the brazier. Its scent drifted on the night air, heavy and cloying. "Mullein and musk, to stir the senses—" She broke off as she caught sight of Kristy.

"Look at her—she wears no mask."

The others stopped to stare at Kristy. Grotesque animal heads fixed glittering eyes on her.

"A stranger—an intruder—"

"She comes among us with no mask—"

"No mask—"

"Seize her—"

Kristy forced aside her fear, and kept walking toward the altar. Then Gwyneth turned and spoke. "Let her pass. She is the chosen one."

As they moved aside to make way for her, she caught their words.

"The master does her great honor—"

"See how fair she is—the master will be pleased with her."

Revulsion surged up inside her. But there was no way they could force her to submit to their "master," not now. She had no need of his help.

She stopped at the foot of the stone altar and confronted Gwyneth. From beneath the mask of the vixen, came the soft, mocking voice of the High Priestess. "So you've conquered your foolish scruples, as I knew you would. Your need to save your lover is greater than your hatred for us. You know you can do nothing without our help and you've come here to plead for—"

"Wrong, Gwyneth!" Kristy's voice rang out, strong and

confident. "I've come to tell you I don't need you or these others."

"You arrogant fool! The master has commanded your presence—"

"As for your master, he can find another 'chosen one.' I came only for Jared's sake. But he is already free and on his way to me."

"Are you sure?" Kristy caught the cruel mockery in the woman's voice, and the underlying threat.

"He'll escape from the fortress. He'll come for me. And I'll be waiting for him."

"You want him to find you here with us?"

Kristy confidence began to waver. If he found her here, he surely would know what unnatural means she'd used to save him. He loathed the witches of the left-hand path.

But she would make him see that there'd been no other way. She would convince him that she had exhausted all the natural means, that she'd been forced to call on her powers of witchcraft to save his life.

Jared loved her. Surely he would understand and forgive.

The silver eyes gleamed with unholy laughter. "You're afraid to have him discover you here at our Sabbat, aren't you?"

"I won't be here. I'll wait for Jared at the Rowan Tree— in the upstairs chamber where we first met." She turned to leave the circle but Gwyneth blocked her way.

"Let me pass."

A hoarse cry went up from the worshippers. It echoed through the firelit circle. They crowded forward. At first she thought they were trying to stop her from leaving. Then she realized they were no longer looking at her.

"He is here . . . he is with us. . . ."

The masked heads turned; the eyes were rapt with adoration. What were they staring at with such awe?

"He walks among us." One spoke the words and the others

echoed them. "He walks among us. . . ." Kristy willed herself not to be caught up in the mass frenzy.

A huge figure stepped into the firelight. A man's voice, deep and commanding, rang through the circle. "Silence, all. Your master is with you."

The worshippers fell silent, their heads thrown back, their arms raised. The drumming stopped, the music of the reed pipes faded away. Kristy heard only the sighing of night wind, the surge of the sea from the beach below the cliff. And the hammering of her heart against her chest.

From the far side of the circle, he came forward to the altar. Kristy could not take her gaze away. She, like the rest, was awed by his commanding presence.

No! You're not one of them, Kristy! You know he's only a man!

A man—but not like other men. He was the living embodiment of a pagan deity, worshipped in different guises and under different names. In ancient Greece and Rome, there'd been Pan and Dionysus. And here too, in Britain and Scotland, Wales and Ireland: Arawn—Cernunnos—Herne the Hunter. They'd been venerated since the Celts and the Druids first had gathered in the forests and on the moors.

The coven master was a deity of nature with the head of a stag and its great, many-branched horns. The firelight played over his powerful body. His massive chest was bare except for its mat of thick, coarse hair. His long legs were sheathed in dark leather breeches and black fur boots fastened with leather thongs. He radiated an aura of crude animal power.

The coven master.

Move, Kristy! Don't stand here, staring like the rest of them.

She must back off slowly, lose herself in the crowd, then disappear into the night. Somehow, she'd find her way across the moors, back to Glenrowan.

But he was looking straight at her. It was already too late.

"Bring her to me."

Hands grasped her arms, her shoulders. She struggled, she fought them with all her strength. . . . A man's arm went around her chest, cutting off her breath. Her heart pounded until she thought it would burst. Her head began to spin and she slumped forward. Her physical powers were no match for theirs. But she wouldn't surrender herself to the hysteria that moved the coven like a tangible force. She would not allow herself to be caught up in their mindless frenzy.

"Let me go!"

"Go?" The coven master's dark gaze locked on hers. "And where will you go? To Jared Ramsey? You have no need of him. I will take you tonight. By the time the Beltane fires burn themselves out, you will have forgotten your mortal lover."

The crowd closed in around her again. The smell of their sweat, their musky, heated flesh sickened her. Now their hands tore at her cape, her gown. Stripped to her shift, she was lifted onto the altar.

"Prepare her," the coven master commanded.

The terror that seized her was like none she'd known since that night long ago. The night of Samhain. A little girl in a white tunic. . . .

But she was no longer a helpless child. She was a woman. Jared's woman.

She tensed her muscles, then started to fight them off with mindless fury, her screams tearing from her throat. She punched and clawed and kicked. She bent one knee, drew up her leg, then thrust it out, ramming her foot into a soft belly. From under the mask of a sow came a woman's squeal of pain.

"She must be punished," Gwyneth's voice called out. "Use the scourge on her."

"No!" The voice of the coven master. "I will not have her flesh marred. I will enjoy the touch her silken skin, its smooth perfection."

"May we bind her, master?"

"That you may do."

Someone seized her arms and pulled them above her head. Pain tore at her shoulders. Another worshipper gripped her legs, forcing them apart. She heard the harsh grating of metal on stone. Rough iron bands closed around her wrists, her ankles. The stone slab was icy cold against her skin. A shiver ran through her, then another. Her whole body began to shake.

"Here are the oils," she heard a woman's voice saying. "To heat her loins . . . to stir her senses . . . to make her ready to receive the master. . . ."

Hands were pushing up her shift; moving underneath it, stroking; rubbing warm heavy-scented oil up along calves, her inner thighs, her belly, her breasts. Others lifting her hips from the stone, kneading the oil into her buttocks. . . . Violating the most intimate places of her body.

Noooo!

"She is ready, master."

She turned her head and saw that the worshippers had formed themselves into three concentric circles. They began to dance around the altar, slowly at first, then faster and faster, spinning, whirling, crying out in their rising frenzy.

The coven master strode to the stone altar. He leaned over her. She pulled against the chains, but they held her fast. The iron bands scraped her wrist and ankles. And now . . . the huge body kneeling over hers, the hairy hands, touching her, sliding over her oiled flesh.

She willed herself to faint. If she lost consciousness, she would be spared the ultimate shame . . . the degradation of her spirit.

She closed her eyes and tried to go limp, insensate, but it was useless. His hairy hands were bruising her breasts and a deep, rumbling laugh welled from his throat. "You won't escape me that way. You will receive me willingly. I will fill you with my power. You will share every moment of ecstasy with me."

She fought for breath—and gagged as she drew in the odors of male sweat, leather, and heavy-scented oils. The chanting of the worshippers beat at her brain. The pounding drums, the squealing pipes seemed to possess every atom of her being.

Then silence. An instant when the night went utterly still.

From the darkness, a voice called her name.

Jared's voice.

She turned her head and she saw him, coming through a space between the stones, his men crowding in after him. His green eyes blazed with a killing rage. Swiftly, he covered the distance between the stones and the altar. He encircled the stag-horned head with his arm, and jerked it back. The master gave a roar of pain. Jared's grip tightened. The master slumped forward across her body.

His weight was crushing her, driving the breath from her lungs. Had Jared strangled him?

But an instant after, the master raised himself and broke free. He rolled off her body, leaped from the altar, and landed on his feet facing Jared.

She saw Jared draw back his arm and smash his fist into the masked face. His opponent swayed, but remained standing. Then he struck back, catching Jared on the side of the head. Jared was thrown against the altar. He braced himself on the stone slab, lunged forward, and seized the master by the throat. As the master struggled to free himself, the stag mask twisted and was pushed aside.

Jared's eyes widened with recognition. He gave a harsh, wordless cry, as he reached out and ripped the mask, hood, horns and all, from the master's head.

She heard the uproar from beyond the stone circle.

"That's Fairfax—the bloody bastard!"

"It's him!" another man yelled. "Puritan hypocrite!"

"Fairfax—the witch master!"

"Cromwell will have him drawn an' quartered!"

These were not the voices of the coven. Raising herself as

far as her chains would allow, she caught sight of Jared's men, surging forward.

Then out of the corner of her eye, she saw a swift movement close by. Fairfax reached for the athame—the ceremonial sword that lay across the foot of the altar.

"Jared—watch out!" she cried.

But Jared had already whipped his sword from its scabbard. He cast aside his cloak. In the firelight, the two men faced off. Steel rang on steel. Fairfax was the heavier of the two, but Jared's body was lean and hard; he moved with the swiftness of a jungle cat. Although she knew nothing of dueling, she sensed they were evenly matched.

The smugglers drove back the members of the coven. Some were already tearing off their masks, tossing them aside. Kristy kept her eyes fixed on Jared and Fairfax.

Jared thrust, and slashed Fairfax across his naked chest. A thin line of blood welled up.

"The master is wounded."

"He bleeds—like any man."

The coven members began muttering to one another.

But the master paid them no heed. He thrust and Jared deflected his blade. He thrust again. Jared parried and retreated a step. Fairfax lunged and caught Jared on the shoulder. Kristy stifled a cry of fear. Fairfax lunged again. Step by step, Fairfax was forcing Jared back.

Now Jared was trapped against one of the standing stones. Fairfax lunged forward, his arm extended to its longest reach, his weight resting on his right leg.

With one swift movement, Jared dodged aside, leaped backward through a space between two of the stones. Fairfax tried to shift his weight, to thrust again, but it was too late. Before he could regain his balance, Jared's sword darted out through the open space. He plunged the blade deep into Fairfax's massive chest.

But Fairfax still stood erect. For an instant, Kristy felt a surge of fear. Was it possible the coven master had taken on the powers of a pagan god—that he could not be killed by any mortal man?

Then she saw him sway and stagger back. He clutched at one of the stones. Slowly his hand slid down the side of the stone. He fell backward, his massive body crashing to the ground. The full moon overhead bathed his face with a white radiance. His body contracted in a brief spasm, then lay still. Jared bent and grasped the hilt of the sword, and she flinched. She knew he'd need a weapon with which to defend himself but even so—she averted her eyes.

The coven members, stunned by the death of their leader, ran in all directions—away from the firelight, into the sheltering darkness of the moor.

Jared came to her side now. His shirt was torn but his shoulder was not wounded as seriously as first she'd feared. He leaned over her, his green eyes searching hers. Would he think that she had taken part in the ceremony willingly? If he did, she feared that no words of hers would change his mind.

He unfastened the iron bands from her wrists and ankles. He spoke softly, his voice filled with wonder. "I heard you calling me, back in the fortress. You set me free. You shattered the cell door. But how?"

"I have powers. A witch's powers. I never wanted them. I didn't know I had them, or why—not until tonight, when the mirror showed me my past. Those years I couldn't remember—they were there, in the mirror—"

"Be still, love," he said softly. He lifted her from the altar and cradled her against him. He wrapped the cloak around her.

His men had begun milling about the circle. One kicked over the brazier and the air thickened with the heavy smell of incense. Another swept the vials of oil from the altar and sent them crashing to the ground.

"Master Ramsey," one of them called. "We can't stay here. Where do we go now?"

"Those troopers are searching the countryside," another shouted. "We'd best head for the coast."

"We'll find us a ship."

But he did not answer; he did not even look at them. His eyes were fixed on Kristy's upturned face. He walked away from the altar, holding her tightly. She reached up and put her arms around his neck. He carried her through a space between two standing stones, and kept going until he reached the clearing beyond the outcropping of jagged rocks.

At the foot of the oak, he lowered himself to the ground. He held her against him, and stroked her hair.

"The dark mirror," he said. "The witch's mirror. You used it to set me free."

"It was the only way. But I promise you—I'll never use it again."

He put his hand over her lips. "Don't promise me that, Kristy."

"But I don't need those powers—not any longer. I don't want them. I never did."

"You still can use the mirror if you wish."

"I think so. But why—"

He cupped her face in his hands and looked down at her as if he were trying to memorize her features. "Use the mirror once more." She heard the driving urgency in his voice. And she heard the sorrow, too. "Use it to carry you to your own time."

"You're sending me away? She searched his eyes. "But you love me—I know you do."

His green eyes locked with hers. "It's because I love you that I want you to go."

She looked up at him, shaken and bewildered.

"I'm a wanted man. The troopers from Ashford are out hunting for me and my men right now."

"Then we'll head for Whitby together—or Robin Hood's Bay. We'll cross the sea—"

"Not this time. Kristy, I'm not only a smuggler now—I'm

a traitor. Cromwell won't rest until I'm captured.''

"I won't leave you!"

He shook his head. ''Back at Lachlan Hall, I let you persuade me to take you along, when every instinct told me I shouldn't. I won't let that happen again.'' His voice was quiet, but implacable. ''I'll have to run and keep on running, hiding. Maybe I'll get across the sea, maybe not. But I won't let you share the danger. You weren't meant to live as a homeless fugitive—hunted like an animal.''

"Haven't I the right to make that choice for myself?"

''Not this time. I'll love you as long as I live. That's why I want you to return to your own time.''

"How can you be sure it's possible?"

"You got me out of Ashford," he reminded her.

"But that was different! I don't know if I can—"

He pulled her close and his mouth covered hers, silencing her. She clung to him with all her strength. Her body molded itself to his. Her hands stroked his hair, his neck, his shoulders. So brief a moment of shared ecstasy, out of the limitless sweep of time. . . .

Then he drew away. ''If you love me, you'll do as I ask. Do it now, Kristy. Return to your own time.''

But even as he spoke, she knew she couldn't leave him. Her mind moved swiftly, seeking another way.

There had to be another way.

Hope stirred inside her. She turned and reached her hand into the hollow under the root of the gnarled oak. She took out the velvet bag.

"You'll do it then?"

"Only if we go together."

"But how? This is my time—the future is yours."

The words came to her, out of the depths of her spirit. ''To those who love as we do, time has no meaning. Our love is stronger than time. Believe that, Jared. Believe it, with all your heart, as I do.''

She undid the strings, took out the mirror, and set it on the ground in front of them. She drew closer to him.

"Take my hands in yours. Hold them tight. Don't let go. Whatever happens, don't let go. And don't take your eyes from the mirror."

He took her hands. "Kristy, I—"

"Don't speak. Don't look at me. Look into the mirror."

The oval was dark, motionless.

She did not speak. She did not move. All the forces within her were centered on the oval of blackness.

There was a movement so slight she could not be sure she was seeing it. A ripple . . . then another. And now the oval, no longer dark, showed her the reflection of her face, her amber eyes wide, her lips parted.

Where was Jared's reflection? The mirror already was drawing her into its depths. . . . She couldn't see his face, only her own.

And then she caught the first indistinct glimpse of his features—faint and wavering. But she was whirling down a tunnel of mist—a tunnel with no beginning and no end. Beyond the reach of time and space. And she was alone.

Not without you. I won't go without you.

With all her inborn powers, she fought the pull of the mirror, willing herself not to be taken away without him. . . .

From the far end of the tunnel, she heard the sound of shrill laughter. Gwyneth's laughter.

She saw Gwyneth, small and far away—growing smaller now—a tiny figure of crimson and silver. But still visible. Gwyneth was reaching for the mirror, smashing it against the tree trunk, holding it high above her head, then casting it over the edge of the cliff.

Jared!

The pull down into the tunnel . . . it was stronger now . . . far too strong for her powers—for any human powers to resist. . . .

Jared!

She whirled faster and faster. The darkness claimed her.

Chapter Twenty

When Kristy opened her eyes, she saw the night sky above her. Slowly she turned her head and stretched out her hand. Her fingers brushed against a rough, hard surface. In the light of the full moon she could see the jagged stump of a tree, all that was left of the twisted oak that had been growing there only a few moments ago. It had been a living tree then, its trunk stretching out over the side of the cliff, its budding branches swaying in the wind. She had hidden the mirror in the hollow under one of its roots.

Fear shot through her, a fear deeper, more agonizing, than she'd ever known before.

"Jared?" She called his name, softly at first. Then with growing urgency.

"Jared!"

But she heard only the sea wind, and the waves breaking against the rocks below. "Jared, where are you?"

And still he did not answer.

Now she caught another sound, mingled with the moaning

of the wind, and the timeless rhythm of the waves against the shore, a sound she had not heard for so long that she did not immediately recognize it.

She raised herself on one arm, and tilted her head to listen more closely. It sounded like muffled, far-off thunder.

She got to her feet, steadied herself against the jagged tree stump, then moved closer to the edge of the cliff and looked down. Her breath caught in her throat, as she stared down at the pinpoints of light moving at incredible speed. Her legs started to tremble. She was seeing the headlights of cars and trucks, traveling along a highway that hadn't been down there, only a few moments ago.

Not moments—centuries.

A highway like that could only have been built in her own time. Her gaze moved beyond the highway to the night sea, where other lights burned bright and steady: the lights from the fishing boats.

Her fingers pressed hard against her forehead, as she tried to sort out her chaotic thoughts.

She had done it.

She had awakened the uncanny forces hidden beneath the dark oval of the scrying mirror. Drawing on all the power within her, she had bent those forces to her will. She had returned to her own century.

But where was Jared?

Again she called his name. He would hear her, and answer. Any minute now, his voice would ring out, over the sound of the wind, the waves, and the roar of the highway. Hands clenched, fingernails digging into her palms, she waited.

Slowly the frightening suspicion began to stir; it forced its way into her consciousness. She had made the journey forward through time—but maybe she had not been able to bring Jared with her. Maybe he had remained behind in his own century.

She turned away from the edge of the cliff. She could not keep on looking at those fast-moving lights, not now; they only confirmed what she had already guessed.

The full moon was lower in the sky; it was moving toward the horizon. By its frosty light, she could make out the grotesque shapes of the standing stones; they jutted up around the slab that had served as an altar for the coven.

Centuries had gone by, generations had come and gone, wars had devastated the land; and still the stones remained. Only now they were relics of a primitive, superstitious age, curiosities to be pointed out to groups of tourists, she supposed. Did a tour bus stop here, so that a guide might tell the visitors how this stone circle had been used for the witches' Sabbats?

The icy wind blew in from the sea. It tore at her cloak, whipping it open, sending a shiver through her body. She looked down and saw that her feet and legs were bare.

The coven had torn off her gown, her petticoat, her shoes and stockings. She had traveled forward in time, clad only in the thin shift she'd worn when they had forced her onto the altar. And the cape Jared had put around her later, when he'd lifted her, held her close against his chest, and carried her away from the circle of stones. His arms had been strong, protective. . . .

No! She mustn't let herself think about Jared, not yet. Later she would have to come to terms with the truth. But how long would it take before she could face the emptiness of a life without him?

She stood still a moment more—her bare feet pressed against the damp ground, her hair tossed by the wind, her body weighed down by the heavy cloak that had belonged to one of Cromwell's troopers.

She heard the distant roar of a plane's engine, high overhead. Looking up, she saw its wing lights moving across the night sky. Was it heading for the airport in Manchester or London? Or maybe it was bound for New York. Her home.

But her mind rebelled at the thought. Her home—the only real home she'd ever known—had been with Jared. Without him, the years ahead would be lonely, meaningless. How would she be able to go through the motions of living, now that he was gone?

She set her jaw and squared her shoulders. Jared had loved her for her courage, the hard core of strength inside her. He would not want her to give way like this.

She had returned to her own world alone, but she must not linger here, helpless with grief. Later, there would come a time for tears. Now she had to keep her emotions in check, to do what must be done. First, she would set out for the nearest village—Glenrowan.

Resolutely, she turned away from the circle of stones, and started walking across the dark sweep of the moors. There were no Beltane fires to guide her now—only the cold, white moonlight. Her ankles were sore; the rough iron bands had bruised them. Stones and brambles tore at the soles of her bare feet; she bit down on her lower lip and forced herself to ignore her physical distress. But it was not so easy to ignore the other, infinitely deeper pain that lay just beneath the surface of her consciousness.

As she walked on, a merciful numbness gradually enveloped her mind. It shielded her as she moved through the shadows of the night.

Little by little, she found that she was able to concentrate on lesser details. What would she find when she reached Glenrowan? She had disappeared from the village on a night in March—nearly two months ago. She'd left her rented car behind, and her luggage. Even her handbag. Mrs. Ainsworth certainly would have reported her disappearance. The executives from Marisol would have made inquiries.

When she returned to the Rowan Tree, the local constable would want to know where she had been all this time. He would be courteous, no doubt; but he would insist on an explanation.

How could she explain? She couldn't tell them the truth; if she did, they would never believe her. If she tried to convince them that she'd gone back in time, if she started babbling about scrying mirrors and witches' Sabbats, they'd be sure they were dealing with a mental case. She'd be sent off to the nearest hospital. The British authorities would send a message to the American Consulate. And someone—Liz, maybe, or a representative of Marisol—would come and take her back to New York. And there she'd be put into another hospital.

But she wouldn't let any of that happen. Her mind began to move, slowly at first, then faster. She would make up a plausible explanation for her disappearance. She'd tell the police she'd fallen asleep behind the wheel. Highway hypnosis, wasn't that what they called it? She'd dozed off only for a minute, but that had been long enough to lose control of the wheel and swerve off the road, to smash up her rented car. She'd felt all right when she'd arrived at the Rowan Tree, but later that same evening she'd started feeling dizzy. And then she'd blacked out. She must have suffered a loss of memory.

But it wouldn't be easy to convince the police of her sanity if they saw her roaming around barefoot, in nothing but a torn shift and a cloak.

All right, she'd find a way to get into the Rowan Tree without being seen. She'd get herself cleaned up. But where would she find a change of clothes? That last point worried her, but she knew she could deal with it. Maybe one of the American tourists Morag had spoken of had left a pair of jeans and a t-shirt behind. And sneakers? She'd have to get hold of them, too.

If she were suitably dressed, if she spoke calmly, the police would believe her. She held a responsible position with Marisol. Surely her connection with a well-known American corporation would add to her credibility. The garage mechanic would have a record of the damages to the rented Toyota, and the date it had been towed in. Mrs. Ainsworth would show them her signature on the desk register.

Temporary loss of memory. Post-traumatic stress syndrome. The police would have to accept that.

The moon had set when she reached the outskirts of Glenrowan. Although she'd stopped along the way to tear strips of cloth from her shift and wrap them around her feet, her soles were throbbing. But she couldn't rest, not yet.

In the grey light of dawn, High Street was deserted. The windows of the small shops were dark. The only light came from a neon sign in front of the garage.

The blacksmith's shop, the wheelwright's shop were gone. What else had she expected? They'd been gone for centuries.

Don't think about it. Don't think about anything except the demands of the moment. She had to keep out of sight. She didn't want some early riser to stop her and ask questions, before she was ready to face the police.

Moving in the shadows, she reached the top of the street, where the Rowan Tree stood out dark against the pale grey sky. It looked exactly as it had the day of her accident. Why not? That had been only two months ago.

She prowled around the square stone building, looking for a way to get in without being seen. At the rear of the building, she found an unlocked window. Slowly, inch by inch, she raised it high enough so she could get over the sill. Once inside, she stopped. It wouldn't be smart to start looking for a light switch; she might crash into a piece of furniture and wake somebody.

Her eyes adjusted to the darkness. She caught the gleam of polished pots and pans on a wall rack. A wooden table and a big six-burner, double-oven gas stove.

Wincing with each step, she gritted her teeth and moved on. Through the kitchen, into the back hallway, then up the stairs to her room.

But it wasn't her room, not after all these weeks. She could only hope nobody else taken it for the night.

She reached the top of the stairs. Her room—the one she'd

301

rented that day in March—had been second from the front landing. Carefully, she turned the knob. Thank heaven, the door wasn't locked; she pushed it open and stepped inside. By the pale light of dawn, she saw that the bed—not the huge canopied bed, but the other one with the polished maple headboard—had not been slept in. The old-fashioned white chenille spread lay smoothly across it. She breathed a deep sigh of relief.

She found the light switch near the door, and blinked at the sudden glare from the fixture overhead. A brief smile touched her lips. She had become accustomed to the softness of candlelight. Electric lighting would take some getting used to.

She took off the heavy cloak and tossed it over the nearest chair. Then she went to the bed, pulled back the spread, and sank down on the edge. The flowered comforter, the plump pillows, looked inviting. Sleep. She needed sleep. But something caught her eye—something that didn't belong here.

Her suitcase, standing at the foot of the bed. And there on the nightstand lay her handbag.

Why hadn't Mrs. Ainsworth put them away in a storage room? Or turned them over to the police?

She looked about the room. There by the window stood the round table where she and Morag had sat opposite one another on that March night, with the scrying mirror between them. She recognized the brass candleholders, too. All right, nothing strange about that. But the candles had burned down to the stubs. Surely after all this time, Mrs. Ainsworth would have replaced them.

Her suitcase, her handbag, had not been moved; but where was her carry-on?

It was back in the past. She shivered as she remembered leaving it behind in this room on Beltane Eve, when she'd set out for the Sabbat.

It wasn't hard to guess what had become of it. Master Prescott had found it, examined the contents, then had gotten rid of it. There had been gossip about his inn—a refuge for smugglers. And his niece's hysterial outburst about a witch in one of the chambers, would have put him at even greater risk. He wouldn't have wanted Cromwell's troopers to find any "witches' tools" on his premises.

When Kristy had set out for the Sabbat, she had carried only the mirror with her, in the pocket of her cape. The scrying mirror. She went cold at the memory. But there was no need to fear its power any longer. The ebony handle, the broken shards had lain scattered beneath the waves for all these years.

She didn't want to think about the mirror, the altar, the Sabbat. But she could no longer fight back those memories. Gwyneth, in crimson and silver. She had smashed the mirror to avenge herself on Kristy for destroying the power of the coven—and on Jared, who had killed her master. How better to take her revenge than by separating them from one another for all eternity?

Kristy tried to draw back from the pain that had lain dormant inside her. She couldn't face her loss, not yet. If she let herself think about Jared now, she wouldn't be able to bear it.

Never to see him again. Never to hear his voice, to feel the touch of his hands stroking her hair, caressing the curves and hollows of her body, until she burned with her need for him. Never to have him take her to the dizzying height of passion, to share the shattering ecstasy of their climax. Then to lie in his embrace, drowsy and fulfilled. . . .

She wrapped her arms around her body, seeking comfort, but instead, she felt a wave of revulsion. The torn shift, her skin, were saturated with those musky oils the witches had rubbed into every part of her. She had to cleanse herself, to get rid of this tangible reminder of her ordeal.

Although her fingers were unsteady, she found her keys in her handbag, opened her suitcase. She went through the carefully folded garments, took out her beige flannel robe, and laid it across the bed. She searched again, came upon her soft shearling slippers.

Swiftly, she crossed to the half-open bathroom door. The room wasn't as luxurious as the one in her hotel suite back in Manchester, but Mrs. Ainsworth had provided all the essentials: two paper-wrapped cakes of soap, clean towels and washcloths. She stripped off her torn shift and shoved it into the corner, Later she'd get rid of it.

She stepped into the spotless tile shower. Hot water streamed down over her upturned face, her body. She scrubbed herself as hard as she could, until her skin began redden. She went on scrubbing, rinsing. She had to get rid of every trace of oil from her body and her hair.

She dried herself, returned to the bedroom, and put on the robe and slippers. As she was fastening the belt around her waist, she heard a light tapping at the door and for a moment, her heart leaped with hope. *Jared? Please let it be Jared— somehow—*

"Good morning, Miss Sinclair." Morag's voice. Mrs. Ainsworth's Morag.

She opened the door. The girl wore a wool skirt, a freshly ironed cotton blouse. Her flaxen hair was short and straight. "I heard you moving about, and the shower running, and Mother said to ask what you wanted for breakfast."

She hesitated a moment. "About last night—" She avoided Kristy's eyes. "I'm sorry I bothered you—about reading my fortune. You won't tell my mother, will you?"

Last night! But that had happened nearly two months ago. Kristy's throat tightened so that she couldn't make a sound.

Morag must have mistaken her silence for cold refusal. "Please, Miss Sinclair. I never meant to upset you. Not after your accident and all. Mother said you needed a good night's sleep—and I was pestering you about that mirror. Why, what's the matter, miss?"

A good night's sleep. What was the girl talking about?

"Morag—" She forced the words past the tightness in her throat. "What's today's date?"

"Why it's Tuesday, miss."

"Yes, but what month is it?"

The girl stepped back and eyed Kristy a little warily. "March. The tenth of March."

It wasn't possible. From the hour she'd landed in England, she had followed the meticulous schedule laid out by her secretary. On the eighth, she'd completed her business in Manchester; on the ninth, she'd been on her way to Leeds. The ninth. The day of her accident.

But what about all those weeks she'd spent with Jared? Spring had come to the moors—new grass carpeting the hills and brookside banks, the buds opening on the branches of oaks and elms, the first translucent leaves. Then Beltane Eve—the last night of April. Yet here in her own time, only a single night had passed.

A single night in which she had found the only man she'd ever love—and had lost him.

The girl shifted awkwardly. "Mother sent me to ask what you want for breakfast. There's bacon and eggs. Or oatmeal with cream and sugar. We make our own blackberry jam. It's really good."

"I'm sure it is but—Morag, I don't want breakfast, not yet." She ignored the girl's curious stare. "Remember last night. After you brought the scrying mirror in from the garden and lit the candles. Tell me exactly what happened then."

"I said I was sorry—and I am, honestly. My mother doesn't like those kinds of goings-on. Please don't tell her."

Kristy forced a reassuring smile. "It'll be our secret. I give you my word. Now tell me everything you can remember."

"Let's see." Morag's pale brows drew together. "We sat there at the table, across from one another, looking into the mirror. I stared as hard as I could but I didn't see anything at all. And I don't think you did either—not at first. But then

305

you caught your breath. Real sharp, like. Your face got so strange. And your eyes—''

''What about my eyes?''

''I don't know how to say it. I guess my granny would have called it a fey look. Like you were seeing into a faraway place. It scared me. Then you cried out as if you were scared, too.'' She gave an embarrassed little smile. ''I felt—all shaky inside. I got up and ran out of the room.''

''And you didn't come back.''

''No, miss. I went straight to bed.''

Morag hadn't seen her fall to the floor. She hadn't left her lying unconscious. She'd already gone running off to bed.

''If you're sure you don't want breakfast, I can bring you a cup of tea.''

Kristy shook her head. ''No thank, Morag. I'm going back to bed. I need another couple of hours' sleep. I'll come down when I'm ready for breakfast.''

''Yes, Miss.'' The girl gave her a shy smile. ''It's real nice your not telling my mother about—you know.'' She started for the door. ''You sleep as late as you like. There's no other guests checked in yet—it'll be quiet.'' She closed the door behind her.

Kristy sank down on the bed and buried her face in the pillow. Now that she was alone, she could no longer keep her grief locked inside her. Hot tears came welling up and she did not try to stop them.

She had been so sure she and Jared could return together. That their love was strong enough to overcome the barriers of time and space.

Jared, come to me. I need you. I'll always need you. . . .

Even as her body shook with the force of her sobbing, she remembered the warmth of his strong hands holding tightly onto hers. If only she'd been given a few moments more. She had just begun to make out the first dim reflection of his face in the mirror: eyes, green and fathomless as the sea; eyes that could be glinting with irony, or hot and smoky with desire.

His angular cheekbones. His mouth a hard slash, but so warm and tender against hers.

She started at a faint, scraping sound not far from the bed. She choked back her tears, raised herself, and wiped her cheeks with her hand.

"Kristy."

She caught her breath. "Jared!" It was his voice. But that couldn't be. Her aching need had made her think she'd heard him call her name.

She wondered if that might keep on happening to her in the years to come. Maybe she'd hear a man's deep voice close behind her, and turn around quickly, thinking it was his. Or she might see a face in a crowd, on a New York street; her heart would lift—hope would stir inside her. But it wouldn't be his voice. His face.

"Kristy! How the hell do I get out of here?"

The baffled anger, the impatience. Jared. She got to her feet, her knees unsteady. She ran toward the direction from which the call had come: the closet near the bed. When she opened the door she saw a row of hangers and an empty shelf lined with flowered paper. What else had she expected? It had seemed so real, but only because her hungry heart had wanted it to be real.

She turned and started back to the bed. Drained of tears, at least for now, she would lie down and rest. Later she would dress; no problem, since she had her own suitcase. She'd put on makeup and go downstairs to face Mrs. Ainsworth and Morag. She closed her eyes and started to drift into sleep—

A loud, screeching noise, a crash of wood. A hand on her shoulder. "Kristy!"

Jared's voice, his breath against her cheek. Not an illusion. His touch was like no other. Her eyes flew open. His strong hands were raising her from the bed. His lips brushed the tears from her cheeks.

His shirt was torn and she saw the cut, livid against his

shoulder. He was real and he was here. Here in her own time. But what power had brought him to her?

Unable to deal with the deeper questions, her thoughts moved to the little, unimportant ones. His wide-sleeved shirt was tattered and streaked with grime. She'd get it off him and throw it away, along with her shift. But what about the rest of his clothes?

He still wore his doeskin breeches and high-topped leather boots. And around his lean waist, she saw the wide belt he'd taken from the trooper back at Ashford. The scabbard held the sword he'd used in the duel with Fairfax.

How was it possible that no one had seen him, stopped him, and questioned his appearance here in Glenrowan, dressed as he was? He stretched out on the bed beside her, and drew her into his arms. She held onto him with all her strength.

"I heard you calling, but I was afraid it was my imagination. How did you know I'd be here?"

"I wasn't sure you would be. I could only hope that since we'd met here, you might have come back."

"Someone could have seen you walking through the village."

"I went to St. Edmund's Abbey. I wasn't sure it would still be here. Not after all this time."

"I suppose it's been taken over by the National Trust."

"The what?"

She stroked his cheek. "I'll explain later."

"The trapdoor's still there. I came through the tunnel," he said. "But the other door, the one that opens into this room—it's in the wrong place." He looked about him. "The room's all wrong, too. What are you smiling about?"

"Don't you remember? I said that, the night you came in and found me here. And you thought I was lying. Now maybe you can understand how I felt."

"Sorry, love," he said. "But about that trapdoor in the closet—"

Obviously, he wanted to change the subject and she let him. "Whenever the inn was remodeled, they left the trapdoor. Only now it opens into the closet."

"But why keep the door at all?"

"As a curiousity for tourists. Maybe they have guided tours through the smugglers' tunnel."

He gave her a baffled stare. "Guided tours—tourists?"

There was so much she'd have to explain to him. Now he was a stranger in her world. Later there would be time for talk. Later she'd tell him about how Dermot had survived, how a Stuart had been restored to England's throne. But all that could wait.

She pressed herself closer to him. "I thought we'd never find each other again. Even now, I'm afraid to believe you're really here."

"You need proof, my love?" He reached out and stroked the curve of her throat, then slid his hand beneath her robe. He cupped her breast, felt the nipple harden under his fingers.

His mouth found hers and her lips parted. His tongue slid inside and her own rose to meet it. Then he lifted his face and looked down, his eyes searching hers. "Something happened to me, out there on the cliff," he said. "Something I don't understand. I was holding your hands, yet I felt you drawing away from me—then you were gone."

"I never would have left you willingly." Kristy didn't want to remember. But she, too, had to understand. Because what had happened to them had been part of a pattern, a greater pattern than she had ever conceived of. She would never understand all of it. But perhaps it would be enough to grasp only a little. She spoke slowly, wonderingly. "I fought to stay until you were with me—but the pull was too strong. And then I saw Gwyneth, far off at the end of a kind of tunnel." A tunnel without beginning or end. A passage that spanned the farthest reaches of eternity.

Gwyneth had smashed the mirror, yet somehow he had

come to her. If the mirror hadn't brought him here, then how had he been able to follow her?

"You didn't come to me through the power of witchcraft," she said. "I think, when Gwyneth destroyed the mirror, that power was lost to me."

"Then how—"

"Don't you know, even now? There's another, far greater power. It's real. We proved that, didn't we?"

She reached up, drew him down to her. She gloried in the fullness of her joy as his arms went around her again.

"A greater power?" But even as he spoke, she knew he understood; the look in his eyes told her so.

A silent prayer of thankfulness rose up inside her. Her lips curved in a tremulous smile. "The power of a love like ours. A love stronger than time."

BELIEVE
Victoria Alexander

Tessa thinks as little of love as she does of the Arthurian legend—it is just a myth. But when an enchanted tome falls into the lovely teacher's hands, she learns that the legend is nothing like she remembers. Galahad the Chaste is everything but—the powerful knight is an expert lover—and not only wizards can weave powerful spells. Still, even in Galahad's muscled embrace, she feels unsure of this man who seemed a myth. But soon the beautiful skeptic is on a quest as real as her heart, and the grail—and Galahad's love—is within reach. All she has to do is believe.

___52267-5 $5.99 US/$6.99 CAN

Dorchester Publishing Co., Inc.
P.O. Box 6640
Wayne, PA 19087-8640

Please add $1.75 for shipping and handling for the first book and $.50 for each book thereafter. NY, NYC, and PA residents, please add appropriate sales tax. No cash, stamps, or C.O.D.s. All orders shipped within 6 weeks via postal service book rate. Canadian orders require $2.00 extra postage and must be paid in U.S. dollars through a U.S. banking facility.

Name_____
Address_____
City_____State_____Zip_____
I have enclosed $_____ in payment for the checked book(s).
Payment <u>must</u> accompany all orders. ❑ Please send a free catalog.
CHECK OUT OUR WEBSITE! www.dorchesterpub.com

Haughty young Lady Kayln D'Arcy only wants what is best for her little sister, Celia, when she travels to the imposing fortress of Hawkhurst. For the brother of Hawkhurst's dark lord has wooed Celia, and Kayln is determined to make him do the honorable thing. Tall, arrogant and imperious, Hawk has the burning eyes of a bird of prey and a gentle touch that can make Kayln nearly forget why she is there. As for Hawk, never before has he encountered a woman like the proud, fiery Kayln. But can Hawk catch his prey? Can he make her...Hawk's lady?

___4312-2 $4.99 US/$5.99 CAN

Dorchester Publishing Co., Inc.
P.O. Box 6640
Wayne, PA 19087-8640

Lady of the Night

Cordia Byers

Manacled to a stone wall is not the way Katharina Fergersen planned to spend her vacation. But a wrong turn in the right place and the haunted English castle she is touring is suddenly full of life—and so is the man who is bathing before her. As the frosty winter days melt into hot passionate nights, she realizes that there is more to Kane than just a well-filled pair of breeches. Katharina is determined not to let this man who has touched her soul escape her, even if it means giving up all to remain Sedgewick's lady of the night.

___4404-8 $5.99 US/$6.99 CAN

Janeen O'Kerry
QUEEN OF THE SUN

Riding along the Irish countryside, Teresa MacEgan is swept into a magical Midsummer's Eve that lands her in ancient Eire. There the dark-haired beauty encounters the quietly seductive King Conaire of Dun Cath. Tall and regal, he kindles a fiery need within her, and she longs to yield to his request to become his queen but can relinquish her independence to no one. But when an enemy endangers Dun Cath's survival, Terri finds herself facing a fearsome choice: desert the only man she'd ever loved, or join her king of the moon and become the queen of the sun.

___52269-1 $4.99 US/$5.99 CAN

Dorchester Publishing Co., Inc.
P.O. Box 6640
Wayne, PA 19087-8640

Please add $1.75 for shipping and handling for the first book and $.50 for each book thereafter. NY, NYC, and PA residents, please add appropriate sales tax. No cash, stamps, or C.O.D.s. All orders shipped within 6 weeks via postal service book rate. Canadian orders require $2.00 extra postage and must be paid in U.S. dollars through a U.S. banking facility.

Name_____
Address_____
City_____ State_____ Zip_____
I have enclosed $_____ in payment for the checked book(s).
Payment <u>must</u> accompany all orders. ☐ Please send a free catalog.
CHECK OUT OUR WEBSITE! www.dorchesterpub.com

THE OUTLAW VIKING

SANDRA HILL

As tall and striking as the Valkyries of legend, Dr. Rain Jordan is proud of her Norse ancestors despite their warlike ways. But she can't believe her eyes when a blow to the head transports her to a nightmarish battlefield and she has to save the barbarian of her dreams. If Selik isn't careful, the stunning siren is sure to capture his heart and make a warrior of love out of the outlaw Viking.

___52273-X $5.50 US/$6.50 CAN

Dorchester Publishing Co., Inc.
P.O. Box 6640
Wayne, PA 19087-8640

Please add $1.75 for shipping and handling for the first book and $.50 for each book thereafter. NY, NYC, and PA residents, please add appropriate sales tax. No cash, stamps, or C.O.D.s. All orders shipped within 6 weeks via postal service book rate. Canadian orders require $2.00 extra postage and must be paid in U.S. dollars through a U.S. banking facility.

Name_____
Address_____
City_____State_____Zip_____
I have enclosed $_____ in payment for the checked book(s).
Payment <u>must</u> accompany all orders. ❑ Please send a free catalog.
     CHECK OUT OUR WEBSITE! www.dorchesterpub.com

TIMESWEPT TRAVELER
ELAINE FOX

With a thriving business and a stalled personal life, Shelby Manning never figures her life is any worse—or better—than the norm. Then a late-night stroll through a Civil War battlefield park leads her to a most intriguing stranger. Bloody, confused, and dressed in Union blue, he insists he has just come from the Battle of Fredericksburg—more than one hundred years in the past.

Maybe Shelby should dismiss Carter Lindsey as crazy—just another history reenactor taking his game a little too seriously. But there is something compelling in the pull of his eyes, something special in his tender touch. And before she knows it, Shelby finds herself swept into a passion like none she's ever known—and willing to defy time itself to keep Carter at her side.

_52074-5 $4.99 US/$6.99 CAN

REFLECTIONS IN TIME

ELIZABETH CRANE

Bestselling Author Of *Time Remembered*

When practical-minded Renata O'Neal submits to hypnosis to cure her insomnia, she never expects to wake up in 1880s Louisiana—or in love with fiery Nathan Blue. But vicious secrets and Victorian sensibilities threaten to keep Renata and Nathan apart...until Renata vows that nothing will separate her from the most deliciously alluring man of any century.

__52089-3 $4.99 US/$6.99 CAN

Dorchester Publishing Co., Inc.
P.O. Box 6640
Wayne, PA 19087-8640

ATTENTION ROMANCE CUSTOMERS!

SPECIAL TOLL-FREE NUMBER
1-800-481-9191

*Call Monday through Friday
10 a.m. to 9 p.m.
Eastern Time
Get a free catalogue,
join the Romance Book Club,
and order books using your
Visa, MasterCard,
or Discover*®

Leisure
Books

Love
Spell

GO ONLINE WITH US AT DORCHESTERPUB.COM